W
H
H
DID

ALSO BY DEBBIE VIGGIANO

WHAT HOLLY'S HUSBAND DID

DEBBIE VIGGIANO

Bookouture

Published by Bookouture in 2018

An imprint of StoryFire Ltd.

Carmelite House
50 Victoria Embankment
London EC4Y 0DZ

www.bookouture.com

ISBN: 978-1-78681-390-9
eBook ISBN: 978-1-78681-389-3

For Kathryn Taussig with immense gratitude

Chapter One

'You only do it once a month?' asked Jeanie, her brow knitting. 'But that's terrible, Holly. Don't you like sex?'

I pursed my lips and did a bit of eye-rolling for effect. If only she knew the truth. Instead I said, 'What's wrong with once a month?'

Jeanie pulled a face. 'Nothing. If you're fifty.'

'My husband has a stressful job. Have you any idea how many mouths Alex peers into every day?'

'Good thing Alex isn't a gynaecologist then,' said Jeanie with a sniff. 'Scrutinising umpteen fannies Monday to Friday must be a major turn-off.'

'Do you have to be so coarse?'

'Hark at you!' said my best friend, adopting a highfalutin voice. 'I remember when you used to like nothing more than discussing the number of times we all did it – *and* how and where. Didn't you let Malcolm Hodge give you one in the back of his dad's car?'

'Most certainly not,' I lied. 'You must be thinking of Caro.'

'I could have sworn it was you,' said Jeanie, her eyes narrowing with suspicion.

'Talking of Caro, where is she?' I was anxious to get off the subject of sex and what we'd all got up to pre-marriage. That was the downside of still being mates with two besties from your secondary-school years. Caro and Jeanie knew all my secrets, as I did theirs. The good, the bad and the downright filthy. But talking about sexual adventures as giggling eighteen-year-olds was one thing. Discussing it a couple of decades later just seemed wrong.

'I did text her and invite her for a cuppa after the school run.'

'Caro had to take Joe to the dentist.'

'Really? Alex didn't mention he was seeing Joe today.'

'She's taken him to an NHS dentist.'

'Why?' I asked in surprise. 'Alex has always seen Joe. What's happened to change things?'

'Cost,' said Jeanie simply. 'Your hubby charges like a wounded rhino.'

'Have you any idea how expensive it is to run your own practice?' I replied, put out.

'But do you have any idea how many fillings Joe needs?' countered Jeanie.

'Well Caro shouldn't allow her son to scoff so many sweets,' I huffed. 'That boy has amalgam in every other tooth and recently had two extractions.'

'I didn't know that,' Jeanie said, raising her eyebrows.

'And nor are you meant to,' I added hastily, realising I'd been remarkably indiscreet about patient confidentiality.

'Anyway, enough about Caro,' said Jeanie, topping up her mug from the enormous teapot hogging half the kitchen table. 'You were saying…?'

'Saying what?' I replied, deliberately vague as I gazed beyond my kitchen window. In the late afternoon sunshine of an early and very golden September, the garden still looked beautiful, although autumn had made her presence known, touching some of the trees and turning several leaves lemon and brown.

'You know perfectly well,' said Jeanie crossly. 'You were telling me about your sex life.'

'No, *you* were asking nosy questions.'

Jeanie took a noisy slurp of tea. 'It's nothing to be ashamed of, you know. When did you go off it? Recently? Or years ago? Is that why you only had one child?'

'For goodness' sake, Jeanie. What is this, an inquisition?' I picked up the teapot and stalked over to the kettle, flicking the switch.

'I wouldn't do that if I were you,' Jeanie said, nodding at the kettle before helping herself to an 'Extra Special' biscuit. Special or not, they tasted like chocolate cardboard.

'Do what?' I growled.

'There's no water in it.'

I snatched the kettle from its base just as it made a strangled noise and puffed a scalding cloud of steam over my wrist.

'Bugger,' I squeaked, nearly dropping the wretched thing. Turning on my heel, I stomped over to the sink and stuck the kettle under the tap. A fountain of water immediately rose up, hitting me squarely in the chest and drenching my top.

'It helps if you flip back the lid,' my friend pointed out.

'Thank you,' I snapped. 'I'd forgotten you had a degree in Stating the Bleeding Obvious.'

'My, my, my,' Jeanie blew out her cheeks, 'we are in a tizzy today.'

'I am *not* in a tizzy.' I grabbed a tea towel and mopped my bosoms in agitation.

'Two minutes ago you were gleefully gossiping about Alex's practice manager and how her bunions were worse than Victoria Beckham's, but the moment the conversation veered towards good old-fashioned bonking, you got all hot and bothered and started chucking water around the kitchen. Your face matches the colour of your kettle.'

I switched on the bright red cause of my soaking, and briefly drummed my fingernails on the worktop as we waited for it to boil. I broke off to stab a forefinger in Jeanie's direction. 'I'll have you know that my sex life is AMAZING.'

'Oh grim,' said my daughter, pushing through the kitchen door, her customary scowl in place. Sophie, not quite fourteen, tossed a look of disgust in my direction. 'The last thing a child wants to know is that her parents still do it. Especially at your age.'

Jeanie hid a smile in the palm of her hand while I volleyed back my daughter's glare.

'Don't be ridiculous,' I blustered, my face now the colour of an aubergine and probably clashing violently with the hateful kettle. 'Jeanie and I were… were practising our lines. We're thinking about starting up an amateur dramatics group.'

'In that case, you'll be a natural…' Sophie gave me a withering look as she raided the biscuit tin, 'because there can't be many actresses who are able to blush to order.'

I turned away, letting my hair fall across my flaming face as I refilled the teapot and tossed another teabag in for good measure. Behind me the door slammed. Sophie had left the kitchen – the child was incapable of shutting a door quietly. I swear that the very second my beautiful, cuddly, super sweet, smiley baby had blown out the thirteen candles on her birthday cake, she'd morphed into a sullen, bad-tempered, sneering stranger with more lip curl than an angry Rottweiler.

'Blimey, you're so red I can feel the heat coming off you from here.' Jeanie picked up my latest copy of a gossip magazine and began fanning herself.

'Oh do give over,' I said sulkily, banging the teapot down on the table.

'You'll be telling me you're menopausal next.'

'I know someone who went through the menopause at thirty-eight,' I huffed.

'Holly, we both know you're not going through the change' – Jeanie arched an eyebrow – 'and judging by the way you fluttered your eyelashes at the proprietor of Serafino's Cucina last week, you're clearly not past it either.'

'Luca Serafino is married. I wouldn't *dream* of flirting with someone else's husband.'

'Hmm, try telling your eyeballs that. Every time he came over to our table your pupils dilated to the size of his meatballs – and we all know how big they are.'

'I've had enough of this,' I said, feeling a rant coming on. 'You'll be shining lights in my eyes and threatening torture next.'

Jeanie reached across the kitchen table and took my hand. 'Hey,' she said gently, 'I'm one of your oldest friends. I'm concerned, that's all. It just seems that, well, lately you've not looked very happy, and I wondered if it might have to do with you and Alex.'

'I'm deliriously happy!' I snarled. 'Listen, Jeanie, just because Alex doesn't come home to a wife dressed like a French maid, who pulls him by his tie up to the bedroom, whips down his trousers and proceeds to tickle his fancy with her feather duster, does not mean there is anything wrong with us between the sheets. I mean, do you and Ray still rip each other's clothes off the moment he comes home from the office?'

'I'd like to,' answered Jeanie calmly, 'but regrettably the kids are always around.'

'But… but you can't possibly!' I protested. 'You've been married the same number of years as me and Alex.'

'A year longer, actually,' Jeanie reminded. 'Sixteen years of wedded bliss to your fifteen.'

'Well bully for you.'

Jeanie's prying had touched a nerve, although she didn't know the whole reason why. I'd considered my marriage perfectly happy until last Christmas when, quite by accident, I'd happened upon a series of flirty texts on my husband's mobile. If the sexts hadn't made Alex's trousers swell, they'd certainly made my eyeballs bulge. And overnight, everything had changed.

Chapter Two

Reading what 'Queenie' had wanted to do with my husband's private parts had transformed our marriage from one that occasionally sizzled and popped, to one full of distrust on my part. That said, our lovemaking had never been particularly wild or experimental, not even when we'd first started dating.

Back then, I was a newly qualified dental nurse and had been delighted that the surgery's practice manager had partnered me up with their new recruit. Alexander Hart, BDS Hons, was every girl's dream guy – good-looking, educated, charming, ambitious and hard-working. He'd also had an elusiveness about him that I couldn't quite put my finger on. Shyness? Naïve sweetness? Whatever the heck it was, it ignited my interest, somehow making him even more wildly attractive. I'd pursued him like a heat-seeking missile. Alex was what my mother called 'a good catch'. And I'd caught him.

Pre-marriage, intimacy was erratic. Our incomes were at junior level and there was no spare cash to splash on dirty weekends away. We were both still living with our parents who were old-fashioned enough not to permit us to share a bed in their homes.

Post-marriage, and finally in a starter home, there were moments where Alex and I engaged in a sort of frantic, almost desperate, sex, that left us both reeling. He would hold me close afterwards, murmuring loving endearments. But it didn't last. I told myself that all relationships settled into a rhythm. That couples didn't carry on bonking like bunnies forever. I tried not to mind too much when Alex yawned his way across the bedroom, and hugged his pillows rather than me. Eventually I got used to his apologetic shrugs accompanied by, 'Sorry, darling. Another time.'

There was only one point in our marriage when I was ruthlessly determined to pick up the pace of our sex life again. Jeanie and Caro were both trying for a baby, and I didn't want to be left out. We'd moved into a family home by this point with spare bedrooms crying out to be filled with cots and teddies. My mother always said the way to a man's heart was through his stomach. So I regularly plied Alex with oysters for dinner laced with chilli peppers and avocado. Oh yes, I'd done my aphrodisiac homework, and we weren't talking Ann Summers' sexy lingerie.

On one particular evening, armed with temperature charts and ovulation kits, I'd seduced Alex's taste buds yet again and nearly wept with joy when he'd torn his eyes away from the rugby to briefly roll on top of me. Less than a minute later, he'd turned his attention back to the screen, happily watching a bunch of muddy men head-butting each other. I'd lain with my legs up against the wall reading a celebrity magazine full of glamorous stars hugging baby bumps. Oh, how I envied them all. But the food of love paid off. A triumphant sperm cosied up with a ripe and ready ovum, and nine months later our daughter burst into the world.

In the year following Sophie's arrival, there was absolutely no intimacy between Alex and myself. He had taken himself off to one of the empty bedrooms to avoid my broken nights impacting upon his patient list.

'Don't be silly, darling,' he said, after I'd been particularly tearful and asked if he no longer found me attractive. 'You're gorgeous. But we have a little baby, and her needs must come first.'

'But what about my needs?' I bleated, refraining from telling him that so desperate was I for male attention there had recently been an exchange of chit-chat with the lorry driver who delivered our fuel. Without quite knowing how, our banter had quickly descended to smutty innuendo about the length of his hosepipe, the size of my oil tank, and the importance of regularly filling it up. Too late I'd noticed the glint in his eye as he'd adjusted his scruffy trousers. Horrified, I'd questioned what the hell I was doing flirting with a pot-bellied, jowly-faced man with dubious body odour, and then backed off faster than a Scalextric car in reverse. That evening I'd sat my husband down for a frank talk, but both my efforts and libido went unrewarded.

'You simply have to understand, sweetie,' Alex reasoned, 'that right now your needs – and mine,' he hastily added, 'must be put aside. Sophie is the priority.'

And right on cue our sleeping daughter had stirred in her cot, opened her eyes and screamed the house down for her feed.

Eventually our intimacy had resumed, but it lacked fire. I devoured the problem pages in every mother and baby magazine where this was, reassuringly, frequently discussed. So many new mothers complained about their husband's lack of sexual interest. All sorts of reasons were given by Aunty Sue or Dear Dorothy, the most common being the 'Madonna-whore complex' in which, after childbirth, some men didn't feel it 'right' that the mother of their child should behave like a trollop between the sheets. I did try talking to Alex about it, but he quickly became irritable. Anxious that I'd offended him – no man likes having their prowess challenged – I'd backed off, telling myself that I should be grateful for our once-a-month lovemaking which, a few more months down the line, became every other month. Alex was always attentive on these occasions, but I couldn't help feeling that it somehow smacked of duty on his part. I made a point never to grumble for fear of offending him again, but also because he always complained about tiredness and work stress, and said he was amazed he could even raise a smile. So I convinced myself that this pace and pattern was quite normal in new families, and told myself to be thankful for what we had together, even if our sex drives were so obviously mismatched. Several years later I'd convinced myself that couples like us had settled into a domestic rhythm, enjoying companionship rather than lust. So, we snuggled together whilst watching telly, or enjoyed laying side by side in bed reading – me with a pile of paperbacks full of bodice-ripping hunks and breathy heroines shrieking, 'No, Sire, no, no, no, oh go on then yes, yes, yessssssss!' and Alex with a stack of dental magazines full of riveting articles about plastic dentures.

But last Christmas, this harmonious slide into premature old age had shattered like a dropped chandelier. Our respective families had descended for the annual festive dinner complete with figgy pudding. Making sure everybody's glasses were filled, I'd disappeared into the kitchen to baste a turkey so vast it had surely been genetically modified. Our recently acquired and food-obsessed rescue dog, Rupert, had immediately walked to heel, willing me to drop the enormous baking tin so he would have an excuse to claim the bird as his own. Shooing Rupert away, I'd squashed everything back into the oven, then checked the slow cooker. A homemade alcohol-laced creation was gently steaming its way to perfection. It was then that a finger of cold dread had prodded me in the stomach. Despite spending hundreds of pounds on food, I'd forgotten to buy enough milk to make the custard.

'Fuckity-fuckity-fuck,' I swore, as Alex came up behind me.

'How long are you going to be in here, Holly?'

I turned to him with wild eyes. 'I'm cooking dinner!'

'Can you come back to the lounge? It's rather bad form, darling, not socialising.'

'I'm doing my best,' I snapped. I began randomly opening cupboard doors. There had to be some Long Life somewhere. 'Surely you can cope with topping up a few champagne glasses and offering around a bowl of nibbles?' I banged a cupboard door shut and wrenched open another, nearly taking it off its hinges.

'Your brother has arrived.'

'And?' My eyes flicked over jars of herbs, condiments, and tins of baked beans.

'I think it's best if you deal with him. Tensions need to be diluted. You know how he and I have never… well, *hit it off*.'

I reversed out of another cupboard and glanced at my husband. 'Well *try* and get along. Just for today? After that you can resume being vile to each other.' I turned my attention to ransacking drawers. There was an outside chance I'd popped a carton of Long Life in with the tea towels during a hormonal moment. 'Just remember, you're not alone. All over the country, families have been thrust together –

Debbie Viggiano

relatives who abhor each other, cousins who can't stand the sight of one another, even brothers-in-law who don't see eye to eye. It's what folk do at this time of year – buy lavish gifts for people they detest.'

'Simon is something else.'

'He's gay, Alex,' I pointed out, throwing tea towels everywhere, 'not an alien from outer space. Are you homophobic?'

'Of course not!' my husband blustered. 'He's just… so rude.'

'You mean bitchy,' I said, sweeping tea towels back into one drawer and emptying the next of tin foil and greaseproof paper. 'He actually has a fabulous sense of humour if you take it with a pinch of salt.'

This wasn't entirely true. Simon was every cliché you could think of. Ultra-camp, he had a habit of tossing his head if annoyed, flicking his hair if flirting and mincing about like a *Strictly* contestant, right hand permanently extended as if an invisible handbag was dangling from one wrist. He didn't know the meaning of the word 'tact' and delivered his barbed comments in a voice that made Alan Carr sound like Brian Blessed. Simon also loved winding people up, and when they finally lost their cool he would deliver his catchphrase:

'Stop being so sensitive. I'm only kidding.'

Although everybody knew he wasn't.

'Anyway, why were you swearing just now?' asked my husband, stepping to one side as I slammed the last drawer. My temper was starting to fray.

'There isn't enough milk for the custard.'

'So?' He shrugged. 'We'll have the pudding without.'

'Are you mad?' I asked, plonking my hands on my hips. 'Or just plain stupid?'

'I beg your pardon?' said Alex, looking affronted.

I narrowed my eyes and began speaking in an enunciated tone – the sort used on idiots. 'The. Pudding. Will. Be. Too. Dry. Without. Custard.'

'Don't. Speak. To. Me. Like. That.'

'I don't believe it!' I roared, clutching my temples dramatically. 'All my efforts are going to be ruined.' My bottom lip jutted out, and began wobbling violently. 'This is just typical,' I whimpered, eyes filling up. 'I've been a good wife, a good daughter, a good daughter-in-law, a good mother, a good bloody everything to bloody everyone, slogged my guts out, brought all and sundry together for one – ONE! – chuffing day of the year in the faint hope of playing happy families, and what for? Hmm? All my cooking will be for nothing. All the hours – no, *days* – spent wrapping presents, not to mention months sourcing the damn things, and for what?' I clawed at my throbbing head. A migraine threatened. 'Everything's spoiled!' I sobbed. 'All because there's no TOSSING MILK FOR THE CUSTARD!'

My voice bounced off the kitchen walls. From the next room, the murmur of conversation ground to an embarrassed halt.

Alex raked a hand through his hair. 'Are you due on?'

'Yes,' I cried.

Alex grabbed his car keys from the kitchen table. 'I've not had a drink. I'll go and get some milk.'

'It's Christmas Day,' I wept, grabbing a tea towel and trumpeting into it. 'Nothing will be open.'

'Mr Patel's shop will be.'

'But his shop is in the next village!'

'I'll be five minutes,' Alex promised. 'Dry your tears, turn the hob down on those veg, then go into the lounge and make conversation with our two families that have absolutely nothing in common apart from us.'

And with that he'd driven off in a spray of gravel – leaving his mobile on the worktop, and me to compose myself. When his phone had dinged with a message, reading it had been unavoidable.

Heyyy there, Mister Sexy!

My eyes widened. Alex had programmed in the sender's name. *Queenie.* Who was this woman? Evidently someone he knew. Why else add a person to your list of contacts? I'd barely gathered my thoughts when it dinged again.

Did you like what I did to you last night?

I gasped and leaned against the worktop, palms flat and splayed out to stop me from reeling.

Dinggggg.

Would you like me to do it again?

Dinggggg.

I keep thinking of that song 'Genie in a Bottle'. It makes me think of what I want to do to you…

Dinggggg.

I'm wiggling my hips and wanna make your day, dance for you, lots of rhythm and sway… dooby do, dooby do (and I absolutely LURVE your dooby do)

Dinggggg

Rubba-dub, rubba-dub, gimme rubba-dub-dub

Dinggggggg

D u b - d u b - d u b - d u b - d u b - d u b - d u b - d u b -
aaaaaaaaaaaaaaaaaaaaaah!

With a shaking hand, I picked up the phone. I didn't know Alex's passcode. Why would I? I'd never had cause to go through his mobile – until now. I pressed the home button. The messages instantly disappeared to reveal the numerical keypad for passcode entry. I entered Sophie's date of birth. The screen prompted me to try again. I tapped in my birthday. No. Alex's. Nope. Gordon Bennett, what was the combination? I was still stabbing away at the screen when Alex walked back in with the milk. He froze. In a nano-second his eyes flicked from me to the phone and then back to me again. And then his face drained of colour.

Chapter Three

'It's not what you think,' he said, but his knuckles were as white as the carton of milk he was gripping.

'Like hell it isn't,' I spat. 'Who is she?'

'She isn't anyone.'

'That's funny,' I said, giving a mirthless hoot of laughter. 'Because it says "Queenie" here.' I stabbed the screen to underline my point.

'Look, Queenie is—'

'—a genie in a bottle,' I interrupted, snatching the six-pint carton from my treacherous husband and brandishing it like a lethal weapon. I wondered if it was possible to kill him with it. I could imagine the newspaper headline now. MAN BLUDGEONED BY MILK CARTON AFTER MARRIAGE CURDLED. I shook my head. God, I was going nuts. 'According to this text, she likes rubbing your dooby-do. What do you have to say about that, eh?'

'Absolutely nothing, because it means absolutely nothing.'

'WELL IT MEANS SOMETHING TO ME!' I bawled.

'Holly, can we have this discussion later? We have our fam—'

'Ay say!' squawked a plummy voice from the next room, 'is everything awl right?'

Alex's mother. I really couldn't cope with Audrey right now. As far as my mother-in-law was concerned, her son was Mr Golden Balls. He could do no wrong. If he'd robbed a bank at gunpoint, she'd have insisted his ulterior motive would be to give money to the poor. If I told her my husband was porking genies, she'd likely tell me I wasn't providing enough bedtime satisfaction, so it must be my fault. I had no doubt that Audrey would then whip out her iPhone and order me an Aladdin outfit off Amazon, complete with magic lamp.

'Everything's fine, Mum!' Alex called. 'Just a small custard catastrophe.'

I shoved the carton of milk into Alex's chest. 'This conversation isn't over,' I snarled. 'And YOU can make the chuffing custard.'

'Darling, don't be silly, I don't know how to make cus—'

'Then google it! You wanted me to deal with my brother, so that's what I'll be doing. That, and getting drunk.'

'Holly, this is all a storm in a teacup. You do realise you're being quite irrational?'

Dingggggg.

Wishing you the horniest Christmas ever, baby xxx

'Look at this!' I sneered, waggling the phone I was still holding at my husband. 'Am I *still* being irrational?'

'Absolutely,' Alex insisted.

'Well if you're going to continue claiming I'm being unreasonable, then I might as well behave in an unreasonable way.' Without missing a beat, I stalked over to the slow cooker where the Christmas pudding was quietly simmering, and dropped Alex's phone into the pot. 'Oh dear,' I said sarcastically, 'it looks like Queenie is in hot water.'

Alex rolled his eyes and gave a theatrical sigh. 'It's of no significance to me, Holly. In fact, I'm glad you did that.'

Too late I now realised that I couldn't demand Alex show me any previous sexts from Queenie.

'I'll level with you,' said my husband. 'Queenie is a patient. Well, an ex-patient. She took a shine to me, so much so I had to tell her I couldn't treat her any more. She didn't take it well.'

'How did she get your mobile number?' I demanded.

'It's on my business cards,' Alex reminded me. 'It's the out-of-hours number. You've just put my emergency phone in the slow cooker.'

I paused. *Was he telling the truth?* It *could* be possible... 'So why did you programme her number into the phone?'

'Because,' Alex said calmly, 'I then know it's her calling me rather than an emergency, and therefore will avoid answering her call. Isn't it obvious? Listen, Holly, the woman is a fantasist. A nutcase. A stalker. What more do you want me to say?'

'Why have you never mentioned this before?' I demanded.

'What, and upset you? I wanted to avoid the very thing that has now happened.'

'I... I... where were you last night?'

'Here!'

'You were late home.'

'Yes, after seeing an emergency! An abscess doesn't stop just because it's Christmas Eve.'

Alex placed the carton of milk on the worktop, and then wrapped his arms around me. I stiffened within his embrace, but he kissed me on the forehead, and when he next spoke it was in a sing-song voice, like that of a parent soothing a distressed child. 'Listen to me, you silly goose. Do you really think I have the time or energy to have an affair?'

I looked at my husband. This was a man with a sex drive smaller than a goldfish. Despite the sexting, it didn't stack up. Suddenly I felt confused.

'I don't know what to believe,' I conceded. 'Are you honestly telling me there is no other woman on the scene?'

'Cross my heart.'

So I accepted what he said. For a while.

Chapter Four

'Sorry I missed out on our catch-up last week,' said Caro, handing me a cup of tea, 'but Joe had a dental emergency.'

'Yes, Jeanie told me.' I was determined not to make any comment about her defection to an NHS dentist, or furiously defend Alex's price plans.

'Anyway, the three of us are together now,' Caro beamed, 'which means you can properly update me.' Her hazel eyes looked at me expectantly.

I looked at her blankly. 'Update you about what?'

'Don't be coy, Holly. Jeanie told me that you and Alex are having bedroom troubles.'

'Sorry,' said Jeanie, giving me an apologetic look. 'But it doesn't really count as gossiping, does it? We've known each other for so long that talking about each other is allowed.'

'For heaven's sake,' I said, glaring at Jeanie, 'who else have you been broadcasting to?'

'Don't be silly, Holly,' said Caro, her voice dismissive. 'It's me. The three of us have been through everything together.'

'Too true,' said Jeanie, biting into an enormous slice of Caro's homemade carrot cake.

'From falling in love, to getting dumped,' said Caro, 'to falling in love again, then getting married, and finally pregnant. We've cried together about fears of being fat and our husbands not fancying us, then ringing each other up in the early hours when we were pacing the floor with colicky babies. We've been there for each other through everything.'

'We even shared our teen years,' Jeanie reminded us. 'And heaps of detentions' – she looked at me reproachfully – 'usually because of sneaking into the boys' changing rooms after PE trying to glimpse what was in their shorts.'

'I thought that was your idea!' said Caro.

'No, it was definitely Holly's.'

'Was it?' Caro's head swivelled to me, dark pencilled eyebrows raised.

'I don't flipping know! What's this got to do with anything? You're making me sound like some sort of pervert.'

'Of course you weren't a pervert,' Jeanie assured me, reaching forward and patting my hand with her sticky fingers, 'you just had an enquiring mind.'

'Particularly where men's private parts were concerned,' Caro smiled.

'You *are* making me out to be a pervert,' I protested.

'Never!' said Jeanie, licking buttercream off her fingers, 'but you have to admit you were the first out of the three of us to notice the opposite sex.'

'So what's wrong with that?'

'Nothing,' said Caro. 'All we're saying is, given your keen early teenage interest in boys—'

'Like bribing the class heartthrob to kiss you behind the bike shed in exchange for a bag of chocolate buttons—'

'What? I never—'

'It just seems crazy that a woman like you,' Caro interrupted, 'who always insisted that blondes had more fun, was the first to pop her cherry and had slept with five men by the time Jeanie and I had finally got off the virginal starting block, should now settle for a once-a-month tumble.'

'I do hope that when Jeanie-Big-Gob was so busy gossiping to you about my private life, she also relayed what I told her: that my husband is absolutely knackered. And me too,' I quickly added. 'Sometimes it's very difficult orchestrating a sex life when one of you has a headache after squinting through a pair of loupes overseeing a tricky dental implant, and the other has a migraine from a slanging match with her teenager.'

'We have teenagers too,' said Jeanie, 'and we don't let the little darlings impact on bedroom time with our hubbies, eh, Caro?'

'Most definitely not,' Caro nodded.

'You two obviously have nothing better to do if you're so concerned about my sex life.'

'You're right,' Jeanie nodded. 'My days are full of a housewife's chores, just like Caro's. We do endless washing, piles of ironing, and constantly clear up after a house full of slobs. Is it any wonder we're reduced to entertaining ourselves dissecting everybody's sex lives? But if you really want to know, Holly, Caro and I have privately thought you've not seemed like yourself for ages. Since last Christmas, actually.' She helped herself to another slice of Caro's cake.

I'd looked at it longingly when I'd first walked into Caro's kitchen, but if I ate any now it would probably stick in my throat.

'Yes, well, there's nothing to dissect,' I said firmly, taking a sip of tea. 'Sometimes, it's about quality, not quantity,' I asserted.

Even though I was batting my besties' observations firmly back at them, there was a part of me that felt quite hurt by their line of questioning. One disadvantage of a long friendship was that, more often than not, we were oblivious to each other's feelings when discussing personally thorny subjects.

Caro tucked a strand of dark hair behind one ear. 'I suppose you have a point about the quality and not quantity thing,' she said, lowering her voice. 'I'll confess to not always being gratified by David's performance under the duvet.'

My ears pricked up. This was more like it. Someone else with a dissatisfied sex life. Hurrah!

'I mean,' Caro continued, 'we might do it two or three times a week—'

Two or three times a *week*?

'—but it's so bloody boring.'

Jeanie nodded. 'And over too quickly.'

Caro giggled. 'How do you know that? Have you been having secret trysts with my David?'

Jeanie laughed, her blue eyes sparkling with amusement. 'Now there's a thought! I wonder how we'd all rate each other's husbands if we could wave a magic wand and morph into the likeness of each other. You might like Ray's style, Caro. He takes bloody ages to come. Drives me nuts. If David's a quick bonker, I think I'd prefer that. It would let me get back to my book. Sometimes I don't know what's more enticing – *Fifty Shades of Grey* or *Fifty Thrusts with Ray*.'

'So tell me then, Holly,' said Caro, 'in what way is your once-a-month coupling so sparkling and worth the wait? You might convert me!'

I flushed. 'Well, unlike you two ladies of leisure, I do work, you know.'

'Yeah, so?' said Jeanie. 'You're not exactly exhausted by it, are you? I mean, being a dental nurse for a couple of days a week is hardly going to give you soaring stress levels on a par with Theresa May.'

'It still takes it out of me,' I said defensively. 'You have no idea what some patients are like. I have to be a professional assistant to Alex and chief hand-holder to the patient, telling them they're doing splendidly, when in fact they're making a massive issue about a simple check-up. It's very wearing.'

'Stop trying to change the subject and spill the beans,' said Caro cosily, leaning forward. 'What's it like having a bonk once a month but knowing it's going to be – as you so succinctly put it – *quality*?'

'Why are you so interested?' I protested.

'Because it's fun discussing our sex lives,' said Jeanie. 'We used to discuss sex all the time.'

'Yes,' I spluttered, 'before our kids came along.'

'Just because we're all now a bit older and more matronly looking, doesn't mean we have to avoid the subject. Come on, Holly. Caro has just told you that David is too quick, and I've confided that Ray takes too long. So tell us about Alex's performance.'

'Oh, for…' I huffed with exasperation. They weren't going to shut up, were they? A pair of bored housewives with nothing better to gossip about. 'Right, well, if you must know, it's… it's… well, exactly that.' I nodded. 'It's the superior bonk. You should try it. Do you know, I think I might have some of that carrot cake after all, Caro.'

In one smooth move, my friend had cut me a slice and handed me the plate. 'And?'

I took an enormous bite, making speech impossible. As Caro waited for me to finish chewing, she turned to Jeanie. 'Have *you* ever had a superior bonk?'

Jeanie considered. 'Mm, yes, but not recently.'

'How long ago?'

Jeanie's brow furrowed as she thought about it. 'About... let me see... before Charlotte and Harry were born?'

'But that's years ago!' Caro gasped.

'I know.' Jeanie pulled a face. 'And you?'

Caro wrinkled her nose. 'It's always a bit hit and miss to be honest. I still fancy the boxer shorts off David, don't get me wrong, but we're very aware of Joe and Lizzie being savvy teenagers, and the walls of our house being paper thin. It does rather put a dampener on things, especially if you're partial to gloriously noisy sex.'

'Hold it right there,' said Jeanie, slapping the cake away from my mouth and stopping me taking a second massive bite, 'I'm still waiting to hear the details about this superior bonk with Alex.'

'Honestly, Jeanie,' I protested, 'it's like being back at secondary school with you all over again, like when you wanted every last detail about the French kiss.'

'Yep,' she said cheerfully, 'you're absolutely right.'

'A sex life should be private,' I said primly. 'Alex would have a fit if he knew the pair of you were asking about his performance.'

'But Alex isn't here,' said Caro, 'so come on, indulge your besties with some details. If we're impressed, we might ration our own husbands in the hope of upping their game.'

It was obvious that my friends weren't going to drop the subject until they had some juicy details. But what could I tell them about Alex? And I'd still not confessed that it was really once every *eight* weeks. They'd be appalled. I'd have to do some serious embellishing – or even downright lying.

'Well,' I said, looking at a spot on the wall above Jeanie's head and allowing my mind to wander back to a time where I'd been infatuated, besotted, and totally in lust with my very first boyfriend, Johnny. He'd been the one to show me the ropes; how to please a man, and how to receive pleasure in return. Unfortunately, he'd traded me in for a cougar who had an extra twenty years' experience under her garter belt. I'd been bereft, until Hugo James had come along with his sexily slicked-back hair, cool shades, and the sort of leather jacket that emphasised the broadness of his shoulders. My loins twanged at a memory, and I cleared my throat. 'Okay, if you really must know, Alex starts off by giving one of his special smouldering looks.'

'Oooh, lovely,' Jeanie sighed, twiddling a strand of her long black hair.

'And the chemistry is so instant,' I murmured, gazing into space as I recalled returning Hugo's smoulders with my own come-hither looks, 'it's so spine-tinglingly perfect, there is no need for words.'

'Keep going,' said Caro, hooked.

'He strides over, sweeps me into his arms, and begins kissing his way down my neck…'

'Yes…'

'… to my shoulders …'

'Yes…'

'… trailing his hot lips over my breasts …'

'Yes, yes …'

'…taking the time to suck both nipples until I'm begging him to resume his tantalising trail of kisses down… down… down a bit more…'

'Oh my God!' said Jeanie, fanning herself. 'Does he actually do *that*, Holly?'

'Oh yes,' I purred. And Hugo had been very good at it too.

'Ray won't. He says it doesn't turn him on.'

'Be quiet,' said Caro bossily, 'and let Holly continue.'

'Alex loves doing it,' I lied. 'It's his speciality.'

'How? Tell me, tell me!' begged Jeanie.

I smirked. 'He does the alphabet with his tongue.'

'No!' said Caro. 'What's it like?'

'Mind-blowing. Every little bit of you zings with pleasure. And he doesn't rush it. We're talking… ooh… a good ten minutes.'

'Ten minutes of foreplay?' Jeanie's eyes rounded.

'No, foreplay is about half an hour – we do other things beside the alphabet. It's probably about, ooh, forty-five minutes before we actually consummate our lust for each other.'

'Bloody hell,' Caro croaked. 'No wonder the pair of you only do it once a month. You must be chuffing knackered afterwards.'

I gave them both a smug look. 'Quality, not quantity. And that, girls, is the superior bonk.'

'Oh, Holly, you're so lucky,' said Jeanie, eyes shining as if she'd just caught a glimpse of the Holy Grail. 'What I'd give for one hour with your hubby.'

'Hands off, Jeanie,' I said, giving her a playful warning, 'because he's all mine.'

Wasn't he?

Chapter Five

Having made out to Jeanie and Caro that my sex life was the next best thing since the carrot cake we'd all indulged in, I felt an urgent need to prove it. Okay, so Alex and I did it very infrequently, but that didn't mean to say our rare couplings couldn't benefit from a bit of imagination, which, in turn, might pick up the pace of things, too. My eyeballs fairly gleamed with fresh hope, and my belly let out an alarming gurgle. Oh yes, there was a definite second wind going on here. I was positively raring to get things back on track. Which was why I found myself, once home after the school run, nipping into the study and furtively logging on to the internet to check out how to seduce a man through the art of burlesque.

Apparently, I needed to think about musical accompaniment – preferably a big band or 1940s show music – and then a fun costume teamed with skyscraper heels. Hmm. I didn't have a *froufrou* petticoat or any elbow-length opera gloves. Perhaps I could find some on eBay? I read on. It was important to peel off the gloves seductively, one finger at a time, and then languidly toss them aside whilst remembering to give a tantalising shimmy, bosom quiver and booty shake. I boggled at the diagram. I was just reading how to strut before stripping, when a pair of hands went over my eyes, making me jump.

'Guess who!' said a camp voice.

'Simon!' I spluttered, hastily shutting the laptop and hoping my nosy brother hadn't seen what I'd been reading.

'Before you even think about undressing, dearest, I'd get yourself off to the gym.'

I gnashed my teeth. This was one of the reasons why my brother always wound me up. Mother Nature had bestowed my sibling with the sort of willowy frame that I'd never achieve at the gym in a million years. As if this weren't enough, while I spent a fortune at the hairdresser's every month adding platinum highlights at vast expense, Simon had never had to splash cash on such a thing, being blessed with naturally golden locks.

'What are you doing here?' I asked rudely.

Simon tossed his head, 'and it's lovely to see you, too.'

'You know what I mean. I wasn't expecting you.'

'Evidently. Sophie let me in. We're going shopping as soon as she's changed out of her school uniform.'

This was another thing that annoyed me about my brother. These days he seemed closer to my daughter than me. I couldn't remember the last time Sophie and I had hit the High Street together, linking arms as we checked out Top Shop, or gossiped in Costa over hot chocolates piled high with whipped cream. My daughter had no interest in hanging out with her mother, but if Uncle Simon appeared in a wiggle of hips, waving his wallet, she was off like our dog Rupert after a rabbit. I'd asked her on one occasion, why she liked spending time with my brother. Her reply was, 'Because Uncle

Simon is so cool and funny, and all my friends are jealous that I have a gay uncle who drives me around in his flashy sports car.'

Whereas presumably I was uncool, not remotely funny, and she was ashamed of my battered unflashy four-by-four.

'Make sure you bring Sophie back in time to do homework.'

'Honestly, Holly, chill. The poor kid has had a day of slaving at that posh school you and Alex insist on sending her to. I don't know why you waste your money when there's a perfectly good comprehensive down the road.'

'Thank you, Simon, but I think Sophie's education is the decision of her parents who have her best interests at heart, not her uncle who scraped his A levels and dropped out of uni.'

'Didn't do me any harm though, did it?' he said, flicking his hair back.

This was true. Simon had gone on to launch a very successful online fashion business and liked nothing more than blowing his spare cash on his niece, indulging her questionable taste, to the envy of her peers. No amount of explaining would make me understand the importance of wearing a four-hundred-quid pair of jeans that looked like they'd been mutilated by Edward Scissorhands.

Simon nodded at my laptop. 'So what was that all about? Trying to spice things up between the sheets?'

'I am *not* having this conversation with you.'

'Bet you've told those two mates of yours, eh? Caro and Jeanie. The three of you are like the Witches of Eastwick. No doubt you were round at one of their houses earlier, stuffing cake, complaining about your men, and trying to convince yourselves that size doesn't matter.'

'Simon—'

'Because size most definitely *does* matter. I should know.'

'You are bang out of order.'

'Bang is the right word, Sis. Why don't you tell me all about it? I might be able to give you some advice. We're not so different you know,' he said, fluttering his eyelashes.

'If I needed advice, you would be the last person I'd ask.'

I could imagine it now: confiding in Simon, then listening to him guffaw as I told him about my burlesque outfit, no doubt sending me up and making comments about taking a hedge trimmer to my bush before I wore anything high-cut over the leg. *Oh no.* My self-esteem wasn't brilliant at best. The last thing I needed was my brother ridiculing me.

Simon theatrically placed a hand upon his chest. 'Too cruel. Your words are like daggers that have pierced my heart. You can be such a bitch, Holly.'

'You too,' I snapped, heading to the kitchen. 'Do you want a cup of tea while you're waiting for Sophie?'

My daughter chose that moment to walk into the kitchen. She was now out of her school uniform but clutching a huge French textbook.

'Uncle Simon, please could you give me twenty minutes to quickly get this bit of homework out the way?'

'Of course, sweets.'

I stared at my daughter, gobsmacked. For a moment there I'd seen my darling girl how she used to be, charming and compliant. What *was* my brother's trick in accessing this side of her personality?

'That's very diligent of you, darling,' I said, smiling with approval.

Whereupon Sophie's head rotated a hundred and eighty degrees and her upper lip peeled back in a sneer.

'Despite you thinking I'm lazy and prefer playing truant rather than reading de Troyes,' she spat, 'I can assure you that I have every intention of passing my French exam next week.' And with that she stalked off, giving the kitchen door its loudest slam to date, and sending Rupert running for cover under the kitchen table.

'Don't worry, Sis. Another four years and she'll be pleasant to you again, and yes I will now have a cup of tea.'

I reached for the kettle. Great. So now I was stuck with Simon. I just hoped he didn't ask me any more probing questions about my burlesque research.

'You still haven't told me about –' Simon jerked his head meaningfully in the direction of the study.

I tossed a teabag into a mug and poured on the boiling water. 'Can you watch what you're saying when Sophie's around?' I said through gritted teeth. 'Everybody seems to want to know about my private life. I had Jeanie in my kitchen recently, thinking it her right to interrogate me, and then Sophie walked in. It was embarrassing.'

'I knew it,' Simon crowed, 'it *is* about sex. What's up? Presumably not Alex.'

I shook my head in exasperation. 'Why do you have to reduce everything to smut level?'

'Because that's the way I am, dearest. But if you don't mind me making an impartial observation…' Simon hesitated, as I slid into a chair opposite him. 'I'm not sure Alex is the sort of man who will appreciate your efforts in that department.'

I blinked. 'Why ever not?'

Simon leaned back in his chair, crossing one long leg over the other. 'Because he's a stuffed shirt, darling.'

'No he's not!'

'Oh, but he is. I just don't know what you ever saw in the guy, Holly. You could have had the pick of them all. Young men were flocking around, but instead you chose a man who surely invented the word *staid*. There's more to marriage than plodding along in an oh-so-respectable fashion. You should have married what's-his-name.'

'What's-his-name?'

'Wanted to be a doctor.'

'I have no idea who you're talking about.'

'Yes you do,' Simon said, waving a limp hand. 'Aunty Shirley's boy.'

'You mean our godmother's son?'

'That's the one.'

'Jack?'

'Why do you keep replying to me with questions? Yes, Jack.'

My mind flipped back through pages of memory. Shirley was my mother's best friend. Mum was from the generation where it was polite to prefix the name of anyone much older with 'aunty' or 'uncle'. Aunty Shirley was therefore no blood relation, although I loved her like one. She was a social butterfly who never stopped talking, but I couldn't say the same for her son. I remembered Jack as a little boy in short trousers and spectacles, dark hair sticking up in all directions. He'd looked a typical nerdy kid, emphasised by his love of science books. Whereas Simon and I had grown up on a television diet of *Danger Mouse*, Jack had preferred *Bellamy's Backyard Safari*. By the time I'd reached the age of fifteen, I'd treated him in much the same way as my own daughter now treated me. Yes, Jack had been sweet, and yes, in hindsight he might well have had a crush on me, but at that point in my life I'd been forced into wearing teeth braces which, back then, were thick metal and most unattractive. I hadn't smiled at anyone for two years, least of all Jack – who had still looked like a nerd.

'If ever there was somebody who defined the word "staid", then it surely has to be Jack,' I said.

'You've got to be kidding,' said Simon, uncrossing his legs and sitting up straight. 'He's a doctor now. He's spent the last two years living in some remote part of Africa doing worthy stuff, but he's back in England for the time being planning his next career move and, in the interim, writing a book about medicine in the Third World.'

'Which means he's still a nerd.'

'*Au contraire*. Doctor Jack is Action Man in human form. He did a charity cycle from Namibia to Cape Town, raising a stack of money towards the cost of clean water and toilets, he's been on overseas television raising awareness about rhinos being slaughtered, and even been sponsored by businesses to go kayaking with crocodiles.'

'Who in their right mind would kayak with crocodiles?'

'Someone hell bent on raising hundreds of thousands of pounds for good causes. He's quite well known in Africa. A bit of a hero. But he's never married, despite a bevvy of beauties regularly appearing on his arm.'

'And how do you know all this?' I asked.

'Because we're Facebook friends.'

'Ah, that means you fancy him.' I rolled my eyes.

'Everybody fancies him,' said Simon, spreading his hands wide. 'If you got yourself on Facebook too, you'd see for yourself. Honestly, Holly, for one still the right side of forty, you just don't keep up with the times. Even Aunty Shirley is on Facebook. Oh, and your boring fart of a husband.'

'Alex is on Facebook?' I was genuinely surprised.

'Ah, that's got your attention, hasn't it!'

It had indeed got my attention. If my husband was on Facebook, presumably he had a number of friends and acquaintances that he regularly spoke to. I wondered if bloody 'Queenie' was one of them.

'I think, in Alex's case, it's a business page though?' Simon added.

'Right,' I nodded, 'that probably explains why he's never talked about it. Perhaps I might investigate Facebook myself, seeing that everybody else is doing it.'

'Don't expect me to friend you. I'm not having you snooping through my timeline ogling all my friends and wondering which ones I've slept with.'

I tutted. 'I'm not remotely interested in your sex life.'

'Which neatly brings us back to yours. You still haven't told me why you want to swing an opera glove around your head and step out of a giant cocktail glass.'

'Look,' I said, through slightly clenched teeth, 'if you really must know—'

'I really must.'

'Alex and I haven't been getting on so well these past few months.'

'Since last Christmas.'

'How do you know that?'

'I think all our family, Alex's included, worked that out when you lost the plot over a bit of custard.'

'Right.' I sighed. 'It wasn't just custard. There were some texts. Or, to give them their correct name, *sexts*. I discovered them quite by accident when Alex went out to buy milk. He left his phone behind. Somebody called Queenie sent a series of messages implying she wanted to rub various bits of Alex's anatomy.'

Simon looked visibly shocked. 'Oh,' was all he said.

'Yes. Oh.'

'I'm so sorry, Holly.'

I gave my brother a sharp look. I wasn't used to genuine sympathy from him.

'Obviously we had a row about it.'

'Did he ever tell you who Queenie was?'

'Yes. Some nutty ex-patient who was stalking him.'

'Ah. So he didn't tell you he was having an affair?'

'He categorically denied there was another woman.'

Simon nodded. 'Why, indeed, would he even be interested in another female when he has a wife as gorgeous as you?'

'Are you being sarcastic?'

'Yes. Believe me, Holly, there is nothing sexy about that upper lip hair you're sporting. You really should do something about your appearance. And tell me, are monobrows the latest must-have?'

Ah, this was more like it. Simon at his bitchy best.

'Thank you for reminding me I need to pluck out a few hairs,' I growled.

'Forget tweezers, dearest, you need a razor. Look, instead of trying to imitate Dita Von Teese, you'd be better off doing things for Alex that he appreciates.'

'Like what?' I frowned.

'It's your husband's fortieth birthday next month.'

'Yes, I know. We'll go out to dinner to celebrate.'

'What about throwing a surprise party for him? It was a really big deal for me when I hit the Big Four-O last year. I'd have loved somebody to do that for me.' His eyes took on a faraway look as his mouth turned down with sadness. 'Alas, it wasn't possible.'

For a moment I was quiet and considered. That was quite a nice idea. Actually, it was a bloody brilliant idea! I'd invite all our relatives, near and far. It would be a real knees-up, like nothing we'd had since our wedding reception. I'd get a band in and we'd dance, and laugh and have fun and be like kids again, giggling at Uncle Bob's terrible disco moves, and then when the singer turned to the slow ballads, we'd smooch with our bodies pressed against each other. And then, at the end of the night, flushed with the success of it all and high on champagne bubbles, we'd retire to our bedroom, arms around each other's waists. I'd briefly disappear into the bathroom, re-emerging in a lace corset with matching suspenders, then hit the button on the bedside radio – naturally, pre-programmed to a station that played smoochy jazz numbers – and immediately proceed to drive Alex mad with lust as I seductively quivered, shimmied and shook.

'It's not often I agree with you, Simon, but on this occasion, I think you could be right.'

'I'm gay, darling. Gay people are always right.'

At that moment Sophie returned. She scowled at me, then beamed at her uncle. For once it didn't bother me. My head was full of other things. Like arranging a party. Oh, and opening a Facebook account.

Chapter Six

The moment Simon and Sophie had left the house, I hurried back to the study. Opening up the laptop, I clicked off burlesque dancing – I'd pretty much got the gist of it anyway – and typed *Facebook* into the search engine. Why hadn't I done this before, I wondered, as the website link presented itself. I mentally shrugged. What was the point in having heaps of virtual friends? It wasn't as nice as sitting in a mate's kitchen putting the world to rights whilst hoovering up a box of cream cakes. But Simon was right. Again. I should try and keep up with the times. At the very least, make a show of it.

Minutes later, I had set up a profile. Now what? I needed some friends. I had stacks of them, didn't I? Well, definitely two.

I typed Jeanie's name into the search bar. Up popped her picture. Good heavens, what was she doing with her mouth? Some sort of peculiar pout? It made her look, well, weird. I sent her a friend request, and then searched for Caro. Oh, for goodness' sake, she was doing the same thing as Jeanie with her mouth. Out of curiosity, I typed in my brother's name. Simon's face immediately filled the screen, complete with camp trout-pout. I reviewed my own profile picture with fresh eyes. Clearly smiles – like flared trousers – came in and out of fashion and, right now, plumped-up lips were in. Moments later, I'd outlined my own with an eyebrow pencil, and filled them in with a dark lipstick. I practised pouting in the same way as Jeanie, Caro and Simon. Bingo. Taking a selfie, I uploaded it to Facebook. It looked nothing like me, but no matter, I now had hip lips.

I then searched for Aunty Shirley. Ah, love her, she didn't change. I sent her a friend request too, then scrolled through her list of friends. Forty of them! I was still struggling to find four. I knew who I was searching for – and there he was. Nerdy Jack. Except I couldn't see what he looked like. He had his back to the camera, standing on the banks of a brown river. Judging from the surrounding parched scrubland, it wasn't England. I clicked the mouse on his name, hoping to see more pictures, but none were forthcoming. Presumably I had to be friends with Jack in order to see them. I then put my husband's name into the search bar.

Up popped Alex with – I gasped – three hundred and twenty-two friends. What? How did he know so many people? Fortunately, Alex hadn't applied any privacy settings to his account, so I was able to take my time and scroll through all the names. Many of the men appeared to be of the florid-faced variety: dentists, dentistry lecturers, members of the Dental Association, also a charity for trigeminal neuralgia, and there were a considerable number of women there too, one of whom was a stunner. I peered at her name. Annabelle Huntingdon-Smyth. Hmm. I'd keep an eye on her. Maybe make discreet enquiries. Ah, there were Jeanie and Caro. Why were they Facebook friends with Alex? They didn't chat to him extensively in person, so why would they do it virtually? Should I, perhaps, friend request their husbands? I wasn't sure. If so, what would I chat to them about?

Hello, Ray! I'm now on Facebook. How's the garden? I liked your picture of what you had for dinner last night. By the way, is it true it takes you ages to come?

Likewise David.

Hey, Dave! I've finally caught up with social media. I know I only saw you a few hours ago when I had tea and cake with Caro in your kitchen, but I just thought I'd mention how tired you looked. Is this because you are exhausting yourself having sex three times a week?

Hell, if Jeanie and Caro could be friends with my husband, then I would be friends with theirs! After all, I needed to urgently swell my number of contacts. At this rate I'd be looking like Billy No-Mates. I sent off friend requests to David and Ray, and then turned my attention to the main box where the cursor was bobbing about.

What's on your mind?

Gosh, I hadn't a clue. Not specifically, anyway. What to have for tea tonight? Whether my daughter would ever willingly kiss me goodnight again? Whether my husband would ever come home from work in a fluster after suffering a miracle testosterone surge and masterfully tell me to get in the bedroom, and NOW, because he'd spotted my trout-pout on Facebook and it had driven him mad with desire? I was just debating what to write, when Facebook gave me a notification that Jeanie had accepted my friend request. Moments later a little box popped up indicating she was direct messaging me.

What are you doing on here?

Supposedly connecting with friends. Except I don't seem to have any.

Don't worry. People have zillions of friends, but they don't actually know them.

So what's the point of being friends with people you don't know?

So you look popular.

I boggled at the screen. What was this? I felt like I was back in primary school all over again with rivalry about who had the most scooby plaits hanging off the zipper of their pencil case.

I bumped into Simon on his way to Bluewater. He said you're planning a party.

I groaned. Trust my big-mouthed brother to start spreading the word.

Yes. Alex is forty next month. It's a surprise. Don't say anything.

Are you going to put it as your status?

What a brilliant idea!

Yes.

In which case, make sure your settings are switched to private so you don't get gatecrashers. Also, make sure Alex can't read it.

Oo-er. I'd not thought of that. Good point.

Will do. Catch you later xx

I clicked off the pop-up box, found the help button and sorted out the privacy settings, and then began to type.

Holly Hart is planning a party…

I sat back in my chair, feeling rather pleased with myself. Who to invite? Family, obviously. Both sides. The fact that they didn't mix very well meant I'd need to dilute the two groups with lots of mutual friends. As Alex had so many Facebook contacts, I thought it might be prudent to vet who was a *friend* friend, and not just an acquaintance. I certainly didn't want to end up with Rent-A-Crowd. When did friendship get so complicated?

I was just about to click off Facebook when another notification appeared, this time advising that Caro was now my friend. The pop-up box appeared again.

You're finally on Facebook! AND having a party? You never said!

I've only just decided. It's for Alex. He's going to be forty.

Ah. What are you going to give him (other than a superior bonk of course)?

I glanced about nervously, even though nobody was home. The last thing I wanted was Simon coming back early with Sophie, sneaking up behind me again, and reading about my fictitious sex life, especially after he'd caught me googling erotic strip moves. He'd think I was having some sort of breakdown. Either that, or suspect his sister was a nymphomaniac.

Let's not talk about things like that online, Caro.

What? Not talk about the party? Or sex?

Sex!

Sigh Fine. So when's the party?

Sometime next month. Need to put my thinking hat on.

Do you want Rachel Weston's phone number? She's a party planner.

Rachel Weston was a pushy school mum. She wasn't my sort of person at all. She had one of those 'fritefly porsh' accents that spoke of elocution and social climbing, rather than being born with a silver spoon in her mouth.

Thanks, but I think I can manage.

Okay. But if you change your mind and use Rachel, she'll expect an invite.

In that case I would definitely manage without her. I mean, how hard could it be to throw a party?

Chapter Seven

I spent a satisfying hour surfing the internet for suitable party venues, ultimately settling on the local golf club. Alex's birthday was the seventh of October, which, this year, fell on a Saturday. Picking up the phone, I spoke to the club's social events manageress. She advised that the Mayflower Suite had unexpectedly become available due to a wedding cancellation.

'Oh dear,' I said, momentarily sorry for the bride whose nuptials had turned to ashes. However, her loss was most definitely my gain.

'These things happen,' said the disembodied voice. 'At such short notice, you'll have to pay the entire fee. No deposit.'

'Right,' I gulped. Alex, whilst not exactly stingy, nonetheless kept a firm hand on the Hart finances. I might have trouble explaining the withdrawal of a large sum of money from the joint account. Thankfully I had squirrelled away enough of my own wages to just about cover the party costs. No matter. This would be my birthday present to him. I rather suspected there wouldn't be much left in the coffers afterwards, so presenting him with an actual gift might not be possible. I had a mental vision of handing Alex a small and beautifully wrapped oblong, his eyes lighting up.

'Holly, you shouldn't have! Is this the gold tie pin I was after?'

'Er—'

'Oh. A bar of chocolate.'

I shook away such thoughts. Too late now. I'd set the wheels in motion. Jeanie, Caro and Simon would never forgive me if I did a party U-turn.

'The Mayflower Suite is the largest function room,' said the voice. 'It has a capacity of one hundred and fifty people, its own bar, and permanent dance floor.'

'Sounds perfect.'

'Now, what about music? Did you have a DJ in mind?'

'I was hoping for a band.'

'This is your lucky day, Mrs Hart! The bride had booked a band, and I know they're still available.'

'Brilliant!'

'One other thing…' The voice hesitated.

'Yes?'

'Would you be interested in karaoke too?'

'I think the band on its own will be enough.'

'Have you heard of band-karaoke? I mention it because the bride booked these musicians specifically because of their diversity. They offer an hour's slot for guests to sing their own songs with live backing. The bride was meant to have been singing a couple of ballads to her new husband, but now sadly it's not to be. However, the karaoke element is very popular with family and friends. It provides a lot of fun, and would definitely make a fortieth birthday party go with an extra swing.'

'You've talked me into it.'

I had a sudden vision of taking the mic and singing something hauntingly beautiful to Alex. But then again, maybe not. My voice, especially after a few drinks, was more Jeremy Clarkson than Kelly Clarkson, but perhaps I could give my husband a rousing rendition of 'Happy Birthday' before someone else took a proper turn.

'And food? I don't suppose you'd like the bride's caterers, would you?'

'A three-course meal would definitely be beyond my budget. But what about a buffet?'

'Yes, that can be arranged.'

We finished off with me agreeing to pop in after the school run the following morning and pay the full amount.

Checking my watch, I headed off to the kitchen to start dinner. Alex wasn't a fan of ready meals, saying they were of no nutritional value and full of unrefined sugar, which was terrible for the teeth. Everything I cooked had to be from scratch. As I was no Nigella, this was sometimes problematical. Like now. My husband would be coming through the door at any moment expecting organic pork chops and a mountain of pesticide-free fresh veg. There was no time for burning the former and peeling the latter. Hurriedly, I tossed pasta into a saucepan and mincemeat into a pan, furtively extracting from the depths of the larder a concealed jar of tomato and basil sauce for a speedy Bolognese. The sound of a key in the door let me know I'd not allowed enough time to nip outside to the wheelie bin and dispose of the evidence. Looking around for somewhere – anywhere – to hide the jar, I spotted my handbag on the kitchen chair. Moments later, the offending jar rested amongst a detritus of crumpled tissues, old sweet wrappers and tampons. I really must sort my bag out. It was shameful.

'Mm, something smells good,' said Alex, walking into the kitchen. He came over to greet me. I raised my mouth up to meet his kiss. He avoided my lips, instead pecking my cheek. I hid my disappointment. Why should tonight be any different to yesterday evening? And the one before that? I wondered if Jeanie and Caro's husbands did the same to them, or whether Ray and David were quite up for ravishing their wives over the potato peelings.

Alex moved over to a stack of mail I'd left on the kitchen worktop. He began thumbing through it. 'The house is incredibly quiet,' he said, grimacing at a brown envelope.

'I expect Sophie will be home any moment.'

'She's out on a school night?'

'Yes,' I nodded, 'but don't worry, she was very conscientious and did her French homework beforehand.'

'Where has she gone?'

'Shopping. She's at Bluewater with Simon.'

At the mention of my brother's name, Alex frowned. 'Is that wise, Holly?'

'What do you mean?' My tone was slightly defensive. I wasn't always my brother's biggest fan, but equally I didn't like Alex insinuating Simon was a dreadful influence on our daughter.

'She'll come home with all sorts of unsuitable clothes, or ridiculous high heels entirely inappropriate for a child of thirteen.'

'She's nearly fourteen, Alex.'

'Yes, fourteen going on twenty-four, and I blame your brother for that.'

I turned the bubbling pasta down and briskly stirred the Bolognese, irritated.

'I think her peers are more likely to be the cause of her trying to look older. All the kids are like it. Have you seen some of the girls that come of the school gates? They look like jail bait.'

'Yes, and as our daughter is one of them, no doubt all the other school parents will be blaming Sophie *and* your brother as the cause.'

'Are you deliberately trying to wind me up?' I asked, tetchy now. I scraped some meat that had caught on the bottom of the pan.

'No.' Alex abandoned the post and turned to me. 'Why are *you* suddenly so protective of him?'

'Listen, just because Simon is sometimes eccentric' – I ignored Alex making a *pffft* sound – 'it doesn't mean he's a nasty person.'

'I didn't say he was nasty. But he *is* irresponsible. The last time he took Sophie shopping, she came home wearing a skirt with splits up to her navel.'

'You're exaggerating.'

'It was for the school disco and most unsuitable.'

'Well at least it was for the school disco and not bloody Stringfellows,' I said tartly.

'No doubt your brother had ideas about borrowing the skirt himself.'

'Oh for God's sake, Alex. He's gay. Not transsexual. And so what if he was, and wanted to borrow the skirt? What is your issue with my brother?'

'Nothing,' said Alex, mutinously. 'I'm going upstairs to change. And I'm not hungry any more.'

I stared at his retreating back, my eyes narrowing, just as his mobile pinged with a text. The words were out of my mouth before I could stop them.

'Hurry up and read your message, Alex. It might be Queenie again, wanting to rub you all over, which is more than I bloody get to do.'

Alex froze. For a moment he remained motionless, facing the other way, but then swung round. His face was a mask of fury.

'That old chestnut *again*, Holly? You're like the proverbial stuck record. How many months has it been? But you can't let it drop. At least once a week you have to bring up the subject of an unhinged ex-patient. Nobody is rubbing me all over, and since when did you want to anyway?' He stalked out of the kitchen.

'You're right!' I yelled after him, 'because I'd like something a bit more than that.' I chucked the spoon down and turned off the hob. Moments later I was striding after him. 'I'd like some SEX,' I shouted. 'Do you hear? SEX-SEX-SEX-SEX!' I charged into the hall – only to come face to face with Simon and Sophie who had just arrived home. From the shocked look on their faces, it was obvious they'd heard every word.

'Darling hearts, are you having a cheeky little row?' asked Simon, attempting to lighten things for Sophie's benefit.

'Oh no, Uncle Simon,' Sophie snarled, 'that will be Mum practising her Am Dram lines again. She's something of a drama queen these days. Eh, Mum?'

'A Drama Mama?' he sniggered, before arching a newly waxed eyebrow at me. 'Whatever next, Holly?'

'Oh sod off, Simon,' I muttered.

'I can see I'm not wanted, so I won't stay,' he said, tossing his head. 'Lovely to spend time with you, Sophie darling.' He kissed his niece on both cheeks. 'If things get too heated here, give your uncle a call. You can always come and live with me.'

'I heard that!' Alex's voice drifted along the landing, before the sound of our bedroom door slammed. Great. No doubt Sophie would be joining in shortly, too.

'Simon, *please*,' I hissed. 'And do you have to wind Alex up?'

'He winds himself up, the pompous pleb.'

'Bye, Uncle Simon,' she said, gathering up her shopping bags, and following in her father's wake. Moments later her own bedroom door banged shut.

'So many tempers in this household,' Simon tutted. 'What's going on, Holly? One minute you're reading about seduction through the art of burlesque, the next you're chasing your husband down the hallway angrily demanding sex. Are you a frustrated dominatrix? Is there a whip hiding in the cupboard, alongside the ironing board and vacuum cleaner?'

'Can we drop the subject, please?' I said, now thoroughly rattled.

'This marriage is plainly in trouble.'

Rupert slunk past, his tail wagging apologetically, as he disappeared up the stairs to find a quiet spot.

'Look, you worry about your own relationships,' I told him irritably. 'Thank you for taking Sophie out, and I'm sorry you caught Alex and me having cross words.'

'I would kiss you goodbye, dearest, but you look all sweaty in the face after shouting.' Simon wrinkled his nose. 'And if you're hoping to get your leg over tonight, shave them first, dah-ling.

They're hairier than mine.' And with that my brother minced off, leaving me inwardly seething.

I stalked back to the kitchen to clear away food nobody wanted and, just to let my husband and daughter know they were in good company, slammed the kitchen door so hard the very foundations of the house shook.

Chapter Eight

I woke up on Friday morning knowing that there were two things I absolutely had to do. The first was pay the events lady at the golf club my entire savings for Alex's fortieth birthday party. The second was to inject some calm into my marriage.

Alex and I had gone to sleep last night with our backs to each other in the dark, bodies tense. Both of us had been doing the sort of enforced slow breathing that indicated we were fast asleep, untroubled, and entirely oblivious to each other, even though we both knew we were lying there awake, seething with ill temper.

When I awoke in the morning, Alex had already left the house. I got out of bed and drooped off to the bathroom. Stepping into the shower, I realised how ridiculous the situation was. How could we have fun at a big celebratory party when we were constantly sniping at each other? I stepped out of the shower and wrapped the towel around me, padding back into the bedroom. Reaching for my mobile phone, I sat down on the edge of the bed and tapped out a message to Alex.

Sorry to mention Queenie. Again. I guess I'm just a jealous old bag. I love you.

Seconds later, there was a reply.

Let's put it behind us. See you later x

I exhaled, partly relieved that I was forgiven, partly sad that he'd not ended his message with the three magic words, as I'd done. Still, I pondered, looking at the text, he'd ended it with a kiss. Just the one. Nothing over the top. Sighing, I went back to the bathroom and quickly finished drying off. I wanted to cook Sophie a proper breakfast before she went off to school. It hadn't escaped my attention that our daughter was watching what she ate. I was well aware that her classmates did the same, trying to emulate the latest reality star. I wasn't quite sure why they thought a pin-thin body and lollipop head looked alluring, but they did, and that was that.

Twenty minutes later, Sophie came into the kitchen looking mutinous. She obviously wanted to let me know she'd not forgotten my shameful outburst in the hall last night. Regrettably life didn't come with a rewind button, so I took the next available option, which was to pretend it had never happened. I ignored my daughter's reproachful stares as she sat down at the kitchen table, and smiled brightly as I set the full English before her. I'd also decided that diversionary tactics were required to help Sophie forget what she'd heard.

'Can you keep a secret?' I said cosily, beaming away.

Sophie looked up from her plate, a mixture of curiosity and rebellion imprinted upon her features.

'Depends what it is.' She speared a sausage and dipped it in egg yolk.

I pulled out a stool and sat down opposite her, hoping to eat my own breakfast companionably with her. There was a time when we'd done so. It seemed long ago.

'It's Dad's birthday next month.'

Sophie shrugged and bit into the sausage. I wasn't telling her anything she didn't already know.

'It's his fortieth,' I pressed on, 'which is quite a big deal, so I thought I'd throw a party to celebrate.'

Sophie looked at me, ready to ridicule. 'Here?'

'Most definitely not,' I replied, suppressing a shudder. Years ago, I'd had a house-warming party, and spent the entirety of the following day deep-cleaning, including bleaching bathroom walls from the evidence of dreadful aims by drunken men, to shampooing the carpets after two women I'd vaguely known had upchucked all over the new Berber. I'd vowed never again.

'If not here, then where?' asked Sophie, puzzled.

'Well, at a venue. The golf club have a fabulous function room available.'

Sophie's face lit up. 'You mean, a proper party? With a DJ and strobe lights?'

'A band, actually.' I saw her expression of delight waver. 'A karaoke band,' I ploughed on. 'They'll sing popular songs for everyone to dance to, but also do a stint where the guests can sing with professional backing.' Sophie's eyes widened with astonishment, and then her whole face became wreathed in smiles. For a moment I basked in her evident joy, and privately thought how pretty she looked without the habitual sneer.

'Omigod, that is so cool, Mum! Will I be allowed to sing a song?'

'Of course!'

'I'm going to be the envy of my class. Everybody's going to want to come, but' – she paused dramatically – 'only those who are in favour with me will receive an invitation.'

'Ah. Just remember this is Daddy's party. Invitations will be to his friends.'

The sullen expression was back in a flash. 'Oh. So it's an old fogey party. No worries. I'll stay over at Lucy's house for the night.'

I immediately back-pedalled. 'Obviously you can invite one or two friends,' I said hastily, 'I want you to have a great time too.'

'Only one or two?'

'Okay, maybe three or four,' I nodded, anxious to recapture the sparkle and fizz of just a few seconds ago.

'Mum, I have *heaps* of friends. There are six of us in our exclusive group, but I'm also pretty good friends with Lucy. I'd like her to come, but if I ask her then Tierney will expect an invite. And if the two of them come, Nicole will demand an invitation. And I can't invite Nicole without Jasmine. She'd have a total bitch fit otherwise, and turn everyone against me in a nanosecond.'

'Oh. Well, I wouldn't want that to happen,' I said, biting my lip, remembering my own school days and the fragility of friendships. 'All right, let's say ten friends.' Excellent, Holly. If you can't agree, compromise. Ten friends was a generous offer.

Sophie instantly reverted back to beaming at me over the fry-up. I mentally sighed with relief. Her good mood continued throughout the school run. She even kissed me goodbye when I pulled over, illegally on yellow zig-zags, to let her out of the car.

'Bye, Mum. Love you.'

I was so shell-shocked at the endearment, I nearly burst into tears on the spot. Instead I blinked rapidly and kissed my daughter as a car horn, somewhere behind, blared angrily at my dire parking.

'One more thing,' I said to Sophie, as she released the door handle, 'not a word to Dad. It's a surprise – my present to him.'

'My lips are sealed,' she nodded, before catching sight of some friends and scrambling out of the car to be with them. 'Hey, guess what!' I heard her shout. 'I'm having a party, and you're invited!' I lingered for a moment on the zig-zags, watching my feisty teenager having a moment of glory as she held court to her delighted mates. I suddenly felt very emotional. I was so used to ducking Sophie's verbal missiles that now, with hostility temporarily suspended, I wanted the moment to be repeated. To last longer. I fought an urge to get out of the car, race after her, and hug her tightly. That would never do. She'd be so embarrassed. A rogue tear spilt from one eye, startling me. I marvelled at how quickly emotion could be conveyed from the heart to the brain, and then on to the eyeball. Swiping it away, I signalled to pull out – and nearly ploughed into Caro whose vehicle was already swooping in front of mine. Joe and Lizzie tumbled out, pavement side. Moments later, Caro's driver door opened – and was nearly removed by a lorry thundering past.

'Holly!' she called, hastening over to my driver's side and taking her life in her hands as a result. She flattened herself against my vehicle as rush-hour traffic sped past. 'We need to discuss Alex's birthday. David and I haven't a clue what to buy him. Come over for coffee. I'll give Jeanie a ring, too.'

'Okay, lovely,' I said, conscious of a pile of ironing awaiting my attention. To hell with it. I'd do it later. 'Give me half an hour. I have a party to pay for,' I grinned. 'It's going to be at the golf club.'

'Ooooh, the *golf* club,' Caro said whilst letting out a low whistle. 'That won't be cheap.'

'Well, it's not every day your husband turns forty,' I shrugged. 'There was a bridal cancellation, but I need to pay for everything now to secure the date.'

'Okay, I won't hold you up. See you soon.'

Caro scampered back to her car, nearly knocking a cyclist off his bike, but attracting the attention of a man driving a white van who buzzed down his window and whistled loudly.

'Nice arse!' I heard him shout.

Fifteen minutes later, I parked between a Bentley and a Jaguar, acutely aware that my dented and dirty vehicle looked very out of place. Once inside the building, I adopted a confident expression – as if frequenting golf clubs was all in a day's work – and made my way over to reception. The events manageress just happened to be behind the desk and greeted me warmly. For one surreal moment I thought she was going to kiss me on both cheeks, continental style.

'So, Mrs, Hart,' she concluded, after running through an A4 sheet of neatly typed costings, 'all I need from you now is a cheque for this amount.' Her manicured finger pointed to a figure that momentarily made my bowels lurch.

'Super!' I said brightly, then immediately cringing. Who said 'super' these days? Possibly drivers of shiny Jags and Bentleys like those in the car park, but most definitely not owners of battered four-by-fours. I reached for my bag but, as I unzipped it, my nostrils twitched as the golf club's reception area filled with the pungent smell of garlic, tomato and basil. 'Ah,' I said, fishing out yesterday's empty jar in front of the wide-eyed manageress. 'Could I possibly trouble you for a bin?'

Chapter Nine

I arrived at Caro's just as Jeanie was pulling up.

'Coo-ee,' said Jeanie, momentarily struggling to get out of her car. 'I'm going to have to go on a diet for this fabulous party you're organising. Caro phoned me from her car and let slip you've booked the golf club. Very posh.'

'Nothing but the best for my hubby,' I grinned.

Jeanie linked my arm companionably as we walked up to Caro's front door. 'And quite right too. Alex deserves it.' She lowered her voice, whispering conspiratorially, 'Between you and me, I didn't sleep much last night. I was all steamed up after you telling me about Alex and his superior bonk.'

I laughed good-naturedly. 'Did you get Ray to oblige?'

'Yes,' Jeanie nodded, 'but I think he wondered what the hell had got into me. I wanted to be a bit more, you know, adventurous, which was rather at odds with the way I looked.'

'A vision in curlers and face cream?'

'Something like that,' Jeanie giggled. 'But he rose to the challenge magnificently.'

'What challenge?' said Caro, opening the front door.

'I've just been telling Holly that Ray and I are practising the superior bonk,' Jeanie said with a wink, stepping into Caro's hall.

'Is that why you look a bit peaky today, Holly?' said Caro, shutting the door after us. 'Were you at it again last night, by any chance?'

'Absolutely,' I nodded. Well, it was only a small lie. We'd certainly been at each other's throats. That counted for something, surely?

Caro led the way into the warmth of her kitchen. The weather had cooled dramatically in the last twenty-four hours. I let out an involuntarily shiver, rubbing a hand over one bare arm, flattening the little hairs now standing up as a result of the rapid change of temperature from outside to indoors. I'd been stupid enough to leave the house without a jacket or little cardi.

'Chocolate cake?' asked Caro, removing from the larder a monster creation covered in rich fondant and sprinkles. I automatically began salivating – a sure sign that every mouthful contained a thousand calories.

'Oh dear,' said Jeanie, looking torn, 'only seconds ago I told Holly I was going on a diet for Alex's party.'

'Tomorrow is another day for diets,' said Caro.

'You're right. Fill it up,' said Jeanie, nodding at the plate Caro had set in front of her.

'I'll put the kettle on while you're cutting us both a slice,' I said.

I stuck the kettle under the tap and, while it was filling, gazed out of the kitchen window. Damn, it had started to rain. Nor had I come out with an umbrella. Ah well, at least my filthy car would get a bit of a wash. I plugged the kettle in and sat back down next to Jeanie, leaving Caro to do the beverages.

'So, give us all the details,' said Jeanie, looking terribly over-excited. Admittedly, it wasn't often us girls got out these days. A film here. A restaurant there. But never a boogie. We lacked the confidence to strut our stuff anywhere other than at a rare wedding or very occasional party. 'Will there be a disco?'

I could imagine Sophie, if she'd been here, ridiculing Jeanie, telling my friend that the word 'disco' went out with Noah's Ark.

'Yes, there will be music and, hopefully, lots of dancing.'

'Wonderful!' Jeanie clapped her hands together, eyes shining. 'And what sound?'

'Eh?'

'You know… eighties… nineties… techno… trance… garage?' Jeanie stood up, and dropping chocolate cake crumbs from her lip, did some voluptuous wiggles. 'Should I be dancing like this?' She then flung her arms wide, brought them together across her ample bosom, dropped the elbows down and started voguing around the kitchen table. 'Or maybe like this? I can do a great impersonation of Madonna – obviously not the figure though, only vocally.'

'Jeanie, sit down,' I laughed, 'and save your energy for the party. And no, it won't be a *disco* because I've booked a band.'

'No!'

'Yes! And…' I added, enjoying the look of delight on her face, 'it's a karaoke-band, so guests get to sing if they want to!'

'Yay!' she squeaked, flinging her arms wide again and nearly sending the chocolate cake flying. 'I'll definitely do a number. Maybe several.' She squirmed with happiness on Caro's kitchen chair. 'Do you remember when I used to be in a band in my early twenties?'

'How could we forget?' said Caro, good-naturedly.

'My speciality was Christina Aguilera,' she beamed. 'Back then I used to have platinum blonde hair and a figure to die for. However, despite the boobs and stomach succumbing to gravity, the voice still has it.' She warbled a few notes by way of demonstration. 'Tell you what,' she said, her eyes lighting up, 'I'll sing a song just for Alex. It can be his birthday present from me.'

'He'll be thrilled, Jeanie,' I said warmly, knowing that Alex would be touched, if a little embarrassed.

She looked thoughtful for a moment. 'Let me see,' she said frowning, then put a finger up in the air, as if a light bulb had just gone off inside her head. There was something theatrical about the pose. Almost – as I would wonder later when replaying this moment – deliberate. 'I'm going to sing "Genie in a Bottle".' She looked at me speculatively. *Defiantly?* 'Because I, for one' – she waggled her eyebrows – 'would secretly love to rub Alex the right way.'

And in that moment, it was as if a pause button had been hit on a giant cosmic remote control. Everyday life around me froze. Jeanie's mouth stopped working. Caro ceased offering me a slice of chocolate cake. Even the rain paused in its lashing against the window pane as my mind zipped back to last Christmas. Re-read *that* text. My eyes widened. No! Or… I gulped… was there an outside chance Jeanie could be Queenie? After all, she'd always been a flirt with the men, Alex included. I'd never really had reason to doubt the cheeky behaviour of one of my best friends before. Until now. Was it just a massive coincidence that Jeanie had mentioned the very words used in the sext messages? Or had she just made a massive faux pas? I didn't know. I knew I wasn't particularly rational in my thinking where those wretched messages were concerned.

I wouldn't confront Jeanie – I needed to be sure. But from this moment on, I vowed to watch Jeanie closer than a hawk hovering over a field mouse.

Chapter Ten

There must have been something in my expression that made Jeanie pause and look at me uncertainly.

'What?' she asked, slightly on the defensive. 'Is it my voice? Do you think I can't sing? I can practise,' she said, looking anxious, desperate not to have her moment under the spotlight thwarted.

'N-no,' I stammered, urgently recovering my composure. 'You sounded great. Fabulous.' I nodded.

'Are you sure?' she looked uncertain now, worried. 'I don't want to make a dick of myself.'

'You can't make a dick of yourself,' said Caro, 'because you haven't got one.'

'I know,' said Jeanie, quietly, 'I said "dick" because it sounds better than "twat".'

'Oh I don't know!' I said brightly, 'nothing wrong with the word "twat" in the right place and the right set of circumstances.' I met her gaze. 'And when in relation to the right person too, of course.'

Jeanie blanched. She was looking at me apprehensively. Caro was frowning, her expression one of bewilderment. She couldn't work out what was suddenly going on, or why the atmosphere had changed from fun chatter to edgy tension.

'I won't sing,' said Jeanie, now looking visibly upset.

'Don't be silly,' said Caro, 'it's a karaoke band. Anyone can sing. That's the whole point of something like this. Having a laugh at people who are out of tune.'

Jeanie looked horrified. 'Was I out of tune?'

'No!' Caro and I chorused together.

'Of course you must sing,' I said, touching her arm, anxious to slap down the cow in me and restore pleasantness. I was imagining things. Making mountains out of molehills. I could almost hear my husband whispering in my ear. *Upsetting your bestie now, Holly? What is it with you? You're beyond paranoid.* I mentally shook my head. 'Your voice is wonderful,' I assured Jeanie. 'Just brilliant. You should audition on *The X Factor.*' I meant it. She did have a great voice. It was just her chosen song that had touched a nerve.

Jeanie swallowed. Nodded. Then exhaled shakily. 'Okay. As long as you're sure.'

'Of course I'm sure! I'm might even take the mic first and sing "Happy Birthday". It will be dire and very off-key, but I don't care. As long as everyone is enjoying themselves.'

'I'll sing something too,' said Caro, grinning. 'When I was a teenager, I used to dream of being a pop star.'

'I think we all used to sing into our hairbrushes in the privacy of our bedrooms,' I smiled, forcing myself to relax, tugging my mind away from last Christmas to the here, the now, in Caro's kitchen.

'What will you sing, Caro?' asked Jeanie, now fully recovered and turning her attention back to the chocolate cake.

'"Total Eclipse of the Heart",' said Caro, without any hesitation. 'I have a voice like a foot rasp, so it's the perfect tune to growl into the microphone.'

'Oooh, I love that song,' said Jeanie, enthusiastically. 'And what are we all going to wear? I'm definitely up for raiding the housekeeping and buying a new frock. The last time I partied I was only a size ten, which shows how long ago that was!' She patted her generous curves.

'I think the three of us should have a shopping day together,' said Caro.

'Great idea,' said Jeanie, her eyes shining. 'Perhaps we could ask Simon to come along, Holly? You know, for guidance. He's very Gok Wan in his manner, isn't he?'

'Believe me, Simon is the last one we want to accompany us. He'll be shredding our self-esteem faster than a kid tearing at birthday wrapping paper.'

'But I like Simon,' Jeanie protested. 'He's so funny.'

I looked at Jeanie incredulously. 'Well, if you don't mind being told your breasts are like socks, and your buttocks resemble a sofa that's lost its stuffing, then go ahead. But count me out.' Perish the thought that my brother joined us. He'd love every moment. Be in his element. I could see him now, looking down his nose at something designer, making loud comments about putting me in trousers to hide the thread veins on my legs. Oh no. Definitely not. 'Quite apart from anything else,' I added, 'remember he has his own online fashion business. He'll be steering you into something hideously expensive and completely crazy, like fuchsia pink covered in ginger feathers teamed with scarlet heels and saying, "Fabulous, dah-ling, now you're speaking to the world and showing the colours of your soul".'

'Okay, okay. Shall we go to Bluewater tomorrow then?' asked Caro. 'Press our noses up to the brightly lit glass windows of Top Shop, before heading over to Evans?'

'I quite like the sound of fuchsia pink and ginger feathers,' said Jeanie, pouting.

Before I could contribute any further to the conversation, my mobile began ringing. I reached into my handbag. The display let me know it was Alex. Caro caught sight of the screen.

'Look out,' said Caro, 'Alex is about to summon Holly to his surgery saying he can't see another patient until he's had the superior bonk.'

Jeanie giggled, and I put a finger to my lips as I answered.

'Hi, darling,' I purred, letting the girls know I was thrilled to hear from my husband who I was still madly in love with and, if I'm absolutely honest, conveying to Jeanie that no matter how many times she sang 'Genie in a Bottle' she didn't stand a chance.

'Holly,' said Alex, his voice full of irritation, 'where are you?'

I laughed seductively and said, 'I can be anywhere you want me to be.'

Caro and Jeanie raised their eyebrows at each other as if to say, 'See! He really is summoning her for that superior bonk!'

'Good,' said Alex, ignoring my innuendo, 'because my nurse has just gone home with a migraine, and I need a dental assistant for this afternoon's patient list. Can you get to the surgery as soon as possible, please?'

'Your wish is my command,' I said huskily.

There was a pause before Alex spoke again.

'Have you been on the sherry?'

I grinned at Caro and Jeanie, letting them think that naughty flirtatious banter between Alex and myself was all in a morning's work. Regrettably, I'd started something here, thanks to being privately embarrassed about sparse couplings with my husband. If I couldn't prove to myself that all was well, if nothing else I'd make damn sure I'd prove it to my girlfriends. Especially Jeanie. I knew perfectly well they'd repeat it back to their respective husbands. I could almost hear Jeanie saying, 'The Harts' marriage is alive and kicking.'

What they didn't know, of course, was that it was just kicking.

Chapter Eleven

Jeanie kindly agreed to drop Sophie home after school, and the three of us promised to meet at Bluewater the next day. I arrived at the dental practice forty minutes later.

As I walked into Alex's surgery room, my husband glanced up from his keyboard and gave me a grateful look. His tone, however, was brisk.

'Get your scrubs on, Holly. There's not a moment to lose. The next patient is due in two minutes.'

'Give me a chance,' I puffed, hanging up my coat and slipping my handbag into a corner. I wasn't keen to leave it in the staff room. There were no lockers, and only last week somebody with light fingers had removed fifty pounds from another nurse's handbag. Not that a thief would have much success with the contents of mine. Unless they liked stinky food jars.

I headed there now though to get changed, emerging seconds later to catch a glimpse of a woman going into Alex's surgery. His patient had arrived. She was tall and slim, with a waterfall of dark hair tumbling down her back. The door shut behind her. I took a deep breath, smoothed down my uniform, and moved down the hallway to Alex's surgery. I was just about to press down the door handle when I heard a throaty laugh on the other side of the wooden panels, followed by Alex joining in. I paused. He sounded so happy. It made me realise that, recently, we hadn't done a lot of laughing in our marriage. The woman said something undistinguishable. I strained to hear:

… ironed things out … questions … problem gone away … dangers of sexting …

I gasped, quickly stilling the noise of my breath to glean any further key words, sifting through the muttering and furtive laughter coming from within. Alex was talking now, but mumbling. I couldn't work out what he was saying and was forced to press one ear flat against the door. The woman was now speaking. It was little more than a murmur. And then she said an audible word that was never very far from the corners of my thoughts. *Queenie.*

'Is everything all right, Mrs Hart?'

I jumped, bashing my forehead hard on the edge of the door frame. I turned, my face a picture of guilt, to see Alex's receptionist Jenny – evidently on her way to the loo – frowning at the sight of the boss's wife eavesdropping.

'Yes,' I spluttered, rubbing my throbbing head, 'just… just listening to see… if it's clear to go in.' I pointed one finger at the door. Made a stabbing motion. 'Someone's in there.'

'Yes, that's right. It's the patient, Mrs Hart,' said Jenny, as if addressing someone very slow, 'and she's waiting for you.'

'Right, yes, thanks,' I nodded. Blasted woman. I had never taken to Jenny. She had a haughty demeanour, and much of the time carried on like she owned the place. 'Thank you for the reminder.'

She gave me a strange look, but didn't move. For goodness' sake. Didn't she have a pee to do? Or did she always loiter in corridors? *A bit like you*, said a little voice in my head. Ignoring it, I shouldered the door open.

It was clear that Alex and his patient had stopped exchanging secrets to listen to me and Jenny outside. My husband's expression was guarded, and the patient had arranged her features into one of neutrality. As I glanced at her, my eyes widened with surprise. I knew her. Well, not personally. But I definitely recognised her. She was one of Alex's Facebook friends, easily recognised because in a sea of jowly-cheeked men and grey-haired women, her photograph had leapt out. I could see it hadn't done her justice. She was, quite simply, stunning. And she knew about Queenie. I gulped. So, was Jeanie 'Queenie', or could this exotic creature be her instead? I checked her left hand. No wedding band. She was a free agent. And a very beautiful free agent, at that. Bugger. And what was her name? Pretty sure it had an upper-class ring to it. Annabelle Arty-Farty-Something-or-Other.

'At last,' said Alex, 'we've been waiting.'

'Yes. Sorry,' I said, meekly bowing my sore head, and scuttling over to the far end of the room where sterilised instruments were set out on a tray. I picked everything up and, moving to the right of the patient, set it down on a bracket table next to my husband's elbow.

'Thanks,' said Alex. 'Okay, we're doing a white filling today.' He pressed a foot pedal so the chair reclined backwards. 'Let's get you numbed up, Annabelle.' He gave her his best chairside smile and picked up a syringe full of local anaesthetic. 'Open wide.'

Annabelle gave a little giggle, as if Alex had said something funny. And naughty. I was standing to her left, slightly behind her head, so couldn't see if she was smiling with her eyes at Alex. I looked at my husband. His eyes were twinkling with... what? Humour? Amusement? I couldn't see his mouth because he'd pulled his dental mask up.

'Oh, that is fan-*tas*-tic,' he murmured. 'Let's just find the right spot' – he paused, as Annabelle made an appreciative noise. 'There it is, now get ready for a big prick,' he said, eyes widening – did his eyebrows just waggle? – as Annabelle gasped like a porn star. What the hell was going on here?

'Perfect,' Alex sighed. 'How was it for you?'

Pardon?

'Would you like to wash your mouth out?' I said, shoving a plastic cup of pink mouth rinse under her nose. 'Sometimes pricks can leave a bitter taste.'

I glared at Alex over Annabelle's head. He glared back.

Annabelle took the cup, swished, but didn't lean over the basin.

'Er, you're meant to spit that out,' I said.

Her head swivelled in my direction, and she looked me straight in the eye. 'I always swallow.'

Bitch! There *was* something going on here.

She sat back again and Alex gazed at her adoringly.

'Are we ready?'

'Oh yes,' she murmured, 'as ready as I'll ever be.'

'Let's begin,' said Alex, *sotto voce*. 'I promise I won't hurt you.'

'You could never hurt me, darling,' she whispered.

Darling?

'I'm ready,' Alex nodded, 'ready to drill into you.'

'Yes, oh yes.'

Suddenly the pair of them were vibrating away, Alex with a look of intense concentration on his face, Annabelle making little squeaks and grunts, gripping the arms of the chair, then digging her fingers into the padded fabric, now raking her nails back and forth leaving tiny scratches, and finally letting out a long, shuddering moan. The drill whirred to a stop.

'I wish all my patients were like you,' Alex crooned.

I gnashed my teeth, aware that I'd been doing it throughout the procedure so far. At this rate I'd chomp through my crowns and need a mouth guard to protect them. Perhaps I should shove Annabelle onto the floor, prostrate myself in front of Alex and cry, 'Quick, I'm grinding, ahhhhhhhh.'

'And now,' said Alex, 'the best bit. I'm going to fill you.'

'Oh, you wonderful man.'

'All in a day's work,' said Alex modestly, as he took the burnisher from me.

Nobody spoke while the cavity was finished off – bonded, light cured, shaped and finally polished.

'All done,' Alex smiled.

Annabelle gave a contented sigh.

'Oh dear,' she said, in a little girl voice, 'I'm all dribbly.'

It was too much. I grabbed the aspirator and shoved it none too gently in her mouth.

'Try sucking on this.'

I'd had enough. First Jeanie telling me she wanted to sing just for Alex, and not any old song, but a song about a magical creature who rubbed phallic objects, and now this woman in my husband's surgery, writhing away in his chair, making sex noises, with Alex doing the equivalent of pillow talk throughout the treatment. Without a doubt one of them was Queenie. And I was on red alert.

Chapter Twelve

The rest of the afternoon passed in a whirl of root canals, extractions and amalgam. I had no chance to quiz Alex about Annabelle and, even if there had been a suitable lull in work, I decided that the surgery wasn't the place to interrogate my husband, especially with my emotions swinging wildly between hurt and boiling anger, and also a beady-eyed receptionist never very far away. I had no doubt Jenny would delight in gossiping to the other associates and their nurses about Mrs Hart making wild accusations about goodness-only-knew-what.

I left the surgery before Alex. He had patient notes to finish off, and a till to cash up. But I wouldn't have too long to wait until he was home. And then I'd resist the temptation to pull up a stool and shine a light in his eyes to ask exactly how he knew Annabelle, and what they had in common – other than a horizontal position in his surgery.

Sophie was already home when I arrived. She was in high spirits and greeted me effusively.

'Hiya!' she beamed. Good heavens. Was this child actually my daughter, or an alien that had stolen her identity? 'I've had such a fab day at school.'

'Lovely, darling,' I said, smiling at her exuberance. No tales today about bullies or bitchiness. A relief on both sides.

'You know you said I could invite ten friends to Dad's party?'

'Er, yes?'

'I'm really sorry, Mummy,' said my daughter, in a sugary sweet voice, 'but it might now be twelve. Is that okay? I just didn't want to upset Amelia and Tara.'

'Oh, right.' Good heavens, we mustn't disappoint *them*, must we? Clearly it was much more important to keep friends happy, as opposed to me. I was about to protest, but then stopped. I didn't want to rankle Sophie. I was still enjoying the novelty of having a cheerful teen. And – confession time – I just wasn't up for any door slamming right now. I chucked my coat over the bannister and went into the kitchen, my mind on what to cook for dinner. Sophie padded after me, possibly anticipating a delayed negative reaction over the two extra friends, but she was pleasantly surprised.

'Okay, darling, I'll agree to Amelia and Tara, but if we could absolutely draw the line there, yes?'

'Of course,' Sophie trilled. She grabbed an apple from the fruit bowl and bit into it happily. 'I'll be upstairs. Homework,' she added, by way of explanation.

I gaped after her retreating back, aware that my daughter was about to attend her studies without any nagging on my part. Amazing. Perhaps I should throw a party more often. Every month. No, week. Make that every day. And talking of parties, I really *must* finish letting everyone know about it.

I set about prepping veg and cooking dinner with the phone tucked between shoulder and ear, ringing contacts, expressing delight at the excited reactions to those who said they hadn't properly danced since Madonna released 'Ray of Light'. Siri was instructed to email everyone the details, and then, finally, I rang my parents. Mum answered on the second ring.

'Darling! How are you? I was just saying to Dad, I must give you a call and let you know the news.'

'Hi, Mum, I'm fine, and I have news too! But you go first.'

'Okay. Well, you remember Aunty Shirley and her son Jack?'

'Yes. As a matter of fact, Simon was talking about them both the other day.'

'She's moving to Kent.'

'Really? That's nice.'

'Yes, she's had enough of Manchester with summers full of rain.'

'So she's going to enjoy the southern summers full of rain instead!'

'I think our weather is marginally better than the North,' Mum laughed. 'She's bought a place off-plan, but even though the conveyancing has completed, she can't move in. The builders royally fudged up. They've been very kind though – paid for all her stuff to go into storage and did a cashback deal.'

'Quite right too,' I said indignantly. 'Where's she living until the new place is ready?'

'Well, that's the thing. The builders offered to put her in a B&B, but Dad and I wouldn't hear of it. We've told her she's welcome to stay here. She'll be arriving tomorrow.'

'How lovely. I haven't seen Aunty Shirley for years. Too long.' I felt a pang of guilt. I'd spoken to her on the phone here and there, but not actually made the journey to Manchester. After all, the city wasn't exactly around the corner from Sevenoaks and somehow, juggling a job with a home to run, an infant child… and then a handful of a child… and then a brat of a teenage child – well, it just hadn't happened.

'You'll be able to do lots of catching up,' said Mum happily. 'And her son will be staying, too. Remember him?'

'Of course I remember nerdy Jack!'

'*Darl*ing,' Mum gently reprimanded, 'make sure you don't call him that when you see him.'

'I *can* be subtle, Mum. Sometimes.'

'Jack was in Africa, but he's been lured back to Blighty.'

'Don't tell me, he missed the weather.'

'I think it's more to do with a book deal and having a base to write. I don't suppose a laptop is much use in the jungle – nowhere to plug it in, surely?'

'I honestly don't know,' I said, having a mental image of a Crocodile Dundee-type of character looking for a socket in a tree trunk.

'Anyway, they'll both be here tomorrow. Dad and I thought we'd let them settle in, and perhaps the whole family can join us for Sunday lunch and give them a proper welcome. I'll do a roast beef dinner. Alex's favourite.'

Mum knew she needed something to tempt Alex to visit if Simon was going to be there. The atmosphere was always strained when my brother and husband were in the same room. It could be quite wearing.

'Fabulous, Mum. About one o'clock?'

'Perfect. Now tell me your news.'

I took a deep breath and said excitedly, 'I'm throwing a fortieth birthday party for Alex.'

'Wow, I'll bet he's chuffed to bits, eh?'

'Ah, that's the thing, Mum. It's a surprise party. It absolutely *has* to be a secret.'

'My lips are sealed.'

'Okay, here's the details.' There was then a bit of page turning in Mum's enormous desk diary as she found the right date to scribble down the venue and time. She had yet to get to grips with diarising electronically, and still thought Siri was a real person. 'Have you invited the Wheelers?' she asked.

'The Wheelers?' I asked, my mind blank.

'Very close friends of ours. You must remember Violet? They'll be so upset if they're not invited.'

I had a vague recollection of a woman with an iron-grey corrugated perm. One word. Formidable.

'It's just that,' said Mum, suddenly anxious, 'she invited us to her Brian's fortieth, and she's not really the sort of person to get on the wrong side of.'

I sighed. 'Yes, fine, why not,' I conceded. 'Two more people won't hurt.'

'I'm so glad you said that,' said Sophie, coming into the kitchen and overhearing, 'only I've just had Tabitha and Zara on the phone, and they absolutely *begged* to be invited. If you say yes, then they'll include me in Zara's belly-piercing celebration.'

'Just a minute, Mum.' I cupped a hand over the receiver and turned to my daughter. 'Sweetheart, this is getting ridiculous.'

'*Please*,' she begged. 'Zara is really cool. I've been wanting to be friends with her for yonks. It would mean so much to me. And you just told Granny she can invite some people we don't even know.

It wouldn't be fair to give Granny preferential treatment over your own daughter.'

'Oh for—' I rolled my eyes and sighed mightily. 'Fine, fine. But that is absolutely it, Sophie, okay?'

'Thanks,' she grinned, and blew me a kiss, before skipping back to her bedroom, no doubt to immediately ring Tabitha and Zara with the good news.

I took my hand away from the phone. 'I'd better go, Mum. The chicken needs basting and Alex could walk in through the door at any moment. I don't want him hearing us furtively talking. He'll wonder what's up.'

'Quite, darling. Toodle-oo!'

I hung up and scooped all the fresh veg into the steamer, all the while thinking about the party. The guest list, like knitting, was growing ever longer, which alarmed me. I still felt unsettled and out of sorts about Jeanie and now Annabelle. It had also occurred to me, as I'd scraped skin from carrots, that if Alex had lied about Queenie's true identity, then it was likely she'd be at the party. All I had to do now was *find out* her true identity. Because, come party night, I wanted to flush her out.

Chapter Thirteen

Alex arrived home just as I was carving up the chicken.

'Thanks for coming into the surgery today,' he said, pecking my cheek.

'That's fine. Working an extra afternoon in addition to a Monday and Wednesday is no big deal.' *Unlike your patient*, I silently added, who was a very big deal to me. However, there was a time to broach a subject that might culminate in a row, and it wasn't until after dinner had been cooked and eaten. I wasn't making that mistake again.

'Obviously you'll get paid for it.'

'Thanks,' I said, setting his meal before him. 'Careful. Plate's hot.'

Just like Annabelle. I wondered if my husband was echoing that thought as he picked up his knife and fork. I went out to the hallway and called up the stairs.

'Sophie? Dinner's ready.'

'Two minutes,' came the muffled reply.

I returned to the kitchen and sat down next to Alex.

'Mum's invited us to Sunday lunch, by the way.'

'Ah. I was thinking about getting in a last game of golf on Sunday, before the weather truly changes.'

'It's roast beef,' I said, and watched him instantly crumble.

'In which case I shall look forward to it,' he replied, smiling.

'Mum said that my godmother and her son are staying with her and Dad for a few weeks. Do you remember Aunty Shirley and Jack? They were at our wedding.'

Alex contemplated. 'Think so. Jolly lady. Son wore specs like Clark Kent.'

'That's them. They will be there too. And, er, probably Simon too.'

Alex groaned.

'Roast beef!' I said again, smiling.

'Clearly your dear old mum knew I'd need coercing. Tell her the roast beef trick worked, and that her son-in-law isn't daft.'

I smiled. 'Will do.' I wanted to steer the conversation in a different direction.

'I quite enjoyed working on a Friday for a change, instead of sitting and gossiping with Caro.' I looked at my husband for any reaction when I added, 'And Jeanie.' Even though the luscious Annabelle was now giving me a bad vibe, I still felt unsettled after Jeanie's declaration about wanting to sing to Alex. And not just any song, but a very pertinent one in relation to those damn sexts.

Alex rolled his eyes. 'I don't know what the three of you find to talk about so much.'

'Oh, you know,' I said lightly, 'this and that.'

'You mean having a snipe about which school mum is standing at the school gate, loudly telling anyone who will listen about her recent holiday to India while the rest of us are looking forward to a week in Cornwall, preferably without having to dodge the raindrops.'

'Something like that,' I nodded, popping a roast potato in my mouth.

Sophie came into the kitchen.

'Sorry, Mum,' she apologised, causing her father to raise his eyebrows at her polite expression of regret over being late to the table. 'I wanted to finish that last bit of homework before I came down.' She turned to Alex. 'Hello, Daddy. How are you?'

Alex eyed her beadily. He wasn't stupid. Why was our daughter behaving so sweetly?

'I'm fine,' he said. 'And you?' He flashed me a sideways look which more or less conveyed, *is she sickening for something*?

'Good,' she beamed. 'I'm so excited about the par—'

I coughed loudly, causing both father and daughter to look at me, the first in surprise and the latter in horror as she realised she'd nearly spilt the party beans. Alex gave her his attention again.

'So excited about what?' he asked.

'The… the party that Tabitha and Zara are having. I've wanted to be besties with them for ages. And… er… they've invited me.'

'I'm glad you're so popular,' Alex smiled.

Sophie flushed and concentrated on eating her dinner.

'That was lovely, Holly,' said Alex, putting his knife and fork together.

'I aim to please,' I replied, thinking momentarily of Annabelle. Did she please my husband in ways that I couldn't?

I cleared away our plates while Sophie finished off her meal.

'I have one more piece of homework to do,' she said, and glided away.

'Is she okay?' Alex asked, when our daughter was out of earshot.

I moved over to the kitchen door and quietly shut it.

'Yes. Perhaps she's finally maturing. She's been very sunny lately. Makes a nice change.'

'Totally agree,' said Alex, before adding, 'What's for pudding?'

'Me!' I said lightly, just to prove I could be sunny, too.

A shadow passed across his face.

'I don't think it's appropriate to talk like that, Holly, when our daughter is around.'

'She's not around,' I said, making sure the sunshine was still very evident in my tone of voice. 'I'm just bantering, darling.' It was important to keep my husband in a relaxed mood. After all, there was a tricky subject to broach. Softly does it…

'Right,' said Alex.

Was it my imagination or did Alex look relieved? I gave a tinkle of laughter.

'After all, I'm hardly likely to ravish you over the dining table when I haven't cleared away the tureen of vegetables and roast potatoes, ha ha!'

'Quite,' he agreed, with forced jollity, 'ha ha ha!'

A part of me thought, somewhat irritably, *and why the hell not?* The presence of a teenager aside, what was so wrong with prostrating oneself over the distressed wood, scattering peas and carrots in all directions, and writhing together in ecstasy? But then again, Alex and I had never *writhed.* It wasn't in his nature. And why was I even thinking it? Perhaps I was having some sort of mid-life crisis? Or a breakdown? But then again, I knew the real reason why my mind was going down this path. It was because of Annabelle's antics this afternoon. Alex made to stand up.

'I really enjoyed the surgical procedures today,' I said, quickly, so that Alex sat back down again. His expression was instantly one of delight. He could talk about his work all day long.

'Really?'

'Definitely.'

'Why's that then? For me, it was just the same old, same old.'

'Not at all,' I said, shaking my head. 'I mean, take the patients.'

'What about them?'

'They were such fun!'

Alex looked perplexed. 'I'm not sure about that. Ancient Mr Robins complained bitterly that his new dentures had made his gums sore. He said he was making it his mission to get me struck off before he died.'

'Oh how amusing,' I hooted, 'the silly old buffer!'

Alex looked put out. Probably not quite the sympathetic response he'd been hoping for. I flapped a hand, dismissing crabby Mr Robins, wanting to shift the conversation to someone who was a million times better looking.

'I'm talking about the other patients. Like… what was her name? Oh yes, Annabelle Huntley-Smith.'

'Huntingdon-Smyth,' said Alex, sounding wary.

'That's the one,' I beamed. 'She's hilarious.'

'Oh?'

'I had terrible trouble keeping a straight face in the surgery, ah ha ha ha!'

'Why?'

'All that writhing, and those funny sex noises.'

'*Sex* noises?'

'Yes, you know.' I leaned back in my chair and made doe-eyes at the ceiling. '*Oooh*, I need a big one. *Ahhh*, right there. Oh yeah, give it to me babe!'

'Holly, I have no idea what you're talking about. Annabelle was a very nervous patient. She was doing her best not to scream, although the odd squeak did escape her lips. And she most definitely didn't call me "babe".'

My sunny smile instantly contorted into a snarl. 'No, but she called you bloody "darling".'

Alex rolled his eyes. 'She's a good friend.'

'Huh,' I spat, eyes narrowed, 'if she's such a good friend, why don't I know her? Answer me that!'

'Why *would* you know her? She's a tireless fundraiser for the trigeminal neuralgia charity that I'm a member of. She was once misdiagnosed by another dentist and ended up having a number of unnecessary dental extractions for pain relief. When she came to me, she was in agony and absolutely distraught. I immediately knew what the problem was and referred her to hospital. She ended up seeing a brain surgeon for a micro-vascular decompression. Annabelle now works closely with the charity, and I see her frequently. She usually accompanies me to their dinner-dance events.'

'Oh she does, does she?' I roared. 'And why haven't you ever invited *me* along to these functions? Could it be that you don't want boring old wifey around because it might cramp your style with a woman who regards you as some sort of real-life hero?'

Alex tutted, pushed back his chair and stood up. 'You never wanted to come along in the early years,' he said, 'so I stopped asking you. It's no big deal.'

'Well it's a big deal now!' I yelled, 'and I'll be coming along to future functions, dressed from head to toe in an outfit that makes the *Strictly* dancers look like they got their costumes out of a clothes recycling bin.'

'Whatever,' said Alex, his lips now a thin line.

'*Whatever*,' I mimicked, in a childish voice. If there was one word in the English language that drove me round the bend, it was that one. 'And I'll just say this to you, Alex,' I hissed, pausing dramatically before adding, 'I'm pretty damn sure I know who Annabelle *really* is.'

There was a resounding silence as we glared at each other and he digested this piece of information. He was the first to speak and, when he did, his voice was low.

'I'm going for a drive.'

Without missing a beat, he snatched up his keys and mobile and stalked out of the kitchen. I didn't try to stop him on account of the fact that I was suddenly shaking. Seconds later his car engine roared into life. I wondered if he'd text Annabelle. Give her the heads-up. *We'll have to be more careful, darling. Holly's on the warpath.* Or would he ring her instead? Even worse, would my husband go to her?

I put my head on the table and silently wept.

Chapter Fourteen

Alex had come home after an hour of – so he said – aimless driving until, tired and fed up, he'd returned to placate the lunatic wife. He'd found me in the bath, face wiped clean of mascara tears, the only sign of upset being slightly pink eyeballs.

He'd reassured me that the jealous outburst over Annabelle was unfounded. I'd apologised. And then, later, when we'd gone to bed, he'd snuggled into me. We'd spooned. I'd desperately wanted to kiss and make up in the way that was most natural between a man and woman, but hadn't dared initiate anything for fear of rejection. I'd finally drifted off to sleep with hazy thoughts about visiting my GP. Maybe it was all in my head. Perhaps I needed antidepressants?

When I awoke the following morning, I told myself that the last thing I needed was to start taking Prozac. Just because my best friend Jeanie had a little crush on my husband, and a nervous female patient made sex noises, it didn't mean either of them were having a raging affair with Alex. *No, Holly, you need to get things into perspective. And maybe if you felt better about yourself, you'd stop fretting that every other woman has the hots for your hubby.* Indeed. Which was why I was now on a mission to buy the most fabulous party dress on the shop rails. To hell with the cost. I'd bash the plastic.

I could hear Alex and Sophie downstairs, chatting. Every now and again Sophie gave a peal of laughter. I sighed contentedly. Our daughter was still happy. Hurrah! With a bit of luck, her good mood would prevail all the way through the lead-up to the party. As for the after-party bit, well we'd cross that bridge when we came to it.

Getting out of bed, I moved over to the window and pulled up the blind. My gaze fell upon the garden, a hectic riot of autumnal colour with the lawn carpeted in leaves of orange and gold. The sun was shining and, if it hadn't been for those leaves, it could easily have been mistaken for a glorious summer's day. I reached up and opened the window. A wasp immediately flew into the bedroom, and I shrieked. What was it about wasps that they had to make an appearance the moment the weather turned warm?

I grabbed one of Alex's dental magazines from his bedside table and thwacked at the wasp until it lay in a squashed heap on the carpet. Chest heaving from exertion, I bent down and peered at the tiny crushed body, instantly overcome with mortification. *Sorry, God. I didn't mean to kill one of your creatures. I'm not really a murderer.* I had a sudden vision of bashing Annabelle and Jeanie with the same magazine, over and over, until they fell to the floor like this wasp. *For goodness' sake, Holly, get a grip. Get OVER this endless inner conflict. Perhaps you should go to your doctor after all. And forget the Prozac. Ask to be sectioned.* I let out a whimper and, dropping the magazine, hastened off to the shower.

Jeanie and Caro were already waiting for me outside M&S when I arrived at Bluewater to shop for our party dresses.

'Sorry, sorry,' I said, hastening over to them both, 'Sophie wanted a last-minute lift. She's been invited to a friend's house for a sleepover.'

'Oooh, no teenager around tonight,' said Jeanie, nudging me heavily in the ribs, 'are you listening to this, Caro?'

'Indeed,' said Caro, giving Jeanie a knowing look. 'What's the betting that Sevenoaks will be on the news tonight?' She affected the voice of a BBC newsreader: 'A minor earthquake has occurred in a small Kentish village disrupting gas and water pipes. One resident, who did not wish to be named, apologised saying it was down to her and her husband having a superior bonk.'

'Shut up, Caro,' I said, but without rancour, although I was starting to wish I'd not been quite so graphic about my fictitious sex life. 'Where to first?'

'Costa,' said Jeanie firmly. 'I know I said I was going to diet for the party, but I'll do it tomorrow. I need cake. And you know what I'm like if I don't have a sugar fix. I get all tetchy.'

'Heaven help us if you get tetchy,' said Caro. 'Go on. Lead the way.'

By the time Jeanie had satisfied her cravings, and we'd had a good moan about our incredibly messy teenagers, the shopping mall was absolutely heaving. We elbowed our way through screaming toddlers, frustrated mothers, buggies festooned with carrier bags, and mini-gangs of gorgeous teenage girls simpering at groups of posturing lads full of spots and testosterone.

We ended up in a huge department store which had a selection of clothes designed for bodies like ours. Jeanie immediately fell in love with a short lacy number that hugged her voluptuous curves in all the right places. Caro opted for some strange chiffon-like trousers in canary yellow that ballooned out around her ankles but which teamed with a corset top somehow 'worked'.

'I think Simon would approve,' I said, nodding.

Ever conscious of my brother's barbed comments about my figure and legs, I opted for a slinky long black evening dress, simple in its design and very understated. It was saved from being boring by enormous side slits that went up to one's knickers. I bought a pair of skyscraper heels with diamanté embellishments to jazz things up and lengthen the leg. With a bit of luck, they might drive Alex mad with desire. Either that or I could stab Queenie with the stilettoes.

Chapter Fifteen

I let myself into the house with a certain amount of stealth. I didn't want Alex welcoming me and seeing expensive-looking shopping bags and then peeking inside – my back-up story about the evening dress being bought for one of his charity functions might be a sore subject after the blow-up about Annabelle.

Rupert greeted me, tail wagging, sticking his wet nose inquisitively inside the carriers, but losing interest in clothes when he spotted an open packet of mints in my handbag. Before I could stop him, he'd grabbed them and run off like all opportunist thieves. Seconds later came the sound of paper being shredded and happy snuffles as he tucked in. Ah well, at least his halitosis would be improved for the next half hour.

I crept upstairs and hung the dress, reverently stroking the creases out of it, loving the softness of the fabric against my fingertips. I pushed the shoes to the back of my wardrobe and, once downstairs again, tucked the carrier bags away in the recycling bin. Sounds of a football game came from the lounge. Wondering if Alex would like a cup of tea, I popped my head around the door.

He was flat on his back, stretched out on the sofa, fast asleep. For a moment, I just gazed at him. He was still a handsome man. No wonder Jeanie had the hots for him. Caro too, I shouldn't wonder. His laptop was open and perched on his stomach, which was slowly rising and falling with each breath. His Facebook page was open. As the screen hadn't timed out, I presumed he'd nodded off only a minute or two ago. Leaning across, I peered at his timeline, almost immediately spotting the open direct message box. My blood pressure rose upon seeing who he'd been talking to. Or, rather, *trying* to talk to. Annabelle Huntingdon-Smyth.

Hi, darling. Saw you were online. Are you there?

I could feel my face contorting with rage. The last thing I wanted was another row over this blasted woman. *She's just a business acquaintance*, I reasoned with myself. *A do-gooder working with a charity that is close to your husband's heart. His friendship with her is just that and means nothing else.*

At that moment Alex's mobile phone rang, startling him into wakefulness. He jumped again when he saw me standing right over him, and the sudden movement dislodged the laptop from his abdomen. His hands shot out as a reflex to stop it crashing to the floor.

'Sorry, didn't mean to frighten you,' I said, passing him the ringing mobile from the coffee table. 'I came in to see if you wanted a cuppa?'

He gave his eyes a cursory rub and took the phone from me.

'Thanks, Holly. A cup of tea would be lovely. Oh no,' he groaned, 'this is the out-of-hours phone. It will be an emergency. Make mine a coffee. I need plenty of caffeine to wake me up.' He touched the mobile's screen. 'Alex Hart here. Can I help you? Right. Throbbing, you say? Could be an abscess.'

I left him to it, and went to make the coffee. Rupert reappeared, trotting at heel and looking at me optimistically. Usually when the kettle went on, that meant the biscuit barrel came out. I looked at his stomach. It was starting to look like the biscuit barrel. I gave him a beady look.

'I suppose nobody has bothered to walk you today.' Well, obviously not. I was the one that walked Rupert, and this morning my intent had been on sniffing out a good dress, not a lamppost. 'It's no good giving me that reprimanding look. If you're trying to make me feel guilty, it won't work. Well, actually, it is working. Yes, all right, all right, I'll take you for a walk.' Rupert wagged his tail appreciatively, and then looked meaningfully at the biscuit barrel. 'Oh, if you must,' I sighed, holding out a digestive. It was only eighty calories. I'd make sure our walk was a brisk one. Rupert trotted off, tail wagging at his good luck. Mints *and* a biscuit. Result!

I took the coffee to Alex who was simultaneously talking to the patient and tapping away at his laptop. He then set it to one side on the sofa and took the coffee from me. The laptop screen was visible. The pop-up box was still open. Annabelle had responded. I tried to read their exchange, but the words were blurry.

'Thanks,' Alex whispered, sipping gratefully. 'Okay, well from what you've told me I think I'd better pop along to the surgery and see you. You are aware of the fees, yes?'

Alex had stopped doing National Health patients years ago, just before we were married. He'd said there was no money in it. I'd thought him terribly mercenary at the time until, after five cancellations in one day, he calculated his day's pay had been less than the minimum wage.

'I didn't study medicine for five years to end up questioning if I had enough money to buy a Walnut Whip,' he'd fumed.

Shortly afterwards, he'd been taken on by a private practice in Sevenoaks. A few more years down the line, and mortgaged up to the eyeballs, the practice was exclusively Alex's.

'Yes, Mastercard is fine,' said my husband, draining his coffee. 'Make your way there and I'll see you shortly.' He ended the call and turned to me. 'Sorry, darling. I know it's Saturday and you hate me working at the weekend, but I'm going to have to slip off. Shouldn't be too long.'

'Okay. Fancy watching a film later?'

'Sounds good. Want to check out Sky Movies and see what's on?'

'I meant at the cinema. Sophie's on a sleepover. We could be romantic' – I waggled my eyebrows – 'and snog in the back row.'

'Sorry, Holly, I'd rather stay at home. It's been a hell of a week and I'm knackered. Not sure actually if I'll even be able to keep my eyes open to watch a movie.'

'Right,' I said lightly. 'Another time.'

And presumably a superior bonk would be out of the question.

Chapter Sixteen

The moment Alex had left, I hastened back to the lounge. The television had been left on. I didn't want to listen to the noise of an overexcited commentator as a pair of muscular legs powered across the pitch, the crowd erupting as the ball went between the goalposts and the football player threw his arms wide, sinking to his knees, skidding forward several feet in the mud, before the rest of the team threw themselves on top of him and they all rolled about looking like they were having a mid-field orgy.

I frowned. Why did my mind bring everything back to sex? *They're playing football, Holly. Not strip poker!* I hit the off button on the remote control, then stared at Alex's laptop. Facebook was still visible, including the pop-up Messenger box. The cursor winked at me invitingly. I'd just have a small peek. Nothing wrong in that.

Hunkering down, I pulled the laptop towards me and scrolled back through the direct messaging.

Hi, darling. Saw you were online. Are you there?

Hey! Sorry to keep you waiting. Postman was at the door. How's the mouth? Sore?

Not at all – all thanks to my brilliant dentist.

My pleasure.

Honestly, the pleasure was all mine.

I'll bet it was, I grimaced.

Lovely to see you.

And you. You truly brightened my day.

Bet you say that to all the ladies.

Only you.

Flirting, or what!

I've got to zip off. Out of hours patient.

pulling face If you fancy swinging by for coffee later, I'm in.

I do fancy!

Wonderful

Well, what an endearing exchange of conversation. I rocked back on my heels, sucking on my teeth, and wondered if I would dare to… no, no, that would be wrong. An invasion of privacy. And… and very out of order. But despite thinking honourable thoughts, my fingers – and paranoia – were having none of it. Was there the smallest chance of getting Annabelle to say something incriminating? My eyes widened in horror as they began tapping out a message to Annabelle.

Should be with you soon.

I'm putting the kettle on!

Forget the coffee. Fancy tea-bagging?

Ha ha! What brand?

The Alex Hart special brand. I have two that are full to bursting.

Darling, your innuendo is hilarious!

They mustn't be steeped for too long.

Why's that, ha ha!

Because the flavour drains and there is danger of being left with something limp.

Good thing I'm a ballsy sort of girl, eh?

Oh Annabelle, you're having such an effect on me. I'm in real hot water now.

Ha ha!

I was interrupted by the phone ringing. Jumping guiltily, I glanced at the handset on the sideboard. I could just about make out the incoming caller ID. Alex. Ignoring it, I stood up, leaving the laptop as it had been on the sofa. Oh God. What had I done? Not for the first time, I wondered about the state of my mind. The landline stopped ringing, but seconds later my mobile, left in the kitchen, let out a merry tune. I scurried out of the lounge, snatching it up just before the last ring sent it to voicemail. Alex again.

'Hi, darling!' I chirruped into the handset, knees slightly quaking.

Quietly, I unlocked the back door and stepped out into the garden. A late afternoon breeze was swishing the branches of overhanging trees, stirring up leaf fall.

'Where are you?' Alex barked.

'I'm out,' I said, quite truthfully. The garden was definitely outside the house. 'Walking Rupert,' I added. A definite lie. But I'd soon rectify that. 'What's up?'

I've just had Annabelle text me. Someone has been sending her ridiculous messages, apparently from me.'

'Oh,' I said, feigning surprise. 'How annoying.'

'You wouldn't know anything about it?'

'No,' I said, reddening with guilt and grateful Alex wasn't around to witness it. 'Why would I know anything about it?' I made my tone sound annoyed. Nothing like accusing the accuser. At that moment Rupert bustled out of the back door. His face visibly lit up as if to say, 'There you are!' and he gave a woof of joy.

'Okay. I can hear you're busy with Rupert. I'll have to change my passwords. It's obviously the work of some bastard hacker.'

'Y-yes,' I stuttered with relief. 'The... the fucker.'

There was a resounding silence before Alex replied. 'I'm glad you're outraged on my behalf, darling, but there's no need to swear.'

'Sorry. Must go. Rupert's done a whoopsie and I need to pick it up.'

I ended the call and then hurried back inside the house. Having pretended that I was out with the dog, I decided to do just that and make myself scarce. Feeling like a criminal, I grabbed the lead and my jacket, locked up and set off at a trot to the Common. I wondered ruefully if anyone had ever used their dog as an alibi before.

Chapter Seventeen

The wind was really coming up now and I huddled down in my collar, shivering slightly. Light was starting to fade. The one thing I disliked about this time of year was the evenings drawing in. It meant the last walk of the day was without the joyful observation of the sun sinking in a glorious bonfire of orange, whilst batting the midges away from bare arms. Usually there were other dog walkers on the Common, but today, given the hour and the deepening shadows, it was empty. I decided to do one circuit before heading home. No doubt Alex would be back by then and I could return, windblown and rosy-cheeked, offering tea and sympathy... no, not tea, Holly... offering wine, then... and lament about the outrageousness of computer hackers. Brilliant idea.

Stepping off the pavement and onto a bridle path, I let Rupert off the lead. He bounded off, tail up, nose down, already on a scent. I followed him along the meandering track, passing a huddle of houses set back from the Common along a private road that hugged its border. Street lamps were coming on now, their light-sensitive photocells activating automatically, glowing in such a way that they looked like they had halos. Ahead, Rupert was directing a series of excited woofs at the base of a tree trunk.

'Leave it, boy,' I said, catching up with him. 'The squirrels will outrun you every time.'

Rupert wagged his tail optimistically, refusing to budge. I left him to it and walked on. He would catch up when he was bored with the lack of action. After fifteen minutes, I had circumnavigated most of the area and was approaching the homeward road. It was only when I was back on the pavement, standing in a lamp's spotlight, that I realised Rupert wasn't with me. I turned and peered into the darkness, scrunching up my eyes, desperately trying to penetrate the gloom and spot a brown-and-white mongrel bobbing towards me.

'Rupert?' I called. 'Here, boy!' I let out a piercing whistle. Nothing.

I sighed. Well I wasn't going to retrace my steps. The Common was a joy to behold in daylight, but not now, with its hint of menace and trees that – if you were inclined to be fanciful, and I most definitely could be – looked like enormous monsters with outstretched arms. I shivered again.

'Rupert!' I yelled. 'Look what I have! Chewy. Come to Mummy… chew-chew!' When that didn't work, I upped the game. There was only one way to deal with a dog that was ruled by its stomach. 'Dinner, Rupert! Din-dins!'

I sighed with relief as a shape came into view, white patches visible in the gloom so it looked as though a series of unconnected blobs were heading my way. He was in full pelt now, no doubt his furry little head full of thoughts about meaty bits covered in rich gravy with a generous sprinkling of doggy biscuits.

'Good boy!' I praised. 'Come, Rupert, come.' I reached into my pocket for one of the treats I always stashed for just such an occasion. It was at this point that I realised Rupert wasn't remotely bothered about going home for a tin of chunks because, only inches from his nose, was a far better choice of menu, and so fresh it was still alive and trying to outpace him. Wild hare. The creature was belting along as if its life depended upon it – which it surely did – and heading straight towards me and... oh God... I was suddenly alive to the sound of a car's engine coming along the lonely road.

'Rupert!' I called urgently, splaying my arms wide like a goal-keeper, ready to snatch up a dog in this case. 'Leave it... LEAVE!'

In my peripheral vision I caught sight of headlights sweeping around a bend in the road, then came the sound of a gear change as the vehicle picked up speed and hurried along the straight bit of tarmac that ran parallel to me. Rupert's quarry was only feet away. It looked terrified. Spotting me, it swerved sharply to my left, past my legs and out into the road. I flung myself sideways, making to grab Rupert who wriggled out of my grasp.

'RUPERT!' I shrieked, as I crashed down on the hard pavement.

It was all over in a second. There was a terrified squeal from Rupert, a horrible thud of metal on bone, the sickening sound of snapping and breaking, a mighty screech of brakes, and then a shape flying through the air and thumping down in front of me.

'OH MY GOD, HELP ME, HELP ME, HELP ME!' I screamed, scrambling to my feet. One hand accidentally touched the inert and twisted form silhouetted in the car's headlights. Suddenly I was vibrating faster than one of my husband's dental drills. For a moment the road spun, and I thought I might faint. There was a clunk of a car door, and the sound of heavy footsteps rushing towards me as I staggered, mindful not to tread on the lifeless body. Suddenly strong arms were holding me up.

'I've got you,' said a man's voice. 'You're all right. Everything's okay, but you're in shock.'

'My d-dog,' I stuttered, teeth chattering like joke dentures out of a Christmas cracker.

'Your dog's fine,' said the man, as Rupert slunk towards me, tail at half-mast, with a flicker of an apologetic wag. 'Here, boy,' said the man, grabbing Rupert's collar. 'May I?' he asked, propping me up with one hand as, with the other, he took the lead from me and dextrously clipped it onto Rupert's collar. I was staring at my dog as if he was Christ risen again.

'B-but,' I stared wildly at the shape on the pavement, 'I thought…'

'It's a hare.'

Rupert looked at it longingly, clearly still thinking of his stomach, but prepared to leave it alone in order to ingratiate himself back into my good books.

'Oh my God,' I said, and promptly burst into tears.

'Listen, you're not in any fit state to walk home. Let me give you a lift.'

'Oh n–no, really, I-I'm fine.' I swiped a fluttering hand across my face, rubbing away tears. 'I-I can walk.' Just as soon as my legs stopped doing an impersonation of blancmange.

'Are you worried about accepting lifts from strangers?' the man asked, kindly.

The thought had flashed through my mind, but I hadn't liked to say.

'I'm a doctor,' he said.

So was Harold Shipman.

'I can call someone, if you prefer?' he suggested.

'I-I'm not sure my husband is available,' I answered.

Alex had planned on 'swinging by' Annabelle's for coffee. I looked up at the man, trying to read his face in the lamp light. Did he look like a serial killer? Were his eyes too close together? Instead, as I took in his features properly, I caught my breath. He was so indecently handsome that he made Alex look ordinary.

'Let me wait with you while you try calling him,' he said. 'It's a bit lonely here.'

I was on a very isolated stretch of road. It occurred to me that if this man wanted to rape or murder me, he could pretty much do it right here and now without any interruption. It was also now pitch black and freezing. Even Rupert was shivering.

'If it's no trouble, then perhaps I will accept a lift,' I said gratefully, thinking that Rupert would surely defend me if the man tried anything dodgy. Not that Rupert was aggressive, but one whiff of his breath was enough to have even the strongest person running for the hills.

The man smiled. Even in the gloom I could see he had very white, even teeth. He was so good-looking it was almost obscene. And unsettling. He reminded me of Patrick Dempsey in his heyday. I was feeling quite weird now, and wasn't sure whether shock was still at play, or whether this man was having an odd effect on me.

He opened the passenger door and I almost fell into the seat, so wobbly were my legs. The man strapped me in, as if I were a child, and then lifted Rupert onto my lap.

'Okay?' he asked, his voice full of kindness.

'Yes. Thank you,' I said, suddenly feeling shy.

Seconds later he was in the driver's seat and we were on the road home. I gave him directions, my voice occasionally catching as I hugged Rupert tightly, so glad that my smelly boy was still of this world. I buried my head in his fur, and he licked a salty tear from my cheek.

'Here we are then,' said my Good Samaritan a few minutes later. The car rolled to a standstill outside my home. 'I recommend a stiff brandy and an early night.'

'Thank you,' I said, 'and I'm so sorry about everything. That must have been quite a shock for you too.'

'I've had worse,' the man smiled. 'Stay there, I'll come around and help you out.'

'Oh, it's fine, I'm—'

But he was already out of the vehicle, striding round to the passenger side, and pulling open the door. Rupert was immediately scooped up and tucked under one strong arm, while the other hauled me out of the car. His hand was warm on mine, and bizarrely a ripple of tingles zinged up and down my spine. *For heaven's sake, Holly, this is not the time nor the place to let a good-looking stranger affect you so. You are very obviously sexually frustrated. Soon you'll be prostrating yourself across the bonnet of any passing male driver, panting, 'Take me, I'm all yours.'*

'Shall I walk you to the door?'

Yes please, and would you like to share that stiff brandy with me?

'N-no, I'm fine. Really.'

'Okay, here's your little chap then,' he said, handing me Rupert. 'Be a good boy for your mum, eh?' he laughed, and rubbed his fingers behind Rupert's ears. I had a sudden overwhelming urge to have my own ears rubbed. Perhaps Alex might like to give it a go the next time the moon turned blue and he had a testosterone surge.

'Thank you so much,' I said, gazing up at him. I had to crane my neck a bit too. He was well over six feet tall.

'Take care.'

Another friendly smile, and then he was gone. As I walked up to the front door, it occurred to me that I suddenly felt bereft. And I had absolutely no idea why.

Chapter Eighteen

When I walked through the door, Alex was already inside. He must have got home just a few minutes ahead of me because, from my viewpoint in the hall, which opened straight into the lounge, I could see he still had his coat on. He was crouched down, in front of the coffee table, staring at his laptop and frowning.

'Hello!' I called warily, putting Rupert down. My heart was still banging away at an extraordinary pace. One way or another it was getting a bit of a work-out today. From shock, to attraction, to trepidation, and all in less than an hour. When Alex finally glanced up at me, he looked livid. My pulse quickened, but for all the wrong reasons. Cancel *trepidation*. Make that *fear*.

'Have we ever lied to each other?' he demanded.

I stared at him with huge eyes. 'No,' I lied. 'Have you ever lied to me?'

'Of course not,' he said, but his eyes slithered away.

Okay, we were both lying. And knew it.

'Did you type these ridiculous messages to Annabelle?' he demanded.

'No,' I lied again, and this time it was my eyes that slithered away.

'Well somebody did!'

'Is she Queenie?' I blurted, my voice cracking.

Alex rubbed a weary hand over his face. 'Oh God, not that again, Holly.'

'IS SHE?' I demanded. 'I heard you talking together about Queenie. Yesterday, in the surgery. When I was outside the door.'

'She once knew the patient. She was just making conversation. Asking if I'd ever had any further problems. That's all.'

I raised my eyebrows in surprise. This time Alex's eyes stayed on mine. Was he telling the truth? Or was he still lying? 'I don't believe you.'

'Do you know what, Holly?' My husband stood up and came towards me. 'I don't actually care whether you believe me or not. Nothing I say or do to reassure you about another woman is ever going to stop you periodically acting like a fruit loop, throwing your weight about, being all sweetness and light one moment but the next' – he clicked his fingers – 'carrying on like someone auditioning for a part in *The Exorcist*.'

'How dare you!' I glared, aware of Rupert creeping off to a quieter corner of the house. My poor dog, all he did was slink about.

'Oh I *dare*,' he said, stopping in front of me. Suddenly he thrust his face into mine. 'I am fed up,' he hissed, 'of constantly being accused by you.'

'And not without just cause,' I hissed back. Our noses were now practically touching. 'How would YOU feel, Alex, if I popped out for a pint of milk and YOU discovered a string of sexy messages on MY mobile phone, eh? Someone quoting lyrics from a song, telling me how they'd like to hit me one more time, baby?' I paused. Was I muddling my lyrics up?

'If you told me there was nothing in it, I would believe you.'

'So it wouldn't rattle you? Wouldn't lay dormant in the back of your mind waiting for a stimulus from an over-familiar person who called your wife *darling*, and regularly accompanied her to dinner-dance functions that you had ABSOLUTELY NO IDEA ABOUT!'

Alex took a step back as some spittle flew into his eye. My heart was pounding away again. I clutched my chest, as if trying to slow the frantic beating to a more sedate rhythm. This surely couldn't be good for one's health. I stood there panting, feeling quite ill. Perhaps I was going to have a heart attack. Maybe the shock of thinking Rupert had been killed had finally caught up with me. I wondered, if I dropped down dead right now, if Alex would even care.

'We've had this discussion a million times before,' said Alex tersely. 'And I'm done with the subject.' He turned on his heel and stalked off to the kitchen. 'Next time you decide to write messages to my Facebook friends,' his voice floated back to me, 'ask my permission first.'

'And next time,' I shrieked, just as the doorbell rang, 'ask MY permission before you sail off for coffee with CHUFFING ANNABELLE HORNYCUM-STIFF.' I staggered slightly, heart now threatening to bounce right out of my chest and boing across the hallway. The doorbell rang again, this time more persistently. I took a deep breath and attempted rearranging my features into a mask of pleasantness, before opening the front door.

'Yes?'

It was Annabelle Huntingdon-Smyth. She glared at me.

'Could you give this to Alex, please?' She thrust a scarf into my hands. 'He left it at my place.'

'Yes, will do,' I said brightly.

'And just to let you know, Mrs Hart, I detest tea.'

Chapter Nineteen

Annabelle's beautiful face was suffused with anger. Looking furtively over my shoulder to make sure Alex was out of earshot, I stepped outside pulling the door after me, so it was not quite shut.

'I do apologise,' I said earnestly, 'for any strange messages you received from my husband, but it would seem Alex's account was hacked.'

I could never confess to Annabelle that it was me who'd done exactly that. She'd think I was barking. And let's be honest, half the time I was. *But not without cause*, protested a little voice in my head, *those sexts upset your world. And anyway, if there was an outside chance of Annabelle being Queenie, then you could consider your action as justifiable karma.* Bloody right too! I straightened my spine.

'He's changed all the passwords,' I said, blasé now, 'so there should be no repeat of anything untoward.'

She gave me a measured look. 'Is that so?'

'Yes,' I nodded, as my heart did a few nervous somersaults in my chest. At this rate, the continued cardiovascular workout would make me a new woman.

Her face softened, but only a smidgen. 'No harm done. Whoever the hacker was, they weren't malicious. Just immature.'

'Quite,' I agreed. 'And, er, I'm so glad to see you again,' I said, ignoring her sudden arched eyebrow, 'because, well, I gather you're a very good friend of Alex's.'

'Meaning?' she said sharply.

'Meaning that it would be lovely to have you at his surprise fortieth birthday party,' I gabbled. 'I do hope you can come. The party is three weeks today. But obviously he knows nothing about it and' – I cast a furtive glance over my shoulder to make sure Alex wasn't hovering – 'obviously your husband is most welcome too.'

'I don't have a husband.'

Oh, yes, I remembered spotting her ring-less fingers in the surgery yesterday.

'Your boyfriend, then.'

'Don't have one of those either.'

'Then any friend, it doesn't matter who,' I ploughed on, giving her a winning smile, anxious to ingratiate myself as *that nice wife of Alex Hart's* and not *Barking Mad of Sevenoaks*.

'I do have a partner,' she drawled, 'but he's married.'

'R-right,' I warbled. 'Well, um, if he's not with his wife that evening, bring him along.' *Oh fabulous, Holly. Now you sound like you're condoning her duplicity.*

She threw back her head and laughed. It wasn't a nice sound. I had the distinct impression she was laughing at me.

'There's no need to bring him along,' she said, giving me a mocking smile.

I was about to ask why not, but the words died on my lips. For just one split second I was riddled with doubt. Was she trying to tell me something? Was she... I blanched... dropping hints that Alex was the married man? Was that why there was no need to bring him along – because he would already be there? 'Well, whether you come alone or accompanied, I'm sure Alex will be thrilled to see you.'

I gave her the venue address and time, then watched her stalk off. What a horrible woman. What on earth did Alex see in her? She was the type who probably had loads of men friends, but few women pals. I tried to imagine her sitting down for a cosy gossip with Jeanie and Caro, but the very thought seemed incongruous.

I shut the door after her and took off the coat I was still wearing from walking Rupert. I slunk into the kitchen – heavens, I was emulating the dog now – to start cooking our evening meal, even though I had no appetite. I felt unsettled, and thoroughly out of sorts. I was just washing my hands at the kitchen sink ready to start prepping food, when Alex came up behind me. Bracing myself for more angry words, I was surprised when he wound his arms around my waist and hugged me to him.

'Sorry,' he said.

Sorry? I was the one in the wrong, yet he was the one apologising? But I was too relieved to question my husband's sudden change of mood, or how either of us had behaved. I was just overjoyed we were no longer fighting.

He turned me round to face him.

'My hands are wet,' I protested, holding them away from his shirt.

'Doesn't matter,' he said, pulling me into his arms.

It felt so nice, I melted against him. 'I didn't mean to make you angry,' I said in a small voice.

'I know,' he murmured, his breath warm against my ear.

I closed my eyes. 'Can I ask you a question?' I felt his body tense. 'No accusations,' I added quickly.

Alex leaned back slightly, so he could look down at me. 'What?'

'Do you ever regret marrying me?'

For a moment he was silent, and I felt my stomach knot with tension.

'No,' he said eventually. 'The only thing I regret is that you saw those ridiculous texts. It has caused a lot of trouble and upset. For both of us.'

'So you don't want a divorce?'

Alex shook his head and gave a faint smile. 'No, I don't want a divorce. We have a nice life. Why would I want to change that?'

'For love,' my voice quavered. *And passion and thrills*, a voice in my head added.

'I have love with you,' Alex said. 'You're one of my best friends.'

'Does that mean you tell me everything – all your secrets?'

I saw the hesitation in his eyes before he answered. 'Of course. Do you tell me yours?'

I found myself hesitating too. Well, no. Not everything. Sometimes I confided in Jeanie and Caro. Other times, my mother. And on the very odd occasion, my brother Simon. It depended on what the secret was, and who the best person was to entrust the secret with. It was no good talking to Alex about the undisclosed course of acupuncture I'd had to help with pre-menstrual tension. He'd have hit the roof at me spending so much money when, possibly, a pot of evening primrose oil might have done the trick. But Jeanie and Caro had understood perfectly when I'd confided about my irrational thoughts and increasingly barmy behaviour. It was Jeanie who'd revealed she'd seen this marvellous man who made her look like a human pin cushion every few weeks but stopped her from murdering Ray when he walked over her newly washed kitchen floor in his grubby shoes.

'That's a long pause,' Alex smiled. 'Are you evaluating your answer?'

'I guess so,' I shrugged. 'I mostly tell you everything. Some of it is girl talk, and you wouldn't be interested.'

'Ah, your partners in crime, Jeanie and Caro. So they know things about you that I don't!'

'Maybe,' I grinned.

'Leave dinner for now, darling,' he whispered, cupping his hand under my chin and tilting my face up to meet his lips.

Astonished at such spontaneity on his part, I didn't dare to presume that it would lead anywhere, and simply enjoyed the moment, feeling his mouth on mine, as my heart once again started to palpitate, but this time in anticipation of pleasure. I instantly batted the thought away. I didn't want to be disappointed. Didn't want him to suddenly step back and say, 'There, glad we got things sorted, you carry on with dinner and I'll just grab the last of Everton playing Liverpool before I have an early night – I'm absolutely shattered.' But no, wait, something was happening on his part, oh my goodness... my heart was fairly galloping now as the tip of Alex's tongue touched my lips, parting them, darting inside my mouth. This was unprecedented behaviour at seven o'clock in the evening. Suddenly he was pulling away. Taking my hand.

'Shall we go upstairs?' he asked.

Shall we? Why was he even asking! It was as much as I could do not to drag him up to the bedroom, throw him down on the bed, rip my clothes off and punch a fist into the air as I raised my face heavenwards and shrieked, 'Yesssssssssss!' *This* was why I didn't want to lose my husband and was desperate to save my marriage. For the love and warmth that I knew was there, below the surface, if only I could just let things be. There had been lovely times in the past, and I needed to let the good times roll again. Like now.

Instead I allowed myself to be led, soft and pliant, up the staircase, stepping over Rupert who was now dozing at the top, and into the master bedroom, where Alex gently proceeded to make love to me. It wasn't by any means the superior bonk. But it would do. My husband was actively demonstrating that he loved me. And this time my heart was singing.

Chapter Twenty

When I awoke the following morning, it was to see my husband setting a cup of tea down on the bedside table. He kissed me on the forehead.

'Morning, sleepyhead,' he smiled.

'Hey,' I yawned, and stretched, letting the duvet slip so he could see my bare breasts. I was more than up for a repeat of last night. Perhaps things were finally, *finally*, changing in the bedroom department. 'How are you?' I caught his hand, squeezed it in mine. With a bit of luck, I was looking tousled and sex-kittenish.

'I'm fine,' he said, gently reclaiming his hand. 'Enjoy your tea. If you don't mind, I want to sit in the conservatory with the Sunday papers and chill for a bit.'

'Sure,' I said lightly. 'Would you pass me my phone, darling?'

Alex handed it to me before disappearing downstairs to claim some downtime. Fair enough. It was Sunday, after all. I looked at my mobile. A text from Sophie.

Can I skip Sunday lunch at Granny's? Only Tabitha's asked me to stay here for roast dinner and it would be really cool if you said yes xx

I tutted. Oh well, why not. At least she wouldn't be bored stiff with all the adults, and I could get reacquainted with Aunty Shirley and Jack without worrying about dashing back home because my teenager was fidgeting.

Sure. Enjoy. But we'll pick you up on our way home. Compromise! Xx

Compromising seemed to be the name of the game when it came to a teenager in a perpetual battle, to not exactly give in but at least meet each other half way.

I then went on Facebook to see what my tiny army of friends were up to. Ooh, goodie! Two friend requests. I frowned. Both were from men I didn't know, good-looking and sporting military uniforms. I ignored them, instead clicking on the messages icon to read a notification.

Greetings! I am contacting you because I can tell from your picture that you are a very kind person and will help me. I am a Nigerian prince with an enormous amount of money that I have to keep secret from my Government. Please can I deposit the money in your account? For this supreme favour, I will give you half. All you have to do is tell me your bank details and passwords. Have a fabulous day, dear friend!

Yeah, right. I blocked 'Prince Tunde Oteduko', and then looked at my status. I hadn't a clue what to write. Did it really matter? Did anybody truly want to know? I looked up as Rupert came into the bedroom, tail wagging optimistically and hoping for walkies.

'In a minute, boy,' I said, picking up my tea and quickly drinking it down.

He took this as his cue to jump on the bed for a cuddle, which prompted me to tap out: *In bed with my hairy man…*

I grinned as I thought of Jeanie reading my status. She loved hirsute men. I could imagine her now demanding to know if Alex's chest had more than five hairs. If I told her it looked like a rug she'd probably faint with desire. I snuggled into Rupert and he sighed contentedly, as did I. Relationships with dogs were far less complicated than relationships with husbands. Yawning, I settled back against the pillows and closed my eyes. Just for five minutes…

'What time did you say we had to be at your mother's for Sunday lunch?' asked Alex.

I opened my eyes again. 'Oh, not for ages. One o'clock.'

'Thought so. Will you be ready in twenty minutes?'

'Twenty minutes? Whatever is the time?'

'Gone noon.'

'What?' I spluttered. I'd fallen back asleep. How had that happened? Yesterday's close shave with Rupert must have taken it out of me far more than I'd realised. Rupert looked at me woefully as if to say, 'You mean to tell me it's too late for walkies?' He presented me with his backside, before jumping off the bed. Dear Lord, if it wasn't my teen sulking, it was the dog.

Flinging back the duvet, I headed off to the bathroom. How was I meant to make myself look beautiful in twenty minutes? Actually, eighteen minutes. My bladder, having held on for almost twelve hours, seemed to be taking forever to empty.

Grabbing my toothbrush, I caught sight of myself in the overhead mirror. No wonder Alex had wanted to distance himself. Rather than a sex-kitten reflecting back, I looked more like a dishevelled tiger with stripes down her face – I should have taken more time to remove yesterday's mascara.

Walking into the shower cubicle, I blasted it all away. With a bit of luck Mum would be running late, but then again Dad was a stickler for time-keeping, especially if Mum had delegated him to make the Yorkshire puddings. I'd never hear the end of it if his batter hadn't risen.

Stepping onto the bath mat, I gave myself a brisk rub-down and hurriedly dressed.

'Darling!' Alex called up the stairs, 'What's happening about Sophie?'

'She's having lunch with her friend,' I yodelled back.

'Okay. I've let Rupert out for a wee and he's in his basket. I'll be getting the car out of the garage.'

'Right, give me two minutes.'

I hopped my way into a pair of jeans and tugged a T-shirt over my head. No time to glam up. Slicking on some lippy, I pulled my hair up into a ponytail, nicking one of Sophie's scrunchies. It would have to do.

Grabbing my bag, I hastened down the stairs, pausing only to remove a couple of bottles of wine from the cooler for Mum and Dad, and rushed out to the car.

'Good thinking,' said Alex, catching sight of the vino. 'Never turn up empty-handed,' he smiled.

'I think it would be good form to stop somewhere and grab some flowers for Aunty Shirley. We haven't seen her for years, and I feel bad about that.'

'Sure, there's a garage en route.'

'Even better,' I said, five minutes later, pointing at a lay-by ahead, 'look, a flower stall. I can buy three times as much for what the garage would charge, and those blooms look absolutely gorgeous.'

Minutes later, I was back in the car with some glorious bouquets. Their scent instantly made Alex sneeze. We pulled up on my parents' drive with five minutes to spare.

'Excellent timing, darling,' I smiled.

Alex took the wine and went ahead, while I fought my way out of the car with all the flowers.

'You're here!' I heard my mother cry. 'Come in, Alex, come in. You remember Aunty Shirley, of course.'

I moved up the path, my face semi-hidden by hundreds of petals and frothy gyp. Stepping into the hall, the perfume of the flowers was momentarily covered by the heavenly smell of beef.

'Hello everyone,' I trilled, moving into the front room where everybody was gathered. Dad was pouring ice-cold Prosecco for the ladies, and beer for the boys. Simon was already here and, for some reason, looking thoroughly overexcited. He was tossing his head about like an impatient horse ready to start running in the Grand National. I spotted my godmother and beamed. 'Aunty Shirley!' I said, heading over. 'It's so good to see you again! These are for you,' I said, handing her the flowers and then kissing her on both cheeks, continental style.

'Holly,' said Aunty Shirley warmly, 'you look wonderful, dear.' She hugged me tightly, briefly squashing some of the flowers, and then, as a tall figure came into the room, said, 'and you remember Jack, of course.'

I turned, a ready smile on my face, and the breath instantly whooshed out of me. It was the looker who'd given Rupert and me a lift home from the Common the night before.

Chapter Twenty-One

It took me a moment to recover, if you can even call it that, because I couldn't quite believe the man walking towards me was the one who'd not only nearly flattened my dog, but rescued him too. My mouth was slowly opening like a fool, and then a blush unfurled from the tips of my toes to the top of my head, so that even my hair felt like it was on fire. This was nerdy Jack? Where were the geeky specs? The skinny body? And the spotty face? I gulped as my eyes flitted over his torso, which, even to my ignorant eye, was both broad and 'built', and then up to his handsome face. His eyes were smiling with pleasure, and I burned with both embarrassment and girlish delight as he stooped to kiss my cheek. My face instantly felt as though it had been torched and, ridiculously, one hand fluttered up to touch where his lips had been. Realising how stupid that must look, I instantly dropped it back by my side. Out of my peripheral vision I could see Simon noting the effect Jack was having on me. Oh God. No doubt this man was the reason why my brother was almost whinnying with delight and pawing the ground.

'What a pleasant surprise,' said Jack, stepping back from me.

'Yes, isn't it?' I said inanely, suddenly tongue-tied. 'You remember Alex?' I said, making a long cartoon-arm and pulling my husband away from Dad and Aunty Shirley.

'Hey, good to see you again, matey,' said Jack, pumping my husband's hand. 'You haven't changed a bit.'

'Well you certainly have,' said my husband affably. 'Where are the *Joe 90* specs? I didn't recognise you!'

'Ah, I had laser treatment a long time ago. Perfect eyes.' He swivelled the perfect eyes to me. 'How are you, Holly? Fully recovered after the excitement of yesterday, I hope?'

Alex frowned. 'You didn't mention you'd seen everyone yesterday, darling.'

'It was just Jack. Although, we didn't recognise each other.'

Alex was looking bemused now. 'That's nice. Where did you see each other?'

'Didn't Holly tell you? I nearly ran over your dog. Rupert, isn't it?'

'Y-yes,' I stammered.

Alex was now looking incredulous. 'Why didn't you say?'

'I, um, forgot.'

'You forgot our dog was nearly run over?'

'She was very shocked,' said Jack smoothly. 'Unfortunately, the hare Rupert was chasing wasn't so lucky.'

'You were walking Rupert off the lead!' exclaimed my husband, sounding aghast.

'Yes, but only around the Common.'

'The Common runs parallel to the road! Whatever were you thinking of, Holly?'

Bloody Annabelle Huntingdon-Smyth! I wanted to howl, but this was neither the time nor the place. 'Rupert needed to stretch his legs,' I said, defensively.

'Well next time take him across the fields where there isn't any traffic, and he can chase wildlife to his heart's content.'

There was an uncomfortable pause where I was embarrassed for being publicly told off by my husband, Jack was embarrassed for landing me in it over Rupert, and Alex was embarrassed for letting his crossness over my stupidity get the better of him in front of Jack. My brother seized upon the awkward lull in conversation to zoom over with a glass of beer for Jack.

'For you,' he said, batting his eyelashes coquettishly. 'Now do tell us, Jack, are you married and, if not, why not?'

Jack threw back his head and roared. 'Ah, Simon, it's refreshing to see that nothing about you has changed over the years. You are as tactful as ever.'

'Discretion is my middle name,' Simon beamed, 'but don't evade the question, you naughty boy.'

'There was nearly a wife,' said Jack, looking amused, 'but she didn't like the idea of creepy-crawlies, or the fact that there would be no en suite bathroom in the jungle. We parted company.'

'Oh, what a shame,' said Simon, sounding about as sincere as Vladimir Putin. 'And no girlfriend?'

'No girlfriend.'

'Or boyfriend?' said Simon, hopefully.

Alex rolled his eyes and removed himself to talk to Aunty Shirley and Mum, who were chatting about the benefits of winter pansies.

'There is neither a girlfriend, nor a boyfriend,' Jack laughed.

'Well I can't help you with the former,' said Simon cosily, 'but if you ever fancy going out for a drink or… anything else… don't hesitate to give me a call.'

'Thank you,' said Jack, smiling. 'I'll remember that.'

I couldn't help feeling ridiculously pleased that Jack wasn't partnered up.

'Will you be going back to Africa eventually?' I asked.

'Never say never, but for now I'm stopping in England. Africa was an adventure, but there is something terribly appealing about running water and a shop at the end of the road.'

I tried to think of something intelligent to say but as my knowledge of Africa could be written on a postage stamp, instead said, 'How amusing', and gave a tinkle of laughter.

'Oh, Holly, please, no,' said Simon, looking pained. 'I hate it when you do that fake laugh. It always sounds like a donkey braying— Ouch!' squealed my brother. 'What did you do that for?'

'I'm so sorry, was that your foot I trod on? Please excuse me, Jack. I'll just see if Dad needs any help carving the beef.'

Seething, I tossed the last of my wine down my throat and went off to the kitchen to find my father. Between my husband and my brother, I was starting to feel more than a little rattled, which didn't mix well with the effect Jack was having on me either. *For God's sake, Holly, you're a married woman. Jack is wonderful eye-candy, but Simon is right. That was a ridiculous bit of laughter – and why were you laughing anyway? Try and be witty and charming. When we sit down to dinner, ask intelligent questions about the book he's writing.*

I was relieved when Mum told us all to sit down. I pulled out a chair next to Aunty Shirley. Dad topped up everybody's glasses, and I took a sip of wine from my refreshed glass.

'You've turned into a bonny lass, Holly,' Aunty Shirley was saying.

'She carries her extra pounds so well,' said Simon sweetly. He hadn't forgiven me for treading on his foot.

'Do tell me about this new house you're buying,' I said, ignoring Simon as Alex sat down to my right. Mum and Dad were sitting at either end of the table. Simon had quickly stationed himself next to Jack who – I palpitated a bit – was now sitting opposite me.

'It's very pretty,' said Aunty Shirley, and launched into a long story about her conveyancing disaster and the builders' bodge-up, leaving me to discreetly study Jack under my eyelashes, then break out in a muck sweat when he glanced up and caught me looking.

'Can I pass you some potatoes, Holly?' he asked, smiling.

God, he was so… so… *sexy*.

'Yes, thank you,' I said, reaching out to take the tureen, but accidentally clipping my wine glass in the process. It instantly tipped over splashing the contents everywhere, but not before it started a domino effect of hitting Alex's glass of beer, which wobbled around on its base. Terrified that the beer would topple over too, my hand shot out to save it, and promptly knocked the bowl of potatoes out of Jack's hand. 'Oh God!' I squeaked.

'Couldn't matter less,' said Mum, looking slightly flustered. She quickly gathered up the scattered potatoes. Alex shot me a livid look and began mopping up spilt liquid with his napkin. 'There!' said Mum. 'No harm done. Here, Holly, help yourself, and then pass them round the table. Horseradish sauce, darling?' she asked, passing me a jar.

'Thanks,' I said gratefully, taking it from her by the lid… which hadn't been secured properly. It immediately parted company with the jar, which upturned into my lap.

'Dar*ling*,' said Alex, a slight edge to his voice, 'you're being very clumsy today.'

'Not a problem,' said Mum, scampering off to the kitchen to fetch a wet cloth.

'It's all right,' I said, as she hastened back, 'most of it landed in my serviette.'

'Good, good. I'll get another jar of horseradish.'

'Holly, dear, if you pass me your plate,' said my father, 'I'll load it up while you sort yourself out.'

'Thanks, Dad,' I said appreciatively, handing him the plate and taking the soggy napkin out to the kitchen bin.

'So,' said Alex to Jack, once I was back at the table and attempting to eat my dinner without further calamity, 'Aunty Shirley was saying earlier that you've been doing exciting things with crocodiles.'

'Be still my beating heart,' said Simon, theatrically. 'The only wildlife I've ever encountered are trouser snakes.'

I flashed my brother a warning look, but Jack seemed unfazed by my brother's risqué humour, and laughed good-naturedly.

'All for charity,' Jack explained. 'The crocs weren't too trouble-some. It was when I was paddling a kayak around the estuary that I had a moment of anxiety. An eight-inch shark fin rose out of the water just moments after leaving the shore. It was only a couple of metres from my kayak, and there had been no mention of sharks during the orientation prior to getting in the water. The guide chose that moment to give me a big smile and reveal that the estuary was home to three different types of sharks.'

'How terrifying,' said Simon, clutching his chest with one hand and allowing his other to momentarily stray to Jack's forearm. Talk about any excuse to get touchy-feely.

'Whatever did you do?' I asked. *Hooray. A sensible question, Holly.*

'Thankfully, it lost interest and swam off. To be honest, I was more concerned by the hippos at this point. They'll snap you in half without a moment's hesitation. The scariest moment was parking the kayak on a river bank for a breather, and discovering it was an entrance point to the river for a small herd nearby. You've never seen us paddle off so quickly. Then they began trailing us along the bank. For big animals they can really shift.'

'How amazing,' gushed Simon.

'How fast can they run?' I asked.

'Almost thirty miles per hour,' said Jack.

'I think I would just faint clean away,' said Simon, swooning, and once again clutching Jack's arm. If Jack minded, he didn't show it, unlike my husband who was tutting with disproval every time Simon flirted outrageously with Jack.

'Yeah, I did feel somewhat unsettled when one of the hippos broke into a jog and entered the water. He proceeded to stick just his eyes above the surface and was watching me intently. I had to pay close attention to my surroundings. It wasn't a comfortable ride.'

'Would you say it was the most frightening thing you've ever done?' Simon simpered.

'Without a doubt,' Jack nodded. 'Scarier than skydiving. Scarier than swimming with whale sharks. Scarier than volcano boarding.'

I boggled into my roast beef. At what point had Nerdy Jack become Action Man?

'I remember being scared when I went skiing,' I said.

'Black run?' asked Jack, sympathetically.

'Er, no. It was a school trip to a dry slope. But my ski fell off and I was terrified.'

'Oh for goodness' sake, Holly,' said Simon, 'it's hardly in the same vein as Jack with his circling sharks, charging hippos and crocodiles snapping their jaws of death.'

'Talking of jaws,' said Jack kindly, 'I gather you're a dental nurse.'

'Holly works for me,' said Alex, interrupting. 'I have my own practice.'

'Impressive,' said Jack. 'You know, I'm long overdue for a check-up. Despite kayaking with fearsome beasts, nothing terrifies me more than a visit to the dentist.'

'Surely not,' said Alex, laughing. 'Come and see me first thing tomorrow morning, before the patient list starts. My surgery prides itself on excellent chairside manner, and my wife will look after you.'

'Thanks. I will. But I warn you now, Holly, you're dealing with a coward.'

'Don't worry,' I said cheerfully, 'I'm happy for you to hold my hand.'

'Excellent,' said Jack, winking, and holding my gaze for slightly longer than was necessary. 'I'll look forward to that.'

Chapter Twenty-Two

'Your brother is outrageous,' Alex seethed, on the drive home. 'Much as I love your parents, Holly, I do wish they'd take Simon to one side and tell him to tone down his behaviour.'

'That will never happen, and anyway, he's not that bad.'

'I disagree. He's rude, and he uses his sexuality to be uncouth. All that touching Jack's arm and leg, and then talking about how he likes to handle trouser snakes. Disgusting. Goodness only knows what Aunty Shirley thought.'

'Aunty Shirley was laughing!' I protested. 'She's not as stuffy as you think. She really likes Simon and thinks he's funny.'

'Well I don't. And thank goodness Sophie wasn't there. I'd have ended up having words with your brother if he'd spoken like that in front of our daughter. Bad example.'

I sighed and looked out of the window. There was no reasoning with Alex when he was in one of his moods about Simon.

'That reminds me,' I said. 'We're picking Sophie up on the way home. Can you detour past Tabitha's house? I have the postcode.' I leaned forward and activated the car's satnav.

'Terrific,' Alex tutted, as the voice activation told us to proceed five miles along the road, 'let us now drive out of our way to top off an irritating day.' He tutted again.

'You're starting to sound like Skippy the kangaroo.'

'Who?'

'Oh never mind,' I tutted. Might as well join in.

For the next five minutes we drove on in silence.

'Who is Tabitha?' Alex eventually asked.

'One of Sophie's wannabe best mates. She's apparently one of the class's cool kids.'

'And what, pray tell, is so cool about Tabitha?'

'I haven't the faintest idea.'

Ten minutes later I had a sneaking idea why everyone wanted to be like Tabitha. We pulled in on a gravel drive that led to an enormous contemporary-looking house that seemed to be made almost entirely of glass. I could see straight through to the rear garden, which looked like a manicured park, complete with swimming pool covered by a clear dome. The front door was answered by Miss Popular herself, a vision in full make-up and short skirt and looking at least six years older than her tender fourteen years. Good God. I wasn't sure I wanted Sophie emulating Tabitha. I'd much prefer my teen to look her age, complete with spots and a slick of puppy fat. Sophie appeared seconds later, and was beaming widely.

'Hi,' said Tabitha, with all the poise and assurance of a more mature woman. 'I think my mum wants a word with you, Mrs Hart.'

'Oh, right,' I said in surprise, as a slightly older model of Tabitha appeared in the hallway, her face lighting up as if she'd known me for years, rather than having ignored me at the school gates as one of the lesser mothers who never looked like that female in the perfume commercial and, even worse, drove a dirty car.

'So lovely to see you, Holly!' she beamed. 'Izzy,' she quickly added, realising that I didn't know her name.

'And, er, you too, Izzy,' I nodded. 'Thank you for having Sophie. Very kind of you.'

'An absolute pleasure. Anytime. Lovely girl,' she gushed, 'a real credit to you, and a wonderful influence on Tabs.'

I glowed from all the compliments about my teen, and noticed Sophie was also pink with pleasure.

'Now I wanted to see you before you drove off.' Izzy looked furtively at the car where Alex was sitting impatiently drumming his fingers on the steering wheel. 'It's about,' she dropped her voice an octave, 'the party.'

I stared at her, clueless as to what she was talking about. And then realisation dawned. She was having a party. Oh wow, and she wanted to invite me! I was going to be allowed access into the clique of glamorous mothers Izzy consorted with. For a moment I felt quite heady and had a flash of insight into how flattered my daughter must feel that Tabitha deigned to hang out with her.

'How marvellous,' I purred. 'We'd be delighted.' I presumed my husband was included. 'Where and when is it?'

'Well that's what I wanted to ask *you*,' said Izzy chummily.

I stared at her in confusion, then glanced at Sophie for a clue as to what Tabitha's mother was talking about. It was then that I noticed my daughter was no longer pink with pleasure, rather red with embarrassment. The penny dropped.

'Do you mean my husband's surprise fortieth birthday party?'

'But of course,' Izzy laughed, 'it's so good of you to invite us all.'

'B-but, it's just a small event, you know, immediate family and a few friends—'

'Hey,' Izzy put a hand on my arm, stopping me in mid flow. She opened her eyes wide and adopted a reassuring tone. 'We may look grand, but we really don't mind a small event. Nothing wrong with that at all. So where do we go?'

'The golf club,' I said faintly.

'Ah, never mind,' said Izzy, for all the world as if I'd just said it was taking place at the local village hall with galloping rising damp. 'I'm sure your hubby will be thrilled nonetheless.'

'Yes,' I said, dazed. 'It's the thought that counts.'

'Super. I'll let the others know and we'll see you there!'

Sensing dismissal from a higher being, I turned and walked back to the car, leaving Sophie and Tabitha to hug each other goodbye. I'd have to talk to Jeanie and Caro about Izzy whatever-her-name-was. See what tips they had for deflecting the Mummy Mafia from coming to the party of a man they didn't know from Adam.

Behind me, I heard Sophie's feet scampering across the gravel as she caught up with me.

'Mum, I'm *so* sorry, she just assumed that she and her friends were invited because Tabitha and my other new friends were coming. I didn't know what to say, so I bottled out and left it to you.'

'And now I've wimped out too,' I said, smiling ruefully at her anxious face. 'Perhaps they won't come. After all,' I said, adopting a naff accent, 'it's only at the golf club, innit.'

Chapter Twenty-Three

The following morning, I was up extra early so I could luxuriate in front of the mirror carefully applying make-up. I then whizzed Rupert up the lane for such a fast walk we must have looked like a speeded-up film. Back home, I returned to the mirror, this time to flat iron the frizz out of my hair. There was something about a silky mane water-falling over the shoulders that looked so seductive, and today that was how I wanted to appear – even if the first official patient of the day was Mr Simms who had terrible gingivitis and halitosis to rival Rupert's.

'You look nice, Mum,' said Sophie, wandering into my bedroom. 'Where are you going?'

'Only to work,' I said, ultra-casually.

'You don't usually bother to glam up for Dad's patients.'

Ah, but it depended on who the patient was.

'I know. But today,' I shrugged carelessly, 'I thought I'd make a bit of an effort.'

'You don't fool me. I know the reason for this,' she said, picking up a lock of my hair and letting it slip through her fingers.

I reddened. 'I'm doing it for me!'

'Oh come off it, Mum,' Sophie scoffed. 'Apart from anything else you've gone the same colour as our front door.' Bugger. Had Alex mentioned Jack to Sophie? Had he happened to say, in passing, that my godmother's son was Hollywood handsome, and this morning the man himself was gracing the surgery for a dental check-up? 'It's because of Tabitha's mother, right?'

I looked at my daughter blankly. 'Izzy?'

'Yes. It's because she's super pretty and mega trendy, and yesterday she made you feel like one of Dad's old slippers. Worn out. And smelly,' she added, as she watched me liberally spraying myself in perfume that was usually only worn on special occasions.

I mentally sighed with relief. 'Ha ha,' I laughed, 'you're right. You've sussed me out!'

'You're so transparent, Mum,' Sophie grinned. 'And you look really nice, by the way.'

'Thanks, sweetheart,' I said, touched.

'Not as gorgeous as Izzy, but keep practising. You should try using an eyebrow pencil too. Do you want to borrow mine? It would frame your face and bring harmony to your features. Your brows are very sparse and need some definition.'

Since when had my daughter been buying eyebrow pencils? Zoella had a lot to answer for.

'Okay,' I said, 'but make it quick. I need to get a wiggle on.'

'Don't rush it, Mum,' said Sophie. 'You need a steady hand.'

'Right. Are you nearly ready for me to take you to school? I'm sorry, but you're going to be a bit earlier than usual. Dad wants to squeeze in a new patient before the list gets underway. It's Aunty Shirley's son, actually. Jack,' I quavered. If Sophie noticed the tremor in my voice, she made no comment.

'You don't need to run me to school this morning,' said Sophie, colouring up slightly but sounding very chipper, 'because Tabitha's mum is taking me.'

'Is she?' I frowned. Right. No doubt come to see what the Harts' house looked like, and whether it was posh enough to permit entrance to the yummy-mummy elite club. Izzy was going to be disappointed.

Sophie skipped off to get the eyebrow pencil, oblivious to school politics and parental one-upmanship.

'Want me to do it for you?' she asked, returning with the pencil.

'I'll manage, thanks.'

'Okay, I'll leave you to it.'

Five minutes later, I had a pair of eyebrows that made Cara Delevingne's look moth-eaten. Wow. Go me.

'Are you ready, Holly?' Alex called up the stairs. 'I can't afford to be late.'

'Coming!' I grabbed my handbag and skipped along the landing, just as Sophie had earlier. I felt like a new woman, and all thanks to an eyebrow pencil. I wondered if it might do the same for Alex. Put some lead in *his* pencil, so to speak. 'Bye, Sophie,' I called, 'don't forget to lock up on your way out.' I heard a grunt of acknowledgement by way of response. Ramming my feet into shoes, I hastened joyfully after Alex, throwing myself into the passenger seat with – it had to be said – far too much enthusiasm for a Monday morning session with grumpy members of the public.

'I don't want to spend too much time on Jack,' said Alex, as he floored the accelerator. 'If he needs treatment, I'll work out a quick dental plan and leave you to go through the price options.'

'Sure,' I said lightly, my heart already quickening at the mention of Jack's name. I instantly felt guilty. But then I thought of Annabelle Huntingdon-Smyth, and wondered whether Alex had joyfully skipped off to the surgery, full of delicious anticipation at seeing such a beautiful woman as he snapped on his gloves, planted his feet wide and huskily said, 'Right, shall we get down to it?' No, actually I wouldn't feel guilty. Jack was just... well, Jack. He was still the same nerdy Jack. Just all grown-up now. And there was no harm in admiring a drop-dead gorgeous guy, was there? It was no different to Alex appreciating Annabelle's loveliness, or Sophie having a girl-crush on Tabitha. It didn't *mean* anything.

Leaving Alex to fetch his briefcase and a bag of clean scrubs from the boot of the car, I went ahead, sweeping into reception with new-found confidence and poise. Jack hadn't arrived yet, and the waiting room was empty. Jenny, the receptionist, was simultaneously switching on her computer and listening to answering-machine messages. She looked up as I came through the door.

'Good morning,' I trilled.

'Hello, Mrs Hart,' she said formally.

She never called me by my Christian name, preferring to keep things professionally chilly, although she was quite happy to call Alex by his first name and flutter her eyelashes whilst doing so. Our dislike for each other was mutual. I nipped into the ladies', ready to change into my scrubs. As the door closed after me, a snort of laughter followed in my wake. I ignored her. Anybody who resorted to sniggering needed to go back to the playground. Some women, like Jenny, just never grew up.

Emerging from the cloakroom, I went into my husband's surgery and began setting out instruments. Alex walked in a minute later, now wearing his own scrubs, and I was thrilled to see Jack was with him too. However, this time I was prepared for my body's knee-jerk reaction to Aunty Shirley's son. Oh yes, indeed. Today there would be no foolish clumsiness. No dropping things or knocking stuff over. Instead, Jack would see a woman in her prime. Confident. Poised. Efficient. Indispensable, and downright glamorous with it.

'Well, hello,' I said, sounding like a female version of Leslie Phillips. *Steady, Holly. You'll be saying 'ding-dong' next.* I cleared my throat. 'Lovely to see you again, Jack. Do take a seat.' I indicated the dental chair.

'Hey there,' said Jack, raising his eyebrows. Was that some sort of secret communication? I raised mine enquiringly. He lowered his and grinned. 'Don't forget you've got to hold my hand.'

'Yes,' I squeaked, composure slipping for a moment. I cleared my throat and tried again. 'I'd be delighted to.' Hell, now I sounded like Jessica Rabbit. I gave another little cough.

'Are you all right, Holly?' asked Alex, turning to me. 'Do you need a glass of wat— Good God!'

'What's the matter?'

'Nothing,' he said quickly, picking up his loupes and slipping them over his nose. 'Are you okay… the cough?'

'I'm fine,' I said crisply, now sounding like I'd sprayed my tonsils with laundry starch. I turned to Jack. 'Let me put these on your face.' I popped some goggles over Jack's very perfect straight nose. 'And this goes around the neck,' I said, tucking a bib under his chin. He was sporting designer stubble this morning. Lovely. Very… rugged.

'Thank you,' Jack whispered.

Why was he whispering? 'Feeling okay?'

'Just a bit nervous,' he said, reaching for my hand.

'You'll be fine,' I assured, as his warm fingers encircled mine. I wasn't sure I would be though; his touch was making parts of my body sparkle like never before. I momentarily clung on to the rinse basin with my free hand in order to steady myself. 'Just remember, it's only a check-up.'

I peered at him. Was it my imagination, or was he turning the colour of putty?

'Now then, Jack,' said Alex, coming over. 'Nothing to worry about. Open wide.' Alex pulled the overhead light down, as Jack obliged and opened his mouth.

'Oh that's brilliant,' I said, stroking Jack's hand. I wasn't entirely sure if that was ethical, so I stopped. 'You're doing really well.'

'No he's not,' said Alex.

'I beg your pardon?'

'He's passed out! Oh, for goodness' sake,' said Alex irritably, 'I thought the man was a doctor.'

'He *is* a doctor!' I cried, 'but even surgeons can have phobias. *Do* something, Alex!' 'Can you stop panicking, Holly?'

'Panicking? Me? What if he dies? Oh God, he's choking, he's choking, listen to the noise he's making,' I gabbled, as an unconscious Jack emitted sounds like a hissing coffee percolator.

'His tongue has rolled to the back of his throat,' said Alex, sliding two hands either side of Jack's jaw, and lifting him so his airway cleared. 'He'll come to in a minute.' Alex reclined the chair so Jack was completely horizontal, and then used a foot button to slowly elevate his legs. 'Loosen his clothing.'

'What?'

'We need to increase blood supply to the brain so it gets more oxygen.'

'Right, loosen clothing, loosen clothing,' I repeated, hands fluttering about. I could feel myself breaking out in a sweat; indeed my whole forehead was damp as I unbuckled Jack's trouser belt and, averting my eyes heavenwards, reached for his zipper.

'His *shirt*, Holly,' Alex barked. 'Don't you recall any of your training?'

'Right, right, shirt, undo shirt,' I gabbled, swiping a shaky hand across my sweaty brow before concentrating on unbuttoning Jack's shirt. As the sight of well-defined pecs came into view, along with a delicious smattering of dark chest hair, I couldn't help gasping aloud.

'What's the matter?' snapped Alex.

'Nothing,' I warbled, trying not to swoon onto Jack's muscular torso. Alex would go barmy if his dental nurse fainted on top of his unconscious patient. My fingers shook as I undid another two buttons revealing an expanse of golden-brown skin, no doubt tanned from his time in Africa. *Stop looking at his chest, Holly. Think about Brexit. The economy. World politics. Whether Donald Trump dyes his hair and, if so, why saffron yellow?*

'I think that's enough buttons, Holly. We don't want the patient coming to and thinking you're stripping him.'

'Oh!' I snatched my hands away. 'What's the matter with Jack's face? He's gone bright red.'

'That's good. I think we'll give him a bit of oxygen just to help him come round. Pass me the tank.'

'What tank?' I looked around wildly.

'Over there. Put the mask over his face and depress the pump switch.'

I grabbed the tank and looked for the button. 'It's not working.' My hands were shaking badly now. 'Can you do it, Alex?'

'I'm holding Jack's head,' Alex snapped, 'so his tongue doesn't slip back down his airway. For heaven's sake, Holly, ring reception. Get Jenny in here. And I strongly suggest you do some nursing revision.'

'I'm sorry, I'm sorry,' I said, lunging for the phone.

'And you might want to take yourself off to the cloakroom and repair your face. I didn't like to say anything earlier, but your eyebrows have turned into two enormous caterpillars, one of which appears to be crawling off your forehead because you've rubbed it.'

Chapter Twenty-Four

Needless to say Jack did eventually come to, and the rest of the check-up proceeded without further hitch.

'I'm delighted to say,' said Alex, looking at an X-ray, 'that despite your aversion to dentists, your teeth are absolutely perfect.'

'Thanks,' said Jack. 'And I'm really sorry about the fainting. I feel so stupid.'

'Happens to the best of us,' said Alex heartily, trying not to look at the clock on the wall. We were now running half an hour late for the first listed patient, who no doubt was sitting in the waiting room impatiently tapping his foot and would complain bitterly once ensconced in the chair. Alex pressed a button, and the dental chair slowly whirred upright. Jack stared in bemusement at his unbuttoned shirt and flapping trouser belt.

'Sorry,' I apologised, 'that was my fault.'

'What a shame I wasn't awake to appreciate it,' he murmured.

Was he flirting? I blushed furiously.

'Now look after those teeth,' said Alex, firmly guiding Jack out of his surgery.

'Do I settle up at reception?' he asked.

'Nothing to pay on this occasion,' said Alex. 'On the house.'

'Well, thanks, buddy. That's very kind of you. And if you ever need a consultation about your bonce, let me reciprocate.'

'Will do,' said Alex, opening the door.

'What do you specialise in?' I asked, causing Jack to pause in the doorway and Alex to fidget from foot to foot.

'Neurosurgery, with specialist clinical interest in skull base surgery for the treatment of acoustic neuromas, pituitary tumours and trigeminal neuralgia.'

At the mention of the last two words, my ears pricked up.

'How amazing. Alex is on the board of directors of a charity that offers chronic pain support for sufferers of trigeminal neuralgia,' I said.

'Fabulous stuff,' said Jack. 'If anybody wants a micro-vascular decompression in their lunch break,' he joked, 'send them over to me. I won't hold you up any further, Alex. I know you are a busy man. Thanks again, both of you.'

And then he was gone, leaving me to soothe a very agitated husband and an irate patient who complained bitterly from start to finish. But, somehow, I was impervious to both and spent the rest of the day feeling strangely elated.

Once off-duty, I tore off to Sophie's school, immediately spotting Caro and Jeanie gossiping in the car park. This area was meant solely for teachers and visiting members of the public, but was nonetheless where every parent congregated at this time of day, always causing obstructions and pandemonium. Jeanie appeared to be talking earnestly to Caro, who was nodding, a frown upon her pretty face.

'Yoo-hoo!' I called, and hurried over to greet them. The moment they saw me, they sprang apart like deflecting magnets. 'Hi, girls,' I said, puffing slightly. Caro greeted me with a smile, but not before I'd noted the worry etched across her forehead. As Jeanie raised her eyes to me, I could see she'd been crying. 'Oh! Whatever's the matter, Jeanie?'

'N-nothing,' she stuttered, her watering eyes suddenly looking shifty, 'I'm just… full of cold.'

I stared at my friend in confusion. Since when had she so obviously lied to me? Caro was clearly privy to whatever was so secret. How strange. And surely rather hurtful?

'Oh look, there's my two coming out,' said Caro, 'I'll catch you both later.'

'Yes, okay. How about we have—'

But Caro had already disappeared into the tidal wave of students pouring out of the school door.

'Looks like somebody is wanting a word with you,' said Jeanie, nodding her head in the direction behind me.

'What? Where?'

'I must go,' Jeanie muttered, already distancing herself. 'I need to see Charlotte's teacher. She's on her fourth detention this term. Apparently, it isn't acceptable.'

'Oh dear. Is that why you've been cry—'

A hand clamped onto my shoulder, and Jeanie instantly scuttled off, head down, pushing through the heaving throng of teenagers as she hastened towards the school's main entrance.

'Holly!' said a familiar voice that definitely wasn't on my Christmas card list. I spun round to see Izzy and her yummy-mummy crowd. 'We're all so delighted to see you,' she gushed.

'Hi, Izzy.' I nodded at the well-turned out mini mob standing with her, identical hair-dos blowing in the late September breeze. They all looked like models in a shampoo commercial.

'Sooo looking forward to the party,' said another mother, whose name evaded me. Mindy? Minty?

Enough was enough. 'Look—'

'Hi, Mum,' said Sophie, suddenly appearing by my side. Her face looked pinched and anxious. 'Can we go please? I've got a stack of homework and need to make a start.'

'Sure.' I turned away from the in-crowd. 'What's up?'

'Tell you in the car,' said Sophie under her breath.

The school was well and truly behind us when she finally turned, glancing at me across the hand brake. Her face was abject with misery.

'I don't know how to tell you this!' she croaked.

Oh God. Please don't tell me my daughter was going to confess to something horrific. A letter had recently gone out to the parents about eating disorders and self-harming, children suffering with body issues and being addicted to scratching their arms with a compass. Not my daughter. Please. I'd rather have her banging the doors at home until they all fell off their hinges, just so long as she was a 'normal' stroppy teenager, in the Kevin and Perry mould.

'You can tell me anything,' I whispered, suddenly not quite trusting my voice. 'Whatever it is, Sophie, I'm here for you.'

Pausing at some traffic lights, I took my hand off the steering wheel and gave hers a quick squeeze of reassurance. She took a deep breath.

'My entire form has invited themselves to Dad's birthday party.'

There was a pause as I digested this, and Sophie stared unhappily ahead.

'Is that all?' I asked. Relief was washing over me in waves.

'What do you mean *is that all*?' she shrieked. 'That's at least *thirty* kids. And let's not forget their awful parents,' she raged, her temper suddenly rushing to the fore. I raised my eyebrows at her outburst. This morning Izzy what's-her-face was super pretty and mega trendy. Now Tabitha's mother was being lumped into the 'awful parents' category. 'I like being more popular, Mum,' my daughter continued, 'but it's getting out of hand. I feel like my friends are false. And actually,' she gulped, 'I reckon that's why everybody sucks up to Tabitha. The kids don't necessarily want to know her. They just want to sashay around her house and eat popcorn in her cinema room or run around her massive garden before heading off to the indoor swimming pool. I'm not into fake friends. But neither am I into being Billy No-Mates. Does that make me pathetic for not standing up to them all and saying, "Clear off, you can't bloody come!" '

'That's quite a speech, darling,' I said, as the traffic lights shifted to green. 'Firstly, don't say "bloody". Secondly, I'm proud of you for recognising phoney friends. Thirdly, I understand you don't want to be left on your Jack Jones if you stop everyone coming along. But we'll go for a compromise,' I said. That word again. 'I'll ring the golf club and tell them to forget the buffet and cancel the free bar. After all, I'm not forking out for a stack of food and drink for people I don't know, but equally I'm not brave enough to stand up to that lot either. However, if they want to come along for a free boogie and swell the crowd, that's up to them.'

Sophie instantly burst into tears. 'You always know what to do, Mum. And you're so wise. I love you.'

Always knew what to do? Wise? Me? The woman who suspected one of her best friends had sent a string of sexts to Alex? Who also distrusted a flirtatious and very beautiful patient around her husband? Who felt like her marriage was hanging by a thread, but equally was behaving like a teenager around another man? But I loved my daughter for thinking it, and I told her so.

Parenting was such unchartered territory. One minute you and your child were at each other's throats. The next the umbilical cord was reeling in a rapidly regressing teen, wanting to pick her up, as if a baby, and fiercely cuddle her. My mind instantly turned to my best friends, Jeanie and Caro. Once home, I'd give them a call. Invite them for coffee tomorrow morning. Have a proper catch-up. And find out exactly why Jeanie had made out she'd had a cold and then rushed off, almost as if she couldn't bear to be around me.

Chapter Twenty-Five

'Caro?' I asked, speaking into the handset. Sometimes I didn't know if I was talking to my friend or her daughter, Lizzie. Both were sounding increasingly alike on the phone.

'Wrong!' said Lizzie gleefully. 'Just a minute, Holly, and I'll get Mum for you.'

'Thanks, sweetie.'

I waited a minute or so whilst Lizzie foghorned and Caro abandoned whatever she was doing to, somewhat breathlessly, take the phone.

'Hi, it's me,' I said.

'Oh, Holly, sorry I had to dash off earlier. I saw that awful woman descending, so I turned and fled. I just can't bear her.'

'You mean Izzy?'

'Yes. She's a nightmare. She was standing there with her hanger-on girlfriends, loudly telling them about how she and Sebastian, her clever businessman of a husband, recently went to some opening by the Prince of Wales and, honestly, it was Charles this and Camilla that, and how Kate is so nice and normal, and that her baby bump is so tiny and cute. Izzy's well-toned arms are nothing to do with visits to the gym but everything to do with aggressive social climbing.

And then Jeanie clapped eyes on her and wanted to run away too. Is Izzy your new bestie?' Caro teased.

'Absolutely not,' I said emphatically. 'But listen, I didn't ring you to discuss Izzy. Caro, why was Jeanie crying?'

There was a moment's silence, as if my friend was thinking how best to answer this question. 'She was upset because she's done something stupid.'

'Surely it's not worth crying about? Hell, I do daft things all the time,' I pointed out, my mind turning back to this morning's fiasco at the surgery. I'd been as much use to Alex as a chocolate teapot.

'Perhaps that's not quite the way to word it. When I say "stupid", I really mean—' Caro broke off and I sensed her raking a hand through her mane, 'more like, downright idiotic.'

'Like what?' I asked.

'Look,' Caro dropped her voice to little more than a murmur, 'I can't really speak. Walls have ears, and all that. I also have a very knowing teenager who is a massive blabbermouth, and I can't risk her overhearing.'

'Is Jeanie in trouble with the law?' I said, my voice rising in alarm, and then instantly dropping again as I realised my own savvy teenager might be close by. 'Has she had one of her hormonal moments,' I whispered into the handset, 'and dashed out of the supermarket with a trolley full of shopping and not paid for it? We've all done it. It's nothing to be ashamed of.'

'No, no, it's nothing like that,' said Caro. 'I think Jeanie would actually cope far better with the outcome of some absent-minded pilfering.' She gave a hollow laugh.

'It surely can't be that terrible!' I reasoned. And then a part of me froze. What if Jeanie had confided in Caro about the very thing I had recently suspected Jeanie of? 'Anyway,' I said, trying not to let the hurt creep into my voice, 'why has she told you and not me?'

'I don't honestly think she meant to tell me, Holly, so don't be peeved.'

'I'm not peeved,' I said, immediately sounding peeved. 'But we've all known each other since exchanging our knee-high socks for stockings. I thought we were close. Why have you been entrusted over me with a secret?' Okay – maybe this was a *bit* hypocritical. After all, there were loads of things I hadn't confided recently.

'She's ashamed, Holly. And she blurted it out in a tumble of words and tears. I just happened to be there in the moment her guilt came to the surface and divested itself.'

'Guilt?' I said, feeling another frisson of alarm.

'She's ashamed. I guess some secrets are so huge, there is an overwhelming desire to relieve yourself by sharing them. But once the words are spoken, they can't be unsaid, and then there is a risk the person you've unburdened to tells someone else.'

'Like me,' I said, asserting myself somewhat.

'Yes, like you,' Caro sighed.

'I'm all ears,' I said pointedly.

There was another long pause, and I sensed Caro looking around, making sure Lizzie couldn't hear what she was about to say. 'If I tell you,' she whispered, 'you absolutely *have* to promise you won't tell a soul.'

'Of course not!'

'Nor must you let on to Jeanie that I've told you.'

'Surely she'll tell me herself when we're next together?'

'I don't know,' said Caro thoughtfully, no doubt chewing her lip as she tried to work out the way our friend's mind worked. 'I suspect she is already regretting spilling the beans to me.'

'Just tell me, Caro,' I said, fighting down a sense of exasperation. 'Perhaps I'll be able to help her.'

'You won't,' she assured. 'Neither of us can help her. She's landed herself into a right old pickle.'

'Which is?'

'You haven't yet promised me you won't let on to Jeanie that I've told you.'

'For God's sake,' I hissed, before raising my eyes heavenwards and silently apologising to God for taking his name in vain. 'Yes, I promise. Now spit it out, or else I'm going to drive round to your house and stick pins in you!'

'Right,' said Caro, taking a deep breath, 'prepare to be rocked. Jeanie has been having an affair with a married man.'

Chapter Twenty-Six

As I listened to Caro's words filtering down the handset, through my ears and into my brain, I felt as though the very foundations of the house were rocking. It was one thing to suspect. Quite another to have it confirmed.

'Jeanie's having an affair?' I croaked.

'Apparently so,' said Caro, sounding very furtive.

No wonder she didn't want our children overhearing. All our kids went to the same school. If either Lizzie or Sophie blabbed and word got out to Charlotte and Harry, well, it didn't bear thinking about.

'Who's she having an affair *with*?' I whispered, tightly clutching the phone.

'I don't know. She wouldn't tell me.'

'Why not?'

'Heck, I don't know. I was so gobsmacked by what Jeanie was saying, I didn't push for her to answer the question about who he was. I was reeling. I mean, I know Jeanie has moaned about Ray from time to time, but I never thought she was unhappy enough to stray. After all, we all complain about our husbands.'

'Yes, quite.' I murmured.

'And how on earth has she even managed to find the opportunity? Both of us know how busy her schedule is.'

I nodded, even though Caro couldn't see me. 'I know what you mean. All those Pilates and Zumba classes, or rushing off to do thirty lengths at the local pool because she reckoned she'd put on a pound just looking at a Mars bar.' It occurred to me those activities always took place in the evening, but I didn't voice it aloud to Caro. 'Jeanie is always on the go, and in between she's busy looking after Ray and the kids.'

'Except,' said Caro pensively, 'perhaps there *was* no Pilates or Zumba or frantic swimming? After all, we were never there with her. Perhaps it was Jeanie's escape clause to rush out the front door for a secret assignation?'

'Yes,' I agreed, 'you're probably right.' I was mentally trying to work out the frequency of Alex dropping everything some evenings to dash off to an emergency that couldn't wait. Did it dovetail with Jeanie's possibly fictitious exercise classes?

'I wonder where they went?' mused Caro. 'It certainly hasn't been her house. There's no way Jeanie would risk bringing a bloke home, not with the sort of neighbours she has. You can't stand on her doorstep and ring the doorbell without all the net curtains in her road twitching like your Rupert when he's asleep. Whoever he is, the pair of them must be having evening trysts. But, equally, they can't be going to *his* house either. After all, he has a wife. And unless she's the very understanding sort, it's hardly likely he'd say, "Alicia, darling, just popping upstairs for a bit of rumpy-pumpy with my floozy. Put the kettle on, because I won't be long".'

'Alicia?' I queried. 'Is that her name?'

'No, Holly,' said Caro patiently, 'I made it up. I have no idea what the name of this guy's wife is, any more than I know what *he* is called. It's just a mystery how two married people can conduct snatched moments without having a handy convenient bed. I don't imagine Jeanie is the sort of person to check in to a cheap motel for an hour, do you?'

'No,' I whispered, as a horrendous thought occurred to me. I knew exactly how my husband could orchestrate snatched moments with a lover, if he so wanted. At the dental surgery. There were all manner of suitable places to flop down upon once hemlines had been lifted and trousers dropped. From the squashy sofas in reception, to the reclining dental chairs in the surgeries, to Jenny's enormous meet-and-greet desk. And after hours there would be no interruptions. None whatsoever, thanks to the front door being firmly locked and the key tucked safely in Alex's pocket.

'Let's do coffee tomorrow morning,' said Caro, interrupting a horribly vivid image of Alex sitting on the receptionist's typing stool, Jeanie astride my husband, and the chair spinning round and round and round as they noisily climaxed. 'Let's see if she confides in you, Holly, and then the two of us can press her to reveal who he is.' She made a clicking noise with her tongue. 'I still can't believe it. I thought her marriage was rock solid. Like ours,' Caro added.

I chewed my lip. One thing I could privately admit to without any shadow of a doubt was that my marriage was *not* solid. Had I once thought it was? Yes. Absolutely. I'd never doubted Alex's reasons to stay married to me until last Christmas… and if he'd wanted out, he could have said so there and then. Indeed, only the other day, after my meltdown over Annabelle Huntingdon-Smyth, I'd asked him if he wanted a divorce, but he'd said no... pointed out we had a lovely life. Was it that? Simply that divorce was expensive and he didn't want to dismantle the 'lovely life'? That it was cheaper and more preferable to stay married to wifey who had never set his boxer shorts on fire but, as a family, collectively gave stability to their child, whilst he quietly got his thrills elsewhere – as Jeanie was apparently now doing? I gulped. Jeanie. With her big smile, buxom hips and billowing cleavage. *Stop it, Holly, stop it. Jeanie is one of your best friends. One of the closest. She wouldn't do that to you!* Wouldn't she? How many times in TV soaps, films, reality shows, was a good friend weeded out and shown to the audience to be a traitor who had smiled to the victim's face and laughed behind their back?

I caught sight of my reflection in an overhead mirror. The woman looking back was pale with scared eyes and a tense expression. I'd been on edge for months. Three-quarters of a year to be precise. I knew, in my heart of hearts, that something wasn't right in my marriage. And it didn't matter how many times Alex vehemently denied it, someone else held his affections in the palm of their hand, had enjoyed his kisses on the curve of their lips. The question was... who? Annabelle or Jeanie? I was ninety-nine point nine per cent certain that my feminine intuition was right.

And in that moment, I knew it was vitally important to stop confronting Alex, to cease behaving like a suspicious wife, to abandon hissy fits, to forget cross-examination and meltdowns, and instead to sit in the wings quietly. Watching. Observing. And not just him, but Annabelle and my dear friend Jeanie too. Because sooner or later, one of them would make a wrong move. And when they did, they'd reveal themselves. And I'd be there to catch them out.

Chapter Twenty-Seven

When I awoke the following morning, I couldn't wait to wave Alex off to the office. I wanted a quiet moment to think. And to trawl through Facebook. To engage in, as my daughter would call it, *stalking*. I felt myself go slightly hot at even acknowledging that I was consorting with such a word. It conjured up a mental image of a paranoid person, desperately flicking through photographs of others, looking at their faces, scrutinising expressions, seeking hidden meanings. Was she touching his arm in such a way because she was claiming ownership of that man's heart? Or was she innocently pulling him round to simply smile at the camera?

Such thoughts raced through my head now as I started by checking Jeanie's Facebook page. She hadn't updated her status for a couple of days. Was that because she'd felt too miserable? Too tearful? Sometimes it was hard to put on a brave face to the world, and no place more so than social media. I'd quickly discovered that there were people who forever posted pictures of themselves with their other halves... *look at me with Derek, aren't we a fabulous couple*!... or pictures with their kids... *we are the perfect family*!... but I'd read somewhere that sometimes, underneath such look-at-me postings, was an unhappy marriage or a dysfunctional family.

Privately I believed that it was those who *didn't* put their husbands and kids under the spotlight of social media who probably had the best relationships.

Sifting through Jeanie's timeline, she was doing a lot of the former. There were stacks of recent images of her with hubby Ray. My cursor hovered over the last and most recent posting. She'd captioned it: *Me and my 'Ray' of sunshine, ha ha!* The pair of them were laughing into the camera, Ray with a hand around Jeanie's shoulders, squeezing her tightly to him, a soppy look about his eyes which said it all: *This is the only woman for me.* Whereas Jeanie was looking radiant, positively blooming, and… triumphant. Would that be because currently she had not one, but two men bolstering her ego?

I scrolled through her list of friends and was amazed to see a headshot of in-crowd Izzy, which didn't make sense considering she and Jeanie barely acknowledged each other outside the school. I clicked on Izzy's profile picture and, as expected, up came photograph after photograph of her family… *aren't we wholesome!*… right down to everyone wearing matching festive sweaters last Christmas… *aren't we hilarious!*… then, later, grouped around the in-house cinema screen sharing popcorn from a bowl the size of a small pond… *aren't we having fun!*… then under the glass dome at the rear of Izzy's house by the pool, all jumping off the side, holding noses as an upward spray of chlorinated water was snapped and forever suspended in mid-air… *don't you wish you were like us?*… before disappearing underwater, vast ripples fanning out on the pool's surface. Izzy's husband, Sebastian, perfectly counterbalanced her fragile beauty, with his battered good looks and the height and build of somebody who regularly played rugby.

I clicked off Izzy's timeline and moved on to Annabelle Hunting-don-Smyth. But... oh, the bitch! She'd changed her privacy settings. All I could see was her profile picture, a professional portrait, studio lighting haloing her glossy mane and emphasising glowing skin, teeth pearly white thanks to either Alex's dental tricks or a spot of photoshopping. Bugger. How could I keep an eye on her now? A part of me wondered whether to try logging on as Alex. I knew my husband's email address, but was clueless about his password. If I tried to hack Alex's account and he found out, he'd go ballistic. Apart from anything else, it would blow my cover on quietly catching him out. After all, I'd already vowed to be more cunning than a stealth aircraft. However, I was also a firm believer of that old saying *action speaks louder than words*. Annabelle's action of changing her privacy settings smacked of something to hide. She was therefore still a suspect.

I looked at my watch. It was time to leave for coffee with Caro and Jeanie. This morning I was going to have an up-close and personal opportunity to question Jeanie – obviously I'd have to be careful that I didn't let on I knew her secret. I wasn't yet sure how to lead her into dropping her guard and confessing that she was Queenie of the saucy sexts, but where there was a will there was a way. And right now, I was feeling very wilful.

I went to sign out but paused as a friend request notification caught my eye. I clicked on it. My eyes widened at the image of Jack smiling out from the computer screen, his eyes seemingly locked on mine. The hormonal effect was instantaneous – armpits instantly breaking out into a muck sweat and my heart turning into a rubber ball that bounced against the underside of my ribs.

'You,' I said, pointing my finger at him, 'need to stop having a strange effect on me. Do you understand? I'm with Alex, and I'm fighting to save my marriage. Stop distracting me with your come-to-bed eyes and sexy smile. Do you hear?'

His profile picture continued to stare unblinkingly at me, and I felt faintly ridiculous speaking aloud. Thank goodness nobody but Rupert was home to hear me talking to a computer image. I looked at Rupert. He'd been trailing me for the last half an hour, and now wagged his tail uncertainly.

'Your mother's going mad,' I told him. His tail picked up speed, and he cocked his head to the side, one ear comically standing up, listening intently to a language he didn't speak but was desperately trying to understand, picking out the odd word that made total doggy sense – *walkies* and *din-dins* being the top two all-time favourites. 'Do you know what Alex is up to, Rupert? Have you heard him making secret phone calls to my friend Jeanie or his beautiful patient, Annabelle?' Rupert replied with a deep baritone bark, as if to say, 'I haven't the faintest idea what you're talking about. Tell me something I understand – like meaty chunks, or chasing squirrels and meaty chunks, or hassling the postman and meaty chunks.'

I sighed and turned my attention back to Jack's friend request and pressed the confirm button. At a later date I would reflect on this moment and wish I'd left time to do some stalking through Jack's timeline. If I'd done so, I'd have discovered something that would have sent shockwaves through me sooner, rather than later.

Chapter Twenty-Eight

Sitting in Caro's kitchen, I noticed Jeanie looked happier today. More relaxed. Gone was the tear-stained face, she seemed able to meet my eyes again, and her body language no longer screamed she'd rather be anywhere except around me.

'How's the cold?' I asked, before taking a sip of my coffee.

'Much better, thanks,' she smiled over the rim of her cup. 'I suspect it was probably one of those twenty-four-hour things. But never mind me, how are *you*? And how's the party planning going?'

I privately acknowledged the change of tack on her part. If you don't want to answer questions about yourself, bend the chit-chat to those around you. But I wasn't going to be so easily deflected.

'The party planning was going splendidly until Izzy and her in-crowd spoiled things. They cornered me at school.'

Jeanie was suddenly looking wary. Was this because I'd managed to steer the timeline of our conversation back to yesterday, when she'd been crying?

'I don't understand,' said Caro, joining in the conversation. 'What's Izzy got to do with Alex's party?' She plonked a plate of biscuits on the table, and then settled down beside us.

'Thanks to my darling girl sucking up to Izzy's daughter, Tabitha, and wanting a bit of Miss Popular's stardust to rub off on her, Sophie just happened to mention to Tabitha that good old Mum was planning a secret party for dear old Dad – and then asked Tabitha if she would like to come along as her guest. Whereupon Izzy presumed that she and Sebastian were also included, along with the rest of the in-crowd who, needless to say, have all said how much they're looking forward to the occasion – even if it is at the lowly golf club,' I added, my expression souring.

'You're kidding!' said Caro, half-eaten biscuit suspended on its way to her mouth.

'I only wish I were,' I said, folding my arms across my chest.

'Have you seen Izzy's house?' said Caro. 'It's incredible. I went there once when the glow of Tabitha's spotlight fell briefly upon Lizzie. She was invited to tea and a swim in their pool. Do you know it has mood lighting?' Caro's eyes rounded in wonder. 'I've never seen anything like it. Who the hell wants to do front crawl in purple water with rainbows arcing across the glass ceiling? When I went to pick Lizzie up, she couldn't resist bragging and showing me. I half-expected a unicorn to wander in and Izzy to say, "And this is Sebastian's latest acquisition. Meet Glitter. Fancy fondling his horn?"' Caro snorted, taking another bite from her biscuit and dropping crumbs all over her lap. 'The whole place must have cost a fortune. Sebastian is seriously loaded. So how are you going to stop Izzy from coming?'

'I can't,' I said, shrugging. 'If I put my foot down, Sophie will be sent to Coventry by the entire class. She'd never get an invitation to anybody's house again. I can't do that to her. So be aware, girls, I've cancelled the free buffet and bar. Apologies. Make sure you eat before arriving and have a bottle of gin in your handbag.'

Jeanie blinked, and I noticed she had gone quite pale. 'It's outrageous that Izzy should invite not just herself but the rest of the school mothers. Are their husbands coming too?'

'Yes. *I* don't even know them, never mind Alex!'

'Then you must be more assertive,' said Jeanie, shifting in her seat.

'Unfortunately Holly cannot do that,' said Caro. 'Apart from risking Sophie being reviled by Tabitha and her cronies, you have to remember that Izzy has serious clout at the school. She's on the board of governors, and a big influence with the Head. Where do you think all the celebs come from when it's prize-giving day? It's all down to that husband of hers. Sebastian has shedloads of media connections with the luvvies.'

'Oh,' said Jeanie, in a small voice. 'I don't care for Izzy at all.'

I saw my moment and swooped. 'But you must like her, Jeanie,' I said casually. 'After all, you're Facebook friends!'

'Are you?' said Caro, looking astonished.

Jeanie instantly arranged her features into an expression of vagueness. 'Oh, yes. That's right.' She shrugged dismissively. 'It was when Charlotte had a very brief friendship with Tabitha and was invited to the house. I've seen it and, yes, it is gorgeous. Afterwards, Izzy friend-requested me. It was yonks ago. I suspect she only did it to add to the swell of her Facebook friends.'

'She hasn't friend-requested me,' I said, frowning.

'Nor me,' added Caro.

'Well, aren't I the lucky one?' said Jeanie lightly.

'Poor you,' I joked. 'It's enough to make you weep.' I looked directly at Jeanie. 'Talking of which, I could have *sworn* you'd been crying in the playground yesterday.'

Caro kicked me under the table. I flinched. It wasn't lost on Jeanie.

'You've been blabbing,' she said accusingly to Caro.

Caro opened her mouth to protest, but I didn't want her telling porkies on my behalf.

'Jeanie, how long have we known each other?' I asked. 'A long time,' I said, when she didn't answer. 'What does Caro know that I don't?' The question sounded innocent enough, but I could feel my stomach muscles knotting. On a scale of nought to ten, my question felt like being only two down from asking Jeanie outright if there was something going on between her and my husband.

'Very well,' she said, taking a deep breath. 'As I'm sure you already know' – she scowled briefly at Caro – 'I've been having an affair.'

I feigned surprise, but I'm no Oscar-winning actress and Jeanie's expression conveyed that she didn't buy my pretence of astonishment. A tiny part of me wondered if Jeanie would crack and go the whole hog with her confession, revealing Alex to be her lover. I felt quite faint at the thought.

'Don't ask me how it started,' she said airily, 'because I don't really know. Actually,' she frowned, 'yes, I do. It was after Ray and I had a row about something ridiculously stupid. I snatched up my car keys and stormed out of the house, then drove around for a bit and, well, to cut a long story short, I had a car crash. Nothing major,' she said quickly, as Caro and I gasped together in alarm. 'It was just a little shunt. I went to pull out on a roundabout, stalled the car, and the vehicle behind went into the back of me. Thankfully, neither of us were hurt. There wasn't a mark on either car, so Ray never knew anything about it. The guy was mortified and kept trying to give me his insurance details, but when I told him not to be silly and refused, he insisted on taking me out to dinner by way of saying thank you. So…' Jeanie paused, and her gaze shifted from us to somewhere beyond the kitchen window as her features softened, recalling the memory, 'I accepted. He was very easy on the eye, plus I wasn't ready to go home. I was still livid with Ray and needed to cool off. The reason for my absence was covered. I certainly didn't have to explain to Ray as to my whereabouts for a few hours. Anyway,' she said, giving a bark of humourless laughter, 'you know me and my appetite. Always hungry.'

I would have smiled if it hadn't been so serious. But I didn't. Like Caro, I was hanging on to Jeanie's every word. But for entirely different reasons.

'So you went to dinner together,' I prompted.

'Yes,' Jeanie nodded, smoothing down her skirt in a demure fashion, as if the action made her more ladylike rather than an unfaithful wife and potential marriage wrecker. 'And he was lovely company. He told me I was funny and wonderful to talk to. He made me feel special.' She flicked back her hair, body language now defiant. 'And then he complimented me on my looks, and said he hoped I didn't think him forward, but he thought I was very beautiful. I can't tell you how much that meant to me,' she lowered her eyes, suddenly pleating her skirt with anxious hands. 'Ray never tells me I'm gorgeous. I'm good old Jeanie with the ample bottom that, if he's feeling affectionate, he slaps heartily whilst making stupid comments like, "That's a fine bit of padding on your rump, love." I don't want to be reminded I've got a fat arse, thank you very much.' She was indignant now, looking for any excuse to justify her actions. 'Whereas this man made me feel incredibly sexy, and not fat but voluptuous. He told me he loved a girl with big curves in all the right places. We drank champagne and he toasted me in the candlelight. Consequently, neither of us could drive immediately afterwards. He suggested we sit in his car and chat for a while.

'We didn't stop talking, but don't ask me what we were nattering about' – she shook her head slightly, eyes faraway now – 'everything and nothing. He said I was fascinating and he wanted to know all my secrets, and what made my heart sing. By now it was him doing the latter to me, and I dared to tell him so,' she said, her voice starting to shake with emotion as she recalled the tipping point, where the conversation took a very different route, from flirting to one of no return. 'I also said he was having a catastrophic effect on not just my heartstrings but my entire body. He didn't say a word. Just looked at me intensely, searching for the signal, the green light, and I nodded, hardly able to breathe as he pressed a button and sent both seats whirring backwards. Our bodies shifted together. Our mouths met. Suddenly we were kissing passionately.' She paused, trying to describe the impact on her emotions. 'It was like… like somebody flicking a switch on the Christmas lights in Oxford Street, except it was going on somewhere internally in my body,' she whispered. 'I honestly felt like every particle of my being was lighting up. It was mind-blowing. I can't remember the last time I felt so desired, or desirable. We didn't go all the way. Despite the privacy glass of his car, we were parked in a side street and neither of us were up for risking arrest with a stationary vehicle's suspension shifting like a rocking horse. But that was the start. The beginning of clandestine meetings. And despite us both being married to other people, and telling ourselves the next time would be the last time, unfortunately it never was. It's proving increasingly difficult to give each other up.'

She stopped talking, and hung her head, contemplating her hands that were still worrying at her skirt. For a moment nobody spoke.

Throughout Jeanie's confession, my heart had been pumping like a jogger's. It picked up speed further when Caro leaned forward to voice the very question I'd been wanting to ask.

'What's his name?'

Jeanie regarded Caro for a moment, before replying.

'I'm not telling you.'

'Can't? Or won't?' I asked. My voice sounded harsher than intended. But Jeanie remained unaffected by my tone, and her expression showed no remorse.

'Both,' she said defiantly, looking me in the eye.

My throat was suddenly very dry, and I felt slightly sick. Alex's car had privacy glass, and the front seats were electric and reclined flat.

Chapter Twenty-Nine

'Does Ray know?' said Caro.

'Of course not!' Jeanie snorted.

'Do you think a tiny part of him might suspect?' I asked.

'Ha!' Jeanie looked angry now. 'Ray would only notice my absence if he ran out of socks and underpants.' She took a sip of coffee and then banged the mug back down on the table. 'He's in his own world. Planet Ray. So long as his fat-arsed wifey puts a steak and kidney pudding in front of him at the end of the day while he watches sport on the telly, he's a contented man. Ray wouldn't notice if I ran around the house stark naked.'

'Maybe an affair isn't the answer. Perhaps you just need to, you know…' I said cautiously, 'put a bit of oomph back into your marriage?'

'Oh yes?' Jeanie said, her face turning to one of scorn. 'You mean like yours?'

Was she ridiculing me? Did she secretly know my love life was more sham than glam?

'N-no,' I stuttered, 'I think sometimes you need to spice things up, and, um, if Ray doesn't realise that, perhaps you should take the lead?'

'Like you?' she demanded.

What was that remark meant to mean? Had Alex told her the true state of our sex life, and that it was mainly like the Gobi Desert with an oasis occurring every time Jupiter was in alignment with Venus? If so, damn the pair of them! No way was I having Jeanie thinking I was some sort of pushover between the sheets. I was determined to fill her with doubt and send her scuttling back to Ray with her tail between her legs.

'Yes, like me!' I asserted. In my peripheral vision I saw Caro raise an eyebrow at the sudden hostility between her two friends. 'In fact,' I said carelessly, 'I recently studied burlesque dancing, and tried it out on Alex.'

'Really?' asked Caro, abandoning her biscuit and leaning closer. 'How exciting! Does this mean you're going to step out of a giant birthday cake at the party, dressed in suspenders and flashing your raspberry ripples? I must warn you now that David might have a coronary, if so. The most excitement he gets from me is when I step out of the bath.'

'Do talk us through your dance routine, Holly,' said Jeanie. Was it my imagination or was she sneering? In which case, why? *Because she's on the defensive, Holly, that's why!*

'Well, I, er, did an impromptu dance only last night, actually.' I cleared my throat. 'I used the dining room chair.'

'Before, during, or after dinner?' Jeanie asked sarcastically.

Oh, she was on the defensive all right!

'After,' I said lightly.

'Oooh, show me your routine,' said Caro, clapping her hands together. 'I'll try it out on David tonight.'

Bugger. Both women were looking at me expectantly. *Right, Holly, give it all you've got.*

I jumped up with alacrity, pulled the kitchen chair out and stood to one side. Raising my arms in the air, I then stroked my palms downwards, brushing my breasts seductively, travelling on down my torso and over my legging-clad thighs, before sitting back down, spine arched, chest out, and then deftly flung one leg over the back of the chair so that I was facing away from them. With legs wide open, I gripped the wooden spindles of the chair with my thighs and leaned slowly backwards – my spine making rather alarming popping noises – as my hair fanned out across Caro's kitchen floor.

'Very seductive,' said Caro, giving me a round of applause.

I noticed Jeanie didn't join in. I raised my torso back up again and then flipped my leg over the back of the chair so that I had moved a hundred and eighty degrees, standing up with a triumphant flourish.

'Amazing,' said Caro. 'Did Alex appreciate it?'

'Totally,' I said, my eyes swivelling over to Jeanie as I added, 'he loves everything I do. He thinks I'm very inventive.'

'You can say that again,' murmured Jeanie.

She so obviously didn't believe me. I shrugged in a couldn't-care-less manner.

'Maybe,' I suggested sweetly, 'instead of playing See Saw Margery Daw with your lover's car seats, you could give it a try with Ray?' I knew fully well that Jeanie wouldn't be able to limbo over the back of a dining chair like I'd just done, and the sudden hurt in her eyes was plain to see. But I didn't care if she was offended. *If* she was bonking Alex, then she should think twice before she messed around with my marriage. Caro was looking bewildered again, not understanding the undercurrents once more whirring backwards and forwards over the kitchen table.

'The trouble is,' said Jeanie, 'I don't want to sleep with Ray at the moment. Somehow it seems deceitful.'

'Haven't you got your loyalty wires crossed?' I asked. 'After all, I'd bet my last fiver your lover is still bonking his wife.'

Jeanie's face wobbled violently, and her eyes filled with tears.

'Don't say that,' she whispered. 'I can't bear the idea of him touching another woman.'

'Better face up to it,' I said starkly.

Caro, a kinder soul than I due to her not having a marriage on the line, reached out and touched Jeanie's hand. 'Don't upset yourself,' she said gently. 'Are you planning on leaving Ray?'

I held my breath, waiting for Jeanie to answer. Oh God. Please say no. But then again, hadn't Alex told me he didn't want a divorce? That he didn't want to change our 'lovely life'?

Jeanie wiped away one of the tears rolling down a plump cheek. 'No,' she whispered. 'I won't be leaving Ray.'

'Why not?' I demanded.

Caro noted my tone and looked at me questioningly. I pretended not to notice.

'Because,' said Jeanie, 'he doesn't want to leave his wife and child.'

I tried to exhale quietly. Breathing was proving very difficult right now and this was nothing to do with the exertion of my chair dance.

'Maybe it's best to give him up now, Jeanie,' I said, 'before your respective spouses find out, and things get turdy.'

'I know you don't approve, Holly,' Jeanie snivelled, 'but don't hate me for it. Please?' she implored. 'We never intended this to happen, and we certainly don't want our partners getting hurt.'

'Then give him up,' I repeated, my eyes pinning hers against Caro's kitchen wall, 'before marriages – and friendships – get ruined.'

Chapter Thirty

There was a resounding silence in Caro's kitchen as my words bounced off the walls. I was giving Jeanie secret messages that only she would understand. Give him up. Before a friendship is ruined. Although it was already ruined, wasn't it? After all, I was simply waiting to catch her and Alex out. I could feel my own eyes filling up, and Caro was again looking at me curiously, like somebody who'd been watching a film on the telly, nipped out to use the loo, only to return and find she'd lost the thread of the drama. She was the first to speak, and when she did her voice was calm, soothing the frazzled tension in the kitchen.

'Look, let's all take a breath here,' she said. 'What's happened has happened. There's no going back, unfortunately.' I noticed Caro was talking to both of us, her eyes flicking from me to Jeanie, like a headmistress talking to two wayward children who'd refused to share their skipping rope, rather than a husband.

I decided to play along – after all, there might be an opportunity here. 'You're right, and I have an idea. Alex's birthday is looming. Let's get our men together pre-party. They can do a bit of male bonding, and perhaps,' I turned to Jeanie, 'you and Ray can get communication lines open again, eh?'

'That's a fab idea,' said Caro, eyes twinkling with happiness. 'Let's make an occasion of it!' she clapped her hands together excitedly, 'and dress up. You can pull out all the stops for your hubby, Jeanie. Get that cleavage on display and wow him over the petit pois!'

I smiled thinly. 'Yes, do that, Jeanie.' And while she was busy wowing Ray, I'd be studying Alex to see if he was wowed too.

'You've done what?' asked Alex, when I interrupted his television viewing later that evening. His expression was one of horror.

'I've invited Caro and Jeanie to dinner this Saturday.'

'And I'm meant to sit at the table and talk to a bunch of women?' my husband asked irritably.

'Of course not,' I soothed. 'The girls will be bringing their husbands along. You do know David and Ray, after all.'

'I have nothing in common with them!' Alex looked aghast.

'Of course you have,' I protested. 'You're all fathers for a start, and your kids all go to the same school. That's two things in common.'

'Holly, unlike you three women who love to analyse your mood swings or bitch about Izzy What's-Her-Face showing off with her Mulberry handbag at the school gate, I haven't a clue what to discuss with Ray and David.'

'Nonsense,' I cried. 'You could chat about golf with Ray. I believe he's partial.'

Alex rolled his eyes. 'Crazy golf isn't quite the same as having a burning desire to play the Old Course at St Andrews.'

'No, but he could learn,' I argued. 'You could talk to him about your bogeys.'

'How disgusting!' said a familiar voice.

'Oh God,' muttered Alex.

Seconds later my brother appeared in the lounge doorway. 'You left your front door unlocked,' he said by way of explanation. 'I was passing and have a little something for Sophie.' Simon shook an unmarked carrier bag in our direction. 'It's a new design, and I *know* it will look *fab*-ulous on my darling niece.'

'That's kind of you,' I said. 'Would you like a cup of tea while you're here?'

'I thought you'd never ask, dah-ling. I'm absolutely parchy-poohed.' Simon turned to my husband who, up until now, had been trying to ignore his brother-in-law. 'And a very good evening to you too, Alex.'

'Good evening,' said Alex, visibly grinding his teeth.

'Enjoying the footie?'

'*Trying* to enjoy the footie,' said Alex pointedly.

'I might join you on the sofa and have a little swoon at all those well-muscled legs, and it's always worth a naughty giggle at the commentator. All that waxing lyrical about penetration in the backfield and going off to the sideline for a quick blow. So titillating!'

'Er, Simon,' I interrupted, catching the thunderous expression on Alex's face, 'come and chat with me whilst I make the tea.'

'Yes, sweets, because I can see I'm not wanted here.' My brother stuck his nose in the air and minced off towards the kitchen.

'You could at least try and be civil,' I hissed to my husband. 'I'm sure he won't stay for long.'

'Your brother is always here,' Alex moaned. 'Why doesn't he just move in with us?'

'I heard that,' Simon's voice floated down the hallway, 'and if it's an invitation, then I accept.'

'Oh for—'

I could see Alex was reaching boiling point. I hastily shut the lounge door, so he could enjoy his precious football without Simon winding him up.

'I do wish the two of you got along,' I complained to my brother, reaching for the kettle.

'Listen, dah-ling, I do my best. It's not my fault you're married to a knobhead.'

'Simon, that's my husband you're bitching about. I don't make disparaging comments about your latest beau, do I?'

Simon shrugged. 'He's a knobhead too.'

'When are we going to meet him? You haven't brought anybody over for ages.'

'Nor am I going to. It's all off again.'

I sighed as I poured hot water over teabags in mugs. 'Do you want me to call Sophie down to have a look at what you've brought over for her? She's in her bedroom at the moment, doing homework.'

'No, dearest. I'll chat with you for five minutes, then I'll go up and see her. So, do you notice anything different about *moi*?' My brother turned his head to the side, flicking back some hair and adopting a haughty expression.

'You've had a shave?'

'Honestly, Holly, your powers of observation are zero. And talking of shaving, your upper lip looks much better. It's so nice to see my sister looking like a woman again, and not impersonating Poirot, but your wax strip missed a bit. Just there,' he pointed.

'Thank you, Simon,' I slapped his finger away. 'What is it I've failed to notice?'

'I've had my ear pierced!'

'Good heavens,' I said, looking at his earlobe. 'Is that a diamond?'

'Do I look like a cubic zirconia person?'

'No,' I replied. My brother always had the best of everything. After all, he could afford it, and had nobody else as such to spend his money on. 'But why have a piercing? Is this some sort of mid-life crisis? A late rebellion?' I teased.

'Dearest, you're not the only one entitled to a hormonal meltdown. I looked in the mirror and thought, "Simon, you're forty-one years old. Why didn't you celebrate last year's landmark birthday with a tattoo, or a Prince Albert?" But I'm not really keen on tattoos, and I thought a willy piercing might be throbbing for all the wrong reasons, so I opted for the ear instead. That was bad enough. The pain was agonising.' He gave an effeminate shudder.

'It suits you,' I nodded. Simon was the sort of guy who was always reinventing himself. From occasional purple streaks in his hair to frills on his trouser hems to colourful shirts slashed to the navel, he always carried off *a look*.

He took a sip of tea and then gazed at me enquiringly. 'I couldn't help overhearing, when I let myself in, that you were talking to Alex about a little din-dins soirée…'

'Oh, Simon, no. You don't know—'

'Of course I know Jeanie and Caro, don't be silly.'

'But not their husbands. Ray and David are very—'

'Boring? Staid? Might be put off their starters by a poofter with a piercing?'

'No,' I hesitated, choosing my words carefully, 'they're men who like to talk to men.'

'How dare you!' Simon snapped, eyes flashing.

'That came out wrong. I'm sorry.'

'I should think so too.' He tossed his head indignantly. 'I would have thought you of all people, Holly, would have known I'm not a girl. Just because I adore pink does not mean I'm a woman, any more than you are a man, even though you often do a very good job of impersonating one with your facial hair.'

Great. I was now going to be on the receiving end of no end of bitchiness for my faux pas.

'We'd love to have you join us,' I said contritely. 'You'll make the evening go with a swing.'

'Just as long as we don't have to put our keys on the coffee table later and play swapsies. I draw the line at getting Alex.'

'Best not to make jokes like that in front of him, Simon.'

'I'm only kidding. And anyway, you have odd numbers now that I'm coming. You'll have to think of someone else to even things out. I know! Invite Jack.'

'Jack?' I repeated, startled.

'Yes. I reckon if he's plied with enough wine and gets to hear what wonderful massages I give, I could persuade him to turn.'

'Actually, that's not a bad idea,' I said, considering.

'What, that I get him to turn?'

'No,' I tutted, 'that I invite him. Alex was moaning about having nothing in common with Caro's and Jeanie's husbands, but he has loads in common with Jack. They've both studied medicine and have an interest in trigeminal neuralgia.'

'Oooh, lovely, I've got a date!' Simon fluttered his eyelashes with delight. 'He's so handsome, don't you think?'

'He's okay,' I shrugged nonchalantly, 'if you like that sort of thing.'

'Oh I do, I do, I do,' Simon clutched his heart theatrically.

I had trouble not clutching mine too.

Chapter Thirty-One

Dinner parties are not really my thing. It's one thing to cook your family a basic meal 'from scratch' every evening, but I was no Jamie or Delia. My cooking was of the straightforward fare. Plenty of roast dinners mixing up the meats, a hearty shepherd's pie, the occasional steak with side salad or, on a night when the winter winds were howling around the rafters of the house and the temperature dropped to zero, comfort was to be found in bangers and buttery mash with chopped red cabbage in a flavoursome red wine jus. Much as I would have liked to spend ages titivating with a hollandaise sauce to accompany a baked salmon, I didn't want to be fretting about stinking the house out with the smell of fish, or getting into a panic about the sauce splitting and fats congealing. I settled on a simple slow-cooker version of coq au vin accompanied by a crème fraîche mash, with melon balls and homemade mint ice cream for dessert.

On the Friday night I prepped everything, left the coq au vin in the fridge overnight and popped a tub full of newly made mint ice cream into the freezer. Easy-peasy. A part of me was very aware that Jack would be sitting around my dining table and I wanted to impress him, to come across as a hostess who wasn't tied to the kitchen labouring over steaming pots and pans thus leaving her guests to make small talk amongst themselves, but instead got stuck into the conversational thick of it. Therefore, I chose to opt out of messing about with starters and instead to conclude with a large platter of cheese and biscuits with coffee and brandy.

Sophie was still Tabitha's new girl crush, and was having a sleepover on Saturday night, which was something of a relief. Izzy had already been on the phone gushing about Sophie being a charming influence on Tabitha, so at least I wouldn't have a bored daughter to worry about and, if things got a bit boozy and raucous, nobody would be disturbing my teenager's Zen or, as Alex preferred to call it, bloody-mindedness.

On the day of the dinner party, I took a great deal of care with my appearance prior to our guests' arrival. I hoped Alex would look at me with eyes that lit up like a Christmas tree's fairy lights. I might not have Jeanie's gargantuan chest, but equally my breasts could in no way be likened to two fried eggs on an ironing board. As I stood back from the full-length mirror to assess the 'overall effect', I sternly addressed my reflection.

'You are a fine-looking woman, Holly Hart. Tonight, you are going to wow everyone with good food, good wine and your good looks. Know it. Believe it. Be it.' It was all very well making affirmations, but sometimes a prayer helped. 'Please God,' I added.

I had let Sophie do my eyeshadow before she left. A pair of seductive smoky eyes stared back at me, and my lips were slicked with a light plum colour filched from my daughter. She'd insisted on doing my eyebrows, properly this time.

'Just remember not to rub them, Mum,' she'd warned.

Yes, I wouldn't be making that mistake again. I was just slipping my feet into some killer heels, when Alex came into the bedroom. He looked very handsome in navy chinos and a soft-grey wool sweater, and I told him so. He didn't return the compliment though, which was disappointing.

'Are you coming downstairs?' he asked, 'only I heard a car pulling up outside and think it might be your friend Jeanie.'

'Your friend too, darling,' I reminded him.

My husband pulled a face. 'I'd rather you greet her.'

'Why?' I asked, slightly irritated. Was this some sort of admission of guilt? Not wanting to be around her, wishing to avoid being the first one to kiss her on both cheeks?

'I don't feel comfortable with Jeanie. She's very loud. Not my type at all.'

'Is that so?' I muttered under my breath. I didn't believe him for one moment. He was clearly trying to set up a smokescreen.

Alex narrowed his eyes at me. 'What did you just mumble?'

'Nothing,' I said brightly, as the doorbell rang. 'I'm sure you'll have a cracking time once you get a glass of wine in you.'

'I'll need a crate to get through this evening.'

I ignored the comment. The last thing I wanted was a fast and furious row prior to greeting our guests. As Alex followed me out of the bedroom, I was aware of him pouting like a child who had been spruced up for a reluctant visit to disliked relatives, and he showed his displeasure by stomping down the stairs after me.

'Jeanie!' I cried, opening the door to my friend. I was immediately knocked back by her enormous breasts, which were trussed up like a pair of turkeys, and positively straining for space in her off-the-shoulder low-cut dress. Ray followed his wife in.

'How lovely to see you both,' said Alex politely.

My head swivelled round. Was he talking to Jeanie *and* Ray, or just Jeanie's breasts? But my attention was immediately diverted by Caro and David tripping into the hallway.

'We came together,' Caro explained.

'Always the most satisfactory way!' trilled a camp voice. Simon was coming up the garden path, staggering slightly, a crate of perfectly chilled champagne in his strong arms.

'Hello, dah-lings,' he chirped to everyone in general. 'I know my company is sparkling enough, but you can never have enough Bolly!' He dumped the crate on the hall's console table, before air-kissing my cheeks. 'Sweetie, those smoky eyes are *fab*-ulous, and your eyebrows look awesome. Just like that rogue hair sprouting out of your chin.' I was about to answer back, but my brother was already moving on to my girlfriends. 'Jeanie, angel! Mwah-mwah! And Caro, helloooo! Such beautiful ladies, I almost wish I wasn't gay' – he batted his eyelids at them –'but sadly I am, so please introduce me to your handsome hubbies.'

And my brother was off, hustling everybody down the hall and into the lounge, taking over Alex's role of host and leaving my husband looking pricklier than a ruffled hedgehog.

'Why on earth did you invite him, Holly?' he seethed.

'He's lonely!' I hissed. 'He's broken up with his boyfriend. Have some compassion, eh? Anyway, Jack will be along shortly. He'll dilute Simon's brashness, plus you'll have somebody to talk to about… stuff.'

'Stuff?' Alex glared at me. 'I graduated from university with a degree in *stuff*?'

'Oh for God's sake, Alex,' I huffed, 'stop bellyaching, and start circulating.'

What a fine start we were off to. It was about time Alex started appreciating me and my good-wife efforts. Anger was flushing my face to an unattractive brick-red as I watched him march off to the lounge. The doorbell rang again. Knowing it would be Jack, I took a deep breath, pasted a welcoming smile on my face and released the door's catch.

'Hey!' he smiled.

'Hi!' I gushed, steadying myself against the door frame as he crossed the threshold. My nose twitched appreciatively as a whiff of expensive aftershave drifted past. Mm, heaven.

I shut the door and, as I turned to face him, he embraced me warmly, his lips brushing my cheek, sending my senses reeling.

'Love your perfume,' he murmured.

'And I love yours,' I whispered back. *Steady, Holly. You're meant to be in the lounge monitoring your husband and Jeanie, not loitering in the hallway feeling overcome with lust for Jack.*

He released me and slipped off his coat. 'Shall I hang it over the bannister?' he asked, nodding at the small pile of jackets and blazers that everybody had slung over the finial, ignoring Alex's offer to hang them in the coat cupboard under the stairs.

'Sure,' I nodded.

'By the way, you look beautiful,' he said, giving me a mega-watt smile that almost finished me off there and then.

'So do you,' I gasped foolishly. *Dear God. Get me into the lounge and into the throng. There was safety in numbers. And have a drink. Now!*

I scuttled off, like a terrified mouse with a sleek cat shadowing it. Everybody was getting well and truly stuck into the champers, laughing and joking. Even Alex, I noticed, and was relieved to see it was Caro he was bantering with, and not Jeanie. Or was that another smokescreen on his part?

'Jack, dah-ling!' called Simon, coming towards us, but bypassing me and smacking his lips against both of Jack's cheeks. 'How wonderful to see you again, sweets. You'll be thrilled to know you're my plus-one. Who's a lucky boy?'

Jack roared with laughter and clapped Simon on the back. 'Good to see you, matey, and I'm thrilled to be sitting next to you at dinner later.'

'Oooh, as charming as ever.' Simon affected a swoon. 'I might have to marry you. Let me get you a drinky-poo. Champagne all right?'

'Definitely,' said Jack appreciatively.

'It's my aim to get you seriously tiddly,' said Simon, as he handed Jack a flute of pale bubbles, 'and seduce you with my charm.'

'In that case,' said Jack gamely, playing along, 'it's a good thing I'm taking a taxi back and not driving.'

'We came by taxi, too,' said Jeanie, edging her way into the conversation, her eyes roving over Jack and evidently liking what she saw. 'I told Ray earlier that tonight I'm getting seriously sloshed. Fill me up, Simon,' she said, holding out her empty glass.

'Alas, dah-ling, I can only give you champagne,' said my brother, 'because I'm saving myself later for Jack.'

I caught Alex's eye and noticed his mouth tighten with irritation. Why couldn't he join in with the jokey atmosphere? Nobody else minded Simon's outrageous humour. In fact, Jeanie was positively encouraging it, shrieking with laughter and wobbling her breasts at Simon, teasing that he didn't know what he was missing, and that someone not a million miles away liked nothing more than oiling her assets.

'Ooooh, a butter mountain!' Simon quipped. 'Stop tempting me, you naughty girl, or I'll leave here all confused. Holly, stop behaving like a wallflower at your own party. Get this down you, and then I'm opening another bottle.'

I took the champagne from my brother and gulped gratefully. If everybody was taking a cab home, it could mean only one thing: they were intent on having a jolly good time. As the bubbles invaded my bloodstream, I felt momentarily light-headed. Even though this was meant to be a bonding get-together in preparation for Alex's party, I mustn't forget there was now a second objective tonight, which was watching Jeanie watching Alex watching Jeanie. I nodded to myself and hoovered up some more champers, deciding there and then to keep up with everybody's alcohol intake. Thank goodness I'd had the nous to prepare dinner the night before.

'Something smells delicious,' said Jack, sniffing the air appreciatively.

'Do tell everyone, Sissy-poo, what have you cooked?' asked Simon.

'Coq au vin,' I replied, throwing the rest of the champagne down my neck and holding my glass out for a refill.

'*Fab*-ulous, dah-ling,' said Simon, handing me a refreshed crystal flute. 'I adore a bit of coq.'

Jeanie giggled into her champagne, then gave me a brazen look. 'Don't we all,' she said with a smirk.

Chapter Thirty-Two

Nobody seemed in any rush to sit down for dinner. The drink continued to flow – on empty stomachs – and it was only when the seventh bottle clanked its way into the recycling bin that I realised everybody was catastrophically pissed.

I staggered off to the kitchen, switched off the slow cooker, microwaved last night's pre-made mash and yodelled for everybody to sit up.

'Tits up?' drawled my brother, swaying into the kitchen.

'Shit up,' I slurred.

'Dah-ling, are you telling me to sit up or shut up?'

'Both,' I nodded. 'Not in here!' I squawked, as Simon pulled out a tall stool by the kitchen island. 'In the dining room. The table is all laid. It looks beautiful. Best china. Silver cutlery. Flickering candlelight.'

'How romantic. I'll be able to gaze at Jack adoringly, and hopefully his pupils will dilate with lust.'

'Can you direct everyone into the dining room and tell Alex to come and help me?' I hiccupped, holding onto the worktop for a moment while the kitchen briefly spun. It was imperative to get food into tummies and alcohol mopped up as soon as possible.

Simon minced off to do my bidding. When the kitchen door opened a second time, it wasn't my husband who came in, but Jack. As he came towards me I grabbed the worktop again, but this time to steady myself against the effect his proximity was having on me.

'Can I give you a hand, Holly?'

'That's very kind, but Alex will help me.'

Jack frowned. 'I don't think so. He's in deep conversation with Jeanie.'

At the mention of my friend and husband having their heads together, I blanched.

'What are they talking about?' I whispered, face paling.

'Divorce, I think.'

'What?' I squeaked, spreading my hands along the worktop again. In the last two minutes it had received quite a lot of fondling.

'Shall we?'

I stared at him blankly. 'Shall we what?'

'Serve dinner?'

'Yes,' I said faintly. *Oh my God.* The treacherous pair had waited for me to take my leave to the kitchen, then gone into a huddle, clearly discussing how to end their respective marriages. This wasn't good. Not good at all.

'Are you all right, Holly?' Jack touched my forearm, and the heat of his hand instantly had me sagging against the cupboards. Dear Lord. Why did this man have such an effect on me? It wasn't right, this conflict of emotions. I shouldn't be reacting with electric jolts every time I clapped eyes on Jack, when all I really wanted was to save my marriage. Was this how it was between Jeanie and Alex? That they just couldn't help themselves because of some invisible current scorching between them, so that any moment now they might both self-combust with desire in my dining room?

'Here,' Jack ordered, 'drink.'

'I've had enough.'

'It's water.' He led me over to one of the tall stools by the island, then helped me perch aloft, pressing the dripping glass into my hand. 'Come on, get that down you, then you'll feel better. Leave the dishing up to me.'

'No!' I protested, as the room rolled again.

'I'll get your brother to help me,' Jack said.

'He'll like that,' I acknowledged, as Jack strode out of the kitchen. I watched him go, slowly laying my head down upon the cool granite. What a great walk Jack had. It was so... I boggled at a vase of flowers inches from my nose... *what was the word?* Masterful, that was it! I squirmed deliciously at the thought of Jack being masterful with me. *Sit down, Holly, drink this water now, and then I'm going to put you over my knee and give you a good spanking for not serving up the dinner.* My eyes widened at the vase of flowers. Oh my God, was I kinky? I tried to imagine Alex ordering me about in the bedroom. *Come here, Holly. I want to tie you up with yards and yards of dental floss... oh wonderful... now I can read my dental mags in peace.* Nope, Alex was definitely not having the same effect on me.

My mind skittered back to Jack, and warm tingles instantly zinged up and down my spine. I closed my eyes in ecstasy as my mind conjured up various pornographic scenarios of Jack bossing me about. I was breathing heavily now, my upper lip beading with a fine dew of sweat as yet another outrageous situation played in full technicolour behind my shut eyelids. *Come here, Holly, you've kept all your guests waiting. Bend over this stool and let me thrash your bare bottom with this oven mitt.* I gasped aloud.

'Is that all right?'

'Try it with rubber gloves,' I whispered.

'Holly? Holly!'

My eyes snapped open and Jack swam into my vision. I sat up, a fine thread of saliva attached from my mouth to the worktop, like a silvery line from a spider's web. I'd been dribbling. How embarrassing. I swiped a hand across my mouth.

'Come on,' he grinned. 'Simon and I have dished up, and everybody is tucking in. Won't you come and join us?'

'Most definitely,' I said, jumping off the stool and rocking slightly on my stilettos. I'd just remembered that I had a bone to pick, and it wasn't with the coq au vin.

Chapter Thirty-Three

When I swayed into the dining room, I realised almost immediately that if I wanted to pick a bone with Jeanie and Alex I would also have to pick my moment to pick that bone. Everybody seemed to be talking at once, and because everyone was drunk there was a tendency to both enunciate and shout to fend off slurring.

Simon was sitting next to Jack, and I was immensely grateful to them both for serving up the dinner. The room looked beautifully ambient with enormous church-style candles flickering away, their flames casting soft shadows around the table. I noticed Caro was sitting next to her husband David, but Jeanie had abandoned Ray and instead was sitting next to Alex. Ray was by himself at the head of the table, leaving me to sit opposite him at the other end. To my right was Jack and to my left was Jeanie.

'Holly, dah-ling!' Simon's voice rose over the clamouring, and he tapped his fork against his wine glass, making a loud dinging noise that went right through my head. 'Everybody, raise your glass to the cook. You've excelled yourself, Holly, with this casserole.'

'Coq au vin,' I corrected, as everybody toasted me. I pulled out my chair and slumped down heavily. Picking up my knife and fork, I concentrated on delivering food into my mouth and not my ears, one of which was straining to hear Jeanie and Alex.

'It's been going on too long,' Jeanie was saying.

'Have you told anyone?'

'God, no!'

'Does Ray know?'

'Absolutely not, he'd go mad.'

'Sooner or later the truth will out. Secrets never stay quiet for long.'

'Don't say that. The shit will well and truly hit the fan if this one gets out.'

'Sometimes family life gets challenged. It goes with the territory.'

Oh my God. They were talking about their affair and the fall-out if they went public. I must have looked stricken, because Jack was gazing at me with concern.

'Feeling better now?' he asked.

I looked at his handsome face, noticing the kindness in his thickly lashed eyes. I nodded.

'Sure? You look' – he put his head on one side and considered for a moment – 'sad. As if the weight of the world is on your shoulders.'

'Yes,' I whispered, 'it does feel a bit like that sometimes.'

'Want to tell me about it? Sometimes a problem shared is a problem halved.'

I shook my head. 'I can't.'

'Is it a secret?'

I nodded miserably.

'Sooner or later the truth will out. Secrets never stay quiet for long.'

Oh my goodness, those were the very words Alex had just said. For a moment I felt like I was in a living nightmare, as if some invisible force was giving me subliminal messages, urging me to rip the very fabric of Alex and Jeanie's secret wide apart so it was out in the open. What would the pair of them do if I stood up, tapped my glass for silence and calmly announced, 'Ladies and gentlemen. Jeanie and Alex are fucking each other. More mashed potato anyone?'

'Isn't that right, Holly?'

My husband had interrupted my thoughts. 'Sorry, I missed the question,' I replied.

'I was telling Jeanie about the trigeminal neuralgia charity I'm involved in.'

'Oh yes?'

My mind rewound the conversation I'd earwigged. No, no that couldn't be right. There were no secrets about Alex's charity work. They'd obviously quickly changed the subject, worried about being overheard. The scheming love rats.

'A little while ago,' said Alex, 'you told me you wanted to be involved in future events.'

'Did I?' I looked at him, horrified. The last thing I wanted was to be sitting in the corner of some dreary room with peeling paint, perched on a chair and taking minutes of an annual general meeting.

'Yes,' he said, his tone chiding, and expression pained. 'It was after your disapproval of my regular partner accompanying me at the dinner-dance functions.'

'What partner?' asked Jeanie, eyes round with surprise.

Was it my imagination or did she look outraged? Proprietorial?

'I have a female friend,' Alex explained, 'who is heavily involved in the charity, and who I used to take as my plus-one, because Holly found it all immensely boring. What were the words you used to describe one of their galas, darling? Oh yes. Full of chinless wonders and stuffed shirts.'

'Chinless wonders, by their very anatomy, do give excellent head,' said Simon, coming in on the conversation, 'although I'm not so sure about stuffed shirts.'

'Anyway,' said Alex, ignoring Simon, 'there was a little misunderstanding between Holly and my lady friend recently, resulting in my wife now availing herself for such functions. However, the lady in question is unable to bring her partner—'

'—because he's married,' I explained sweetly to everyone around the table.

'That's her business,' said Alex curtly. I realised drink had made him punchy. Well, he wasn't alone. I was feeling pretty punchy too. 'As I was saying, the lady in question has nobody to accompany her to the next function—'

'My heart bleeds,' I said sarcastically, noting that Jeanie had gone very quiet.

'—and I thought, Jack,' said my husband looking across the table, 'that as you're a neurosurgeon and share the same interest, perhaps you might like to come to the event and also be the lady's plus-one for the evening?'

My mouth dropped open. My husband was volunteering Jack to partner Annabelle Huntingdon-Smyth? I appreciated Alex had his hands full pretending to be happily married to me whilst bonking Jeanie and having a relationship with Annabelle that I hadn't yet quite got to the bottom of, but volunteering Jack? *My* Jack? I instantly went cold, as if somebody had thrown a bucket of iced water in my face. Suddenly I was stone-cold sober. Where the hell had *that* bit of exclusive ownership come from? Jack wasn't *my* Jack. I picked up my glass with a slightly trembling hand and took a sip of water.

'What an excellent idea,' I said, my voice quavering. Jack was single. As was Annabelle. In fact, I could visualise the two of them together. A truly good-looking couple. Perhaps they would fall madly in love with each other at the dinner-dance. The thought made my stomach contract, and I could feel the earlier booze mixing unhappily with dinner. *Look on the bright side, Holly*! said the little voice in my head, *if Jack and Annabelle fall in love, that's one less woman prowling around your husband*. I looked at Jack. 'You must come!' I said brightly. 'It will be such fun.'

'Why not?' Jack smiled.

'Excellent,' said Alex. 'I'll let my friend know. She'll be delighted.'

'When is it?' asked Jack.

I tensed, as a thought struck me. Oh no. Please don't let Alex say it's the day of the surprise birthday party.

'A week today,' said Alex. 'The last Saturday in September.'

I exhaled gustily, drawing a curious look from my husband. The party was the first Saturday in October. Thank you, God. I mentally blew a kiss heavenwards.

'Can others attend this function?' asked Caro. 'David and I are up for it, if so.'

'Sadly no,' said Alex, not sounding very sincere.

I was aware my husband hadn't bothered to talk very much to either Caro or David, and that it had been Simon who'd kept them entertained at that end of the table with outrageous stories about his fashion business, and how he'd once designed special pantyhose for a pop star who hadn't had her willy removed. 'It was either that or six rolls of duct tape,' he'd said, making them laugh, 'and even *I* crossed my legs when I saw what a big girl she was.'

Alex gave Jack a grateful nod for agreeing to partner Annabelle, and promptly went back into a huddle with Jeanie. I couldn't quite catch what they were saying. He sounded like he was placating her. Was she angry with him because she wasn't invited to the dinner-dance? I was determined, before the night was over, to find out what the hell was going on here, and seemingly right under my nose. A warm hand landed on mind, scattering my thoughts and sending a million volts through my body, right up to my eyeballs, which were possibly lighting up like a fruit machine.

'I'm looking forward to this charity dinner-dance,' said Jack.

'Me too,' I gasped. He hadn't removed his hand, and his touch was playing havoc with my pulse, which seemed to have relocated between my legs.

'Will it really be full of chinless wonders and stuffed shirts?' He looked amused, and his eyes upon mine were teasing.

I shrugged, embarrassed that Alex had publicly vocalised a private opinion. 'Maybe one or two.'

'Then we'll have to liven it up a little,' he said with a wink.

'Oh?' I said, trying not to stare at him wantonly.

'As a thank you for dishing up dinner while you took a cat nap on your kitchen island, I want you to promise you'll have a dance with me.'

'Sure,' I said lightly, as if it was no big deal. Which it wasn't. I just wished my body would take heed of that.

Chapter Thirty-Four

The dinner party rumbled on. Simon's champagne was long finished and Alex had divested the cooler of several more bottles. I was slowly drinking myself sober with glasses of water and noticed Jack was doing the same. Wordlessly, he stood up at the same time as me, and began collecting up dinner plates and dirty cutlery, helping me carry it all out to the kitchen. Alex and Jeanie were almost nose to nose. They'd be snogging each other in a minute. I was amazed Ray hadn't noticed anything amiss. I stacked the tureens and looked at him under my eyelashes. He seemed quite unperturbed, yakking away to Caro, David and Simon.

By the time the ice cream had been transferred to an attractively frosted dish, and Jack and I had returned to the dining room with pudding bowls and a large crystal platter heaped with the melon balls, conversation had changed to the subject of social media. Jeanie and Alex seemed to have finally emerged from their private bubble. After all, I thought sourly, there's only so much huddling a couple can do in public without excusing themselves and getting a room. I banged the ice cream down on the table harder than intended, making everybody jump. There was a moment's silence, then Simon peered in horror at the contents of the frosted dish.

'What in God's name is that, dah-ling?' he said, shuddering. 'It looks like something one of my ex-lovers once produced. And I don't mean in the kitchen.'

For once I was in agreement with Alex about my brother's jokey innuendo. This was overstepping the mark.

'Do you have to be so disgusting?' I snapped.

'I'm not,' said Simon, affronted. 'It was my ex-lover who was disgusting. It turned out he had an infection.'

'This is homemade mint sorbet!' I roared, 'and it's bloody delicious.'

Simon opened his mouth to say something, but I waved a serving spoon aloft.

'Do *not*,' I warned, eyes flashing, 'make any further comment. Now, who wants some of this?' I asked, looking around the table.

Needless to say, after that nobody wanted any of the ice cream, and only the melon balls were eaten.

Alex squinted at me across the table.

'I didn't know you were on Facebook,' he said accusingly. 'Why haven't you friended me?'

'Because,' I blustered, 'there is surely no point. After all, I'm married to you.'

'Well perhaps you *should* friend me,' he said petulantly, 'and then you would be able to see what I'm up to and won't feel the need to use my laptop and make ridiculous conversation with my friends.'

'Oh?' said Jeanie, looking at me speculatively. 'What's naughty Holly been up to then?'

'Nothing,' I spluttered, flushing with embarrassment. I'd bloody kill Alex later. 'It was just a silly misunderstanding.' I glared at my husband, daring him to elaborate on the subject.

'Well I'm glad you haven't friended *me*,' said Simon imperiously, 'because frankly, Holly, if you saw my timeline you'd be shocked.'

'Do not tell me it's full of gorgeous willies,' I said through clenched teeth, 'otherwise I might just lose my temper.'

Simon looked outraged. 'What a thing to say! Do you honestly think I want reporting to the Facebook police?' He tossed his head with annoyance. 'I have a business page full of fashion, littered with pics of gorgeous models wearing fabric you'd want to caress and clothes you'd want to make love to. Something you wouldn't know much about if both your peeved expression and that awful rag you're wearing are anything to go by.'

'How dare you!' I seethed.

'Joke, dah-ling, *joke*,' said Simon, his tone suddenly bored.

'I'm Facebook friends with Ray,' said Jeanie.

'And I'm Facebook friends with Caro,' said David.

'Awww, that's because he loves me,' Caro smiled drunkenly.

'No, it's so I can keep tabs on what you're up to,' said David dryly. 'All that claiming to being knackered because you've been doing the housework all day long. The other day a Facebook notification pinged me that you were shopping at Bluewater with Jeanie and Holly.'

'Oh yes,' said Ray, 'Jeanie came home with an amazing outfit for the party.'

'What party?' asked Alex, just as Jeanie applied a hefty kick to Ray's ankle under the table.

'This party,' I said brightly. 'Isn't it wonderful?'

Alex looked confused, as well he might. 'Are we talking about the dress Jeanie's wearing or tonight's gathering?'

'Both,' I smiled. 'More wine anyone?'

David held out his glass for topping up. 'So, as I was saying, Facebook lets me know what Caro's really been up to, and then she gets home and squirts a bit of furniture polish in the air and makes out she's exhausted.'

'Oooh, Detective David is after me, eh?' Caro nudged her husband playfully.

'Yes, and I might have to arrest you for telling fibs.'

'In which case you'll have to handcuff me,' Caro purred, 'and let me play with your truncheon.'

'Not here, darling,' David murmured.

'Obviously.' Caro rolled her eyes. 'I meant at home.'

I glared at the unappetising mint sorbet. I wasn't usually envious of my friends, but hearing Caro and David engage in a bit of sexy banter suddenly made me feel resentful about my own slightly sterile marriage.

Jack put his hand on my arm, and once again I nearly hit the ceiling. I wished he'd stop doing that, especially after Caro's sexy banter with David. I was feeling rather hot and bothered. If Jack wasn't careful I'd grab hold of his hand, kiss its palm and work my way up his forearm and not stop until I reached his mouth.

'Thanks for accepting my friend request,' he said.

'Pleasure,' I said, thinking more of his touch on my arm than our friendship on social media.

I could see Jeanie was now very drunk. She leaned forward to say something and for one awful moment I thought her breasts were going to slip out of their awning. I looked at Alex for his reaction, but he seemed unmoved, although David's and Ray's eyes were on stalks. Jack wasn't looking. Thankfully, he'd removed his hand from my arm and was now talking to Simon about his fashion business.

'I must shay…' Jeanie slurred, 'that when I've had too much to drink' – she smacked her lips together lasciviously – 'I get very randy.' She turned to Alex and, eyes almost crossing, let out a little giggle. 'Fancy doing the alphabet?' she asked him slyly.

'Sorry?' said Alex.

'Jeanie,' I said warningly.

She ignored me and instead continued to stare at Alex, her pupils now dilated to the size of my dinner plates as she stuck her tongue between her parted lips, flicked it back and forth a few times and then started to sing, 'Ayyy, bee, cee, dee—'

'I think it's time for coffee,' I said, standing up abruptly, 'and you can give me a hand, Jeanie.' In one deft movement I was by her side, yanking her to her feet. The bosom mountain wobbled violently as I practically dragged her out to the kitchen.

'What the hell are you playing at?' I demanded, once we were out of earshot and I'd shut the kitchen door after me.

'Eh?' Jeanie squinted at me, angrily shaking me off.

'You know perfectly well,' I glared at her.

'Why are you getting all huffy with me?' she demanded, putting her hands on her hips and adopting a narked pose.

'You heard,' I hissed. *Careful, Holly, careful. Jeanie's drunken singing of the alphabet isn't actually proof of a raging affair.* I changed tack. 'I don't appreciate you leaking secrets I've shared about what goes on between me and my husband in the bedroom.'

'Sorry,' she said sulkily. 'It was just a bit of fun.'

'For you maybe, but not me. That's private stuff, understand?'

'I said *sorry*,' Jeanie harrumphed.

'And another thing,' I said, seeing that now was as good a time as any to interrogate her, 'why were you and Alex talking about divorce earlier?'

'No particular reason,' she shrugged, 'Caro had brought up the subject of Brangelina's messy public showdown, and Alex and I ended up talking about the cost of divorce and how expensive it is.'

'Oh yeah? Why's that then? Planning on getting divorced?'

'Wha—' She stared at me incredulously.

'I heard you at the dinner table, Jeanie,' I said angrily.

She shook her head, bewildered. 'What are you on about?'

'Your conversation with Alex. You said it had been going on too long, but you hadn't told anyone, that Ray didn't know and he'd go mad if he did, and Alex said that sooner or later the truth would out because secrets never stayed quiet for long and that sometimes family life gets challenged. You were talking about your affair and getting divorced, right?

Jeanie's eyes narrowed to slits. 'Stop shouting your big mouth off, Holly,' she hissed. 'My husband is on the other side of that wall,' she pointed in the direction of the dining room. 'If you must know—'

'Yes, I really must,' I glared at her.

'I was talking to Alex about Charlotte. She needs dental braces and I don't want to use the National Health. They've already messed up her teeth, and she's in bits about it. I secretly took my daughter along to see Alex, but obviously he only does private work and Ray doesn't earn the sort of money to cover Charlotte's orthodontics. So Alex is doing mates' rates, and I'm filching from the housekeeping to pay for it. I was telling Alex that Ray would go mad if he found out. Satisfied? Or do you want to shout that out for my husband to hear too?'

I stared at her, open-mouthed. Was she telling the truth? Or was she lying? There always seemed to be plausible explanations from Alex every time I distrusted him. Was Jeanie doing the same thing? Giving me a plausible explanation? I didn't know for sure. Perhaps, for now, I should give her the benefit of the doubt…?

'Right,' I said eventually. 'Sorry.'

'Apology accepted,' she snapped. 'And I'm not helping you with the sodding coffee either. I feel dizzy and want to sit down.' And with that she lurched her way out of the kitchen, leaving me alone with my thoughts while I put the kettle on.

A couple of minutes later, as I was pouring scalding water into the coffee pot, Jack came into the kitchen.

'I think you and I are the only sober ones left,' he grinned.

'Yes,' I acknowledged, and cranked up a smile. I was still smarting over Jeanie's anger, which was fair enough if I had got things so catastrophically wrong. I sighed.

'Penny for them?' said Jack, working with me as I pulled cups out of cupboards and found plates for the cheeseboard.

'Just wishing I hadn't bothered with this dinner party.' For a horrible moment, tears stung the back of my eyelids. 'It's been a bit of a disaster.'

'Nonsense,' he said, giving my shoulders a squeeze, and nearly causing me to drop the percolator on the kitchen floor. 'It's been a resounding success. Everyone's having a great time, and I've never had so much fun in my life.'

*

By the time everyone stumbled out to their minicabs, it was nearly two in the morning. I chucked a tablet in the dishwasher, let Rupert out for a last wee, and then wearily climbed the stairs. Alex had passed out diagonally across the bed, on top of the covers. I wasn't going to attempt moving him. Walking across the room to the wardrobe, I hung up my dress, slipped into my pyjamas, then went off to Sophie's bedroom. As I curled up under her duvet, I felt severely out of sorts, but couldn't put a finger on why. It was only as my mind wandered down the corridor of sleep that the reason struck me.

I felt so lonely.

Chapter Thirty-Five

Alex had a blinding hangover the following morning and was grumpy with it.

'I still don't know why you insisted on having a dinner party,' he complained, sipping his morning coffee as I emptied the dishwasher. 'The next time you feel the urge to wow a crowd with your coq au vin, let's invite some educated people over who can offer decent conversation and, oh I don't know,' he sighed gustily, 'debate intelligently about Brexit or a worthy cause.'

'Someone like Annabelle, I suppose,' I said, crashing some plates into a cupboard so hard it was a wonder they didn't chip.

'Yes, why not!' said Alex, missing the sarcasm in my voice. 'A lovely warm-hearted girl. Did you know she's fluent in three languages and knowledgeable about' – he stretched his arms wide – 'so many things.'

'Fascinating,' I said, my tone withering.

'That's the difference between you and me, Holly. You see, I'm really not interested in discussing *I'm a Celebrity* and which one is Ant and which one is Dec. Mind you, the evening would have been vastly improved if your flipping brother hadn't been there telling everybody that the purple grapes we were having with the

cheeseboard looked like his haemorrhoids. Everyone was a philistine
– apart from Jack,' he added.

I could feel my temper rising. Slamming the empty dishwasher
lid shut, I turned my attention to the recycling bin under the sink.
It was stuffed with empty bottles which clanked noisily as I heaved
the container out of its unit.

'Do you have to make such a racket?' Alex snapped, looking
pained. 'I have a headache.'

'Nobody forced you to drink umpteen glasses of champagne.
And how dare you call our friends *philistines*,' I retorted, annoyed.
What a way to talk about such lovely people. There were times I
thoroughly disliked my husband, and this was one of them. 'If you
ever needed a favour off David or Ray, they are the sort of people
who would drop everything to help. Which is more than you do
for them. I was so embarrassed when you recently refused to treat
Ray's toothache.'

'What are you talking about?' Alex huffed.

'I'm talking about when you told Ray to go to A&E,' I reminded
him.

Alex rolled his eyes. 'Yes, Holly. You're right, I did. I remember
now. Ray telephoned at three in the morning. Forgive me if I didn't
rush off to my surgery in the middle of the night, when I had my
own patient list kicking off less than five hours later and needed a
clear head to do Mrs Grayson's tricky dental implants for the paltry
sum of four grand. Much better that I'd told Mrs Grayson to take
her big fat cheque and bog off so I could charge Ray fifty quid for
a dental extraction. Thank you for reminding me that my priorities
are cock-eyed.'

'You could have told him to go to the surgery the following day and wait for a slot.'

'No, I could not,' said Alex tetchily. 'Ray insisted he was in agony and needed immediate treatment. Hospital was the best place. Now please stop being so argumentative with me and for GOD'S SAKE,' Alex bellowed, as the overloaded recycling box tipped over and glass bottles rolled noisily across the tiled floor, 'DO THAT QUIETLY.'

I stooped like a cotton picker, grabbing bottles as they moved this way and that.

'This is a man's job,' I seethed. 'You should be doing this. You're not the only one who is tired.'

'Listen, Holly,' said my husband wearily, 'you are the one who insisted on having a dinner party. It's not my fault your brother brought over enough champagne to stock a supermarket for a year, or that everybody fell on it like parched travellers in a desert.'

'Of which you were one,' I reminded. Straightening up, I hauled the box to the back door.

Alex put his hands in the air. 'Guilty as charged, Your Honour. I've already said, they were your friends, not mine. How else was I meant to get through an interminable evening with such boring people?'

'Jack isn't boring,' I protested.

'Granted, he was the one person there with half a brain and a bit of wit. However, he wasn't sitting next to me, so I wasn't able to properly talk to him, and I certainly wasn't going to spend the evening shouting across the dinner table to him.'

My eyes narrowed as I remembered who he *had* been sitting next to.

'You seemed to be getting on famously with Jeanie,' I pointed out.

Alex threw back his head and hooted with laughter, except there was no mirth to the sound. 'Don't get me started on Jeanie,' he said, rolling his eyes. 'She nearly bored the pants off me.'

'Did she indeed?' I said dryly, as a picture of Alex popped into my brain complete with bare backside and Jeanie looking delighted.

'You didn't look bored,' I continued, pausing to unlock the back door. 'In fact, you seemed positively captivated.'

'Do me a favour,' Alex scoffed. 'The woman is completely off her trolley. And what the hell was she on about wanting me to sing the alphabet song, as if we were two presenters in *Sesame Street*?' Alex shook his head in bemusement.

'I don't know,' I said quickly, as the back door swung open. I lugged everything over the threshold. 'I'm going to the bottle bank. I'll be back in a bit.'

'Have fun,' said Alex sarcastically.

On impulse, I turned back to face my husband. 'Can you keep a secret?' I blurted.

Alex sighed. 'Listen, Holly. If you're about to confide a piece of gossip about one of your girlfriends, I'm not interested.'

I stared at him, weighing up his words, noting the expression on his face.

'Jeanie told me she's having an affair.'

Alex blinked. There was a moment's silence. When he finally spoke, his words seemed guarded. His tone exceptionally casual. Or was I just being paranoid?

'That was remarkably indiscreet of her. Did she tell you who with?'

'No. I was going to ask you the same question.'

Alex shrugged. 'I can't help you, I'm afraid.'

'Apparently they bonk in her lover's car. It has privacy glass and electric seats that recline flat.' I stared at my husband, searching for the slightest flinch in body language that could be construed as an admission of guilt. There was none, but his eyes flickered, and he was the first to turn away.

Chapter Thirty-Six

Caro telephoned me later that afternoon to thank me for inviting her and David to dinner.

'We had a lovely time,' she said politely.

'Did you?' I asked miserably. 'I feel like everybody was talking in their own little huddle and not really chatting all together.'

'Nonsense,' she said stoically. 'I could see Jeanie had buttonholed your husband, but your brother kept us both thoroughly entertained. He's such a laugh.'

So Caro had also noticed Jeanie's focus being solely on Alex.

'Do you think Jeanie's all right?' I asked my friend. 'She wasn't herself.'

'That's because she was pissed,' Caro tutted. 'And no, I don't think she's all right. I think she's riddled with guilt about' – she lowered her voice at the other end of the phone –'you-know-what. And I have something terrible to confess,' Caro whispered.

'What?' I asked, my mouth suddenly going a bit dry.

'I accidentally told David about Jeanie having an affair. It just popped out. He was feeling all randy last night – for which I totally blame Jeanie by the way, parading around with three-quarters of her chest exposed. David couldn't keep his eyes off her boobs and the moment we were home he couldn't wait to get me into bed. I'll bet anything he was thinking about Jeanie's tits as he bonked me,' she laughed good-naturedly. 'Anyway, you know what it's like afterwards – pillow talk and whatnot. We were reflecting about the dinner party, and David said that Jeanie seemed totally transformed, far more confident about herself. David said he wouldn't have been at all surprised if Jeanie was having an affair. He even suggested Jeanie was bonking Alex, ah ha ha ha!'

'Ha ha!' I laughed back, gripping the handset so hard my knuckles turned white. 'How absurd.'

'That's what I said to David. However, I was still quite drunk and indiscretion got the better of me. I ended up saying that Jeanie *was* having an affair, but we didn't know who with. David slapped his thigh and said, "I knew it!", but he was also appalled. After all, he really likes Ray, and feels disloyal knowing something about Jeanie that Ray isn't privy to. But I've assured David it's just a marital storm in a teacup; that Jeanie feels so guilty over the whole matter the fling is as good as over. He's promised to keep schtum.'

'Good, good,' I nodded, 'and, um, I was indiscreet, too. I told Alex.'

Caro sighed. 'What are we like?' I could hear her tutting at the other end of the phone. 'I'm sure Alex is the soul of discretion, but *we* must watch ourselves. There must be no further slip-ups. I genuinely think Jeanie's just had some sort of mid-life crisis.'

'I hope so,' I murmured. Was that what my husband was having? A mid-life crisis? He *was* nearly forty, after all. Wasn't that supposed to be the age where a person questioned everything about their life, before going ever so slightly off the rails?

'Anyway, we loved the party and the company. Simon was hysterical. And just between you and me,' Caro whispered, 'I absolutely adored your other guest, Jack. If he crooked a finger in my direction, I'd be seriously tempted to follow Jeanie's bad example. He's an absolutely stunner! And somebody said he's a doctor. Is that right?'

'Yes, a brain surgeon, no less.'

'He can fiddle with my neurotransmitters any time he likes,' Caro laughed smuttily, just as the doorbell rang. 'I heard that,' she said. 'You obviously have a visitor, so I'll catch you later.'

We rang off and I hurried into the hall, annoyed that Alex wasn't shifting to answer the door for me. He'd taken his hangover to the sofa, retiring to a horizontal length in front of the sports channel. The lounge door was firmly shut, letting me know he didn't want to be disturbed.

Standing on the doorstep was Jeanie.

'Hi,' I said, surprised to see her.

'Hello,' she said, her manner subdued. 'Can I come in?'

'Of course,' I said, stepping to one side, 'you don't need to ask.'

She gave the ghost of a smile. 'I wasn't sure if you'd want me over the threshold after the way I behaved last night.'

'Don't be silly,' I said, leading her into the kitchen. 'Coffee?'

'Please. Make it black. I'm never drinking alcohol again.'

'Ah, we all say that after a skinful.'

'Yes, well, I think an apology is in order,' she said contritely. 'Ray told me I was bang out of order getting so smashed.'

'Everybody was smashed.'

'Yes, but me more than anyone else.' She pulled out a tall stool and sat at the kitchen island. Propping her elbows on the granite surface, she rubbed her eyes wearily. 'I can't even remember the last half of the evening,' she sighed, 'but I do recall you being very cross with me at one point.'

I shrugged. I didn't want to go over old ground about her apparently chatting to Alex about divorce and me getting the wrong end of the stick, or the fact that I'd misconstrued talk about her daughter's teeth braces as something entirely different. After all, whilst I hadn't been as catastrophically pissed as Jeanie, I'd initially shipped enough booze at the start of the evening to drift off for a few minutes with my head down on the very island Jeanie was now perched at.

'I think,' I said carefully, 'that alcohol can colour things so matters get out of perspective.'

'Like making a mountain out of a molehill?'

'Yes,' I nodded, bringing my own coffee over and sitting alongside her.

'That's good to know. But I also came over to clear the air.'

'Oh?'

'Yes,' Jeanie licked her lips nervously, 'I feel like something has changed between us, but I can't put my finger on it. Have I done something to offend you?'

I looked at my friend. Her expression was an open book. She looked guileless. So innocent. Her face was currently scrubbed free of make-up, and last night's glamour-girl chest now concealed under a baggy top. She looked like a middle-aged mum, not a cougar out to snatch another woman's husband whilst wrestling with a guilty conscience.

'Jeanie, lately I've had some… issues. I don't want to go into what they are but…' I hesitated, unsure how to feel my way through the questions I'd so like to ask without revealing my own marriage concerns and anxiety over Alex being unfaithful, 'it would help me enormously if you told me who you're having an affair with.'

'I truly can't,' she said, shaking her head.

'Would it compromise our friendship?' I asked. Quite brave of me to ask that, I thought.

'I feel like our friendship has already been compromised,' she said. 'You're cross with me about the affair, and angry that I'm deceiving Ray.'

'Look—'

'It's okay. I understand. You think I'm a two-faced bitch, sitting at your dinner table with my lovely husband, who is completely oblivious to what's going on in his marriage.'

'I'm not judging you, Jeanie, honest. But, well, surely Ray must know something's up.'

'Why should he?'

'Well, you know' – I spread my hands out, palms up in a helpless gesture – 'you're not sleeping with him any more, you're bonking another man. Ray must wonder why his sex life has dried up.'

'Who says I'm not sleeping with Ray?'

I stared at her. 'You mean' – my eyes rounded – 'that you're still having sex with Ray?'

'I wasn't in the beginning, but I am now, yes.'

'You're bonking two men?'

'Yes.'

'Both at the same time?'

Jeanie folded her arms across her chest, her body language letting me know she was on the defensive. 'Obviously I'm not bonking them both at *exactly* the same time,' she said through pursed lips, 'otherwise my husband would have something to say about that. It's always been his fantasy to have a threesome, but not with another man.'

'Oh, Jeanie, too much information!' I clapped my hands over my ears. Yuck, yuck. I'd never be able to look Ray in the eye again without thinking of him being turned on by his wife rolling around with another woman and him sandwiched somewhere in the middle.

'Well you did ask,' she tutted.

'I thought women rumbled husbands who were having affairs because they stopped sleeping with their wives.'

Jeanie shrugged. 'I don't know. Maybe men are like that. But I'm a woman, and I can tell you one thing, Holly, and that is my libido has gone through the roof. I'm insatiable. Can't get enough of it. There I am, parked up some lonely lane miles from nowhere, flat on my back in my lover's car having orgasm after orgasm and yelling my head off, and then I go home, jump in the shower and then jump on Ray. He thinks all his birthdays have come at once. In fact, he's chuffing exhausted.'

I stared at Jeanie, incredulous. Orgasm after orgasm? And then home again to hubby to have a few more earth-moving moments? I suddenly felt incredibly jealous. When was the last time I'd had an orgasm? Actually, what the flipping heck *was* an orgasm because, now I came to think about it, I wasn't entirely sure I'd ever had one. Oh yes, my privates had heated up a few times, but I wasn't convinced they'd ever ignited because I'd never felt the need to yell my head off. Ever.

'Jeanie, please,' I said in a low voice, 'tell me who he is.'

'I'd like to, Holly. Honest I would. But I can't. Truly. I just can't.

Ask her, said the voice in my head. *Go on! Ask her now*!

'Jeanie, just tell me. Is it Al—' My husband's name died on my lips as the doorbell rang. 'Just a moment,' I said. 'I'll be right back.'

I hastened off to the front door again. It was Sophie, home from her sleepover with Tabitha. My daughter looked tired and not a little tetchy. No doubt my teen hadn't had much sleep last night. Izzy was standing next to her, smiling brightly.

'That's so kind of you to drop her back,' I said, cringing as I realised that perhaps I should have collected my own daughter, instead of leaving Izzy to taxi Sophie home.

'No trouble at all, and it's so lovely to see you, Holly,' she gushed, clearly angling for an invitation over the threshold.

'Would you like a cup of tea?' I asked politely, desperately hoping she'd say no.

'Go on then,' she said, as if I'd twisted her arm. 'Oh, coo-ee!' She waved to Alex as he stuck his head out of the lounge, his curiosity getting the better of him and wanting to see the owner of the highly elocuted voice which was now ringing right up to the rafters of the house. Izzy made *The Good Life*'s Margo sound like a chav. Alex smiled pleasantly but then disappeared back into the lounge, firmly shutting the door behind him again. I let his indifference go over my head. My husband was nothing like Izzy's. Alex couldn't give a toss about what the other school mums thought of him, whereas I had once or twice briefly seen Sebastian in action. He was a charmer, and something of a flirt – not that he'd ever batted his eyelids at me – but I could imagine he held a certain appeal for many of the mothers, not least because he rubbed shoulders with the glitterati and had a celebrity-sized bank balance.

'I'm going up to my room,' Sophie said, yawning hugely. 'There's some homework to finish.'

'Oh, okay, darling,' I smiled at my daughter as she scampered up the staircase, leaving me with Izzy who was looking at me expectantly. 'Um, well, let's go into the kitchen. Sorry, Alex is…' I gestured helplessly as we passed the lounge door.

Izzy finished my sentence for me. 'Watching football,' she grinned. 'Sebastian is the same. Works his little socks off all week, all hours God sends. Sometimes I don't see him until midnight and come Sunday he's exhausted. All he wants to do is hug a cushion and hold the remote control.'

'Yes, quite,' I said, pushing open the kitchen door. 'Look who's here!' I trilled to Jeanie, as if Izzy was a long-lost relative we couldn't wait to get into a bear hug.

'Oh, hello,' said Izzy to Jeanie, her dazzling smile shrinking to a thin line.

Jeanie took one look at Izzy and was suddenly a whirring mass of movement, reaching for her handbag, casting around for her car keys, grabbing her mobile phone which she'd abandoned on the worktop, scooping everything together and nearly falling off the tall stool in her haste to be off.

'You don't have to go, do you?' I asked her.

'Yes, sorry,' said Jeanie, clearly flustered. 'I've left something in the oven. I'd better get back or it will be incinerated and set all the smoke alarms off.'

'Oh, right,' I said, leaving Izzy to sit on Jeanie's vacated seat. I followed my friend through the hallway to the front door.

'Sorry,' she said, when we were away from Izzy and out of earshot, 'but I can't abide that woman.'

I nodded. 'See you soon.'

'Yes. Bye.' Jeanie pulled the door shut after her as I stood for a moment, watching her scurry towards her car.

I walked back to the kitchen and gave Izzy a forced smile. 'What a shame Jeanie had to rush off. Tea or coffee?'

'Tea, please, and I, for one, am delighted she's left.' Izzy smoothed down her top and then, echoing Jeanie's words, said, 'I can't abide that woman.'

As I put the kettle on again, I wondered why. It transpired that I wouldn't have to wait too much longer to find out.

Chapter Thirty-Seven

The following week passed quickly. Alex was fully booked at the surgery, and my own Monday and Wednesday slots passed in a whirl of activity. I'd also put myself on a crash diet, aware that the charity dinner-dance was looming. I didn't want to be sitting next to the willowy Annabelle Huntingdon-Smyth looking like one of the Teletubbies. It was promising to be quite a flashy 'do', especially as Alex's co-trustees wanted a last-minute celebrity to make a guest appearance and draw the raffle. Alex had ended up buttonholing Izzy for advice while she'd had tea with me. She'd been delighted to get Sebastian on the phone and sort something out with a local celeb, an ex-movie star who was making a comeback and would do anything for publicity so long as Alex and the trustees were in agreement to the paparazzi being there.

'She's a total diva,' Sebastian had warned Alex, 'and she'd sell her granny if it meant good coverage for her.'

'Who have you got in mind?' Alex had asked.

'Harriet Montgomery. A name-dropping pain in the arse, but she knows how to work a crowd and your mob will love her. She's apparently starring in Angelina Jolie's next film.'

I spent the days in between getting to grips with the house, tackling a backlog of ironing, and going for long jogs with Rupert in an attempt to tone my thighs. By Friday they didn't look any different, but Rupert's were positively rippling.

'Are you looking forward to the dinner-dance tomorrow night?' I asked Alex conversationally, as we sat down to dinner that evening.

'I could do without it, to be honest,' he said, picking up his knife and fork. 'It's been a hell of a week, and I'm shattered.'

'Have a lie-in tomorrow morning,' I suggested.

'Who's looking after Sophie while we're out? Please don't tell me she's going to Tabitha's house for yet another sleepover. I'm very grateful to Izzy's husband for providing a last-minute celeb, but Izzy isn't my sort of person, Holly, and I'd rather not be indebted to her.'

'None of my friends are your type, are they?' I said somewhat caustically.

'Oh, is Izzy one of your new best friends then?'

'As it happens, no, she's not. But sometimes, Alex, it seems to me that you don't like any of my girlfriends.'

'O-*kay*,' Alex tutted, 'I can see my wife's in one of her funny moods again.'

'I am not in a funny mood,' I protested. 'Oh, for goodness' sake, can we just forget it? And no, Sophie isn't having a sleepover at Izzy's place. She's going to Caro's instead.'

Alex rolled his eyes, his body language conveying the unsaid message that he didn't approve of that plan either.

'It strikes me,' he said, 'that lately our daughter has been farmed out here, there and everywhere.'

My fork paused, mid-air. 'What's that comment supposed to mean?' I asked, stung. 'Sophie has had a couple of invitations recently to a friend's house. I didn't ask for her to be invited, for heaven's sake. You make it sound like I'm a negligent mother.'

'Don't start manipulating words,' said Alex with a resigned air of *here she goes again.*

'I'm coming to the charity dinner-dance to support *you,*' I said. 'What else am I meant to do regarding Sophie's welfare this weekend? Leave her on her own for the night with Rupert?'

'Now you're being facetious,' said Alex, wiping his mouth on a paper napkin. 'And you aren't supporting *me* at all, Holly.' My husband's tone was suddenly cold. 'You were the one who insisted I take you as my partner. I already had a plus-one, remember?'

'Indeed I do, Alex,' I said, my tone dangerously quiet. 'But surely to take one's *wife* to such functions is the done thing? Doesn't it look a little odd parading another woman on your arm?'

'Hardly,' Alex snapped. 'Annabelle is completely immersed in the charity's work, as am I. Nobody raises an eyebrow at her being on my arm, or anybody else's for that matter. It's business. She will be talking knowledgeably tomorrow, not just at the after-dinner speeches, but mingling with those who have suffered TN – as has she. She can talk about drug therapies, treatment options, and generally reassure anybody investigating such avenues. Even Jack, as a neurosurgeon, will be able to talk intelligently to everyone. But what exactly are *you* able to offer, Holly? An opinion on the shade of nail polish you're wearing, or the best shop to buy an evening gown for such an event?'

'How dare you!' I seethed. 'You should be proud of me, instead of trivialising my role.'

'Are we done?' asked Alex, standing up. 'I have some business to see to.'

He stalked off leaving me sitting at the table, opening and closing my mouth impotently, trying to form words and failing. How had an innocent enquiry, asking if my husband was looking forward to tomorrow night's charity function, deteriorated so rapidly into a biting exchange of words? And exactly what business did my husband have to oversee on a Friday night, when his dental surgery was locked up and in darkness?

I could hear Alex moving around in the hallway, retrieving his shoes from the cupboard under the stairs, searching for his car keys, the jingle as he picked them up, the pat-pat-pat of pockets ensuring his mobile phone was to hand, and it suddenly dawned on me where he might be going and, more importantly, who he could be seeing.

Pushing back my chair, I quietly picked up my own keys that were languishing on the worktop just as the front door shut behind Alex. I tore out to the hallway and hollered up the stairs.

'Sophie?'

'Yes,' came a muffled response.

'I have to go out for half an hour. There's been an out-of-hours emergency. Dad's gone ahead. Will you be all right if I leave you?'

'Yes,' came the bored reply.

'Are you sure?'

Oh God. Alex would go mad if he knew I'd left our young teen alone. My words about being a negligent mother who left Rupert to babysit our daughter were fast coming back to bite me on the bum. Anxiety was already gnawing at the pit of my stomach.

Sophie came out of her bedroom and leaned against the banister rail on the landing.

'For God's sake, Mum,' she said huffily, 'of course I'll be all right. I'm nearly fourteen. Everyone else in my class is left on their own when their parents go somewhere. You are the only mother who insists I have a babysitter or sleep at a friend's house when you are out. I'll be fine. And anyway, Rupert's with me.'

'Yes,' I nodded, aware that the dog was now definitely in the role of babysitter, and not necessarily even a good one. I had a sudden alarming vision of an opportunist burglar sitting outside the house, watching two parents leave, then smashing his way through the back door to be joyfully greeted by the family dog. Rupert would obligingly lead the burglar to the bedside drawer where a surplus of cash was kept, and then the other bedside drawer where a few pretty pieces of jewellery languished, before he stumbled upon my vulnerable daughter who would immediately be sold on to some human trafficker on speed dial. I let out a whimper of anguish.

Sophie rolled her eyes. 'Mum, your expression is so easy to read. Nobody is going to abduct me. Would it make you feel better if I put the burglar alarm on after you've left?'

I nodded. 'Thanks, darling. I promise I won't be long.'

Outside came the sound of Alex's car engine turning over. There wasn't a second to lose. Ramming my feet into my trainers, I peered through the front door's spy glass and watched Alex's car reverse off the drive and disappear around the corner. Darting out of the house, I almost threw myself behind the wheel of my car.

The engine roared into life and, grinding the gears noisily, I lurched backwards, then screeched after my husband. I thanked God in his Heaven for the cover of dark autumn nights that cloaked my trailing vehicle. I spotted Alex ahead, and took my foot off the accelerator. If I kept him in my line of vision, there was no need to get so close. The last thing I wanted was him reading my number plate in his rear-view mirror, and my cover being blown. Better to hang back, so all he saw was a pair of headlights some distance behind.

On we drove, taking a left, then a couple of rights, out of the village and onto the main road now, heading towards Sophie's school, which was shrouded in darkness, padlocked chains around its metal gates. I wondered where we were going, my eyes firmly on the road as my mind replayed the image of Burglar Bill looking furtively at the family home and then getting out of his car, a twisted smile upon his evil face. *No, stop it, Holly. You'll send yourself mad if you keep catastrophising things that haven't even happened.* But the anxiety wouldn't go away. I shouldn't have left Sophie. Alex was right. I was a negligent mother, once again acting on impulse, never stopping to think things through, always assuming my husband was up to no good, getting ready to point the finger at him with wild accusations about meeting secret lovers… oh, hello… this route was looking extremely familiar.

We'd crossed a roundabout and taken a couple of lefts into a residential road that I'd visited a thousand times before. I slowed the car down, dropped it into second, now first gear as, ahead, Alex appeared to be scanning the pavement. I glanced in my rear-view mirror to make sure no vehicle was coming up behind me. Nonetheless, I couldn't stay like this, out in the road crawling along at three miles per hour. I found a gap and pulled over on a yellow line, my heart thudding painfully as I spotted a familiar figure standing under the glow of a street lamp. A hand came up, fluttering a wave at Alex, and his car rocked to a gentle halt. The passenger door opened, and the figure slipped inside. Moments later, Alex signalled, pulled out and accelerated off. The brake lights glowed red when the vehicle reached the end of the road, the left indicator blinking, and then the pair of them disappeared out of sight. I didn't follow. I couldn't, because suddenly my body was shaking so violently I wasn't sure my feet would stay on the pedals of my vehicle. But I'd seen enough. My husband didn't need his dental practice to conduct his out-of-hours affair. All he had to do was jump in his car and drive off to some lonely layby, recline his seats and merge with his lover. For the person getting into Alex's car had been my dear friend. Jeanie.

Chapter Thirty-Eight

In that moment, I was too shocked to cry. I simply sat in my car, not far from Jeanie's marital home, shaking like Rupert on a trip to the vet. A part of me wondered whether to take a deep breath and vibrate my way over to her front door, bang the knocker hard against its wooden panels and unburden to her husband. This wasn't just about me, after all. Ray was as much a victim in all this, except he was an unwitting one, whereas I had had my suspicions for months. My marriage had been limping along but was now in injury time. The signs had been obvious – from sexting and excuses, to scant romance and absence of physical contact. But for Ray, had there been any clues? I wasn't so sure about that. He had a wife who excused herself a couple of nights a week on the pretext of visiting the gym – nothing suspicious about that, thousands of women did it – but then returned home in high spirits, grinning manically from ear to ear as she led her husband up to their bedroom and stripped him down to his smalls. I was almost positive that Ray had no idea anything was amiss.

So should I be the one to shatter his world? Break the dreadful news that not only was his wife playing away but, right now, she was in my husband's car getting her leg over his gearstick? Would

Ray cry out with pain as I told him? Would his children rush to see what was the matter with their father? Would their faces crumple as they heard that their mother was not only betraying her best friend, but their father too? Shouldn't it be Jeanie herself sitting down, snivelling into a hankie, as she ripped her family apart? I gulped, as my own tears started to spurt from my eyes. As much as I wanted to unburden to Ray, I couldn't. Jeanie was the marriage wrecker. It was her duty to deal with the fallout, not mine.

The shaking had subsided enough for me to start the engine up. Numbness was descending over me, as if someone had given me an invisible injection, temporarily blocking the pain and allowing my brain to function enough to drive my vehicle past that group of teenagers laughing and joking as they strolled down the road, one kicking an empty beer can into the gutter. Not a care in the world for them. Just worrying whether they had enough money in their pocket to buy a few tinnies to sup with mates, and whether they might get to second base with a new girlfriend this weekend. I stopped at the traffic lights, watching a woman hasten across the pedestrian crossing, collar up against the chill night wind. What did she have to trouble her? Whether to have baked beans or mushy peas with tonight's fish and chips tea? Around me, life was going on, but I felt peculiarly detached from it all. Did the man on the motorbike in front of me have murderous thoughts screaming through his head? What about that van driver to my left? Was he sitting behind the wheel of his vehicle trying to calm an inwardly raging torrent of emotions, or was he listening to some music station and thinking about a Friday night pizza? I didn't know. And I wasn't sure how I got home without writing off the car, because whilst I went through the motions of driving it, my mind was a million miles away, and I had no recollection of the journey.

Pulling up on the driveway, it came as no surprise to discover Alex wasn't back. Struggling to compose myself for Sophie's sake, I took a steadying breath then stumbled out of the car and up to the front door. My hands were so stiff from gripping the steering wheel for the last half an hour that, for a moment or two, I couldn't get my fingers to work. Clumsily, I shook out the key fob, separating the house key from the others, then let myself into the warmth of the hall. Almost immediately there was a cacophony of sound, and I screamed loudly. Sophie erupted out of her bedroom brandishing her unplugged bedside lamp, Rupert at her heels barking hysterically. I fell against the wall, clutching my hammering heart, as Sophie darted past me and turned off the burglar alarm.

'You made me jump,' she said accusingly. 'Why didn't you phone ahead and let me know you were on your way back? Rupert, shut up, you're giving me a headache. Honestly, Mum, sometimes I think you reside on a different planet and… oh! What's the matter?' My daughter came towards me and peered at my pinched face. 'Oh God, what's happened? You look awful. Tell me! Has someone died? Mum, speak to me!'

I stared at my daughter in horror and, despite my best efforts not to, burst into a fresh round of tears. Sophie put the lamp down on the floor and threw her arms around me, hugging me tightly.

'Mum, tell me what's happened. Is it Dad? He's not with you. Has he had an accident?'

I caught the worry in her tone, and it snapped me out of the horror of the last hour.

'Dad's fine, darling,' I managed to say between sobs. 'I've left him at the surgery. He's finished with the patient and just doing a bit of paperwork.'

Sophie scrutinised me. Her father was doing paperwork at the office on a Friday night? I could see she didn't buy it.

'You're shaking. And you *never* cry. Tell me the truth. What's happened?'

I said the first thing that came into my head. 'On the way home, I ran over a fox.'

'Oh no! Did you kill him?'

I shook my head, as I thought of Alex driving off with Jeanie. 'N-no, he got away.'

'Oh, Mum. Poor you. Let me give you a hug.' My daughter once again wrestled me into her arms, squeezing me the way I used to tightly enfold her as a little girl when she'd scraped a knee. It made me cry even harder. Suddenly, and for the first time ever, my daughter was the one in the parental role.

'I-I'll be fine,' I stammered, whipping out a tissue from my sleeve and dabbing frantically at my eyes.

'You're in shock.'

'Yes.' Too bloody right.

'Come into the kitchen,' said Sophie, taking me by the arm and leading me gently, as if I was a five-year-old. 'I'll make you a nice cup of tea with lots of sugar. It's meant to be good in situations like this.'

'Thank you,' I replied, thinking that a brandy might be preferable, and no messing about with glasses, just neck it straight from the bottle. I had an overwhelming desire to pass out. Anything to make the hurt stop.

I sat hunched on one of the tall stools while my daughter busied herself filling the kettle, grabbing a mug, sniffing the milk dubiously from the fridge and ladling sugar into boiling water. At this rate I'd be drinking syrup, not tea. My body was now giving involuntary shakes, as if it couldn't quite decide whether it was cold.

'Here,' said Sophie, 'get this down you. Do you want a chocolate biscuit?'

I shook my head and glugged gratefully. The hot liquid scalded my throat and the sweetness instantly coated my teeth with a sugary film. Sophie monitored me, rather like a beady-eyed nurse, as I worked my way through the half-pint mug. Gradually the shudders ceased. I was left feeling wrung out.

'Better?' she asked, taking one of my hands in hers.

'Much,' I said, giving her a watery smile. 'You'll make a great mum one day.'

She grinned back. 'That's because I've had a great mum to teach me.'

I damn well nearly burst into tears again.

'Will you be okay if I go back to my room? Only I promised Lizzie I'd give her a call before nine o'clock. We need to sort out what we're doing tomorrow night when I have a sleepover with her. Caro has suggested we watch a film, but we're quite keen to stay in with a pile of sweets, and practise giving each other a make-over.'

'I'm fine now,' I patted her hand reassuringly, ready to take back the parenting reins from my girl who was keen to revert to teenage mode. 'You go and ring Lizzie. In fact, I might give her dear mama a call. Caro is always good at lending an ear.' I wasn't quite sure what Caro would have to say when I told her that I'd discovered exactly who our friend was having a fling with, and that her husband's jokey comment about Alex and Jeanie having an affair was an unhappy truth.

'Here,' said Sophie, handing me my mobile. 'Have a good chinwag with Caro.'

'Thanks, darling.'

My daughter skipped off, and I ran one hand wearily over my face. But before I could even tap out Caro's number, the phone dinged with a text message. I read it with disinterest and then, as horror registered, read it again.

Holly, we need to talk. Urgently.

I went cold. The text was from Ray.

Chapter Thirty-Nine

I'd barely finished re-reading the text message when my mobile exploded into life, making me jump violently and drop the damn thing. It skittered across the worktop, striking out precariously at the edge, but fortunately didn't smash to the floor below. I snatched it up.

'Hello?'

'Holly, it's Ray.'

As if I didn't know. 'Hello, Ray.'

'You sound nervous.'

'Er, yes, I am a little.'

'As well you might.' God, he sounded livid. 'I've tried ringing Alex, but he's not picking up.'

'Ah.' Well if I was Alex, I wouldn't want to pick up the phone to a husband on the warpath either.

'I take it you know what's been going on,' Ray demanded.

'I've had my suspicions.'

'How long have they been meeting like this?'

'Well I don't know for sure, but certainly since last Christmas.'

'Last *Christmas*?' Ray's voice was harsh. 'Why didn't you tell me about it?'

'How could I?'

'How could you *not*?' he spluttered.

'Sometimes ignorance is bliss,' I countered, my voice low.

'What sort of attitude is that? Actually, I'll tell you,' he spat, not waiting for me to answer. 'It's a cop-out, that's what it is.'

'I'm sorry you think that,' I said, my voice starting to quaver with emotion, 'but actually this isn't just about *you*, you know.'

'Isn't it?' he asked, sounding incredulous. 'Who else is involved?'

'Me!' I cried. 'For God's sake, Ray,' I said, aware that my tone was getting shrill, 'Jeanie has mentioned in the past that you can be insensitive but—'

'Oh she has, has she!'

'But this takes the flaming biscuit! I have feelings too, or is this just all about you?'

'You've got a cheek, Holly,' Ray growled. 'Your husband earns wads of money—'

'I beg your pardon?' Good heavens, was he already jumping down the divorce route, thinking about settlements, pointing out I'd be all right because of what my husband earned?

'And you work part-time for Alex, no doubt at a hugely inflated salary thanks to your name being down as a Company Secretary, or some such fancy wording. The pair of you are rolling in clover, but in *this* household, it's just the one person working.'

Oh my God, he really was only interested in the financial side of it all. Never mind about broken hearts, or his children's devastation that their parents would be separating. For Ray, it all boiled down to money, and the fact that he was going to be out of pocket when he had to give half the house to Jeanie.

'I must say, Ray, I don't care for your attitude at all. I thought you might be just a tiny bit compassionate about *my* feelings in all this.' My voice wobbled alarmingly and once again I found my eyes filling up.

'Don't try and pull the overflowing tear-duct trick on me,' he sneered. 'I've already got Jeanie here trying to defend her actions.'

'Jeanie's home?' I asked, deeply shocked.

'Yes. She has been for the last ten minutes, frantically trying to plead with me and make me understand there were good reasons why she did it.'

'Good reasons?' I repeated, my gaze falling upon the riot of tiny dots within the granite worktop, the odd one glittering underneath the kitchen spotlights. What the hell was Ray talking about?

'Don't play dumb, Holly. You know perfectly well that Jeanie has been meeting Alex secretly.'

'Y-yes,' I stammered. That much was true. But I wasn't quite sure how my treacherous friend was trying to blag her way out of things by saying it was justified. At that moment I heard Alex's key in the front door.

'I want a word with that chuffing husband of yours. Is he home yet?'

As Alex came into the kitchen, I looked at him with narrowed eyes. 'Yes, he's literally just walked in.'

'Put him on the phone, Holly. Now!'

'My pleasure,' I said sarcastically, before rounding on my husband. 'Guess who wants to speak to you?' I enquired sweetly. 'Ray. He wants some questions answered. And frankly, so do I.' Alex scowled, and held out a hand for the phone. Angered, I slapped the mobile into his palm, then folded my arms across my chest. All I needed was a rolling pin and hair-rollers, and I'd look like Andy Capp's wife.

'Ray!' Alex barked. 'Was there really a need to ring my wife? I'd have been more than happy to have talked directly to you. I see. Well, to answer your question, yes I have been seeing Jeanie.' What a good thing I wasn't armed with that rolling pin otherwise I might have physically struck Alex. 'Your wife has paid me a total of one thousand pounds.'

Pardon?

'Yes, I agree Jeanie shouldn't have gone behind your back, but surely you want your daughter to have a smile she's not self-conscious about? The other guy she saw wasn't prepared to do anything about it. My treatment is in Charlotte's best interests. Okay, I'm sorry you feel that way, but I gave Jeanie a discount of two thousand pounds as a favour, and frankly I don't need to listen to your stream of invective. Goodbye.' Alex disconnected the call and handed me back the mobile. 'Blasted man. You try and do someone a favour and it just comes back to bite you on the bum.'

'Alex, where have you been?'

'Isn't it obvious?' he huffed. 'I've been with Jeanie. This month's instalment on Charlotte's brace was due.'

Charlotte's brace. Yes, Jeanie had told me as such at my dinner party. But how long did it take to pick up an instalment?

'You've been gone ages,' I said carefully. I didn't want to make accusations if there was a genuine reason for Jeanie and Alex meeting, but nonetheless my husband had been gone for over two hours.

'I can tell the time, Holly,' my husband snapped, his tone now one of irritation. 'I made a private arrangement with Jeanie to treat her daughter with an orthodontic brace. She didn't want Ray knowing about it, because he'd already said no to Charlotte having the treatment. I warned Jeanie at our dinner party that secrets have a horrible way of coming out.'

I listened intently, as the pennies rolled around in my brain, clattering into place one by one. 'I drove over to Jeanie to collect this month's instalment for Charlotte's treatment, but Jeanie texted me ahead saying Ray was home early and to meet her further up the road. She was bawling, so I told her to get in the car and took her for a quick drink. She said Ray had seen their bank statement and was questioning why they were overdrawn.'

'Oh,' I said.

'Oh indeed,' Alex sighed. 'Anyway, what's the matter with you? You look like you've been crying.'

I stared at my husband, wide-eyed. There was a perfectly plausible explanation for him being with Jeanie. He wasn't having an affair with my friend. The relief was so enormous I thought I might faint. Adrenalin was whooshing around my body. This wasn't good. I seemed to be in constant fight-or-flight mode, with my whole being overreacting. One minute I was in tears, the next I was accusing my husband of all sorts and behaving atrociously – from stalking Facebook folk like Annabelle, to shadowing my husband in my car. Was I going mad? I let out a whimper.

'Well have you?' asked Alex.

'No,' I lied. 'I'm just tired.'

'You look it,' said Alex, his tone gentler this time. 'Would you like me to make you a cup of tea?'

'Please,' I said, thinking I'd be swimming in tea at this rate. Suddenly I felt ashamed at the way I'd been carrying on. Thank God

Alex hadn't spotted me earlier in his rear-view mirror. I offered up another prayer of thanks that I hadn't blurted anything about an affair to Ray. I closed my eyes for a moment. That had been a close call. Too close. It was quite obvious I was losing the plot. Maybe even going mad. I needed to see my GP. Ask for some antidepressants, or something. Maybe have counselling. Cognitive Brain Therapy, or whatever it was called.

'Here,' said Alex, putting a steaming mug in front of me.

'Thanks,' I murmured. On impulse, I leaped off the stool and flung my arms around his neck.

'Steady,' he said, as I nearly sent him flying backwards. 'It's only a cup of tea I've given you, not diamonds.'

I let out a shaky laugh. 'I need a hug,' I said, my words muffling against his shoulder.

He patted me on the back, a bit like one would burp a baby, then gently disengaged himself. 'I'm a bit tired, Holly,' he said, by way of explanation.

Immediately my spirits sank. Being too tired for sex was one thing, but since when was a husband too tired to give his wife a hug?

Chapter Forty

The following morning, when I was putting the breakfast plates in the dishwasher, the telephone rang.

'Hello?'

'Holly, it's me,' said a subdued voice.

I paused, mid-stack. 'Jeanie, hi. How are you?'

'Feeling wretched,' she sighed. 'I've rung to apologise for my husband being so rude to you and Alex last night.'

'Shouldn't he be the one to do that?' I said lightly.

'Yes, except he's a pig-headed, stubborn-minded, idiotic—'

'I get the picture,' I interrupted. 'So where is Mr Angry this morning?'

'Out. Don't ask where, because I don't know. We're not talking. He's still livid about me paying for Charlotte's orthodontics behind his back, plus lying to him that it was being done on the NHS, rather than privately with Alex.'

'Well, never mind,' I sighed. 'What's done is done. I'm sure things will blow over.'

'I'm sorry you got roped into it, Holly.'

'No worries. Alex and I had our own exchange of words last night, culminating in him removing himself from the dinner table and taking himself off for a drive. I did wonder, at the time, where he was going.'

'Oh?' she said, curiosity piqued. 'I didn't think Mr and Mrs Perfect ever rowed.'

'We're not Mr and Mrs Perfect,' I said, slightly irritated. 'And we hadn't *rowed*, as such. It was more… a difference of opinion.'

'About what? Tell me, Holly. I like to know other couples have "a difference of opinion" and it's not just me and Ray currently at loggerheads.'

'I can't really talk,' I said, lowering my voice, and glancing beyond the kitchen door to make sure Alex wasn't hovering. I was pretty sure he was in his usual Saturday-morning repose – horizontal on the sofa in front of a sports channel. 'It was something and nothing,' I murmured into the handset. 'He took umbrage about a comment I made regarding one of his colleagues involved with the trigeminal neuralgia charity. It didn't go down too well.'

'Ah. Yes, never ridicule or complain about their stuffy male friends, even if they are the most boring farts on the planet.'

'Except this particular friend is female, very beautiful, and has probably never farted in her life – or if she has, it's most likely puffs of glitter.'

Jeanie giggled and I joined in. Oh the relief that my dear friend wasn't having an affair with my husband! I abandoned the dishwasher and, handset clamped to one ear, walked off to the study. Grabbing a biro from the pen pot, I flicked through my desk diary and turned to the upcoming page for Monday. The ink flew across the paper. *Make an appointment to see GP regarding rampant imagination and discuss counselling!* I chucked the pen down on the page and returned to the kitchen.

'Are you still seeing you-know-who?' I whispered.

At the other end of the phone there was a pause. When Jeanie next spoke, it was to address her daughter.

'Charlotte, you've left the fridge door open… Well if you don't close it, things will go off! It's a perfectly reasonable request to ask you to shut the—'

There was the sound of an almighty bang and my handset positively reverberated from the noise. I gathered Charlotte had slammed the kitchen door in Jeanie's face. Nice to know it wasn't just my teenager who was partial to rocking wooden panels off their hinges.

'That girl!' Jeanie hissed. 'Honestly, where's the gratitude?'

'So, now the door is shut – to both the fridge and the kitchen – you can answer my question,' I prompted.

Jeanie heaved a sigh that sounded like it was coming from the very foundations of her house. 'If you must know, we've decided to try and stop seeing each other.'

'Try?' I queried.

'He's intoxicating, Holly. But, yes, I'm definitely going to try and stay away from him, and he has said the same thing about me.'

'Good. I'm sure you're both doing the right thing,' I said. 'So, given that you've both made this decision, can you now tell me who he is?'

'No, Holly,' Jeanie's reply was both instant and adamant. 'I haven't told Caro either, so don't be miffed. It's better this way. Some secrets must be exactly that. Secrets.'

I privately conceded that Jeanie had a point. After all, Caro had already been careless in a drunken moment and told David about Jeanie's infidelity, and I'd done the same with Alex.

'When did you both make the decision to stay away from each other?' I asked.

'Last night.'

The doorbell interrupted our conversation. I knew Alex wouldn't get up to answer it, so padded through to the hallway with the phone still to one ear.

'Someone's at the door, Jeanie. I'd better go. We'll catch up next week.'

'Sure. Oh, and enjoy your dinner-dance. It's tonight, isn't it?'

'Yes,' I grimaced. Today was the day I was going to transform myself into The Most Amazing-Looking Woman in Great Britain. Well, one could hope. 'See you soon. Bye.' I hung up, and then opened the door. Ray was standing on the doorstep, and looking sheepish.

'I'm not stopping,' he said gruffly. 'I've been driving around, getting my head together, cooling off after my ding-dong with Jeanie. I found myself in your road, so thought I'd do the decent thing and apologise for my outburst last night.'

'Apology accepted,' I said. 'We all say things in the heat of the moment, and I can appreciate you were cheesed off about the deception.'

Ray nodded. 'It's not too big a deal really. I'll do some overtime to get the bank balance back into the black. We're not *that* over-drawn. I panicked and overreacted. Jeanie's been quite canny with the housekeeping, although I was starting to wonder why we were eating so much beans on toast,' he said, attempting to joke.

'Would you like to come in for a coffee?'

'Thanks, Holly, but I won't. Is Alex in? It's only right I should see him too.'

'Sure, I'll get him for you.'

Alex was initially prickly with Ray, and I decided to leave the two men alone to smooth their respective ruffled feathers. I wandered back into the kitchen to finish stacking the dishwasher, listening to the odd word float after me as both men chatted about misunderstandings and wanting to clear the air. I still had the telephone in my hand after talking to Jeanie. I popped it back on its base and stooped to resume stacking the dishwasher. But as I slotted a plate into the rack, I froze. Suddenly I was rewinding the conversation with Jeanie. She'd said that she and her lover were going to stop seeing each other. And she'd also said that the two of them had made that decision *last night*.

Last night, she'd been with Alex.

Chapter Forty-One

'You look nice,' said Alex, as he slipped on his dinner jacket and stood back to admire himself in the full-length bedroom mirror.

'Thank you,' I said. Three hours of exfoliating, tweezing, blow-drying, curling, manicuring and following one of Sophie's recommended beauty vloggers on how to apply evening make-up, all for the lukewarm compliment of 'nice'. Such a bland word.

'So do you,' I added.

'So do I what?' asked Alex.

'Look nice.'

'I was hoping you might say dashing and handsome,' Alex replied, adjusting his dickie bow and preening at his reflection.

I didn't respond. It was taking every ounce of effort on my part not to start a full-scale row after Jeanie had disclosed chatting to her lover last night, and 'trying' to stop the affair. I now realised that both Jeanie and Alex had given ridiculous excuses for their meeting. If such a rendezvous had truly been to hand over a payment towards Charlotte's secret orthodontics treatment, then why hadn't Jeanie just given me the money to pass on to Alex the last time we'd had coffee together? 'Shh, Holly. Don't tell Ray, because he doesn't know I've been raiding the housekeeping, but make sure you give this envelope to Alex, please. There's one hundred quid inside.' Their excuses were so rotten, they stank. And Ray was just as big a fool as me for not spotting it.

'You're looking very po-faced,' said Alex, turning away from the mirror. 'What's up?'

I gave my newly tonged curls a quick spritz of hairspray and prayed they wouldn't drop, then reached for my evening bag.

'Nothing's up,' I snapped, instantly thinking of Jeanie again, who'd recently bragged that a certain part of her lover's anatomy was always up. Up and up and awayyy, as her tingling fanny exploded into a climax of shooting stars, rockets and intergalactic, orgasmic—

'Are you sure you're okay?' Alex frowned. 'You were grimacing just then. As if in pain.'

Oh I was in pain, all right. But it wasn't physical. It was emotional. A terrible gnawing ache swooshing around my body, as if it had taken up residence in my circulatory system.

'I told you,' I scowled, 'I'm fine.'

'If you say so,' Alex replied, sounding peeved. He followed me out of the bedroom and down the stairs. 'By the way, it would have been nice if Sophie had bothered to say goodbye to me before going off to Caro's. Our daughter's manners seem to be on the poor side an awful lot these days.'

'She did say goodbye,' I said defensively, 'but you were flat out on the sofa in front of the telly. It's not her fault you were fast asleep.'

'Okay, no need to get narky.' Alex raised his hands in a gesture of surrender. 'I can't help it if my job knackers me out.'

'*Some*thing certainly knackers you out,' I said caustically, 'or should I say some*one*?'

'One or two of my patients are very demanding,' Alex agreed.

'Yes, I had heard,' I replied, the lid lifting slightly on my simmering anger. 'A little bird told me you're going to *try* and refrain from such demands. Awfully good of you both.'

'I have no idea what you're wittering on about,' said Alex, sitting himself down on the bottom step of the staircase and slipping on his shoes. He leaned forward to do up the laces. 'Are you putting Rupert out for a last wee, or shall I?'

'I'll do it,' I said sweetly. 'You conserve your energy for tying both your shoelaces and self into knots.'

I walked off in a cloud of perfume, Rupert at my heels, and opened the back door. A gust of wind blew in, raising goose bumps on my bare arms. I was wearing the slinky long black evening dress I'd bought to wear to Alex's surprise birthday party next Saturday. It was a shame he'd see me in it twice in as many weeks, but then again, after his earlier tepid compliment, would he even notice? The dress's front panel blew out slightly as another cold draught curled around my legs, separating the split that went nearly all the way up to my pants. I'd be flashing a lot of flesh tonight. Good. I wanted other men to stop and stare, and Alex to be proud and say to whoever he was talking to, 'The woman over there who's turning so many heads, you say? Yes, of course I know her. She's my wife.'

Rupert hopped back in, and I locked the door. He clambered into his basket with the sigh of one who had the weight of his owners' problems on his hairy shoulders. Perhaps he noticed the atmosphere in this house sometimes and didn't like it. I paused to consider him for a moment. He *did* look sad.

Alex appeared in the kitchen doorway. 'Can you stop prevaricating. The minicab is here.'

'Hang on a minute. I'm worried about Rupert.'

'Why, what's wrong with him?'

'He looks depressed.'

'Don't be ridiculous,' Alex tutted. 'Give him a chew, and then get your coat on. I don't want us being late.'

I went to the cupboard under the sink and pulled out a plastic container full of doggy treats. Rupert instantly bounced out of his basket, ears up, eyes alight, tail beating a tattoo against the floor.

'You old fraud,' I said, as he gently took the dental stick from my hand. But then again, he wasn't the only one good at deception in this household.

When we arrived at the venue, Jack was already there. Alex was immediately waylaid by one of the portly trustees, leaving me to greet Jack on my own. As he kissed me on both cheeks, my stomach did an enormous flip-flop. He was looking impossibly handsome in his tuxedo, like someone out of a James Bond movie.

'You look stunning, Holly,' he said, appreciatively eyeing my dress's side splits. 'You'll be upstaging the celebrity they've booked to draw the raffle later.'

'Give over,' I said, blushing with delight.

'I hear it's Harriet Montgomery.'

'You hear correct,' said Alex, coming over and shaking Jack's hand. 'Harriet is on the verge of a massive comeback. We're very lucky to have her here tonight. Let's have a drink, Jack, while we're waiting for your plus-one to arrive. I've just had a message that there was a mix-up with the taxi firm, but her car is now on its way.'

'No problem,' said Jack. 'I'm sure your lovely wife will look after me until she arrives.'

'Of course,' said Alex, signalling to one of the waiters who was circulating with a silver tray loaded with champagne.

The waiter glided over, inclining his head respectfully, as if we were royalty. We took our drinks and thanked him, and he reversed away, almost bowing and scraping. Alex spotted somebody of importance and excused himself.

'Oh good, I have you all to myself,' said Jack lightly. His eyes twinkled as they met mine. I nearly fainted. 'Here's to a lovely evening,' he raised his glass, 'and, indeed, all lovely things.'

Oh my God, was he flirting?

'Y-yes,' I nodded, 'lovely... lovelies.'

I took a greedy sip. Well, glug, actually. *Steady, Holly. You don't want to get disastrously pissed and show him your caesarean scar, do you?*

The reception area was filling up with hundreds of tuxes and glittery evening gowns. And to think I'd been boycotting events like this! I took another sip of champagne and reflected. I was pretty damn sure Alex had hugely played down these occasions, making them out to be very dull and full of old fogeys with dandruff over their dinner jackets. Across the room, I could hear Alex poshing up his accent as he haw-haw-hawed with Sir Digby Something-or-Other, a revered patron of the organisation.

'How's the book coming along?' I asked Jack.

'Brilliantly,' he smiled. 'But never mind that. What have you been up to since your thoroughly entertaining dinner party?' He was doing that thing again with his eyes. Twinkling.

'Oh, nothing much,' I shrugged. 'Just a two-day stint at Alex's practice, and then—'

I paused, taking care over what I wanted to say. How exactly *did* one describe feeling like you were going mad as you lurched from doubt to suspicion regarding your husband and best friend pulling a fast one?

'—being very busy wasting a lot of time,' I concluded vaguely, and gave a little laugh. It came out sounding horribly brittle.

'Is something troubling you?' asked Jack. 'I can't help noticing that whenever I see you, you always look so sad.'

Embarrassed, I necked the rest of my champagne and grabbed another from a circulating waiter.

'Well,' I blustered, 'not so much sad, probably more mad.' I nodded my head. 'After all, I'm the mother of a teenager who has quite a lot of surly moments.'

Jack smiled. 'And the sister of a brother who loves to wind you up.'

'Well, quite!' I nodded, gulping down more champagne. 'Simon loves nothing more than making jokes at the expense of others.' Absent-mindedly I ran one hand along my chin, making sure the little hair he'd teased me about was not, even now, sticking out. My brother would have me believe that I had rogue hairs so long they trailed across the ground tripping everyone up.

'And,' continued Jack, softly, 'let's not forget the husband who barely notices you.'

My glass, en route to my mouth, froze mid-air. I couldn't quite believe what Jack had just said. Did I truly look sad all the time? And was it really so glaringly obvious to others that I had a husband so disinterested in me? But before I could deny such a statement, the man himself was bearing down upon us with Annabelle Huntingdon-Smyth on his arm. My heart sank. She was holding on to Alex in a very proprietorial way. I saw the heads turning, as I'd rather hoped they might for me, thus making Alex so proud. Instead, as he bore Annabelle across the room, quietly acknowledging the waves of envy directed at him, he looked like the cat who'd discovered the stolen milk was ice cream with a 99 Flake stuck in the middle.

'Jack,' said Alex, all smiles, 'I'm so sorry to have left you alone with Holly. You must have been bored to tears.' I opened my mouth to say something, but then shut it again and went bright red. How acutely embarrassing. And probably true. I *had* been boring, talking about my daughter's moods and my brother's iffy banter. Jack was a neurosurgeon attending a related charity event, for goodness' sake. I should have been attempting to make intelligent conversation about... about... cranial stuff. *No, Holly, not 'stuff'! Don't you remember how scathing Alex was the last time you used that word?* I stared at the floor, wishing it would open up and swallow me. I shouldn't have come. Alex would have been much better holding court with the intellectual Annabelle.

'She's here at last!' Alex was saying, his mood jocular. 'Let me introduce the two of you without further ado. Jack, this is—'

'I know who she is,' Jack interrupted.

My head snapped up just in time to see Jack looking politely at Annabelle who, it had to be said, was staring at Jack as if he had leprosy. Her lip curled into a sneer.

'Well look who it is,' she mocked.

Alex's face, previously wreathed in smiles, was swiftly transforming into an expression of bewilderment. 'Have you two met?'

'Indeed,' said Jack pleasantly. 'Annabelle is my ex-fiancé.'

Chapter Forty-Two

As the four of us stood in our little group, it seemed as though the background noise and crowd receded at warp speed leaving us in our own private bubble. For a moment nobody spoke. The undercurrents were whizzing around, like orbiting electrons with us as the nucleus.

'How are you, Annabelle?' said Jack, eventually.

His tone was so devoid of emotion he could have been talking to Aunty Shirley, rather than a woman he was once, presumably, passionately in love with. I looked from his face to hers. Jack's expression was benign, but Annabelle's features had contorted into one of pure rage. She reminded me of Rupert when he was squaring up to another dog. All peeled-back lips and bared teeth. A sneaky look at my husband revealed a shell-shocked expression that conveyed he was a little put out that the luscious Annabelle had ever consorted with Jack.

'How am I?' Annabelle hissed. 'How *am* I?' she repeated, this time sounding incredulous. 'How the hell do you *think* I am?' This last sentence was delivered at increased volume causing heads to turn, this time out of nosiness rather than admiration.

'I have no idea,' said Jack mildly, 'otherwise I wouldn't have asked.'

'You went off to Africa without me!' she said, her tone now one of accusation.

'You were invited to come along.'

'I didn't want to go.'

'Evidently.'

'You should have abandoned the trip and put me first.'

'It was work, Annabelle. Not a holiday.'

'You could have taken a different job. I'd have done it for you,' she said bitterly.

'I wanted to help people elsewhere in the world. A golden opportunity arose. It wasn't forever. As you can see, I'm back.'

'Well don't expect to crook your finger and have me come running. Because it won't happen.'

'I wouldn't dream of it,' said Jack pleasantly.

'Anyway, I'm with someone else now,' her eyes flicked briefly to Alex, and the action wasn't lost on me.

'In which case I'm very happy for you. Presumably the gentleman isn't here, or he would have been able to accompany you tonight?'

Annabelle's eyes flicked to Alex again, but this time he didn't catch her look and appeared to be discreetly studying his fingernails. My inner antenna roared into life. It was now swivelling about, on red alert, watching body language, listening for clues.

'The gentleman can't accompany me because…' she paused, as if thinking how best to answer Jack's question. 'It's complicated,' she concluded.

I gulped. So… so she wasn't actually *denying* her man was here, just answering evasively. Stating that the romantic situation was difficult. Which, of course, it was. I already knew that her lover was a married man. And, of course, if that man were Alex it would indeed be doubly complex. Her man was here, but not *with* her. As such. Seemingly, Jack was alive to Annabelle's caginess.

'Yes, it's always complicated when we love someone who is married to someone else,' he said smoothly.

Too flipping right. My brain was working overtime here. Did my husband have two lovers? Or was I going doubly mad?

Annabelle's eyes narrowed, and she was about to reply when Sir Digby walked over to our little group and tapped Annabelle on the arm. Immediately the background noise roared into life and the crowd zoomed back into focus.

'Annabelle, darling,' said Sir Digby, 'our celebrity is here. I'd love to introduce you before we go in to dinner.'

'Of course,' said Annabelle, finally letting go of Alex's arm and instead accepting Sir Digby's proffered elbow. She turned and walked away without a backward glance.

'Well.' Alex blew out his cheeks, evidently rattled.

'Well, well, well,' said Jack dryly. 'That will teach me to ask the name, in future, of anyone you team me up with, Alex.'

Alex was looking at Jack like one might regard a piece of dog poo on the bottom of a shoe.

'This puts a very different complexion on things,' he said. 'Annabelle looked absolutely shattered to see you, Jack. Forgive me, but as a long-standing supporter of this charity, her feelings come before yours. Therefore, for the rest of the evening, I would ask that you permit Holly to partner you, and I shall look after Annabelle. I will ask Sir Digby to take care of adjusting the seating arrangements.'

I opened my mouth to protest, but then shut it again. It was the perfect excuse for Alex to spend the entire evening with Annabelle, seemingly coming to her rescue like a knight in shining armour – albeit without the bloody horse. I glared at him, but he avoided my gaze.

'I hope you don't get too fed up with Holly's company,' said my husband, reminding me that I had nothing of interest to contribute to conversation or, indeed, this evening, 'but I will endeavour to rescue you wherever I can.' And with that Alex hastened after Annabelle and Sir Digby, leaving me once again with flaming cheeks and feeling totally inadequate. As I watched my husband disappear through the throng, I turned to Jack apologetically.

'This isn't turning into a very good evening for you,' I murmured.

'I disagree,' said Jack. 'I now have the most beautiful woman in the room all to myself.'

I reddened a bit more, but out of embarrassment. It was obvious he had only said that to make me feel better, especially after my husband had let it be known that poor Jack was now saddled with a mind-numbingly boring woman.

'Um,' I said, uncertain what to say next, so terrified was I of making tedious conversation. 'Look, if you don't want to talk to me, I'll quite understand. In fact, I'm happy to take a taxi home and let you circulate without me hampering you. I'm clueless about trigeminal neuralgia and brain surgery – don't know the frontal lobe from my elbow – so you mustn't be afraid to say so.'

Suddenly one of Jack's hands was reaching for mine. A warm palm folded around my fingers. It was so unexpected, and so totally electrifying, I nearly shot out of my stilettos.

'Holly,' he said, his face deadly serious, 'I meant what I said. Every single word.'

As my hand fizzed and popped within his, I looked at him. Properly. Searched his face for truth and saw it shine out from his eyes. There were no twinkles right now, just absolute sincerity. I gulped, suddenly tongue-tied, and was relieved when Sir Digby interrupted everyone, speaking into a hand-held microphone, welcoming all, and inviting them to take their seats for dinner.

From this point on the evening became pleasantly blurry around the edges. I'd drunk a couple of champagnes on an empty stomach and was feeling nicely fuzzy, a sensation I clung to. It helped me forget that my husband might as well have nominated me for an award of *Most Boring Person in the Universe*. I didn't want to think about that, or Annabelle hanging onto my husband's arm, or her 'complicated' relationship, or ponder who the hell her lover was. Circumstances had pushed Jack and me together for the next few hours, and as he was so charming, witty and attentive, I'd make the most of it. The fact that he was sex on legs was the icing on the cake of good company.

As we sat at our table, we were duty-bound to make small talk with those around us but, bit by bit, the lights dimmed on the crowd so that it felt as though the two of us were in our own spotlight of a moment. We'd discussed everything and nothing, including childhood memories. His parents and mine had sometimes got together and we'd all set off to the coast on sunny Sundays, catching minnows in fishing nets and pointing out tiny crabs in rock pools, Jack always a bit weedy and puny back then, and me – tall for my age – towering over him, whilst Simon minced about in the shallows.

Yes, even then my brother had been a mincer. Nobody was surprised when he came out at fourteen. The conversation progressed to the awkward teens and, eventually, dating.

'So, you and Annabelle?' I asked nosily. 'How did you meet?'

'She was a patient,' Jack smiled.

I raised an eyebrow. 'I didn't think doctors could date their patients.'

'Let me rephrase that. She was *once* a patient. She was referred to me via a consultant. I was the surgeon who performed her micro-vascular decompression at London's Wellington Hospital.'

'Good heavens.'

'The op went well, she was duly discharged, and that was that. But I bumped into her about eighteen months later, quite by chance, at The Royal London where I was doing skull base surgery and neural oncology. We just happened to be in a lift together, and she recognised me. Annabelle was there visiting a friend who'd had her appendix out and said how very grateful she was to me for changing the quality of her life. She asked if I was available for coffee. I was no longer her doctor, she was no longer my patient, and a considerable time had elapsed in accordance with the updated doctors' handbook. It's called "Good Medical Practice", if you're interested.'

I wasn't. I just wanted to hear how they'd met and become romantically involved.

'Patient groups,' Jack continued, 'welcomed the change, saying it was about time the watchdog moved into the twenty-first century, so I thought, why not accept her invitation? She was very attractive, so we went for coffee.'

'Splendid,' I said, trying to keep the sour note out of my voice. I could imagine Jack and Annabelle together. Her, beautiful and glamorous. Him, handsome and swoon-makingly swoon-making. I was swooning quite a bit myself now and sat up straighter in case I swooned across the short distance between us and nosedived into his groin.

'The coffee turned into dinner, which led to a date, and then another one, and suddenly she'd moved in with me and proposed marriage.'

'*She* proposed?'

Jack laughed. 'Yes, welcome to modern times, Holly. I do believe there are women out there who are prepared to go down on one knee.'

'Wow. So, you were all set to live happily ever after. What went wrong?'

Jack paused. He was too much of a gentleman to rubbish his ex-fiancée, that much was clear.

'Annabelle might be pretty, but she's also extremely high maintenance.'

Oh good. I was keen to get off the bit about Annabelle's gorgeous-ness and far more eager to hear about her not-so-attractive side.

'She has a huge circle of friends, all frightfully well connected, from society types to influences with royalty. She'd think nothing of demanding I cancel a patient's operation to attend a garden party at Buck House, which I simply wouldn't do. It caused terrible rows. A surgeon's life doesn't blend well with a fiancée endlessly on the social circuit and enjoying the party life. In the beginning, I did my best to join in, but excusing yourself at ten o'clock at night because of operating the following morning and needing your eight hours' kip didn't go down too well. She was a bit of a diva.'

I could imagine only too well Annabelle stamping one Loubou-tin-shod foot at not getting her own way over spending the weekend at Lord and Lady La-de-da's country pile, rubbing shoulder pads with the local gentry.

'Anyway, I knew things weren't working, and rather hoped Annabelle would call time on our relationship.'

'Why didn't you end it?'

'She's terribly proud – she'd have been devastated telling people I'd called off the engagement, that she'd been dumped. Much better for her to be seen as the one in the driving seat, the one to do the dumping. When the post came along in Africa, I jumped at the chance, knowing full well Annabelle would be horrified. No way on earth would she give up her weekly nail appointments, regular highlights at a top London salon, or the hot-yoga classes. It was my escape route from the relationship, and I grabbed it with both hands. She threw the ring at me, but then scrabbled about on the floor to reclaim it saying she'd be buggered if she didn't get some money for it, and I went off to Heathrow Airport heaving huge sighs of relief. I stayed away long enough for her to meet someone else and for her to move on with her life.'

'And now you're back.'

'Now I'm back,' he acknowledged, his eyes locking on mine.

He was playing havoc with my heart which, one way or another, was getting a very good work-out right now, both from the chemistry with Jack, and the anxiety over Annabelle and my husband cosying up together. I could see Alex in my peripheral vision across the room, his arm slung casually along the back of Annabelle's chair. They looked for all the world like a couple. And indeed, after rousing speeches from Sir Digby, Annabelle, and actress Harriet Montgomery, it seemed only natural that my husband should take

Annabelle in his arms and whirl her around the dance floor. I'd had no idea my husband could waltz. What else didn't I know about him?

'Shall we?' said Jack, standing up and holding out one hand.

'I'd be delighted,' I twinkled. Oh yes, he wasn't the only one with the monopoly on gleaming eyeballs. Mine were positively shining as he led me onto the dance floor. And there we stayed, pausing for the occasional champagne refill, before the music switched to smoochy songs.

Annabelle was now draped over my husband like a limpet, arms tight around his neck, cheek against his. I should have been astonished that Alex hadn't signalled to a fellow mate to look after Annabelle so he could at least have one dance with his wife, but strangely I didn't care. Instead I was quite happy being held in Jack's arms – arms that felt peculiarly right as they gently wrapped around my body. I even dared to copy Annabelle and let my head rest against Jack's shoulder. I wasn't tall enough to do the cheek-to-cheek thing, but this was very nice. Very nice indeed. And it got even nicer when I felt Jack gently drop a kiss on my head. It was so soft that at first, I thought I'd been mistaken, but my body was telling me otherwise, revving up like a car starved of petrol for so long, feeling fuel rush along its injectors, roaring the engine into life. Any moment now I'd be saying *brmmm brmmm*. I recognised that I was tipsy enough to have dropped my guard, and a little voice in my head cautioned me not to embarrass myself. The last thing Jack needed was Alex's wife untying that dickie bow with her teeth, leading him over to one of the tables, tumbling him backwards amongst the discarded china, and snogging him senseless.

'I need to visit the restroom,' I gasped and, not waiting for an answer, broke away, hastening towards the big double doors, then out of the charity's suite, back through the foyer, around the corner to the ladies' by that huge potted palm and… oh! I skidded to a halt, heart clamouring unpleasantly now as I took in the couple doing their damnedest to blend in amongst the fronds.

'I can't take any more,' the woman was sobbing into the man's dinner jacket. Her head was buried in his shoulder, and his arms were firmly around her narrow waist, pulling her tight against his body. 'Why can't she be the one to leave?' the woman cried. 'I just want her gone so I can live my life without all this ducking and diving.'

I gulped, and held on to my evening bag tightly, as if it were a lifebelt in a choppy sea. I could only presume the weeping woman was talking about me, wishing I'd leave my husband, for the couple in front of my astonished eyes were Annabelle and Alex.

Chapter Forty-Three

I awoke on Sunday morning feeling sick. And it wasn't just from the mild hangover pulsing behind my eyes. I felt sick from the suspicion that my husband was having an affair with not one but two women. My God, he certainly knew how to spread himself about. Did the weeping Annabelle, who had asked why I wouldn't do the decent thing and leave my husband, have any idea that even if I did go, she'd still have somebody else vying for his attention? That other woman, of course, being my best friend Jeanie.

I felt numb. Shattered. Disbelieving. Hurt. Angry. And any other word you can think of to describe yet another duplicity. My mind conjured up several possible scenarios on how to deal with my husband, from reclaiming last night's stilettos and stamping all over his privates whilst he was asleep in bed, to walloping him with the frying pan while he tucked into his morning bacon and eggs. Equally, I veered from those emotions to wanting to fall at his feet and beg him to end both relationships, even wondering if we could sell up and start afresh elsewhere. Put the past behind us. I would be willing to do that. I'd do anything to save my marriage. I wanted my daughter to grow up with two parents. I wanted my husband to love me again, as I loved him.

Although now, with yet another calamity, I was also starting to dislike Alex too. And then I chastised myself. How could I not like my own husband? The fact that I was so desperate to stay married to him surely proved that not to be the case. *Really?* argued the little voice in my head. *And what exactly is so lovable about a man who puts you down in public, gets his rocks off over sexting, and shags two different women with a – very occasional – third thrown into the mix? A man who looks down his nose at your friends, deeming them never quite as classy as his, and can't stand your own brother visiting?* When put like that, it made me wonder. Certainly, Alex had done nothing of late to endear himself. So why was I hanging on so tightly to this marriage? Was it because – as Alex had said only the other week – we had a comfortable life together? That rocking the financial boat would simply cause further upset? Well, the latter wouldn't be so awful for me, but definitely less agreeable for him. If we went down the divorce route, he'd lose half his treasured pension for a kick-off.

I couldn't think straight. Not with this champagne-induced headache. My mind lurched back to last night. From the moment I'd been seated with Jack, everything had felt magical. Even now, as I cleared away the breakfast detritus, I could remember the touch of his hands on my back as we danced. The warmth of his breath against my skin. The kiss that he'd dropped on my head. I paused, and gripped the breakfast table, as the memory zinged through my body, lighting my innards up like the National Grid. Flipping heck, that had been a bit daring hadn't it? Kissing me like that in front of Alex? But then again, perhaps I was getting ahead of myself. Jack was an old friend from childhood days. Maybe it was perfectly permissible to lightly brush one's lips against a female friend's hair in such a situation. I tried to imagine Simon doing the same. Despite our love-hate relationship, when he was being charming and caring, I *could* imagine him doing such a thing, and it would be nothing more than brotherly affection. But… oh. I contemplated the salt and pepper pots with disappointment. Jack's kiss had been nothing more than that. A bit of 'brotherly' affection. You fool, Holly.

I pressed my mouth into a thin line as the realisation dawned. *You read it wrong, Holly. Too much drink, and too much time spent with a gorgeous guy who was, remember, simply looking after you because his plus-one wouldn't have anything to do with him.* There was no imagined lust. Well, plenty on my part, but not on Jack's. And the only reason I'd felt my loins twanging was because my own husband was neglecting me not just physically, but mentally and emotionally too.

I slipped on my yellow rubber gloves, grabbed a cloth and began energetically wiping down all the kitchen surfaces. I didn't know what to do. Many a woman would shriek, 'LEAVE THE TWO-TIMING BASTARD!' But the simple truth was, I was too scared to do it. So, it was a case of shut up and put up. *For now*, I told myself, as I began stacking plates in the dishwasher. *Just for now.* Best not to get on the internet looking up Family Law solicitors when the hangover headache was threatening to renew its efforts. Maybe wait until after Christmas, depending on whether we came to blows over the turkey in front of our combined families…? I poured myself a glass of water and downed it swiftly, just as Alex came into the kitchen. He had his jacket on.

'I'm popping out,' he said.

'Oh,' I replied, my brain whirring. Where was he going? For a Sunday bonk in the car with Jeanie? Or to meet Annabelle for a party post-mortem? 'Where are you off to?'

'Bluewater. I want to get myself a couple of new shirts.'

'Lovely!' I said, peeling off my gloves. 'If you wait a second, I'll come with you.'

'Whatever for?' said Alex, looking aghast.

'Because it would be nice to spend some time together,' I said, giving him my sunniest smile.

'I'm buying shirts, Holly. Man shopping. You'll be bored rigid.'

'No I won't!' I protested. 'I'll help you choose a colour, and then we can have a coffee together. Pull up a chair somewhere and watch the world go buy. Have a bit of "us" time.'

'We had "us" time last night.'

'No we didn't,' I countered, annoyance whooshing upwards like soup in a blender without the lid on. 'You spent the entire time with Annabelle Hunt-Me-Down-Milf wrapped around you like bindweed.'

'Here we go,' said Alex, looking pained.

'What's that supposed to mean?' I snapped. *Careful, Holly, don't antagonise him. Not while you're hungover. Wait until you have your wits about you.* But I was finding it jolly difficult. Hurt was getting the better of me.

'For a start,' said Alex, 'Annabelle is not a "milf" because she's too young and doesn't have children and—'

'Bugger Annabelle!' I screeched, hoping to God he hadn't. 'You completely ignored me throughout the entire evening. Fancy not asking your own wife to dance!'

'I was looking after Annabelle,' said Alex, his teeth visibly clenching.

'Is the woman so helpless she can't look after herself?'

'She was upset, Holly.'

'AND SO WAS I!' I roared, smacking the rubber gloves down on the worktop and resisting the desire to stride over to Alex and slap them around his face. 'And how DARE you embarrass me in front of that supercilious cow.'

'What the heck are you talking about now?'

'You insinuated I was boring!' I shouted.

'I did no such thing!' Alex protested, 'but surely you can understand the guy was expecting the company of a plus-one with a degree in science, not to find himself partnered-up with the mother of a teenager.'

'What the HELL is that supposed to mean?' I demanded.

'I've had enough of this conversation, Holly,' said Alex, moving towards the kitchen door. 'Frankly your jealous outbursts are both childish and draining.'

I rushed over to the kitchen door and blocked Alex's exit.

'You're not leaving here until we've sorted this out,' I hissed, eyes narrowing dangerously.

'There is nothing to sort out,' said Alex, calmly.

But there was no reasoning with me now. I was on a mission. A mission for truth.

'I saw you both, Alex,' I said, my tone deadly.

'Yes, that would figure,' Alex replied, affecting an air of boredom. 'You were there last night, remember? Or are you totally losing the plot, Holly?'

'I saw you with Annabelle in the foyer.'

Alex looked at me, puzzled.

'Does the potted palm ring any bells, Alex?' I enquired. 'If not, let me refresh your memory. The two of you were hiding behind it whilst in your amorous clinch.'

Alex rolled his eyes. 'Do me a favour,' he snorted. 'I was comforting Annabelle.'

'Yes, I did see that,' I sneered. 'I also heard WHAT she was distressed about. Well you can tell her from me, Alex, that I'm not giving up.' I marched over to him and waggled a finger in front of his nose. *I'd* decide if – and when – I was getting out of this marriage. And right now, I wasn't upping and leaving just to suit flaming Annabelle. 'I'm not going anywhere, *comprendez?*' My eyes were blazing now, as was my brain. My head felt so hot, I thought it might explode.

'Have you finished shouting your preposterous nonsense,' Alex demanded, 'or are you going to shut up and hear an explanation as to why I took Annabelle out to a quiet spot?' 'Go on,' I scoffed, folding my arms across my chest, 'let's hear what excuse you're going to rustle up now. I'm all ears!'

'Annabelle was crying because she's fed up not being able to be with her married lover.'

'Tell me something I don't know!' I spat.

'But her lover isn't me, Holly.'

And then my husband said something that totally took the wind out of my billowing sails.

'Annabelle's lover is Sir Digby.'

Chapter Forty-Four

Alex brushed past me, slamming out of the house and leaving me, as always, feeling wrong-footed. My mind flipped back to last night. Indeed, Annabelle had spent quite a bit of time chatting and laughing with Sir Digby and, now that I thought about it, I *did* remember Sir Digby's wife giving Annabelle some very frosty glances. But in the moment, I'd made nothing of it.

I finished cleaning up the kitchen, took Rupert for a brisk walk, and then drove over to Caro's to collect Sophie.

'Aw, Mum,' Sophie complained, 'I'm not ready to go home. Lizzie and I are half way through making a vlog.'

'Leave them to it,' Caro laughed, 'and tell me how the dinner-dance went. You look awful, so it must have been good.'

I pulled up a chair at Caro's kitchen table and flopped down. 'No, it wasn't good.'

'You're kidding,' said Caro, busying herself with the kettle and mugs. 'That's a shame. Was it awful disco music? I always think a rubbish DJ can make or break an event.'

'No, it was nothing like that, although I did end up dancing to somebody else's tune.'

Caro gave me a sidelong glance. 'What's that comment supposed to mean?'

'Alex arranged a plus-one for a female charity colleague, Annabelle Huntingdon-Smyth. She was meant to be partnering up with Jack.'

'Jack? Are you talking about that heavenly man who was at your dinner party?'

'The one and same,' I nodded. 'Except the universe was having a laugh last night, and it transpired that Annabelle was Jack's ex-fiancé.'

'That's a coincidence. Did they have a good laugh about it?'

'On the contrary. Annabelle had a hissy fit, so Alex was forced to be her partner for the rest of the night.'

'Oh dear. So that left you all alone with the delectable Doctor Jack,' Caro chuckled.

'Yes,' I said, colouring up. 'I'll admit he's easy on the eye but—'

'Easy on the eye?' Caro hooted with laughter. 'That man is easy on *every*thing!' She waggled her eyebrows, then put two of her fingers together and kissed them. 'One word. Yummy.'

'Yes, all right, he's yummy,' I agreed. 'But Jack isn't the reason why the evening was spoiled.'

'So what happened?'

I contemplated my hands, twisting them together in my lap. The desire to unburden was immense.

'If I tell you something, can you keep it to yourself?'

'That goes without saying.'

'Including not sharing it with David?'

I saw Caro's hesitation. 'It's hard not to let things sometimes slip out,' she said. 'I didn't mean to tell David about Jeanie having an affair with a mystery man, but unfortunately drink loosens the tongue, and I can be rather partial to half a bottle of red on a Saturday night. Maybe if you're hugging a secret, better not to tell me.'

'Just try your best, eh?' I said grimly, before continuing. 'I'm making an appointment with a doctor on Monday.'

Caro visibly paled as she set the coffees down on the table. 'Why? Is it a health scare? Do you want me to come with you?'

I smiled, despite my misery. 'Bless you, no, it's nothing like that. I think I need anti-depressants. Or counselling.'

Caro's brows knitted. 'Holly, what are you talking about? Just tell me what is troubling you. And from the beginning, please.'

I took a sip of coffee and deliberated whether to let everything spill out. But my mouth had already made the decision for me, forming words, spewing out the whole sorry mess of my marriage, from Alex's sext messages last Christmas, to my lies about the superior bonk, the revelation that my sex life amounted to nothing more than half a dozen very brief couplings in a year, plus my suspicions about Alex's erratic work hours dovetailing with Jeanie's fictitious visits to the gym, and that I didn't know whether Alex was having an affair with Annabelle, Jeanie or both.

'Good God,' said Caro, as I rattled to a close.

'God's not interested,' I sighed, 'because none of my fervent prayers have been answered. Oh, tell a lie. He answered my prayer for conceiving a child fourteen years ago. Believe me, that was nothing short of a miracle.'

'Holly, you can't seriously be telling me that you've been married all these years and, well, that it's always been like this?'

I nodded sadly. 'Yes. But I just put it down to his job. Busy lives. Investing energies in a business and a home.' I gave a hollow laugh.

'Instead he was saying "open wide" to other women. And why stop at Annabelle or Jeanie? How many more mistresses have there been over the years? The fact is, I don't excite my husband. And probably never have.' And with that, I burst into tears.

It was such a relief to have confided in someone. I hoped Caro would keep her promise not to tell David, but then again, so what if she did tell him? It wouldn't go any further. And anyway, I hadn't forgotten that David had been alive to the way Jeanie and Alex had huddled together at my dinner party, with David even suggesting the pair of them were having a fling. It wasn't just *my* imagination running amok here; somebody else had noticed things weren't quite right.

'So where is Alex at the moment?' asked Caro eventually.

'Supposedly at Bluewater buying shirts,' I sniffed, and wiped a hand across my eyes.

'Perhaps he is!' she said, injecting optimism into her voice.

'Maybe,' I acknowledged. 'It will be interesting to see if he comes home with any shopping.'

Our daughters suddenly appeared, in high spirits, keen to show us the vlog they'd made. I let my hair fall across my face, so Sophie wouldn't see my pink eyes, but Caro firmly waved the girls away.

'Not now,' she said, 'we're chatting. You two aren't the only ones with the monopoly on girly talk.'

'But, M-*uum*,' wheedled Lizzie. 'We want you to check out our vlog!'

'Later. Meanwhile, go and make another one!'

The girls shuffled out, but not before raiding Caro's fridge of chocolate and cola.

'That will keep them quiet for a bit,' she nodded, watching them go. She stood up and shut the kitchen door behind them. 'Listen to me, Holly,' she said, returning to her seat with a thoughtful expression. 'I think you're wrong. Jeanie wouldn't do that to you. She's our best friend. She's admitted to having a fling, but she hates herself for it. I think even Jeanie would draw the line at bonking one of her bestie's husbands and then bragging about it.'

'You think?'

'Yes, I do!' she said.

I shook my head. 'I just don't know what to believe, Caro. One minute I think everything is fine, that Alex and I are rocking along nicely together. Then suddenly Jeanie is hopping into Alex's car for a rendezvous. Alex always comes up with a plausible explanation – a cash payment for Charlotte's braces. But last night, another question arose. I found Annabelle Huntingdon-Smyth in a clinch with Alex behind a potted palm. When I confronted him, he said he was consoling her because she was upset about her married lover being there with his wife. There's always a credible excuse. It's reached the point where I think he's either an extremely good liar, or I'm going around the bend.'

'No you're not,' Caro assured. 'Look, it might well be that the explanations Alex gave you about being with Annabelle and Jeanie are completely genuine. And as for his sex drive, well, he *does* work hard. It's perfectly understandable that his dental practice takes all his attention and energy. I do agree with you, however, that the pace of your sex life is a little…' Caro paused to think how best to tactfully describe it '…quiet,' she concluded.

'Quiet?' I snorted. 'Alex's libido is so flipping quiet I swear I hear it snoring. Which is why' – I frowned – 'it doesn't make sense that he's having affairs.' I rubbed my eyes wearily. 'I don't know what to think any more. Perhaps I'm nothing more than a sexually frustrated overly suspicious wife giving him a lot of grief over nothing.'

Caro stood up again and went to her handbag perched on the worktop. She rummaged around for a moment, then pulled out her mobile.

'I don't know about Annabelle Huntingdon-Smyth,' she said, sitting back down at the table, 'and certainly don't have her contact details to track where she is right now. But both of us have Jeanie's number programmed into our phones. Let's rule Jeanie out of the equation once and for all by finding out who her mystery lover is. I'll call her on the pretext of asking about some homework. Let's see if she's at home with Ray, or whether she's made an excuse to go out – like you feel Alex has.' She gave a crafty smile. 'Detective Caro is on the case!' she said, flashing a smile to try and lighten my mood. She pressed the button by Jeanie's contact details, switching the phone to loudspeaker so I could hear the conversation. The line connected and began to ring. 'There's nothing to worry about,' she assured me, reaching across the table and patting one of my hands.

'Hello?' said Jeanie, sounding breathless.

'Hiya, it's only me,' Caro trilled. 'I just wanted to ask you about a homework assignment that was set for this weekend, and whether it needs handing in tomorrow or—'

'I'm out at the moment,' said Jeanie. 'Give Ray a call. He'll know.'

'Oh,' said Caro, in surprise. 'Okay, will do. Er, where are you?'

Jeanie gave a throaty laugh. 'Use your imagination,' she said, before disconnecting the call.

Caro slowly put the mobile down on the table. For a moment, we both regarded it in silence. When she next looked at me, her eyes were troubled.

Chapter Forty-Five

'It must be a coincidence,' said Caro quietly. 'It *must* be, Holly. She wouldn't do that to you, I *know* she wouldn't.'

Tears were running down my cheeks again. I tore off a piece of kitchen towel from the roll sitting on Caro's table, patting my cheeks frantically, fearful of Sophie and Lizzie returning, and my daughter being alarmed that something was clearly wrong.

'I disagree.' I shook my head. 'If she can deceive her husband – the father of her children and supposedly her soulmate – then betraying a friend is nothing more than' – I cast around for a comparison – 'I don't know, brushing a bit of fluff off one's skirt.'

'Have you thought about confronting her?'

'I came perilously close to it at my dinner party. Instead of asking her outright if it was Alex she was having the affair with, I wimped out and simply asked who her lover was. I've asked her a couple of times now, and she's refused to tell me. That, in itself, is surely suspicious?'

Caro shrugged. 'I'm not sure. I would have thought she'd have confided in me, but she hasn't.'

'She wouldn't confide in you, because you're best friends with me.'

'Maybe,' Caro nodded. 'But hypothesising about whether Jeanie is or isn't having an affair with Alex doesn't give an answer. The best person to ask is your husband.'

'Caro, I keep accusing him of all sorts, and he keeps denying it. If I ask him outright whether he's bonking Jeanie, what do you think he's going to say?'

'Tell him you demand to know the truth,' Caro said firmly.

'And he'll give me another display of eye-rolling facial expressions, hands on hips, heavy sighs, and stomping off with the hump. He doesn't want a divorce, I *do* know that much.'

'My God, you've discussed divorce?' Caro shrieked, looking horrified.

'Not in the way you're thinking,' I gave a ghost of a smile. 'It was more, sort of, asking him if he was happy being married to a wife who, in the last year, has given him a hard time.'

'And what did he say?'

'He said he wanted to stay married because we had a lovely life together.'

'Well there you go then!' said Caro, her tone placating.

'That doesn't mean anything' – I gave a bark of laughter – 'Some men simply thrive on having a mistress. Or mistresses,' I said miserably.

'Holly, you're going around in circles again. Would you like to know what I would do in your shoes?'

'What?' I sighed.

'I'd forget making an appointment with your doctor for anti-depressants. It's a marriage guidance counsellor you need to see.'

I chewed my lip. Caro was right. It would be blissful to unload to an impartial person who would supervise us, listen to our grievances, and no doubt come up with some good old-fashioned common sense on sorting our marriage out. I wasn't quite sure how to persuade Alex we needed marriage guidance counselling, but maybe I'd tentatively discuss it with him later. If he hadn't, in the meantime, eloped with Jeanie.

I left Caro's house feeling slightly better. By the time Sophie and I arrived home, Alex was back from Bluewater. Rupert greeted us ecstatically, and then bounded upstairs with Sophie. Suddenly I was alone in the hallway with Alex. He watched me pull off my shoes, a thoughtful expression on his face. Why was he hovering?

'What's up?' I asked, shoving my feet into my comfortable old slippers.

'Nothing,' he shrugged.

I brushed past him and padded off to the kitchen. It was then that I spotted my largest crystal vase, usually hidden away in a cupboard, out on the kitchen island. It was filled with flowers. The arrangement was huge, full of extravagant blooms, including white velvety roses and tangerine tiger lilies. Their perfume invaded the air, and I sniffed appreciatively.

'Like them?' asked Alex.

'Yes,' I said quietly. 'They're beautiful.'

'They're a sorry present,' he said, coming over and putting his arms around me.

I looked up at him, feeling a mixture of hope and despair.

'Tell me what you're apologising for,' I said quietly.

He blew out his cheeks. 'Lots of things.'

'Oh?'

He nodded. 'You're right. I should have asked you to dance last night. That was very remiss of me. I spent too long trying to keep Annabelle occupied and away from Sir Digby's wife who, it must be said, suspects her husband of being overly fond of Annabelle. I won't deny that I was hoping the blind date with Jack would be a roaring success, and that they'd fall for each other. Such rotten luck that they'd already done that, and then fallen out as well.'

'Yes, that was one hell of a coincidence.'

'I'm also sorry that I implied you were boring. Everyone has different qualities. Just because Annabelle is an intellectual—'

'Careful,' I warned, 'you were doing so well just then, don't spoil it.'

'Let me finish,' said Alex. 'You're not dull, Holly. You have qualities that Annabelle doesn't have. You're a wonderful mother, a good cook and a great homemaker. I can't imagine Annabelle peeling a mountain of vegetables and whisking up one of your incredible roast dinners. She's more likely to exist on edamame beans and mineral water. Nor can I visualise her colour co-ordinating cushions and curtains and soft furnishings. You've put this house together and made it the home it is. It's beautiful. I suspect Annabelle would probably employ an interior decorator and furnish everything in ice-white.' Alex tightened his grip around my waist. 'And finally, I'm sorry I didn't ask you to come along to Bluewater with me. You were right, it would have been nice to have had some "us" time together. It was selfish of me to exclude you.'

'Okay. Apology accepted. Did you buy any shirts?'

'Several, and in lots of different colours. If you put them all together, they look like a rainbow.'

'Good heavens, that sounds very flamboyant.'

He smiled. 'Yes, it is a bit. Your brother made a bitchy comment to me at our dinner party about how I always wear black shirts, and had I thought about giving up dentistry and opening a funeral parlour?'

I looked at my husband in amazement. 'Since when did you start taking fashion advice from Simon?'

'Since never,' Alex said adamantly. 'As it happens, M&S had huge posters in store of David Gandy modelling. He was lolling around in various poses with a cashmere sweater slung around his shoulders, and a long blade of grass stuck between his teeth. You know the type of pose.'

I smiled. 'Ah, so because David Gandy was wearing colourful shirts, and not Simon, that made buying them okay, yes?'

'Precisely,' Alex nodded. 'As it's my birthday next Saturday I thought I'd treat myself. I even bought the cashmere sweater,' he added, looking a bit sheepish, 'although you'll be pleased to know I didn't flag down a sales lady and ask if they sold grass.'

'Yes, that might have been misconstrued,' I smiled.

'I'm not sure what Jenny will say when I walk into reception on Monday morning dressed in lilac. She'll probably think I've been sniffing the patients' laughing gas.'

'And you'll find yourself the subject of gossip with all the nurses for the rest of the day,' I giggled.

'Perish the thought.' Alex gave a mock shudder. 'Anyway, enough about them. Are we good again?'

I nodded my head slowly. 'I guess.'

'You guess?'

'Alex, can I ask you a question without you hitting the roof?'

There was a pause while he looked at me. 'I know what you're going to ask, Holly.'

'Do you?'

'Yes,' he nodded his head sadly. 'You don't trust me, do you?'

I opened my mouth to speak, but nothing came out other than a strangled sob.

'Don't cry,' he said, holding me even tighter. 'Ever since those blasted, stupid, ridiculous, damned bloody texts last Christmas—'

'It's not just that,' I blurted.

'Everything was fine until that happened.'

I shook my head, willing the tears back into their ducts. 'The thing is, Alex, I don't think things were fine even before that.'

'Don't be silly, darling, of course they were. We hardly ever had a cross word in all our years of marriage until that happened.'

'Look, I'm going to say something that might… might…' I gulped, 'outrage you.'

Alex gave me an evaluating look. 'Just spit it out, eh?'

'It's about our sex life.'

Alex frowned. 'What about it?'

'It's rather… lacking.' Oh God. I'd said it. I took a deep breath to steady my nerves.

'What do you mean?' said Alex, looking offended. 'Are you complaining?'

'Noooo,' I said hastily. I knew it, I should have kept my gob shut. 'It's… lovely. It's just… we don't, you know, do it very often.'

Alex sighed. 'That's because we're busy people. We get tired. At our time of life we are winding down, not revving up.'

I wasn't entirely sure about that. Lately I seemed to have been revving up like a boy racer's old Ford Fiesta with a reconditioned engine. If my body was meant to be winding down, then why did

I react so strongly to Jack being around me? Apart from anything else, I wasn't yet forty years old. Surely women didn't 'wind down' until they'd gone through the menopause. And even then, there was hormone replacement therapy to keep one's libido fizzing and popping. I was fairly confident fifty-nine-year-old Madonna didn't invite her latest lover home for a mug of cocoa and game of Scrabble.

'Yes,' I nodded, not wishing to upset my husband any further. The male ego was a fragile thing. In that moment I dismissed suggesting marriage guidance counselling… at least for now. 'You're quite right.' After all, I was a woman who wore old, comfortable slippers. Perhaps I'd do well to remember that the next time my libido decided to light up like a firework.

'I *know* I'm right,' said Alex, gently. His tone was one of tenderness. 'Now can we please, darling, put aside these jealous outbursts you periodically have?'

I looked at my husband and nodded. He was right. The sexts had upset my world and, with it, my marriage. We were back to square one. Everything boiled down to me and my misconceptions, misunderstandings, looking for problems where there weren't any, and being jealous of women like Annabelle and Jeanie because of my own insecurities and lack of self-esteem. And regarding our romantic intimacy being scant, unfortunately the simple fact was we had mismatched sex drives. There wasn't much I could do about that. But I had a lot to be grateful for. And then my husband said something that reassured me once and for all.

'Look at me, Holly,' he said. 'No, *really* look at me… gaze into my eyes. I want you to see for yourself that I'm speaking the truth when I tell you that you are the only, and I really do mean this, you are the *only* woman for me.'

'Good,' I whispered.

Alex hugged me tightly and then, just like Jack had the night before, brushed his lips against my hair. There were no zings or jolts of lust, which was probably just as well because Alex was already releasing me, ready to take himself off for a bit of telly time. But right now, I didn't mind. My husband wasn't satiating Annabelle or Jeanie. My marriage was back on track. Alex had told me that I was the only woman for him. It was enough. And with that I buried my nose in the flowers and inhaled gratefully.

Chapter Forty-Six

'A pinch and a punch, first day of the month,' said Sophie, thumping her fist painfully against my arm.

'Ouch!' I shrieked. 'Heavens, child, you don't know your own strength. And you're wrong. Today is the second of October. It was the first yesterday. Why are you rummaging in my bedside drawer?' I asked.

I was standing in front of my bedroom mirror, hastily applying a bit of make-up before going into work. Monday was always a busy day at the surgery. Alex had already gone ahead to open the practice and put the heating on. The weather had taken a dip over the weekend and was definitely nippy.

'All my tights are laddered,' complained Sophie, extracting a pair of mine from the drawer, 'so I need to borrow a pair of yours.'

'That means they'll be wrecked by the end of the day.' I smiled good-naturedly. My joy knew no bounds today. I felt so ecstatic, almost as if I could take a flying leap, ballerina-style, and travel through the air for hundreds of feet. What a great feeling! 'Fine, take them, they're all yours.' I returned to the task in hand, mouth half-open as I stood in front of the mirror stroking mascara onto my lashes.

'By the way, what on *earth* was Dad wearing this morning?' said Sophie, extracting the tights and slamming the drawer shut. 'He looked like a tangerine.'

'Yes, well, between you and me, I think he's having a bit of a mid-life crisis.'

'What does that mean?' Sophie frowned, running the tights over her hands and checking for ladders.

'It's something middle-aged people are meant to have at some point. It a sort of' – I considered – 'psychological phase where the person frets about getting older, and maybe hankers after lost youth. As a result, they sometimes do something rather drastic.'

I immediately thought about Jeanie, chasing lost youth as she pursued somebody else's husband. In the old days, she, Caro and I had been svelte and beautiful, footloose and fancy-free, embarking on the occasional one-night stand, flirting with as many lads as possible, boosting our egos, and knowing that no matter what hour we crashed into bed, we'd always look attractively wan the next day, rather than raddled old bags – which was now always the case if we weren't in bed by eleven. I was overjoyed to know that, unlike Jeanie's mid-life crisis, my husband was simply chasing lost youth by attempting to dress younger. I'd much rather he went to work in an orange shirt, hair parted in such a way as to conceal the area where it was thinning, than pursue some woman in a short skirt and appease his ego by seeing if he could still pull. I finished putting on the mascara and noted the sparkle in my eyes. Good. This was the first time in a long while that I had felt so relaxed about everything.

'I saw Dad hanging up his new shirts yesterday,' said Sophie, sitting down on the edge of my bed, and sticking her left foot in one leg of the tights. 'The lilac one wasn't too bad, and the lemon was so-so' – she seesawed one hand in mid-air – 'but that orange shirt made him look like he'd been Tango'd.' She rolled her eyes as she pulled up the tights.

'Please don't tell him that, darling,' I said, my voice gently chiding. 'Let him think he's a bit cool, eh!'

Sophie snorted. 'He should be so lucky.' She stood up and smoothed down her school skirt. 'I'm ready. Will you be long?'

'Nope, another thirty seconds.' I slotted the mascara wand back into the plastic tube and tossed it into my make-up bag. 'You sort yourself out and get your shoes on, and I'll make sure Rupert's done a wee. He's on his own for a good few hours today, so I don't want him cross-legged.'

'Okay.'

My daughter took herself off, leaving me to gather up my handbag and keys. Downstairs, I was just shooing a reluctant Rupert outside, when my mobile dinged with a text message. It was from Caro.

Everything all right? Been worried about you! Xx

I sent her a quick reply.

Yes. Alex and I had a chat. He bought me beautiful flowers and insisted I was the only woman for him. I believe him. So happy! xx

Caro replied almost instantly.

You silly goose for getting so worked up! Sooo pleased all is well xx

Humming, I popped the mobile into my handbag, and let Rupert back in. Feeling another wave of happiness engulf me, I dropped

Sophie off at school, gave her a cheery wave and then headed off to work. Pausing at some traffic lights, I snapped on my favourite radio station – one that Sophie deemed uncool – and sang loudly along to Wham! How very apposite. The DJ was playing 'I'm Your Man'. I grinned to myself. How fantastic. Alex was *my* man. Not Annabelle's. Not Jeanie's. The lights changed to green and I zoomed off, singing away, secure in the knowledge that all was well in the world of Mrs Holly Hart.

Little did I know then that in a few more days I would look back on this moment and realise that happiness can be very short-lived.

Chapter Forty-Seven

My little bubble of contentment lasted all through Monday, even when Jenny the receptionist visibly boggled at Alex's orange shirt before he went off to change into his scrubs, and one or two dental nurses sniggered behind their hands. As the week progressed, Alex wore a different pastel-coloured shirt every day. His mood was buoyant, as was mine, and things remained calm in the Hart household. I was longing for Alex to make love to me, just to reaffirm that we were – in his own words – 'good again', but knew it was unlikely after our discussion about winding down. Nor did I want to risk upsetting his ego by forcing the issue, so I didn't make any sexual overtures, instead telling myself that it was just as nice having my husband spoon into me a couple of times, especially when he nuzzled my neck for a whole ten seconds.

As I lay awake listening to Alex's rhythmic snores, I plotted. I wanted my husband to be delighted with his surprise party – and I wanted to enjoy it, too, for the right reasons. I would make sure that this wasn't just a birthday celebration, but also a celebration of our marriage. Perhaps I'd even make a little speech to that effect. Great idea! Roll on Saturday night! And afterwards, once home, high on joy and tiddly on alcohol, who knew what might happen?

I hugged myself with delight. *This* time Alex would catch plenty of glimpses of me flashing my thighs in the evening dress he hadn't had a chance to appreciate last weekend, so that by the time we got home he'd be David Beckham to my Victoria and panting, 'Quick, grab my golden balls'. My husband was going to forget about grumpy patients and astronomical overheads and, for one night, ride high on laughter and lust.

Suddenly it was Saturday morning.

'Happy birthday, Daddy!' cried Sophie, opening our bedroom door, Rupert at her heels. She was holding a tray with tea and toast for us both. 'Breakfast in bed is one of my presents to you,' she beamed, as Alex sat up, bleary-eyed, and pummelled his pillows into place against the headboard.

'Thanks, sweetheart,' he said, taking the tray from her. 'Ooh, and I see birthday cards too! How lovely. Let's be careful not to slop tea on them.'

'The cards are from me and Mum,' Sophie grinned, 'but there are lots more waiting to be opened downstairs.'

'Happy birthday, darling,' I said, propping myself upright. I leaned across and kissed Alex on the cheek. 'Sorry if I've got dog-breath. I'll go and clean my teeth before I do anything else.' I flipped back the duvet, and Sophie immediately took the vacated side of the bed, snuggling into her dad.

'Open my card first,' I heard her say. By the time I returned, she had produced a present from her bulging dressing-gown pocket. 'I think you'll like this,' she beamed.

Alex ripped open the paper. 'Socks!' he exclaimed.

'And not just any old socks,' Sophie pointed out. 'These match your new shirts.'

'Indeed they do,' said Alex, gulping at the vision of custard yellow, bright purple and scarlet red. 'They're... colourful.'

'And cheerful,' Sophie nodded.

'Budge up,' I said, getting in next to my girl.

The three of us lay in bed, Sophie, the glue in our marriage, sandwiched between Alex and I, and I felt a sense of contentment. Who needed sex and superior bonks when I had this – my handsome husband and beautiful daughter. Rupert chose that moment to jump on the bed and flopped down, tongue hanging out. I regretted not having my camera to hand to take a picture of the four of us. A happy family, complete with hairy mutt. It was a perfect blissful moment.

'I'll give you my present tonight,' I said to Alex. 'It's a surprise.'

'Lovely,' he said, smiling over Sophie's head. 'Shall I book the three of us a table somewhere?'

'No!' Sophie and I said in unison.

'Ah,' Alex beamed, 'I think you two girls have been conspiring behind my back. You've booked us into the local Indian, haven't you!'

'Maybe,' I said.

Sophie let out a squeal of excitement, causing Rupert to woof and leap off the bed. She squealed again and, unable to contain herself, clambered out of the bed, nearly sending the tea tray flying. She ran off down the landing letting out little whoops of delight with Rupert who, caught up in her exhilaration, zoomed after her.

'Well it's nice to see our daughter in such good spirits,' said Alex, taking a bite of toast. 'I haven't heard a door slam for at least a fortnight. And what's up with the dog? Rupert is behaving like he's found a new lamppost to sniff.'

'He's happy,' I said.

'Last week you said he was depressed.'

'Yes, well, he must have been mood swinging.'

Alex threw back his head and laughed. 'Are you sure you wouldn't prefer to stay in tonight and have a takeaway? We can invite the family over. I'll even suffer your brother, as long as you order an exceptionally hot vindaloo to frazzle his tonsils so he can't speak to anyone.'

I tutted, but smiled. 'Thanks, but no thanks. By the way, the dress code is smart for where I'm taking you tonight.'

'Okay,' said Alex, looking puzzled as he licked a dollop of butter from one finger. 'In that case, I'll wear one of my new shirts again. I haven't worn the raspberry one yet.'

'Whatever makes you happy,' I said, privately thinking that I'd have a few words to say to my brother tonight for making bitchy comments about my husband's fashion sense.

The day passed without incident. Various family members rang to convey their birthday wishes to Alex, and said they hoped to see him soon and to have a lovely day. Both windowsills in the lounge were now full of colourful cards, and Sophie was still periodically emitting squeaks of hyper-excitement. I'd put on party make-up between finishing off a pile of ironing and running the vacuum cleaner around, and my plan was to slither into my evening dress last-minute so Alex's suspicions weren't aroused to soon.

'What time do you want to leave for the restaurant?' he asked, flicking through the telly channels.

'In ten minutes,' I replied.

'Okay, well I'm ready when you are.'

'Good. I'll just pop upstairs and change.'

When Sophie and I came downstairs again, dressed to party, Alex looked startled.

'What sort of restaurant are we going to?' he asked in surprise.

'Dad!' Sophie chided. 'You're meant to say, "Omigod, you both look stunning."'

Alex clapped his hands together and jumped off the sofa. 'OMIGOD, YOU BOTH LOOK STUNNING!' he shouted, grabbing hold of Sophie and dancing her round and round the room. She shrieked with delight, as Rupert bounded after them both, wanting to join in and barking his head off.

'The taxi is here,' I said, as the doorbell rang.

'Oh, there was no need to do that, darling, I could have driven the three of us.'

'Nonsense,' I smiled. 'It's your birthday. You and I are going to celebrate with a few drinks, and not worry about our licences.'

'Fine by me. Okay, which of the two lovely ladies in my life is going to take me by the hand and walk me to our awaiting chariot? I'm an ancient person now. Forty years old,' Alex groaned in mock horror.

'Sophie can do it,' I said, laughing. 'You both go ahead while I let Rupert out quickly. I'll lock up.'

Five minutes later I was in the taxi with my husband and daughter. As we set off, I determined it would be a night to remember. And it was. For all the wrong reasons.

Chapter Forty-Eight

When the minicab drew up outside the golf club, Alex looked a bit surprised.

'The restaurant here is quite pricey, darling,' he said. 'The Indian would have been cheaper.'

'Sweetheart, can you stop fretting about money?' I chided. 'We're not exactly on the breadline, and your fortieth birthday doesn't occur more than once in a lifetime.'

'I know,' Alex said, paying the taxi and taking me by the hand as Sophie ran ahead. 'It's nice of you to spoil me,' he added, giving my fingers a quick squeeze.

'This way,' I said, as we went through the double doors of the main building.

'The restaurant is over there,' said Alex, tugging my hand and making to go in the opposite direction.

'Dad!' Sophie grinned. 'Come with us, please.'

He followed obediently as I led him towards the Mayflower Suite.

'But,' said Alex, looking puzzled, 'I don't understand—'

'Everything will become crystal clear any second now,' I smiled, pulling the suite's enormous door back on its hinges.

'SURPRISE!' shrieked a jam-packed room full of people as the karaoke band launched into an incredibly loud rendition of 'Happy Birthday'.

Alex did a fairly good impression of a fish, opening and closing his mouth several times as the crowd, already with a few sherbets inside them judging from the flushed faces, sang to a rousing crescendo accompanied by the drummer beating his sticks against the snare drums before crashing them down on the cymbal.

Alex stared at the sea of strangers and then at me.

'Who are all these people?' he hissed.

I gulped nervously, anxious that the surprise party didn't backfire.

'Well, they're friends, darling,' I muttered, although I hadn't a clue who at least half of them were. I caught sight of Sophie's headmistress propped up against the bar, and boggled slightly. The Head was here? Gazing at all the beaming faces, I realised that most of them belonged to people I was barely on nodding terms with at the school gates. I glanced at Sophie who was looking at me and visibly cringing.

'Sorry, Mum,' she gulped, 'I had no idea the entire year was going to turn out.'

'Doesn't matter,' I assured. And it didn't. All that counted was my husband being pleasantly surprised, rather than horrified, and that he had an enjoyable evening.

'Speech!' someone yelled, and which another voice seconded. Within moments, a cacophony of demands filled the air that Alex take the microphone and address everyone.

Suddenly my brother jumped up on stage, grabbing the lead singer's mic.

'Come on, Alex. Get your bootylicious butt up here and say a few words.'

Alex's face momentarily darkened, but in front of an audience he could hardly complain about his brother-in-law, ever the extrovert and lapping up attention as he momentarily hogged the limelight. The crowd parted and Alex, never one to be entirely at ease as the centre of attention, walked self-consciously towards the stage as everyone began to clap and cheer.

'Look at this fine specimen of a man,' said Simon into the microphone. 'He doesn't look a day over fifty, eh? Oh, what's that? He's forty, you say! Come on, Alex. As you can see, ladies and gentlemen, these days he's built for comfort, not speed. That's it, keep walking towards me, you don't need to look left and right as you cross a room. And don't suck in your gut, otherwise your ankles will swell. I do love a surprise party. It's always a surprise if anyone turns up!'

Even though my husband had his back to me, I could tell from his rigid posture that he was glowering at Simon. Just as Alex was about to climb onto the stage, a woman darted forward, seized him by the shoulders and kissed him hard on the lips. The crowd roared their approval and Alex, caught off guard, was compliant as her scarlet lipstick pressed against his mouth. I gasped with surprise, as did Sophie by my side.

'That's a bit cheeky, isn't it, Mum?' murmured Sophie, wide-eyed.

That was an understatement. It was downright weird. What the hell was going on here? Jeanie was grinning up at Alex. She then took a showy step away from my husband, and did a little shimmy, her curves and ample bosom – which was firmly on display – wobbling dramatically. Everybody whooped in delight at Jeanie's audacity and she gave a low curtsy, ensuring the entire room was able to have a good look down her cleavage.

'That woman is *such* a tart,' said a plummy voice to my left.

Tearing my eyes away from Jeanie, I turned and found Izzy by my side. Her husband, Sebastian, was watching Jeanie with a lascivious look on his face.

'I-I think she's just in high spirits,' I stuttered, not quite knowing why I was sticking up for my best friend when, in front of all these people, including Ray, she'd just demonstrated a very public display of affection for my husband.

'And here he is at last, ladies and gentleman,' said Simon, as Alex finally reached the stage. He was now wearing Jeanie's bright red lipstick and looking like a drag queen on an off day. 'Your wife has bought you a dictionary for your birthday, Alex, so later you can find the words to thank her for this party.'

The crowd erupted into applause as Simon took a dramatic bow and, blowing kisses to everyone, passed Alex the microphone.

'Good evening, everyone,' said my husband, gazing upon the crowd with a bewildered expression. 'This party certainly is a huge surprise. I had no idea I knew so many people,' he added dryly, as his gaze roved across the upturned faces that he definitely could not put names to. 'But thank you for joining me and, without further ado, I wish you all a good time.'

Suddenly a woman stepped up onto the stage. I immediately noticed the look of genuine pleasure that suffused Alex's face. She took the microphone from him.

'Ladies and gentlemen. I want you all to know that this man is very special to me.'

'Who's that?' asked Sophie.

It was as much as I could do not to shoulder my way through the crowd, snatch the microphone from her perfectly manicured fingers, and bop her on the nose with it. I might have invited her, but it wasn't her place to take over.

'Mum?' Sophie turned to me enquiringly, but blanched when she saw that I was so angry I was almost foaming at the mouth.

'Her name,' I spat, 'is Annabelle Huntingdon-Smyth.'

'This man,' said Annabelle, 'is a hero for so many reasons, but above all,' she turned and looked at him tenderly, 'he is *my* hero.'

'That must be his wife,' said a woman in front of me.

'Chuffing hell,' said the woman's husband, 'she's a right stunner.'

'Dear Alex,' said Annabelle, 'on your fortieth birthday I want you to know how much I love you. You've been by my side through thick and thin. For those of you who don't know, Alex is one of the trustees of a fabulous charity that I'm very much involved in. I would like everybody here to show their appreciation of this wonderful evening by giving just one pound. Come Monday morning, I'll be able to hand over a fantastic donation. Meanwhile, let's put our hands together one more time,' she beamed proprietarily at my husband, 'FOR ALEX!'

The crowd erupted, as Alex and Annabelle kissed. It's fair to say that at this point, any hope I'd had of taking the microphone myself disappeared. I felt absolutely paralysed by this astonishing turn of events with two women who – let's face it – I'd so recently suspected were having affairs with my husband.

Simon, presumably out of loyalty to me, playfully shoved Annabelle to one side, as if fighting over Alex, and gave him a big smacker on the mouth too. To the crowd, Alex looked like he was going along with it. Only I, the woman who knew him best, could see he was apoplectic with rage. The audience, delighted at Simon's camped-up audacity, roared their approval. The female lead singer took the microphone from a laughing Annabelle and launched into her own cover of 'I'm Coming Out', which caused much hilarity, until everybody started dancing. Alex turned his back on Simon and jumped off the stage. Seconds later Annabelle had claimed him for the opening dance, while I stood on the fringes feeling like an outsider looking in.

Chapter Forty-Nine

'Are you all right, Mum?' asked Sophie, raising her voice over the music.

'Never better,' I lied. Refreshment was urgently needed. Preferably a gin and tonic. Or six. Then I'd be good as new. I'd dance in time to the music as I made my way across the floor, past Jeanie, pausing briefly to fling my drink in her face, then move swiftly on to Annabelle, hit her over the head with my evening bag, and then reclaim my husband.

'Only you look a bit…'

'What, darling?'

'Upset. And angry.' My daughter's eyebrows did a Mexican wave on her forehead as she critically assessed my facial expression.

'Nonsense!'

'Are you sure?'

'Quite sure,' I insisted. 'You go and say hello to all those friends of yours and have a good time.'

'If you say so,' said Sophie, uncertainly. 'Actually, I can see Tabitha over there, and I'd quite like to join her.'

'Go,' I urged. 'I've spotted Granny, and anyway, I need to work this crowd and say hello to family and friends.' People that I *did* know. I could see Mum and Dad talking to Simon and Aunty Shirley over by the bar, which meant Jack was here somewhere. I started to move towards Mum, but a hand held me back. Turning, I saw Izzy. Her expression was strained.

'Can I have a word?' she asked.

I glanced in Mum's direction, mentally marking where she was in the enormous crowd, then looked back at Izzy.

'Sorry,' she apologised, 'I quite understand that you need to network with everybody.'

'I don't know half the people here,' I gave a deprecating laugh, aware that Izzy was responsible for inviting a goodly proportion of them. I didn't feel inclined to cosy up with her and make small talk, but equally I wasn't the type to be blatantly rude. 'What's up?' I asked.

'It's regarding Jeanie.'

'Oh?'

My tone must have immediately sounded guarded, because I noticed Izzy's expression veer from apology to annoyance.

'Is she a good friend of yours?' she demanded.

I felt my stomach tighten at Izzy's question. 'She's meant to be,' I said lightly, whilst inwardly vowing that Jeanie would never be on my Christmas card list again after tonight. I was absolutely seething over her kissing Alex. And as for Annabelle… well, I'd deal with her later. 'What about Jeanie?' I asked.

'Don't you think her behaviour with your husband just then was rather over the top?'

Annoyance at Izzy's directness stopped me from agreeing with her. I really wasn't up for being further aggravated.

'Has she always been an appalling flirt?' she persisted.

'Yes.' My answer was immediate. I didn't owe Jeanie any favours, which was just as well because I couldn't keep the bitchiness out of my voice. 'Lately, she has taken to flirting with my husband quite outrageously.' I noticed Izzy's eyes widen. If the woman thought she had told me something new, she was mistaken. 'In short, Izzy, Jeanie is a bitch. Does that answer your question?'

Izzy looked aghast.

'Sorry if that sounds rude,' I said, not sounding remotely apologetic.

'No, no, it's okay,' she said hurriedly.

'I've known her since school days,' I said, 'but more recently can honestly say I have no idea who she is.'

'Yes, yes, quite,' Izzy nodded, 'I understand what you're saying. It must be very difficult for you.'

Oh, marvellous. Izzy suspected Jeanie and Alex had a thing going on between them too.

'Rest assured,' I said crisply, 'it is *extremely* difficult for me. And now, if you don't mind, I'm going to get a drink. I really do need one.'

'Of course,' Izzy nodded, 'I'll leave you in peace.'

I gave her a tight smile and stalked across the room to where Mum had been, only to find she'd disappeared elsewhere in the crowd. No matter. I really *did* need that drink. I elbowed my way over to the bar and was just about to order a double G&T, when a warm hand glided around my waist sending six million volts scorching up and down my spine. In all my life, only one person had even done that to me. I turned and gazed up into the handsome face of Jack.

'Your tipple is on me,' he smiled, signalling to the barman.

'Thanks,' I said, steadying myself against the bar, as Jack paid for our drinks.

'Let's go over here where there aren't quite so many bodies leaping about,' he said, steering me by the elbow. His touch once again had me juddering about and I was glad for the excuse of revellers jostling against me, disguising the effect he was having on me. I really should try and get a grip on the commotion this man caused within me, because it wasn't right that he had the power to make me want to keel over and gasp, 'Take me, I'm all yours'.

'How are you, Holly?' he asked, when the two of us were finally in a quieter corner away from the main throng.

'Fine, thanks,' I lied, as my eyes snagged on Alex in the crowd. He was still dancing with the insufferable Annabelle.

Jack followed my gaze. 'Don't let her bother you,' he said.

I gave a dry laugh. 'She's meant to be having an affair with a married man.'

'I heard,' Jack nodded. 'Sir Digby. Patron of the trigeminal neuralgia charity she likes to bang a gong about.'

'That's right. She's already hijacked my surprise party demanding everyone donate to her good cause, *and* publicly announced Alex to be her personal hero. I think she's got some flaming front, if you don't mind my saying.'

'Annabelle means nothing to me, so I don't mind at all,' Jack shrugged carelessly. 'She evidently means something to my husband,' I said irritably. 'Some people here even presumed her to be Alex's wife, you know.'

Jack gave a hoot of laughter. 'Some women are not wife material. Annabelle is one of them.' He gazed at me thoughtfully. 'Do you feel threatened by her?'

I sighed. 'Is it that obvious?'

'Yes.'

'I once wondered if… if… oh, never mind,' I trailed off miserably.

'Wondered what?'

'If you must know, I recently suspected her of having an affair with my husband.'

'Unlikely. You mustn't let her intimidate you,' he said. 'Really, there's no need.'

'I'm not so sure about that,' I sniffed.

'Trust me, I'm a doctor,' Jack quipped.

The lead singer finished her medley of songs and then, speaking into her microphone, addressed the crowd.

'Ladies and gentlemen, is everyone enjoying the music?'

The crowd hollered their appreciation.

'Excellent! But now it's the band's turn to appreciate *you*. We are a karaoke group and, for the next hour, will cover pretty much any song you can think of, giving *you* the chance to entertain everyone here tonight. So, if anyone reckons they can sing like Madonna, or have missed their chance on *The X Factor*, now is the time for your star to shine! Who would like to go first?'

'Me!' shouted a voice, which I instantly recognised. Moments later, Jeanie was pushing past Alex and Annabelle, hastening over to the stage. Her face was pink and shiny, glowing with excitement. I could tell she had shipped a fair amount of alcohol. I looked around for Ray, and spotted him talking to Caro and David, who had only just arrived. I really needed to circulate and say hello to people. Just as soon as the G&T had hit the spot.

Annabelle had now moved away from Alex, and was talking to Simon, leaving Alex chatting to Izzy's husband, Sebastian. The two men shook hands, and I lip-read Sebastian wishing Alex a happy birthday. They then appeared to be making small talk while Jeanie, looking very full of herself up on the stage, conferred with the lead singer and also one of the guitarists about her chosen song. The guitarist shouted something to the keyboard player who raised an enquiring eyebrow at the drummer who, in turn, gave the thumbs up. Suddenly the opening bars were being played to a song so familiar I found myself freezing to the spot, and in no time at all Jeanie was crooning seductively into the microphone the oh-so-familiar song about being a genie in a bottle. Her gaze was fixed on one person in the crowd. I followed it and wasn't surprised to see her staring intently at Alex as she wiggled and squirmed, her enormous breasts jostling like over-inflated beach balls in a bag. Most of the men in the crowd were egging her on, one or two wannabe studs giving piercing wolf whistles. Alex folded his arms across his chest and looked stony-faced. Even Sebastian was joining in with the crowd and clapping his hands, his eyes like twin lasers on Jeanie's chest. God, men were so transparent. Apart from my husband, of course, who was doing his best to feign disinterest.

Jeanie's husband was now also standing next to Alex and Sebastian, but Ray wasn't joining in with the whooping crowd. Instead his expression was puzzled as he glanced at Jeanie and then Alex, standing by his side. I wondered if Ray was starting to put two and two together about his wife's behaviour. He surely couldn't have been impressed seeing her plant a resounding smacker on Alex's mouth at the start of the evening. My insides clenched as I stood there playing out various scenarios in my head on how to deal with Jeanie. The earlier idea of throwing my drink at her was no longer viable because I'd necked the rest of it and my glass was empty.

'Can I get you another?' asked Jack.

'Please,' I nodded gratefully, not taking my eyes from the gyrating Jeanie as she turned slowly on the spot, presenting her ample bottom to the audience and… good heavens… was she *twerking*?

As Jeanie shimmied and writhed to the close of the song, my attention was caught by two things. Firstly, Jeanie's daughter Charlotte was pushing her way through the crowd wearing an expression that read like an open book. *Mum*, her face so clearly said, *you are seriously embarrassing me in front of my friends*. Not far behind Charlotte, a second female was torpedoing her way towards the stage, but unlike Charlotte, this woman looked like the human equivalent of Mount Vesuvius, and it was clear from her face that she was about to erupt. My body stiffened as my eyes tracked the two females' progress. The latter beat Charlotte by a good ten seconds. As Jeanie held the final note of the song and everybody put their hands together, exploding into loud applause, she was up on the stage, walking swiftly towards Jeanie who was now bowing low, breasts bulging along with, no doubt, every male pair of eyeballs in the room.

The band's lead singer was stepping forward, clapping briefly before extending one hand to take the microphone from Jeanie and pass it to the other woman who, it was presumed, wanted to also try her hand at some karaoke. Jeanie was beaming widely, but when she turned to see who the newcomer was, her grin wavered, and when the woman spoke into the microphone, Jeanie's smile disappeared faster than a snuffer extinguishing a burning candle.

'Ladies and gentleman,' said the woman, her voice trembling violently, 'I'm sorry to interrupt the party, but I want everyone here to know that I'm divorcing my husband.'

There was a stunned pause and for a moment nobody spoke. From one corner of the room came the sound of buzzing, like a swarm of bees, as a large group of school mothers went into a huddle, clearly shocked, but whispering and nodding amongst themselves, as the woman on stage cleared her throat and continued to address the crowd.

'And the reason I'm getting divorced is because of this woman.' She pointed a finger at Jeanie, who visibly shrank away, her previously pink and glowing face now ashen. 'Because this woman is having an affair with my husband.' She turned on Jeanie, her face a mask of hatred. 'Well, you're welcome to him,' she spat. 'He's all yours. Here, you can have this too.' And with that, she pulled off her wedding ring and flung it at Jeanie. The gold band glinted briefly as it soared through the air. It landed with a dull clink on the floor. 'Your outrageous performance singing directly to my enthralled husband, was the last straw.'

I gasped. Jeanie had been singing to Alex. Hadn't she? If she hadn't been singing to Alex, then who the hell *had* she been singing to? My eyes pinged back to my husband who was still standing with both Ray and… oh my goodness.

Jeanie's married lover was *Sebastian*!

Chapter Fifty

Satisfied that she'd exacted revenge by publicly humiliating Jeanie, Izzy calmly returned the microphone to the gobsmacked lead singer, before jumping down from the stage and exiting the double doors of the Mayflower Suite. Two seconds later, a distraught Tabitha and white-faced Sebastian ran after her. Izzy had been determined to shame Jeanie, and had succeeded, but acting in the moment of red-hot anger she'd given no consideration to the feelings of her own daughter, nor to Jeanie's children, and most definitely not to Jeanie's husband.

Now that Izzy, Sebastian and Tabitha were out of the picture, all eyes were on Ray, the cuckolded husband. He seemed to be welded to the spot, weeping openly with his stunned son and daughter now by his side, their arms wrapped around each other as they sobbed together. Simon and Alex moved as one, guiding the three of them towards the very doors that, only moments earlier, Izzy and her splintered family had moved through. As the doors swung shut after them, the crowd's focus switched to Jeanie who was still standing on the stage, not knowing which way to turn, visibly reeling from her private world publicly crashing down around her. She was shivering violently, her face contorted with shock and grief. Had it been only moments ago that the crowd had been loving her, revelling in her audaciously sexy performance, her figure the envy of so many women and lusted after by many of the men? But now, she was reviled. A marriage wrecker. Trollop. The sort of woman that the sisterhood despised, and men wanted to stay away from in case their wives gave them a hard time. It was one thing to flirt with the idea of extra-marital temptation, but quite another to give in to it and have everything blow up in your face. From the expressions on the faces of some men, it was apparent they were identifying with Sebastian's demise.

'What an idiot,' one man was saying to another. 'He's lost it all. A lovely wife, nice kid, and have you seen the family home? Bloody incredible. He won't be living there for much longer now he's got a wife to pay off.'

'Quite,' said another. 'No way would I risk losing my missus and kids for a few minutes of stolen fun with some tart who happens to have tits the size of watermelons. What a fool Sebastian has been!'

The audience were chuntering now, their anger growing as one of the men pointed a finger at Jeanie and yelled, 'Homewrecker!'

She burst into tears, just as Caro and David climbed onto the stage, rushing towards her, David flinging his jacket over Jeanie's shoulders as someone in the crowd lobbed a plastic beer glass which was quickly followed by another, and then a plastic wine flute.

'Rubbish to rubbish!' screamed a woman, who I recognised as one of Izzy's loyal cronies.

The whole drama, from start to finish, had barely lasted thirty seconds, but somehow it felt like thirty minutes.

'I must go to her,' I said to Jack, immediately circumnavigating around the angry crowd's perimeter as Caro and David guided

Jeanie through the double doors and out into the foyer beyond. I wondered what was happening out there. Had Ray caught up with Sebastian and recovered enough to throw him a punch?

Before I'd even reached the exit doors, I was aware of Jack, now on stage, talking into the microphone.

'The show's over, folks, but the party is still on.'

The band immediately launched into 'Tainted Love', which might have been appalling coincidence, but I didn't pause to give it further consideration.

As I crashed through the doors, I saw no sign of Izzy, Sebastian or their daughter, but in the foyer all hell was breaking out between Ray and Jeanie, with their kids firmly in their father's camp.

'You BITCH!' Charlotte was screaming at her mother.

'Don't talk to your mother like that,' Ray automatically chided, before wiping a hand across his eyes and saying, 'but Charlotte's right. You ARE a bitch, Jeanie.'

'How could you *do* that to Dad?' demanded Harry. 'And how are we meant to face our mates at school on Monday?'

Harry wasn't old enough to think about anything other than his world and what his gossiping classmates would make of it all. He'd yet to register the bigger picture, the upheaval of his parents' marriage that had been tossed without any warning into an emotional shredder, or the very serious fall-out of addressing which child would live with which parent if things weren't salvageable. And right now, I had no idea if Jeanie's marriage was beyond repair, or if Ray would even want to stick around to fix it. His eyes were brimming as he looked at Jeanie.

'Why?' he asked.

'I'm sorry!' Jeanie cried, making to go to him, but Ray instantly put his hands up, as if to push her away. She stopped in her tracks, her face crumpling. 'Please, Ray. Don't do this to me.'

'Don't do this to you?' he cried, tears rolling down his face. 'Jeanie, this is all your own doing.'

'I know!' she wailed, 'and I'm so sorry. I don't know what got into me.'

It was in that moment that Ray's face changed from abject hurt and sorrow, to full-blown fury.

'I think everyone here knows damn well it was Sebastian that got into you.'

Jeanie looked like she'd been physically struck.

'Please, Ray,' she whispered, 'don't speak like that in front of the kids.'

'You forget, Mum,' Charlotte piped up, 'that we might be kids, but we're not tiny any more. We know exactly what you've been up to. I can't believe that my own mother has been cheating on my dad. And did you have any idea what you looked like up on that stage?' Charlotte's eyes were blazing. 'You looked like some sad middle-aged woman trying to convince herself she still has sex appeal. Instead you made the biggest fool of yourself and, ultimately, us. You're an embarrassment to your family. But most of all, you're an embarrassment to yourself.'

'Charlotte, you don't understand,' Jeanie sobbed.

'No, she doesn't,' Ray spat. 'None of us do. Come on, kids. Let's go home. And you'– he stabbed a finger at his wife – 'you can find somewhere else to sleep tonight. Go to your lover.'

'I don't want to go to Sebastian!' Jeanie cried, her chest heaving as she burst into fresh tears. 'I want to go home with you. I love you.'

But Ray and the children weren't listening. They'd already turned on their heels and were striding along the corridor, towards the car park. Alex and Simon followed, Alex talking in a low voice to Ray, keeping him calm, uttering soothing advice, urging him to sleep on things and not do anything rash.

Caro moved over to Jeanie, as did I.

'What am I going to do?' she sobbed.

'Nothing,' I said, taking hold of her hand. It was cold in mine, the fingers wet from where she'd been wiping her face. 'Ray is devastated. Right now, he needs some space.'

'Come home with us,' said David. 'Holly's right. You *both* need some space.'

'I don't want space,' Jeanie sobbed, 'I just want my husband.'

I stared helplessly at my friend. She'd had a mid-life crisis and gone off the rails, taking so many people with her into the sidings. Even though I now knew the name of her lover – knew it wasn't Alex – there was a part of me that held back from Jeanie still. I knew why. It was because she'd flagrantly kissed my husband at the start of the night. What had that been about? Simply a case of riding high on over-confidence? Or trying to make Sebastian jealous? Either way, I didn't feel able to extend the hand of friendship and offer her a bed for the night in the Hart household.

'Let's go,' said Caro gently.

'Do you want me to come with you?' I asked Caro. 'Just for a while.'

'No,' said David, replying for his wife. 'I think you're forgetting that this is your husband's birthday party. You need to stay here, with him.'

'Of course,' I said, relieved that I could step out of this drama. I felt I'd had enough of my own recently.

'Can you do me a favour, Holly?' asked Caro.

'Absolutely, just name it,' I replied.

'Let our kids stay at yours tonight? I don't think young ears should be listening to all this, especially if Ray comes around later to talk to Jeanie.'

'You're right,' I agreed.

I gave Jeanie's hand a final squeeze, before Caro and David led her away.

Chapter Fifty-One

Despite it being Alex's party, he wasn't interested in staying. He seemed out of sorts, and I put it down to the very public melt-down of Jeanie and Ray's marriage.

'I'm tired, Holly,' he said, as we stood outside the Mayflower Suite, the pounding music making the double doors reverberate. 'If you want to stay, then do so.'

'But it's your birthday, darling,' I said, trying not to wheedle. 'You can't leave.'

'I can, and I am,' he said firmly. 'I'll go and say my goodbyes, and then order a minicab. Are you coming with me, or not?'

Disappointment flooded through me. Bugger Jeanie and her sordid love affair for wrecking Alex's party, not to mention the considerable financial outlay it had cost me. Everything was spoiled. Why did the best-laid plans never work out? And bugger Alex for always being tired. I was fed up with it. Sophie had already gone back inside, Caro's children trailing happily after her. I could see them through one of the thin glass oblongs in the doors, dancing energetically and looking, luckily, like nothing awful had happened. Why should I further spoil her evening by saying we had to go home? I was also still smarting with annoyance at Annabelle. Still, if Alex went home, at least Annabelle wouldn't have the opportunity to appropriate my husband for the rest of the evening. It was true – every cloud *did* have a silver lining.

I sighed. 'If you really want to go, then do,' I said, waving a hand dismissively. 'But if you don't mind, I'll stay. After all,' I smiled tightly, 'the suite and the band cost a fair bit, so the rest of us might as well get my money's worth.' I realised the comment sounded rather bitter, but was beyond caring. 'I won't cancel the return minicab. I'll be back with all the children a little after midnight.'

'Okay, and I'm sorry to do a bunk from my own birthday party but' – Alex shrugged – 'all that business with Jeanie and Ray has left rather a sour taste in my mouth.'

'I thought you were tired,' I said accusingly.

'That as well,' said Alex hurriedly. 'Look, I'll see you later.' And with that he planted a hasty kiss on my cheek and made off to reception to call a cab. I stared after my husband wondering what sort of man was constantly tired, so much so that he couldn't even stay at his own party. I looked at my wristwatch. It was only half past eight.

I walked back into the Mayflower Suite and caught Sophie's eye. She grinned and waved as she danced with Lizzie, Joe and a large group of schoolmates. At least they were all having a good time. It made up for the disappointment of Alex not being here. And actually, perhaps I should take a leaf out of Sophie's book? I'd paid for this chuffing party, so I might as well enjoy it. I spotted Mum and Dad with Aunty Shirley, Jack and Simon. I'd quite like to buttonhole my brother and see if Ray had given any last-minute indication of things being repairable with Jeanie. They were all laughing and dancing rather badly. For them, the earlier drama was forgotten. Perhaps I would ask Simon about Ray tomorrow instead. For now, it was nicer to let the music claim me. Moving across the floor, I joined them. But within five minutes, Simon made his excuses to leave, saying his ex had texted him and wanted to talk.

'Good luck,' said Dad, clapping Simon on the back.

I spent the next few hours happily doing ceroc with my father and jiving with Jack, washing down copious amounts of booze to cool me down when hot and out of breath. When the band switched tempo and the lead singer sang a love ballad, I found myself once again swaying with Jack, my body pressed up against his, and familiar stirrings rippling through me.

'For the second week running,' he whispered into my ear, 'I'm dancing with the most beautiful woman in the room.'

I laughed. 'You do say the nicest of things.'

'Only because it's true,' he assured.

I was too happy to protest. I leaned into him, enjoying his proximity, the smell of aftershave on his skin, the warmth of his body through the thin fabric of his shirt, and the touch of his hair tickling my hands that were now lightly meeting at the back of his neck. The urge to run my fingers through his hair was overwhelming. I wasn't the most beautiful woman in the room. In fact, I wasn't beautiful at all. Attractive on a good day. But Jack certainly made me feel beautiful. It was late now. Indeed, nearly time to go home. As we moved slowly in a tight circle, my eyes scanned the crowd for a woman who was most definitely very beautiful. Annabelle. My gaze flicked from left to right, my irises like searchlights in a prison camp, seeking the enemy out. For, in my head, Annabelle was indeed an enemy. She wasn't here. I tensed as the sickening realisation dawned that I hadn't seen Annabelle for ages. Not since my husband had left his own party.

Chapter Fifty-Two

When the minicab came to a stop outside our house, I practically threw the fare at the driver, so keen was I to get inside the front door. Sophie, Joe and Lizzie were taking an extraordinary amount of time to get out of the cab, and I suspected they'd shipped a few sneaky drinks at the party and were slightly the worse for wear. Leaving them to sort themselves out, I stuck the key in the lock and almost fell into the hallway in my haste. Rupert jumped out of his basket, bug-eyed, yawning, tail wagging in welcome as he stretched his front paws out, head down, bum up, and went off to greet the children.

'Alex?' I called.

The lights were off downstairs, and I took the stairs two at a time, practically crashing into our bedroom. As the door flew backwards, Alex regarded me in annoyance.

'Do you have to make such a racket?' he complained.

'I thought you were ash-leep,' I slurred.

'Well if I was, I'm not now,' he said petulantly. He was sitting up in bed, glasses perched on the end of his nose, a book between his hands.

'You said you were tired,' I said accusingly.

'I was,' he replied, 'and still am.'

'So why aren't you ash-leep?' I demanded.

'I've been dozing on and off, but didn't nod off completely because I found myself listening out for you.'

'Is that so?' I squinted at him suspiciously.

'You're sounding very punchy,' he sighed. 'What's up?'

'What's up?' I stared at him incredulously. In the last few hours Annabelle Huntingdon-Smyth had called *my* husband *her* hero before suspiciously vanishing, one of my best friends had publicly wrecked her marriage, my carefully planned surprise celebration had backfired, the birthday boy had abandoned his own party, and now he had the audacity to ask me what was up?

'Where's Annabelle?' I demanded.

'How should I know?'

'Where is she?' I repeated, my eyes full of accusation.

'If you're going to create a scene, Holly, shut the bedroom door.'

I flicked the door shut with my foot. It clipped a hovering Rupert on the nose and he let out a squeak. I was momentarily torn between whipping the door open again to give the dog a cuddle or marching over to Alex and slapping him.

'I'll ask for the last time, where is she?'

Alex lifted the duvet. 'Not under here.' He leaned out of bed, peering underneath. 'Nor here,' came his muffled voice. Straightening up, he opened a bedside drawer. 'Nope, she's not in there either.'

I narrowed my eyes at him. 'She was here earlier.'

'What, in this drawer?'

'Don't be facetious!' I howled. 'She left the party soon after you did. Now why might that be, hmm? Was it, perchance, because you are her hero? Did she follow you home, Alex, while you dashed ahead, hastening into the bedroom, twirling around in the en suite, before emerging in your superhero tights and cape all set to wow her?'

'I'm not sure Annabelle likes her men dressed in tights and capes,' said Alex, stroking his chin thoughtfully.

'I can't carry on like this,' I said, drink and shredded nerves catching up with me. I stuck out a hand and leaned against the wall, suddenly feeling a need to be propped up.

Alex got out of bed and came over to me. He was naked and his body smelled of lemon shower gel. He put his arms around me and hugged me tight.

'You're doing it again, Holly.'

'Doing what?' I demanded.

'Making drama where there is none.'

I froze. Was I? Oh my God, he was right. My anger, riding so high until that moment, did an instant U-turn, evaporating faster than a kettle that had boiled itself dry. Silent, I slowly nodded. It was true. I was running old patterns again. Jealousy. Insecurity. Wild accusations. My thoughts once more turned to seeing my doctor for a psychiatric referral. Here we go again. Round and round in never-ending circles. This had to stop, once and for all.

'Hey,' Alex said softly, 'go downstairs and get a nightcap for the two of us. We'll drink it in bed together. Have a snuggle.'

'Can't you get it?' I asked in a small voice.

Alex released me and stood back, arms outstretched, indicating that I look at his body.

'I'm not dressed. I don't want Caro's kids and our daughter seeing me.'

'Oh, right. Okay, I'll go. Brandy?'

'Lovely,' he replied.

I paused, looking at his face. Was I mistaken or… did he just waggle his eyebrows? In which case… oh my goodness! My husband was sending out secret signals. He wanted to cosy down in bed together. Have a brandy. Warm his extremities up. And *snuggle*. Secret code for getting intimate. I didn't need telling twice.

Once again the bedroom door nearly came off its hinges as I wrenched it open and almost flew down the stairs, heading off to the drinks cabinet, extracting the best crystal, slopping amber liquid into both glasses, doubling and then tripling the dose to help Alex's *extremities*. I cackled to myself as I nearly filled the balloons to the brim. *Get that into you Alex, and then you can get into me*, I sniggered. And then a light bulb went off in my head. *Oh yes, perfect, Holly. Brilliant idea, just brilliant.* I hastened into the kitchen, found what I was looking for, then on to the lounge, prowling around in the dark like a burglar as I gathered up my booty, then stole back upstairs with the swag wedged under my armpits, brandy balloons held aloft.

'Here we are,' I said, placing one drink on the dressing table, and passing the other to Alex. I turned away and headed off to the bathroom, pausing briefly to swig some brandy. I felt it scorch down my throat and warm me all over. I was momentarily transported back to being in Jack's arms at the party, feeling the heat from his body against mine and the familiar sensation of zings zipping up and down my spine, and downright lust in my loins. I shoved the feelings away. Now was not the time to be thinking about Jack.

'Where are you going, darling?'

'Just going to freshen up,' I trilled.

'What have you got under your armpits?'

'Nothing,' I said, smartly shutting the bathroom door. I hadn't had much time to put any thought into my burlesque outfit. No matter. These props would suffice. One just needed a little imagination.

I foraged in the bathroom cabinet and removed some eyelash glue for fake lashes I'd never worn. The box had promised that they would stick to your eyelids for a week if required. With a bit of luck, it would do the trick for what I had in mind. I stripped down to my pants and, leaving on my stilettoes, quickly got to work squeezing out a sticky circle around both my nipples.

'Will you be long?' Alex called.

'Coming!' I replied, squeaking with excitement. And hopefully, we would be in the next few minutes! *Such smutty thoughts, Holly, so naughty!* Sliding open the bathroom door, I let one leg appear, slowly waving it up and down, before the rest of me emerged. 'Ta-daaaaa!' I chirruped, flinging my arms wide.

'Good God,' said Alex, as he surveyed his wife, a vision in elbow-length washing-up gloves and strategically placed curtain tassels. It was a shame my pants were size generous from M&S rather than size miniscule from Victoria's Secret, but at least they were black and not my purple-and-white spotty pair. And… damn… I didn't have any music. No matter. If Jeanie could sing at a party, I could belt out a song in my bedroom.

As I launched into Shirley Bassey's 'Big Spender', I pulled out the stool from under the dressing table and put one leg on it, sticking my bum out, whooshing my yellow rubber gloves up into the air, then stroking them slowly down my body as I warned my startled husband in a muddle of lyrics that I didn't pop my cork for the postman every day of the week. I kicked the stool out from under me and planted my legs wide, slapping my Marigolds against my thighs, and then proceeded to bend low, all the way down to the floor, backside out again as I asked my gob-smacked husband if he'd like to have some fun, fun, fun. My curtain tassels swayed gamely as I regarded the bedroom door upside-down through my parted legs and yodelled to my husband that he was going to have a good time, such a good time, and—

'For God's sake, Mum,' said Sophie, barging in unannounced, 'it sounds like a cat's being strangled in here, and… oh!' She froze, mouth open, her expression one of horror as we regarded each other through my legs. Beyond her, I caught sight of Lizzie and Joe, wide-eyed, hands flying to their mouths as they sniggered like Mutley. Through a haze of alcohol, my brain struggled to find an excuse.

'I was just… just—'

'Yes, I can see that you were just-just,' she snarled, before reversing backwards and slamming the door shut.

'Oh my God,' I said to the door panels.

'Holly, please can you straighten up and come to bed.'

I could tell from the impatient tone of my husband's voice that he wasn't requesting my presence by his side for anything other than putting the light out and going to sleep.

'I can't,' I whimpered.

'Why not?'

'I think I've put my back out. Help. I can't move.'

What happened next was possibly even more shameful than being seen by my daughter in such a ridiculous state of undress. When

Alex realised I literally couldn't straighten up, he rang Jack who, fortunately, was still awake and having a party post-mortem with Aunty Shirley and my parents.

'Sorry to trouble you at this hour, Jack, but Holly's put her back out and can't move.'

'I'll be right over,' said Jack.

Minutes later, he was ringing the doorbell.

'For heaven's sake,' I screeched to Alex, as he made to answer the door to our late-night caller, 'give me my dressing gown.'

Alex bundled it up and chucked it at me, then disappeared along the landing. I had pulled off the rubber gloves, which now lay discarded on the floor. However, the curtain tassels were still attached to my boobs. Attempts to remove them had had me squeaking with pain. What the heck had been in that tube? Superglue? I had managed to shuffle forward and was now leaning on my elbows over the bed, backside still out as if demanding a good spanking. I felt myself go hot and cold with mortification as I heard Alex greet Jack.

'Go on up,' Alex said. 'I was just having a nightcap. I might as well have it in the lounge and watch a bit of late-night telly.

'Sure, no worries,' Jack replied.

There was the sound of footsteps on the stairs and, seconds later, the man himself walked into the bedroom.

'I'm so sorry,' I whimpered, 'this is beyond embarrassing.'

He gave me a smile. 'I've seen all sorts in my time, Holly. Black pants are nothing.'

I clutched my bundled-up dressing gown to my chest, hoping to God he didn't catch sight of my lounge's curtain tassels grafted to my breasts. No way was I going to ask him to surgically remove those. I'd soak them off in the shower later. Just as soon as I could stand upright again.

'Right, let's see what's going on here,' said Jack, placing his hands on my back.

Zinnnngggggggggggg.

I let out a low moan and collapsed on the bed as Jack's touch left me shuddering and gasping aloud, so much so that I was worried my nipple tassels would soon be standing to attention.

'This just needs some massage,' said Jack, 'I apologise in advance, but this requires some firmness.'

'Go ahead,' I panted, as his fingers got to work, kneading and unkinking my spine and other parts that I had no idea were so knotted up. As I alternated between sounding like a woman in labour and a studio full of porn stars, I could only thank God in his heaven that Jack thought I was shouting out in pain, and not because every one of my nerve-endings was wide awake with arousal.

'There,' he said eventually, as I finally stopped writhing like a serpent, 'I think you're done.'

He was wrong. I was nowhere near done. I could have kept going all night and felt heady from so much pleasure.

'I know it's really late, Holly, but if you're not too tired, I'd advise you to have a hot shower, then take a couple of paracetamol. You should be good as new in the morning.'

'Thank you,' I murmured, avoiding direct eye contact. I had a feeling my pupils had dilated to the size of my bedside lampshades.

'I'll see myself out. You get into that shower.'

As he shut the bedroom door after him, I tottered off to the bathroom feeling like I'd undergone ten rounds with Cupid and come out of the boxing ring covered in sprinkles, stardust and glitter-tipped arrows. Taking a deep breath, I exhaled shakily and slid back the shower door. As I stepped inside the cubicle, I let out a cry of pain, but it was nothing to do with my back. I'd stood on something sharp. Carefully bending down, I plucked the tiny object from the shower base. Straightening up, I examined it under one of the overhead spotlights, and then gasped as shockwaves ricocheted through me. For there, glinting away in the palm of my hand, was a pretty diamond-stud earring.

Chapter Fifty-Three

As I stood in the shower cubicle, I began to shake. I didn't own diamond earrings. And despite Sophie mithering me to let her have her ears pierced for her impending fourteenth birthday, as yet she had no jewellery collection save for a silver baby christening bracelet. Carefully, I placed the stud on the edge of the basin, then stepped back into the shower. Shivering violently now, from both cold and shock, I let scalding hot water jet over my body, attempting to blast away both the wretched curtain tassels and the horror of what I'd discovered. There was no safe explanation for this. None at all. Alex couldn't possibly tell me this was all in my head. Not unless I had suddenly made a supernatural connection and my paranoia was so deep I was manifesting things. Finally, I had evidence. He'd brought his floozy back to the house while I'd been at the party.

I deliberately stayed in the shower for a good half an hour. I couldn't address this tonight. Not while Caro's kids were here. Nor did I want Sophie hearing me let rip at her father. This needed dealing with when my head was clear. In the light of day. When no children were around. And preferably no knives, or I might be in danger of giving my husband a castration without anaesthetic.

By the time I emerged from the bathroom, with throbbing nipples and a pounding headache, Alex was fast asleep. I regarded my husband in the soft lamplight, sleeping so peacefully. How could he do this to me? And not just me, but our daughter? He'd wrecked everything. In the last few hours, three marriages had gone into crisis. First, Izzy and Sebastian's. Then Jeanie and Ray's. Now mine. As I swallowed down some painkillers and slid under the duvet, its crispness struck me. I inhaled deeply as the scent of fresh linen shot up my nostrils. The cheating bastard had even changed the bedding, and I'd been too befuddled earlier to notice. I recalled how, previously, Alex had got out of bed to hug me, and how I'd noticed the scent of lemon shower gel on his skin. After he and Annabelle had writhed around all over my marital bed, the pair of them had showered together. My headache threatened to go into overdrive, and I closed my eyes, trying to blot out the pain in my temples as well as the ache in my heart.

I found myself replaying the events of the party, over and over. Annabelle on the stage. Laughing at Alex. Telling him he was her hero. Had she been wearing earrings? I didn't recall seeing anything long and dangly glinting through the strands of her hair and re-ran the moment she'd gazed up at my husband, smiling adoringly, shaking back her glossy mane, slowing the memory down, frame by frame, to revealing one earlobe. For just the smallest moment, something tiny had sparkled under the lights.

I had no memory of falling asleep, but awoke exhausted. As I swam to the surface of consciousness, two things struck me. The first was that Alex wasn't in the bed. The second was that I'd left the earring on the basin in the bathroom. Horrified, I threw back the covers and made to jump out of bed, only to feel my back creak alarmingly. I took a deep breath, and carefully slid my legs sideways, before gingerly standing up. My back protested briefly, but behaved. Padding swiftly across the bedroom on bare feet, I went into the en suite and looked fearfully at the basin. An involuntary gasp escaped my lips. The earring had gone. Nooo. No, no, no. Without it, I couldn't confront Alex. He'd tell me I'd been drunk. Imagining things. I could hear the condescending tone of his voice now.

'An earring, you say? What, on the basin? Don't be ridiculous. Holly, I know you don't like Annabelle, but have you any idea how tiresome your accusations are?'

Where was he? Where had he gone? To her?

'Annabelle, darling, the shit has hit the metaphorical fan. Holly discovered your diamond stud. Here, take it. Hide them, and deny all knowledge, because she's bound to roar round here and confront you.'

Annabelle didn't want to marry Alex. Jack had already pointed out that she wasn't 'wife material'. And Alex didn't want to divorce me. He'd said on several occasions that we had a nice life and he didn't want to take it apart. But he'd lied about me being the only woman for him. It seems I was nothing more than a housekeeper – the woman who kept his home clean and tidy, washed and ironed his shirts, put a nice nutritious meal on the table every night, and with who he had the very occasional bit of duty sex. Whereas Annabelle was his lover and got the best of him. No smelly socks to wash, no dog-breath first thing in the morning, no marks around the toilet bowl or whiffy dental scrubs. Well stuff that. The earring might have gone, but there was bound to be further evidence. Because there had to be something, somewhere. And I was going to find it.

Chapter Fifty-Four

Alex rang me as I was getting dressed.

'Morning, darling!' he trilled.

'Hello,' I said uncertainly, my gung-ho spirit momentarily deserting me. 'Where are you?'

'Out on the Common with Rupert. I thought I'd leave you to lie in. David has already been round to collect Lizzie and Joe, and Sophie went back to bed looking like death warmed up. I swear our daughter has a hangover.'

God, he sounded chirpy. And normal. For one crazy moment I actually wondered if I *had* imagined treading on an earring in the shower cubicle.

'I think Caro is anxious to catch up with you,' Alex continued. 'Apparently Jeanie went home to Ray this morning. Their kids are going to Jeanie's mother for a week and they're hoping to quietly thrash things out.'

'That's good.' Actually, I wasn't interested in Jeanie's marriage. I was only interested in mine. 'When will you be home?'

'About an hour. Poor old Rupert hasn't had a decent walk for ages, and he's having a great time. I wondered if you fancied me stopping at that little coffee shop around the corner from ours, and picking you up a warm pain au chocolat? We can have one together, if you like, when I'm back.'

'Sure,' I said. If he wanted to play games, so would I.

'Okay, darling. See you in a bit.'

'Lovely,' I said, putting a smile in my voice. Hanging up, I realised I didn't have much time to find further evidence of Annabelle having been in my house last night or, indeed, at any time before that. Raking a brush quickly through my hair, I got to work.

I started off systematically going through Alex's wardrobe. No trouser pocket was left unchecked, no jacket untouched, as my fingers burrowed and invaded every garment. Next, every drawer was opened and searched, even the insides of each individual sock. Boxer shorts were unfolded and swiftly re-folded, shoes tipped upside down, and his wash-bag emptied out in a tumble of products and then quickly replaced. Thirty minutes later, I was none the wiser. *Think, Holly, think. Where would you hide something – anything – that might be significant in some way, and that you wouldn't want Alex to see?*

I marched over to the bed and upended the mattress onto the floor. A piece of A4 paper gently floated down onto the carpet, coming to rest under the radiator. For a moment, I just stared at it. Hurrying, I hauled the heavy mattress back into place, and quickly straightened the duvet. Scooping up the paper, I hastened into the en suite and shut the door, locking it for good measure. Whatever this was, I wanted to examine it without interruption.

My hands fluttered around the paper's edges as I placed it on the floor. Squatting down, I immediately realised it was a love letter, written in Alex's hand, but for some reason never given to the addressee. The content was an outpouring of a deep love that could never be.

My darling

Oh yes, you are indeed my darling. This is the letter that gets written, but never sent. The letter that is meant to ease the troubled heart, soothe the tormented mind and bring peace to the disturbed soul. My counsellor told me to write this for – ha! – therapy, can you believe?

I paused. Rocked back on my heels. Alex had been seeing a counsellor? What sort of counsellor? A marriage guidance one? For how long? And why? *Well, presumably to discuss his terrible angst about this bloody woman, Holly, that's why!* I sucked on my teeth, eyes filling with tears as I stared in horror at the blurring words. I swiped the tears away with the heel of one hand, anxious that none splash onto the paper, which was now flapping about as if caught in a breeze, so bad were my hands shaking. I couldn't work out whether my emotions were one of devastating hurt, or incandescent rage.

The moment I met you, I knew my life would never be the same again. Does that sound corny? Sorry. I'm a dentist, not a poet. However, I am a lover. And oh, how I've loved you… still love you.

I let out an involuntary sob and stuffed a fist against my mouth, biting down hard on the knuckles. Oh my God. This was real. My husband had, without a shred of doubt, been with someone else.

Perversely I cursed you too. It takes all my willpower not to give in to such feelings. So instead, I remain outwardly calm, but inwardly, oh inwardly, you have no idea what you have done to me. Still do to me. I can remember once, in a moment of intense misery, using every ounce of my being to wish that you would appear. I shouted out loud, to the sky. Can you believe that? Me of all people! Down to earth, sensible me! I don't go in for all that cosmic ordering nonsense. But the universe answered. It delivered you to my front door. Like a genie.

Tears were rolling down my face now. Oh my God. Alex had actually written 'like a genie'. It was there in black and white. Don't tell me this was nothing to do with Annabelle, but everything to do with Jeanie again? It couldn't be… could it? Or was Alex juggling Annabelle *and* Jeanie, and Jeanie juggling Sebastian *and* Alex? How many lovers could one person have, for heaven's sake?

Each time I wanted you, I'd wish with all my being, and you'd appear! How crazy is that! It's beyond crazy. It's downright bizarre. And I came to think of you as a kind of magical being. Indeed, just your presence was magic. I wanted to reach out and touch you, hold you, kiss you, make love to you. Again and again and again.

Make love again and again and again? This, from a man who I'd always believed had a low sex drive? No wonder he could only manage six times a year with me. Whenever he'd staggered into our bedroom, hand clutching his forehead as he'd yawned his way over to the bed declaring he was exhausted, it was because he truly was shagged. Annabelle might be a lover, but it was my best friend who was the love of his life. I wondered feverishly how long it had been going on. I blanched. Well, years. Probably all our married lives if our pathetic excuse of a sex life was anything to go by. All that crap Jeanie had spun about having a shunt in her car with Sebastian and only recently falling for a lover. Sebastian meant the same to her as Annabelle meant to Alex. They were just distractions. So why hadn't they simply gone off with each other right at the start? Before the children came along? Before there were so many hearts to break? I shook my head. I didn't understand. Just didn't understand at all.

You loved that I likened you to a genie. Believe me when I say I wish things could have been different. Even now I wish that with all my heart. But I'm a coward, darling. I can't do it. I will no doubt go to my grave regretting it. But in death I hope we will one day find each other, and finally be together.

Flipping heck. That was a bit dramatic, wasn't it? How chuffing marvellous did the pair of them think they were, doing the decent thing in keeping their respective families together? My lip curled as I mentally sneered at my husband's so-called virtue. Pathetic, Alex. Absolutely pathetic. And as for you, Jeanie. To think I've had you in this house, under my husband's nose, time and time again, getting him all in a lather, with you so coolly acting out the charade of being my best friend, when all along the two of you couldn't wait until you were together, ripping each other's clothes off, and fucking each other's brains out. I stood up and, swaying like a drunk, lurched over to the toilet bowl and threw up and up and up.

Chapter Fifty-Five

Wiping my mouth, I came out of the en suite and replaced the letter back under the mattress just as Alex arrived home with Rupert.

'Yoo hoo!' he called. 'Hot croissants for everyone!'

I came out onto the landing and stuck my head over the bannister rail.

'Hi,' I said pleasantly.

Alex held the paper bag of goodies aloft, smiling triumphantly. 'Breakfast for the two ladies in my life,' he grinned.

'I thought I was the only woman,' I said, careful to keep my tone neutral.

'Sometimes you have to make room for Sophie, darling,' said Alex, his voice teasing as he slung his jacket over the bannister and released Rupert's lead. 'His paws are clean, by the way. It's not wet outside.'

'Good, that makes a change,' I said, coming down the stairs. My brain was whirring. 'You put the kettle on, darling,' I said, 'only I need to ring Caro. She left a message on my mobile while I was in the loo asking me to call her back.' The lie slipped off my tongue so easily.

'Sure.' Alex headed off to the kitchen and I heard him greet Sophie, who was now downstairs and evidently slumped over the table judging by the gist of conversation that floated back to me. That would teach our daughter to filch alcohol. I marvelled at such normal thoughts when another part of my brain was in turmoil. I moved along the hallway to the study and shut the door after me. Caro answered almost immediately.

'Oh, Holly,' she sighed, 'what a flipping night I've had. I've spoken to Jeanie, but I'll update you properly if you fancy coming over for coffee later.'

'Caro, I don't give two hoots about Jeanie. Something terrible has happened—'

'Ah, yes,' she interrupted, 'I did hear. You might as well know that when David collected Lizzie and Joe they were full of glee about you doing a lap dance for Alex. Nice to know things are—'

'Fuck the lap dance,' I spat.

There was an astonished silence.

'Holly? What's the matter?'

'Everything. I can't talk. Listen, there's something I need to do. And I need to do it tonight. Will you have Sophie for me and take her to school tomorrow? It's urgent.'

'Of course. You don't need to ask. Is there anything I can help with?'

'Just Sophie. I'll explain properly tomorrow, when I pick her up.'

'Okay,' said Caro, sounding worried. 'Just remember I'm only a phone call away, right?'

I gulped, and nodded, not that she could see that. 'Thanks,' I said. 'See you later.'

I hung up and walked out of the study and into the kitchen where my husband was seated at the island with Sophie, the two of them munching companionably on their croissants, as Sophie filled him in on how Joe, last night, had gone around knocking back unguarded drinks.

'No wonder that boy looked rough this morning,' Alex laughed. 'Ah well, we've all done it.' He looked up at me as I joined them, and grinned. 'How's the hangover?'

'Not too bad,' I said, cranking up a smile.

'And the back?'

I saw Sophie roll her eyes.

'As good as new.'

'Excellent.'

My husband pushed a plate towards me as I sat down.

'I've been invited to a school reunion,' I said brightly.

'Lovely,' said Alex. 'When is it?'

'Tonight.'

Alex looked surprised. 'That's rather short notice, isn't it?'

'Yes,' I nodded. 'But I'd really like to go. It's in' – I glanced about for inspiration, noticed the clock on the wall bearing the name 'Cambridge Clocks' – 'Cambridgeshire,' I blurted.

'That's a bit of a trek,' Alex frowned.

'Yes,' I nodded. 'And there's a chance to stay the night. I hope you don't mind, darling, but I've said yes. Can you text Jenny and ask her to arrange for my shift tomorrow to be covered by someone else? I'm sorry it's such short notice, but it was rather sprung upon me,' I gabbled, 'and who knows when another get-together will be organi—'

'Fine, it's fine,' said Alex, putting up a hand to halt my prattle.

'How will I get to school tomorrow if you're not here?' Sophie turned to me, her face surly. Now the party was over, normal teenage stroppiness had resumed.

'I'll take you,' said Alex smoothly.

'You go to work at silly o'clock on a Monday,' said Sophie, 'I'm not standing at the school gates at half past seven in the morning.'

'Then take the bus,' said Alex, refusing to rise to our daughter's impending tantrum.

'It's freezing!' Sophie cried. 'I'm not waiting at the bus stop in this weather.'

'I've already spoken to Caro,' I interrupted my daughter, before she went off on a tirade, wound up her father and our Sunday morning erupted into a blazing row. 'You can stay the night at theirs.'

'Good,' said Sophie, looking slightly mollified. She glanced across at my half-eaten croissant. 'Don't you want that?'

'Think I'm still a bit hungover,' I said, 'you have it.'

I passed her my plate. She took it from me and hopped down from her tall stool. 'I'm taking this up to my room. I'll leave you two to talk in peace.' Her lip curled slightly. 'Just don't do anything risqué with those washing-up gloves while I'm gone, Mum.'

And she bounced off with Rupert skipping at her heels, his hairy face full of hope that he'd shortly be licking all the crumbs off her plate. I was left staring into space, feeling slightly sick at the plans I'd started to lay down. It was finally going to happen. I was setting a trap.

Chapter Fifty-Six

Even though I now had fresh evidence of Alex's involvement with another person, I wasn't prepared to confront him with it. Why? Because I wanted to see this woman with him. Discover first-hand exactly who she was. I was at the end of my tether with the seesawing of emotions and constant guessing games. It was time to catch this woman in my bed. And I had no doubt that I would.

Minutes after Sophie had excused herself, Alex did the same, going off to the study and shutting the door. I had no idea what he was doing in there, whether he was secretly texting on his mobile, private messaging on Facebook, or murmuring quietly into the telephone. But it would have been one of those three things, for sure.

As late afternoon darkness descended, I went through the motions of packing an overnight bag for myself, and another for Sophie, then gaily trilled goodbye to my husband as he hugged Sophie and reminded her not to stay up too late talking to Lizzie and Joe, that it was a school day tomorrow, and to be good. He turned to me and squeezed me quickly.

'Have a lovely time, darling. Don't elope with any old school crushes, eh!' he said good-humouredly.

'I'll try not to,' I chortled, feeling slightly sick as he let me go. Would that be the last time he held me as his wife?

Alex stood on the doorstep, and waved us off, Rupert at his heels. This was my last chance to turn a blind eye, not go ahead with what I'd put in motion. I could drop Sophie off, turn around and say to Alex, 'I've had a change of heart. Stuff the school reunion, let's go out to dinner, just the two of us!' and he would discreetly text the love of his life that there had been a change of plan, and then Alex and I could carry on living our lovely life, in our lovely house, living a lovely lie. For a moment I was tempted. But then I remembered the words in the love letter, and they burned a pain deep into my soul with an ache that I knew would never go away. I wanted someone to love *me* like that. To vow to seek me out in the afterlife and be together forever. I hastily blinked back tears that threatened to spill and told myself to man up and see this through to the bitter end.

By the time we pulled up outside Caro's house a few minutes later, my daughter had recovered some humour, and scampered off to greet Lizzie and Joe with barely a backward glance at her mother. Caro came out to the car, arms folded across her chest as if to ward off the chilly night air and stood by my open driver's window.

'Can you tell me quickly what's up?' she asked. 'I'm worried about you. First there's all this upset with Jeanie, and now you're causing me to fret. I'll be totally grey at this rate.'

'Sorry,' I quavered, not trusting myself to speak, 'but I can't right now. I absolutely promise we'll talk tomorrow.'

She nodded, her face full of concern, as I buzzed up the window. Indicating, I pulled away, pointing the car in the direction of home.

Arriving back in my road where everything was so familiar and dear, I saw the house lights on, and caught a glimpse of Alex sitting alone in front of the television in the lounge, the curtains not yet drawn against the winter darkness. I motored on, slowing down as I approached a curve in the road just a few yards from the house. It marked the entrance to playing fields where local school football teams played, mostly at weekends. But now the metal gates were shut and padlocked, and overhanging trees would afford me shadowy concealment, set back from street lamps. I pulled over, executed an awkward three-point turn, and then parked facing the house. From this distance I could no longer view Alex clearly, but I could see enough – certainly the arrival of a visitor.

After five minutes, Alex briefly appeared in the lounge window. He pulled the curtains together. Lights were on everywhere. Another ten minutes passed, and I began to shiver. I wasn't sure if it was out of nerves, anticipation or the freezing cold temperature. A few more minutes ticked by painfully slowly, during which the heavens suddenly opened. As rain lashed against the car's windscreen, the glass began to steam up. And then I heard an approaching engine. Seconds later, a minicab from a local firm swept into my road, its telephone number just about visible on the signage across its bumper. I leaned forward in my seat, rubbing my sleeve against the glass, peering through the smeariness, my eyes straining to see who was getting out of the cab as it stopped outside the marital home. The taxi's rear door opened, a large umbrella went up and a pair of slim jeaned legs alighted on the pavement. My nose was practically pressed up against the windscreen. Who was it?

The figure hurried up the garden path, body hidden by the angle of the enormous umbrella. The door opened and Rupert – the traitor – greeted her with a wagging tail. The minicab moved forward, obscuring the visitor as she collapsed her umbrella. By the time the car had moved away to give me a much-needed clear view, our front door had closed. I watched, taking short quick breaths as my heart raced unpleasantly, wondering what to do next. Lights were now being turned off, one by one, until just a single solitary window remained shining like a golden square against the black of night. It was the master bedroom – mine and Alex's room. Seconds later, Alex once again appeared, and flicked the curtains shut. I inhaled sharply. Mission accomplished. The trap had been set, and both Alex and his lover had fallen headlong into it.

Releasing my seat belt, I pulled up my coat collar against the awful weather and opened the car door. With my head down against the freezing and relentless rain, and hands stuffed deep inside my pockets, I walked with purpose towards the marital home, up the garden path, and quietly let myself into the hallway. Rupert looked surprised to see me, but didn't bark in greeting. After all, he knew me. He didn't bother getting out of his basket and wagged his tail apologetically. I slipped past him and, dripping all over the carpet, quietly moved up the staircase, my heart pounding in time to every stealthy footstep. Avoiding the area on the landing where the floorboard creaked, I tiptoed along until I was outside my bedroom door. From within came the sound of much hilarity, snorts and giggles, and I realised with a pang that Alex and I had never collapsed against each other, laughing weakly until our sides ached. But then again, I didn't hold Alex's heart in the palm of my hand. I reached for the door handle and pushed it down.

My eyes widened at the scene that greeted me. Alex and his lover were naked. The two of them were messing about with my curtain tassels, which I'd left on the bedside table. They were taking it in turns to put them over their nipples, swish them about and crease up with hilarity. Something briefly sparkled in an earlobe, and I recognised the diamond stud I'd found on the floor in the shower cubicle. They were making such a racket laughing, and so absorbed in each other, that for a good five seconds my presence didn't even register. But in that moment, standing in the bedroom doorway, time stood still for me. Those five seconds seemed like an eternity during which everything fell into place. Suddenly it all made sense. This was why my husband wasn't interested in sex with me. Because lying in my husband's arms was my brother. Simon.

Chapter Fifty-Seven

When the two of them did notice me, it was as if someone had pressed the pause button on a remote control. Everyone and everything froze. Nobody moved. Even the fringe on the curtain tassels seemed to be suspended in mid-air. Both Simon and Alex were looking at me, their mouths turned up at both corners in mid-laugh, but their eyes were no longer matching that mood. They say the eyes are the windows to the soul. Right now, Alex's eyes were full of fear, whereas Simon's showed regret. *I'm sorry you had to find out like this, Sis.*

So this was it. The end of a fifteen-year marriage. It seemed to rocket past like a high-speed train, each carriage blurred but full of memories... meeting each other, dating, marrying, starting a family, Sophie crawling, pulling herself upright, starting school, secondary school, a succession of family pets from tiny hamsters to Rupert lolling around on our daughter's bed having his claws painted scarlet while we howled with laughter as Sophie declared she was giving Rupert 'a make-over'.

But other parts of the train were now rocking violently on the track, ready to derail because some of those carriages were full of dark shadows – such sadness, loneliness, frustration at Alex being so emotionally distanced from me, the lack of hugs, warmth, the joy of a spontaneous kiss. I realised now that so much had been missing, indeed had never been there. I felt almost faint as the train disappeared, leaving me standing on the station, rocking with emotion as I stood in that bedroom doorway staring at Alex, my husband but never my soulmate. I wondered if he felt it too, as he silently regarded me. Something registered, behind his eyes, but then he quickly looked away. Simon was the first to speak.

'Holly, sweetie, please forgive me.'

I nodded, incapable of speech, because something weird was happening to my breathing. It seemed to be coming in great chuggy gasps, in and out, in and out, faster and faster, until I felt like I was going to pass out. In a flash Simon had leapt out of bed, and I instantly averted my eyes, because it wasn't just the curtain tassels that were swaying.

'Don't hyperventilate, sweetie,' he said, his arms fluttering around me. 'Breathe slowly, Holly. Nothing is ever as bad as it seems.'

At that moment, I wasn't inclined to agree with him. I'd like to say that my husband attempted to comfort me, but he didn't. He had nothing to say. No words to offer. No explanation to give. He left it all to my brother, who wept on my shoulder, as I wept on his.

Chapter Fifty-Eight

In the initial days that followed, I felt frozen. But over the weeks, and then months, that passed, somewhere a thaw began to take place. I went from feeling shell-shocked to just... well... astonished. It was one thing to have a gay brother but... my husband? How on earth had I never rumbled Alex? Was it because, unlike my brother, he'd never been flamboyant or camp, so out of naivety I'd never twigged?

Certainly Alex's parents had never doubted that their son – who'd played rugby in his younger days, sunk pints with the boys and turned women's heads in every room he'd entered – was anything other than straight. When they first heard the news, my in-laws were so angry and upset that they didn't speak to Alex. They were from a different generation, another era, where you didn't discuss things like that and instead married a nice woman, had two-point-four children and led a discreet double life that nobody knew anything about. Which, of course, was what Alex had done. Eventually though, Alex's parents had lowered the drawbridge over the moat of their emotions and waved a white flag of surrender. Ultimately, they wanted their son to be happy, and an invitation to dinner had been issued to both Alex and Simon.

Regarding Simon, I made my peace with him relatively quickly. Like all siblings, we had times when we seemed to hate each other, but ultimately, we loved each other too. And it was the love that saw us through. It was harder between Alex and myself. He distanced himself for weeks afterwards, coldly retreating, angry that I'd forced him out, and in turn I was livid with him. I found it outrageous that he'd delivered me a massive shock, lied to me for God knows how long, but then selfishly attempted to put his feelings before mine.

'I told you, Holly, that you were the only woman for me. And you were. Why couldn't you have just left things as they were?'

I'd blasted him with both barrels.

'Never mind your feelings!' I'd yelled angrily. 'How about thinking of mine for once?'

Eventually we'd had to talk. It was inevitable. I'd forced the situation whereby we were now leading separate lives and, anyway, I was desperate to move on. As time passed, I realised more and more that there had never been chemistry in our marriage, and that was nothing to do with whether Alex had been having an affair. Any woman leaving a marriage will know in her heart that, whatever the reason for the relationship breakdown, ultimately she deserves happiness. But it takes time to dissect all these feelings, and it also takes time to realise this. It came to me, a couple of months or so later, when I was staring listlessly out of the kitchen window one morning. The sun had peaked out from behind a dark cloud, lighting up the path ahead, and in that moment it dawned on me that it was time to make my own happiness.

Alex and I were no longer part of each other's futures, but we had a daughter together, so there would always be a relationship between us, even if it had completely changed. Alex admitted he'd been seeing a counsellor about his sexuality for some time, feeling torn between being true to himself and conforming to the expectations of others. In the end, my heart went out to him, for all his years of torment. After all, he was entitled to be happy, too.

The family member who was the least shocked by it all was Sophie. Our daughter was initially surprised, but unlike me, she seemed to recover within minutes.

'So many people are coming out, Mum,' she'd said sagely. 'Did you know our headmistress's partner is Mrs Lloyd, our science teacher?'

I'd looked at Sophie as if she'd just said that Donald Trump was resigning as President in order to pursue a career in ballet dancing.

'But Mrs Lloyd is married,' I'd protested. 'I've met her husband. He was on the tombola at the school's summer fete.'

'Yes, I know. But she and the Head apparently locked eyes over Mrs Lloyd's Bunsen burners in the lab one morning, and there was no going back.'

'Good heavens,' I'd said faintly.

'It's actually quite hip to be gay,' Sophie had assured. 'And everyone thinks I'm the coolest girl in the school for having a gay uncle *and* a gay dad!'

In the early days it had just seemed to be me who was alone and miserable. I had briefly wondered whether to get myself on some dating website in a search for the longed-for soulmate, that elusive person who would kiss me at the end of a date and make me feel like an inner part had arrived home. But only one person had ever had that effect on me, and I was suddenly very aware of him, waiting in the wings, looking on with concern, finding excuses to pop in and see how I was… whether I'd like him to walk Rupert, leaving me to howl in peace at the kitchen table or, perhaps, if I'd like to join them both?

So I did. It put fresh air in my lungs and roses in my cheeks and became a regular habit. In time, we found ourselves stopping at the little café afterwards by the woods for a reviving coffee and cake, and then, when the café was shut one day due to staff sickness, Jack said we couldn't possibly forfeit our sugar fix because we'd get terrible withdrawal. So why didn't he take me out to dinner that evening? He knew a smashing country pub that cooked a mean steak and served a delectable cheesecake. And over the after-dinner coffees and in the flickering candlelight, I'd looked across the table and smiled shyly at him, as if seeing him for the first time. He'd taken my hand across the distressed oak and, with it, taken my heart too which, let's face it, had been hammering away with longing every time I'd seen him.

'Holly, I know it's miles too soon, and that you're still mourning your marriage, but…' Jack hesitated, and for a moment I'd caught a glimpse of the uncertain spotty lad I'd known as a teenager, 'would you like to do this again?'

'Definitely,' I'd replied, my heart leaping with joy.

That evening, he'd dropped me home, and kissed me. I'd nearly passed out. It was only the fact that Sophie was home with my mother that stopped me from dragging Jack up to the bedroom and impaling myself upon him.

But all fledgling romances have to eventually bloom, and ours was no exception. And now, eighteen months later, as I sat in Caro's kitchen, gossiping with her and Jeanie, naturally the subject of sex was being put under the microscope by the three of us.

Jeanie, reconciled with Ray after a very turbulent few months and aghast that I had ever suspected her of having an affair with Alex, was keen to hear all the details about my relationship with Jack. So, I told them about it. How Jack had gone on to say that he'd always loved me, from when we were little kids together, through to the teenage years, my braces, his spots, but always thought I was out of his league.

'Aw, this is such a lovely story,' said Jeanie, looking dreamy. 'So why didn't he know who you were when he nearly ran over Rupert with his car?'

'Because,' I said, turning a bit red, 'he reckoned I'd turned into such a raving beauty he hadn't recognised me, ha ha.' I laughed, adding, 'As if I'm anything special!'

'But you *are* beautiful,' Caro said, 'you mustn't do yourself down, Holly. All those years with Alex really didn't do your self-esteem any favours.'

'True,' Jeanie nodded.

And I'd continued telling the girls how Jack had been devastated when Alex had come along and claimed me. Yes, there had been other women eventually, including Annabelle, but apparently nobody had ever captured his heart the way I had. And then his mother, Aunty Shirley, had let slip that my own mother was worried about me, how unhappy I seemed, and suspected my marriage wasn't too great these days. Apparently, Sophie had been confiding many a time to her grandma about the rows, and Jack had taken a last look at Africa and thought, 'Perhaps it's time to go home.'

'I cried when he told me that,' I said to Caro and Jeanie.

Jack had been adamant that there should be no rebound romance on my part. He'd insisted on that. So if I wanted to be a single mum putting my energies into her daughter and pooch, so be it. He said he'd waited years for me. He could wait a bit longer. And in the end, I kept him waiting for just the one year. At that point I was very aware of everybody moving on with their lives. Alex and Simon were living together, no longer giving a stuff about the gossips. Sir Digby's wife had walked out on him. Sir Digby had wasted no time in whisking Annabelle off to live in France. It transpired that Annabelle and Alex had been each other's confidantes. Annabelle was the only person who had known Alex was gay and had known all about 'Queenie' and the sexts.

Izzy and Sebastian were still together and making a go of it, although it was fair to say that Izzy and Jeanie studiously avoided each other at the school gates. Jeanie had declared the affair as the most foolish thing she'd ever done and how she'd nearly thrown away a diamond for a rock, that might have looked big and flashy but actually had lots of sharp bits.

'So tell me, Holly,' she said slyly, 'do you now do it more than once a month?'

'Oh yes,' I purred, helping myself to one of Caro's chocolate biscuits. 'I can truthfully tell you that we do it every day.'

'Every day?' Caro squeaked. 'Surely that's not normal?'

'I thought you were looking peaky,' Jeanie said, peering at me intently. 'Too much bed, and not enough sleep.'

I laughed. 'I'm sure at some point the pace will settle down, but right now it's just lovely. It's so wonderful to be desired and feel desirable.'

And it was. Jack had long finished writing his book and returned to work at London's Wellington Hospital. We'd bought a house together. New home. New start. Sophie alternated between ours, and Alex and Simon's trendy pad.

'And how's the burlesque dancing going?' asked Jeanie, giving me a cheeky wink. Despite the disastrous attempt to woo Alex with my Marigolds and curtain tassels, it was something I could laugh about now. Curiosity had got the better of Jack and he'd asked why there had been a pair of bright yellow washing-up gloves on the floor of the bedroom when he'd come over to manipulate my back. When I'd told him, he'd hooted with laughter, only to then buy me a burlesque outfit off eBay, which he was only too happy to see me wear on a regular basis.

'So all's well that ends well,' said Caro. 'Well I, for one, am very glad that everybody's love lives are sorted.'

'Just think,' said Jeanie, looking at Caro, 'out of all of us, you and David are the only ones who have never had a marital blip.'

Caro raised her eyebrows. 'You think?'

'What's that remark meant to mean?' I asked, suddenly very alive to my friend's cheeks glowing as red as a setting sun.

'Ah, that's another story,' said Caro. She hesitated, as if making up her mind whether to confide, then stood up abruptly and walked over to the kettle. 'Let me make us all another coffee, and I'll tell you all about it.'

A Letter from Debbie

I want to say a huge thank you for reading *What Holly's Husband Did*. If you enjoyed it, and want to keep up to date with all my latest releases, just sign up at the following link. Your email address will never be shared, and you can unsubscribe at any time.

www.bookouture.com/debbie-viggiano

I find relationships fascinating. They can be so complicated. Every family has a skeleton in the cupboard – sometimes so many the door is positively rattling for them all to spill out. How often do we catch snippets of someone telling a friend a disastrous tale of woe? Frequently! From the two young mums blocking a supermarket aisle with their baby buggies as they put their personal worlds to right, to the women in the fitting room next to ours speaking in hushed tones about a life-changing event. It happens around us everywhere. In my days of commuting to London on a packed train, it was unavoidable overhearing someone unburdening. I would discreetly study the listener, noting her facial expression, which was as easy to read as this page... horror, outrage, shock, sympathy... but above all else relief not to be living their friend's drama. Let's face it, we all love a bit of gossip – just so long as we are not the subject of it, or the one having the bumpy ride! After hearing bits of other people's lives, I was always left wondering what happened? What was that person going to do? How would they cope? What were they feeling? What direction would their life now go in? And – the really crucial part – would there be a happy ending?

What Holly's Husband Did is set in a Kent village – my own stomping ground – and features real places, like Bluewater Shopping Mall, which Holly and her besties love to frequent (along with the author!). Holly's dog, Rupert, is a male version of my own rescue pooch and has the same endearing charm and halitosis!

I hope you loved *What Holly's Husband Did* and, if so, would be very grateful if you would write a review. I'd be thrilled to hear what you think, and it makes such a difference helping new readers discover one of my books for the first time.

I always like hearing from my readers, so do look me up on Facebook, Twitter, Goodreads or my blog or website.

With love,
Debbie

 @DebbieViggiano

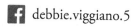 debbie.viggiano.5

 www.debbieviggiano.com

Acknowledgements

This is my ninth novel, but the first with the incredible Bookouture. I have dedicated *What Holly's Husband Did* to the lovely Kathryn Taussig, Associate Publisher, who emailed me out of the blue just as I was galloping towards the finishing line of my last novel, *The Woman Who Knew Everything*. Kathryn had a proposal. Would I consider writing two romcoms for Bookouture? I nearly fainted with shock. I'd been an independent author for so long, the proposition absolutely terrified me. It's one thing to write because you love it and have some readers who follow you, it's quite another to sign a contract and know you have to deliver! I am deeply grateful for her believing in me, dishing out major encouragement as I furiously wrote, and hand-holding me through the edits. Likewise, I would like to thank all the authors under the wing of Bookouture for their friendship and amazing humour, Yeti Lambregts for the wonderfully fun cover design, and Kim Nash, Bookouture's Publicity and Social Media Manager, for her tireless work and amusing stories about Roni, the Greek rescue dog. As I'm also the 'mother' of a Cretan rescue pup, it is nice to sometimes 'talk dog' with another pooch-potty person. Finally, I want to thank you, my reader. Without you, there is no book. I very much hope you enjoy this one.

Debbie xx

33649236R00209

Printed in Great Britain
by Amazon